NCIS:™
LOS ANGELES
EXTREMIS

Coming soon from Titan Books

NCIS Los Angeles™: Bolthole

(November 2016)

NCIS:™
LOS ANGELES
EXTREMIS

Jerome Preisler

Based on the CBS television series
created by Shane Brennan

TITAN BOOKS

For SWP, YWP, HWP and SMP
—with a plan.

NCIS Los Angeles: Extremis
Print edition ISBN: 9781783296316
E-book edition ISBN: 9781783296323

Published by Titan Books
A division of Titan Publishing Group Ltd
144 Southwark Street, London SE1 0UP

First edition: August 2016
1 3 5 7 9 10 8 6 4 2

A CIP catalogue record for this title is available from the British Library.

Printed and bound in the United States.

PROLOGUE I

Port Hueneme, California
May, 1945

Lieutenant Elias P. Sutton stood on the wooden dock gazing northward at the two red-and-white escort tugs and their large, low slung captive. They had appeared to him just minutes ago, rounding the Channel Islands, wending their way toward harbor over the clear blue Pacific water. Behind them, specks of gray in the middle distance, were the two destroyers that had intercepted the U-boat at sea.

Sutton raised his binoculars to his eyes for a better look, the breeze snapping his uniform shirt around his broad six-foot frame. As he understood, the USS *Linette* and USS *Phillips* had sailed from Pearl Harbor shortly after the German skipper radioed his intention to surrender. He had also heard the U-boat, a Type IXD2 longrunner, was cruising somewhere out near Malaysia when Doenitz gave his fleet the order to surface and raise their black flags. The Nazis had finally called it a war.

"Ever do any fishing, Lieutenant?"

Sutton lowered the field glasses and turned toward Holloway, thinking the OSS officer walked like a ghost on tiptoes. He made no sound at all coming up behind him.

Tall, lean and in his mid twenties, Holloway regarded him through the lenses of his aviator sunglasses. He was wearing expensive, perfectly tailored civvies—a tan sport coat with a monogramed pocket square, cuffed brown pants, and a snap brim fedora with a pleated silk hatband. The tops of his polished leather wingtips gleamed in the abundant sunlight.

"I've caught my share of brook trout," Sutton replied. "That sort of thing."

"I mean big game," Holloway said. "Marlin, tuna… the kind of deep-water fish that puts up a serious fight, so you think it might pull your arms right out of their sockets."

Sutton looked at him. "Can't say I've had the pleasure of that experience," he said.

Holloway chuckled mildly. Then he reached into his pocket for a pack of Camels, shook out a cigarette, and put it in his mouth.

"The gratifying part is when you finally haul in one of those bastards," he said, holding a lighter to the tip of his smoke. "You see a nine foot, five-hundred pound marlin come up in the rigging, and know it's something exceptional. A creature that God put some real work into."

Sutton considered that. "Are you telling me size is the measure of something's value, Tip?"

"No," Holloway said. "But it sure as hell doesn't hurt." He came up beside the lieutenant, poked his chin out at the approaching vessels. "ULTRA hit a goldmine with this one. I have a stack of cables between Tokyo and Berlin. I have the sub's crew list and unofficial passenger list. And I have a full cargo manifest… unless there was an eleventh hour change of plans."

Sutton looked around at the quay, where about two dozen seamen in blue denim working uniforms stood at ease. Beyond them, a large group of print and newsreel journalists waited in the shadows of the tall shipyard cranes, their camera gear ready. Gathered behind a rope, they'd arrived to take pictures of the prisoners as they disembarked.

"We've instructed the news people that they can take their snapshots, but are not to ask any questions, or speak to the prisoners at all," Holloway said. "The Germans are being brought to NAS Point Mogu, where they'll board a plane for Washington. The other four will remain on the boat and be debriefed separately. And I've personally selected the agents who will conduct the interrogations."

"Do those agents all dress to kill like you?"

"What?"

"Never mind," Sutton said.

Holloway blew out a stream of tobacco smoke.

"I'm confident Reynolds will keep his end of the arrangement," he said. "We don't want the beast. Just what's in its belly."

The lieutenant was silent a moment. Then he turned toward the channel again, bringing the goggles back up to his eyes. The group of vessels was now less than a half mile from port, and he could see some of the American sailors who'd boarded the U-boat standing on its foredeck.

"'Strange things have happened like never before'," he mouthed under his breath.

Holloway looked at him. "What's that?"

"They're lyrics," Sutton said. "From an old phonograph recording."

"On one of those Edison cylinders you collect?"

7

Holloway chuckled. "I remember you recording on your parents' gramophone when we were boys. You were quite the young performer."

Sutton nodded. "I enjoy my music," he said. "'World Is Going Wrong'… that's the song's name."

Holloway gave a shrug. "Sounds depressing," he said.

"Not when you pay attention to the words."

"I *never* listen to the words, Elias. To me music is about a randy, long-legged girl, a dance floor, and hot swing trumpets playing into the night."

Sutton was silent. It occurred to him that might be everything there really was to say about the differences between them.

"Those tugs will have that boat here before we know it," he said after a moment, nodding toward the seamen on the pier. "We better prepare."

Forty minutes later Sutton hopped onto the submarine's puddled, seaweed-draped foredeck. Holloway followed right behind him on the gangway, holding onto his hat in the gusty breeze. Three hundred feet long, pulled horizontal to the pier, the boat listed gently on the water, held fast by her mooring lines.

A young officer approached the lieutenant, snapped him a crisp salute.

"Boyd, sir… USS *Linette*," he said. "Welcome."

Sutton returned the salutation, noting the expression on his face. Boyd seemed downcast, somehow, even grim. It was unusual for a sailor looking forward to two weeks of shore leave in the States… and whose ship had netted a significant prize. But, Sutton thought, maybe he was reading him wrong. Misinterpreting his weariness after an extended stint at sea.

According to Holloway, U-437 had gone on one hell of a trip of her own. After embarking from northern Germany in January, she'd made her only stop in the Atlantic at Kristiansand, Norway, where the ballast in her keel hold was replaced with her secret cargo. From there, she looped southwest around the English coast, crossed the equator into the South Atlantic, rounded the Cape of Good Hope into the Indian Ocean, and then sailed south of Madagascar to Kobe, Japan.

Quite the journey, indeed, Sutton thought. All told, her crew had traveled almost two thousand nautical miles, and spent three months in a cramped steel tube without setting foot on land.

"Okay, Boyd," he said now. "Show us below decks, will you?"

"Amen," Holloway said before he could respond. His hand still on his hat, he sniffed and wrinkled his nose. "What's that awful stink?"

Old salt that he was, Sutton had barely noticed.

"Life on a submarine, Tip," he said. "Rotting seaweed, dead fish—they get stuck on the rails antenna—you name it. And count on it being even smellier down below." He glanced at the OSS man's feet. "You might want to clean those fancy puppies of yours before they stain."

Holloway looked down at his shoes, then frowned in disgust. Wet ribbons of kelp hung limply from his laces.

"My God!" he said, and leaned forward to pluck them off.

Sutton looked at Boyd. "All right," he said. "Lead the way."

"Yes sir," he said, nodding. Then hesitated. "There's something you should know. About the scientists."

Sutton stared at him.

"Tell me," he said.

Boyd told him.

"I don't understand how this could happen," Holloway said, his face pale. He turned from the dead men on the bunks, pulled his handkerchief from his pocket, and covered his nose and mouth. "These prisoners were supposed to be under constant watch."

"They were, sir," Boyd said. "To the best of our ability."

"And you call this your best?" He waved his free hand at the bunks without looking back at them. "The fact remains you were under strict orders."

Boyd looked uncomfortable. "It's a tight fit in here. Seventy-five German seamen, plus all the cargo and supplies... As you can see, it didn't leave us much room. We managed a detachment of twelve guards, besides myself."

Holloway breathed through the handkerchief, staring at Boyd in the dimness of the crew compartment. He seemed at a loss for words.

Or maybe he was just trying to keep his stomach down, Sutton thought. Walking aft between the stacked wooden crates that lined the hull from stem to stern, he'd smelled metal, machine oil, stale sweat, and above all the diesel smoke that had left a dark coat of soot over everything around them. That was typical eau-de-pigboat; Sutton had commanded one for a full year and hadn't been surprised.

But four men poisoning themselves to death left a different kind of smell. From the looks of their contorted bodies and soiled hammocks—and the sickening puddles on the floor underneath them—Sutton knew they hadn't gone gently. Or held a lot inside their bowels and bladders.

"Run through everything for us," he said to Boyd. "I think we could both use some clarification."

Boyd nodded.

"The U-boat's officers told us their Japanese guests demanded privacy for their sleeping area," he said, and motioned to the canvas hanging he'd yanked down from an overhead pipe. "They had this fabric aboard, and let them use it as a curtain."

"On a German boat that amounts to five-star accommodations," Sutton said.

"Yes," Boyd said, glancing at the occupants of the hammocks. "They were ranking officers. A major, a full colonel, and two lieutenant commanders."

Sutton knew better.

None of them were military men. Their uniforms and ranks were assigned for the journey, so they would not be prosecuted as spies if captured.

"All right," he said. "Go on."

"A week ago, the German Naval Command radioed out orders for its whole submarine fleet to surrender. When these officers insisted that the sub take them to Japan, there was a dispute about it, and they lost…"

"I think that's plain," Holloway said through his handkerchief. He made an impatient winding gesture. "Can we cut to the chase?"

"The Japanese insisted their country was still at war, and refused to give up," Boyd said. "They finally asked for two bottles of luminal tablets and some extra drinking water… and then pulled the curtain."

"Tojo must have a shortage of cyanide," Sutton said.

11

"That would have been quicker, and probably a little neater."

"I wouldn't say the Germans were hunky dory with it," Boyd said. "The men stayed alive for three days... and it wasn't pretty."

"That's more of the obvious, Lieutenant," Holloway said. "Did your crew search the bodies for documents?"

Boyd did a quick side-to-side head wobble.

"I assumed it would be done when we brought them ashore to be processed."

"Listen," he said in a low voice. "Before the crews of the *Linette* and *Phillips* come ashore, they will be sworn to secrecy about the details of this submarine's capture. In writing." His eyes narrowed. "It isn't to be discussed with anyone. That means wives, girlfriends, barroom floozies... nobody, but nobody, including their pet cocker spaniels. Under penalty of court martial."

Boyd was quiet a second. Then his eyes went to Sutton.

"May I speak freely?"

The lieutenant nodded. "Go ahead."

"This is very irregular. I can't presume to respond for my captain."

"And his name is...?"

"Taylor, sir."

Sutton felt some empathy for the lieutenant.

"I'll get it squared with Captain Taylor," he said. "In the meantime, you're excused."

"Sir?"

"Return to the control room and stand by. I'll let you know when we're done in here."

Boyd hesitated a beat. Then he saluted, spun around, and moved back toward the nose of the submarine, his footsteps clanking dully on the riveted metal floor.

Sutton waited until he passed through the forward hatch to break his silence.

"He's Navy," he said to Holloway. "Stay out of my area. I won't stand for it."

Holloway met his gaze and shrugged.

"I'm not here to start a fight," he said. "We're in this thing together."

Sutton nodded. "Tell me what you intend to do with the bodies."

A pause. Then the agent gave another shrug.

"I'm going to undress these sons of bitches, then search them inside and out," he said. "Feel free to help."

Sutton folded his arms across his chest.

"If it's all the same," he said, "I'll stand lookout."

Holloway stuffed his handkerchief into his pocket, clearly irked. Then he went to work on one of the corpses, his face creasing in revulsion as he bent to unfasten its pants.

Thirty seconds later, he vomited on his shoes.

Sutton gave the agent credit.

He hadn't expected him to last more than twenty-five.

PROLOGUE 2

Santa Barbara, California
Present Day

The old man's wife had always insisted he was a creature of habit, and he understood her reasons for believing it. But even now, with Mara gone five years to the day, he would have said she was wrong, arguing the difference between habit and routine.

She never quite understood, he thought, and in many ways that exemplified their years together. Theirs was not so much a conjugal bond as a cold, comfortable peace—the archetypical marriage of convenience, a passionless merger between families. The top-of-the-class Annapolis grad with political aspirations, and the beautiful, young socialite with her Vermont roots, social connections, and horseback riding trophies. Each gave the other entrée to new worlds, and the arrangement had worked to their mutual benefit.

He had enjoyed his share of peccadilloes, of course—a man of responsibility needed the occasional diversion. Most of the women were married, the wives of officers and gentlemen, with no intention of leaving their spouses. He had selected his partners as carefully and sensibly as he'd chosen his bride.

When she died, his tears were real—and mostly for

himself. Already in his eighties, he had wondered how much of his life he would have traded for true love's embrace. But it was a fleeting regret.

It was four-fifteen in the afternoon when he returned from the cemetery. Swinging off the main road that climbed uphill to his Montecito cape house, his driver Ronald eased into the palm-lined access drive, then brought the BMW to a halt in the shade of his porte-cochere.

"Can I see you inside, Admiral?" Ronald said over his shoulder.

The old man reached for the cane beside him on the backseat, his fingers closing stiffly around its silver eagle's head handle.

See you, he thought. Not *"help you."*

His staffers were careful—some might even say gun-shy—choosing their words around him.

"That's okay, I'm fine." He shifted around to his door. "Angie's here if I need anything. You go on over to the filling station and gas up… and please be so kind as to bring back today's paper."

Ronald nodded, waiting with his hands on the steering wheel, his expression saying he understood his employer's stubborn independence all too well.

The old man got out of the car slowly, leading with the cane and then boosting himself to his feet. His painful left hip, his cranky knees, and worst of all his thickened, arthritic knuckles… there was a good deal of wear and tear on his parts. But he would never carp. It had been quite the journey from his boyhood in landlocked Illinois to his commission as the youngest submarine commander in U.S. naval history, to the action in the South Pacific that had marked his path to the Admiralty—and, with Mara's ties, eventually propelled him to a three-term stint on Capitol Hill. Things could have turned out far, far worse.

No, he thought, stepping up to his door. *No complaints.* He'd experienced much in his time, reaching great heights of achievement—more than any man could wish for. And if there was a single mistake he would have liked to undo, at least it was hidden in one of the safest vaults imaginable.

He turned toward the BMW, saw Ronald pretending not to watch him, and waved him off. As the car eased from under the portico, he took his house key from his trouser pocket, raised it to unlock the door... and then paused with his hand hovering at the keyhole, his head tilted with mild puzzlement.

The door was ajar, its bolt withdrawn. That seemed somewhat odd—he'd never known Angie to leave it open. He had also realized the dog wasn't barking, although that was less unusual. He typically walked his Airedale after drinking his four P.M. cognac, but knew the housekeeper would let Colin out onto the veranda if he had an urgent need to relieve himself.

Still...

Odd, he thought.

Pushing the door open, he stepped into his sky-lit living room.

"Angie?"

The housekeeper didn't answer.

"Hello?" He rapped on the jamb with his cane. "Anyone here?"

No answer.

He shut the door and walked through the room, his favorite in the house with its rustic stone fireplace, mission furniture, and antique Navajo rugs. An inscribed photograph of Admiral Nimitz onboard the battleship *Missouri* hung on the wall adjacent to the veranda doors.

"Colin?" he said. "I'm home, boy!"

Silence.

Confused, he turned past the fireplace, moved toward the wide Spanish archway that opened into the dining area... and then halted.

He could hear something dripping in there, pattering rhythmically onto the floor.

His eyes went to the foot of the table. The first thing he noticed was the broken snifter, cognac spilled around the shards of glass, puddled on the lacquered hardwood. Then, on the tabletop, an overturned bottle of Rémy Martin, its contents streaming from its mouth.

He tensed, his pulse throbbing in his ears.

"Angie? Angie, are you all right?"

Nothing.

Stepping forward into the dining area, he saw the tall wooden doors giving into the kitchen had been thrown wide open...

His gaze dropped to the floor between the double doors.

A sharp breath escaped his mouth.

Angie laid sprawled there on her side, jags of glass all around her, a bloody hole in the middle of her forehead, her blouse and apron splattered with red.

"*My God*," he said, his voice a hoarse croak. "*Angie.*"

He was still staring at her body in horror when he heard a noise behind him... the soft clack-clack-clack of doors swinging in a light breeze.

He turned back into the living room, his cane repeatedly tapping the floor as he half-limped, half-shambled along on his spavined legs. Passing the fireplace, cursing his own slowness, he glanced left toward the glass-paneled veranda doors, and realized they were slightly open.

His brow wrinkled. He hadn't noticed before. But his attention was elsewhere when he came into the house, and the bright afternoon sun pouring through the glass had made it hard to see.

Moving around the sofa toward the doors, he pushed them fully open, the breeze coming through as he went out to stand under the vine-clad trellis.

"Colin... are you out here?" he shouted, squinting into the sunlight.

There was no sign of the dog.

He stood looking around the yard, his eyes going to the patches of variegated grass that bordered the path... the tall shade palms on three sides of the yard... and then the thick bougainvillea hedge over to his right...

"Colin—"

He saw the Airedale on its side against the hedge, lying in a broad patch of shade, its lips peeled back over its teeth in a grotesque death rictus. The blood matting its fur to its chest had partially dried in the hot Southern California sun, giving it a dark, tarry appearance.

The old man stared at the dog for a shocked moment, producing a wordless groan of anguish. Then he forced himself to move toward the dog. Walking blindly off the footpath in his agitation, he caught his cane on a small hummock, dropped it to the ground, and stumbled forward, barely managing to keep his balance.

Bending to pick up the cane, he started to lift it... and then jolted upright at the sudden noise behind him.

Terrified, he turned toward his house.

There was someone standing between the veranda doors, a compact submachine gun with a silencer on its barrel held out in front of his chest.

The cloth mask pulled over his face was black, exposing only his narrowed eyes.

The old man looked back at him, his cane slipping from his fingers. Was someone moving about in the living room, behind the intruder? The contrasting splashes of glare and shadow made it impossible to be sure. But he thought he saw somebody... and hoped against hope it might be his driver.

"What do you want?" he asked.

The intruder's eyes locked him in a cold, hard stare.

"Nothing," he said, his voice muffled by the mask. "It's already ours."

The old man's eyes filled with a mixture of understanding and regret. Drawing up straight, he inhaled deeply, smelling the sweet perfume of the bougainvilleas. Then he nodded in sober acknowledgment.

A second later the masked intruder pulled the trigger, firing a three-round burst into his face.

1

"*Path to Glory*," Sam Hanna said to himself.

He looked soberly at a framed black-and-white photo on the wall, thinking that when Hetty Lange had first called him into headquarters to investigate a new case, he never in a million years expected it to be the murder of a longtime military hero.

Callen came up beside him, stepping clear of the open veranda doors to make room for a crime scene tech heading outside with her camera. He had his cellphone out after hearing from Hetty for the second time in under five minutes. This one, she had stressed, was to be handled with particular discretion.

"I saw that flick," he said. "Not bad."

Hanna turned from the photo. "I think you mean *Paths of Glory*," he said. "With Kirk Douglas. About those French soldiers in World War One."

"Actually," Callen said, "I mean the documentary *Path to Glory*. About Arabian horses in Poland."

Hanna was confused. "Why would I bring up a movie about *horses*?"

"That's what I was wondering. Seemed kind of odd under the circumstances."

A powerfully built man of over six foot with a smooth, clean-shaven head, astute brown eyes, and skin the color of caramel syrup, Sam took a deep, exasperated breath, his tee shirt straining over his muscular upper back.

"Look, G, forget the damn horses, okay?" he said. "The movies too. I'm talking about a book."

Callen regarded him a second. "Oh," he said. "Big difference."

"Very big," Hanna said. "It's the senator's autobiography. *Path to Glory, The Making of Admiral Elias P. Sutton.* About his career before politics." He nodded toward the picture. "This shot was taken on the USS *Missouri*—Big Mo', they called her—on September second, nineteen forty-five."

"When the Japanese formally surrendered."

Hanna nodded. "Admiral Chester Nimitz and General Douglas MacArthur were the two American signatories, though MacArthur was there for the combined Allied Powers and Nimitz accepted on behalf of the United States."

Callen studied the photo. It showed Admiral Nimitz seated at a table on the battleship's deck, preparing to sign the documents. Standing immediately behind him were MacArthur, British Admiral William F. Halsey, and another man he didn't recognize.

"Is that Sutton?" he asked, motioning with his chin.

Hanna shook his head. "Uh-uh," he said. "He's Rear Admiral Forrest Sherman, Nimitz's deputy chief of staff. Sutton's right behind him with the guys further back in the shot." He pointed to the crescent-shaped assemblage of military officers viewing the ceremony. "Toward the war's end, Nimitz appointed him a special advisor. Before that he was commander at Port Hueneme up the coast. But his actions at sea made him a legend. In 'forty-three or so, he skippered a Gato-class submarine in the Pacific…"

Listening, Callen saw a pair of detectives from the coroner's bureau enter the house, exchange a few words with one of the uniformed cops at the front door, and then turn toward the dining area, where the housekeeper's body was still being sketched, photographed, and video-recorded. He recognized one of them, an old-timer named Frank Varno, who made sure Callen noticed his unhappy frown as he strode past. If their history was any indication, he would be less than pleased about turning the case over to federal agents.

But Deeks would handle that. As interagency liaison, it was his job to coordinate things with the Santa Barbara police. Well, sort of. Technically, he was the go-between with LAPD, and *their* jurisdiction fell a hundred miles north on Highway 101. But you couldn't pick and choose where crimes involving Navy—or in this instance, *former* Navy—people happened. The operatives with NCIS Los Angeles's Office of Special Projects were by far the closest to the scene.

"…sunk more Japanese supply ships in the war than any other fleet boat captain," Sam was saying now. "Seven years later, Sutton led a task force of destroyers against a pack of Soviet subs during the evac of Inchon."

Callen looked at him. "Hang on," he said. "The Soviets aren't supposed to have fought in Korea."

Sam nodded. "Right," he said. "The Navy kept that battle secret for decades. They didn't want to start World War Three by letting on that the Russians tried to get us massacred." He paused. "My pop was with X Corps—First Marine Division—and they desperately needed evac. He and thousands of other guys would have died without Sutton fighting off those subs."

"And you never would've been a twinkle in his eye."

Sam shrugged his shoulders. "If Dad's eyes ever twinkled, he would've disciplined them," he said with a chuckle. "The man had two looks... hardass and harder hardass."

"Romantic."

Sam gave another shrug. "I'm standing with you today, ain't I?"

Callen smiled a little.

"Got me there, dude," he said, glancing quickly toward the veranda doors.

It was now a quarter past six in the evening, the April sun on the wane, its light slanting almost horizontally over the large, well-tended backyard. Outside, the crime scene photographer had moved from Sutton's body to the shrubs where his dog was found shot to death. She crouched over the animal, snapping away with her camera.

Callen turned back to his partner, who was reading the personalized inscription near the bottom of the picture. It said:

> *To Commander Elias P. Sutton,*
> *Leadership consists of picking good men.*
> *You make me look like a good leader.*
>
> *With Best Wishes and Warm Regards,*
> *C.W. Nimitz, Fleet Admiral, USN*

"Sutton led a hero's life," Sam said quietly. "What kind of world has it end with him being murdered at ninety-three?"

Callen wasn't sure how to answer.

"We better have a look around," he said with a heavy sigh. "How 'bout I take the house, and you take the backyard?"

Sam finally tore his eyes from the picture, looking past Callen into the dining room. Then he clapped a hand down on his shoulder.

"Sure," he said. "Just because I know how much you like talking to Detective Varno."

"I'm touched that you care," Callen said.

Sam mustered a grin.

"Always, man," he said.

"Evening," Varno said with a nod. He was standing over the housekeeper's body. "How nice to see you."

To Callen, the detective sounded as resolutely displeased as he'd looked a few minutes ago.

"That sarcasm I detect?" he said.

Varno touched a hand to his own chest. Like the agents, he was wearing gloves.

"Sarcasm?" he said. "From me?"

Callen nodded. "Oodles," he said.

"I have no clue why you'd think such a thing," Varno said. "I mean, is there a reason it *wouldn't* be nice to see you?"

Callen sighed. The last time the OSP had worked a case in Santa Barbara was a year or so back. A Mexican panga boat carrying a hundred pounds of heroin and a partially decomposed corpse had washed ashore on Arroyo Burro Beach, and that turned out to be part of a three-way deal gone sour—the other part of it having involved a black market shipment of guns and explosives to jihadist revolutionaries in Afghanistan.

Although Deeks and Blye had led the investigation, Callen had wound up in the thick of things... and they'd gotten dicey.

"Look," he said. "That mansion blowing up wasn't my fault."

"Who said it was?" Varno said. "First, I'm sarcastic. Now I'm blaming you for an incident that got me in all kinds of hot water with the millionaire taxpayers in the hills here, not that you would've lost a minute's sleep over my problems." He shrugged. "If you have any other accusations, might as well get them out of the way right now."

Callen frowned. "Okay, Detective," he said. "Maybe we should start over."

"Sure, Agent," Varno said. His mustache was thick and white under a flat, wide nose. "Then maybe you can tell me why you're gracing *my* crime scene with your presence."

Callen motioned to the body in a puddle of blood, her arms and legs flung out at odd angles, her clothes stained red, a large entrance wound in the center of her forehead. A numbered yellow evidence marker had been set beside her.

"She's one reason," he said.

"But she wouldn't make this a case for Naval."

"No," Callen said.

"The senator's a different story, though."

"Yeah."

"Being he was an admiral once upon a time."

"Right."

"Not that his murder's likely to pose a threat to national security," Varno said. "I mean, Sutton was ninety-three and retired from public life for decades. I wouldn't figure he'd be carrying state secrets in his pocket. That would usually leave the investigation up to the local authorities."

Callen remained silent.

"I figure you and your buddy were assigned this case as a favor to somebody," Varno went on. "Could be a politician. Or a Navy bigwig, maybe. A person with ties to the old man who wants you to oversee things, make sure the dumbass hicks from the Santa Barbara County Sheriff's Office don't bungle in the jungle."

Callen still said nothing.

"Good of you to open up to me," Varno said. "Thanks for sharing."

Callen knelt to examine the housekeeper's body, his eyebrows lifting with interest. The entry wound was neat and almost perfectly centered in her forehead—made by a small to medium sized round, he guessed. But while the absence of powder residue indicated the shooter was standing at a distance, a quick glance at the back of her skull showed a very large and messy exit wound—the skin hanging in ragged flaps from the back of her skull, clots of bone, tissue, and hair in the pooled blood underneath it. Normally that kind of damage meant she'd taken a closeup shot.

"This looks like it was made by a nine mil... but not a standard round," he said, glancing up at Varno. "You recover the shell casing?"

The detective reached into his carryall, produced a sealed and labeled plastic evidence bag, and held it out toward Callen.

"Here you go," he said. "For your perusal. In the spirit of friendly and harmonious cooperation."

Callen took the bag from his hand. "A plus-pee-plus load," he said, studying the empty brass cylinder inside. "Pressurized for more oomph."

Varno made a face.

"What's with you and all these double-o words?" he said.

Callen's blue eyes held on him. "Didn't realize I was using them that much."

"Well, you are. And it's kind of peculiar."

"Peculiar?"

"Absolutely," Varno said. "Weird, even. Like you've got an *oo* fixation or something."

The two men looked at each other a moment. Then Callen dropped the plastic bag back into Varno's palm and glanced down at the floor again, his eyes going to the broken glass near the housekeeper's corpse.

"Let's see if I've got this straight," he said. "About four-thirty, a neighbor's kid is riding his bike past the house when he hears multiple gunshots coming from the backyard—"

"He called it a 'burst,'" Varno said. "Teens these days, they're up on all the lingo." He shrugged. "They play those video games, think it makes them black ops. You know what they say about a little knowledge being a dangerous thing."

Callen nodded. Although in this instance, he was thinking it might have helped the kid give an accurate account of what he'd heard.

"So, anyway, he's got more guts than caution and pedals up the driveway—"

"Jumps off the bike and walks it up, actually," Varno said. "The drive's at a steep incline from the road."

"Right, I noticed—"

"This place being at the top of a hill," Varno said. "And I really think we should both call the kid a teen. For consistency's sake."

"Sure," Callen said. "So the *teen* sees that the side door's open—"

"Well, actually," Varno said, "it's ajar."

Callen inhaled. "He notices it's *ajar* and calls nine-one-one on his cell. Then you and the sheriff's deputies arrive to find everything the way it is right now. Sutton and the dog are in the backyard, and the housekeeper…"

"Angelica DeFalco according to her driver's license."

"…Angelica's inside the house, where it appears she was pouring a brandy—"

"Cognac, there's a difference," Varno cut in. "The rule being that every cognac is a brandy, but not every brandy is a cognac."

Callen looked at him. "Right."

"Cognac being a high quality brandy made in a certain part of France."

"Uh huh…."

"The cognac on the table being very high end stuff," Varno said. "Rémy Martin XO Excellence. A one-point-seven-five liter bottle goes for a half grand to a grand, depending where you buy it."

Callen stared up at the detective. Varno's repeated interruptions were really starting to get on his nerves.

"I doubt she was hitting her boss's prime stock herself," he said. "More likely she's pouring it for Sutton while he's waiting for the dog to do its business. Then the killer enters the house, shoots her, goes outside, and takes out the old man and the dog."

"Could be," Varno said. "Or maybe Sutton's killed first. We can't be positive."

Callen considered that. A thought had come to mind.

"Let's get back to the kid with the bike."

"Oops," Varno said.

"What?"

"*Oops*, you called the teen a 'kid' again," Varno said, and grinned. "You see what I did there, incidentally?"

Callen inhaled, ignoring that last comment.

"He hears gunfire in the backyard. Comes up the drive, sees the open side door, calls the sheriff pretty much at once."

"Yeah."

"And there's no sign of the killer."

"Right."

"No more gunshots afterward according to your earwitness."

"Right."

"Meaning the housekeeper was shot *before* Sutton and his dog," Callen said. "Assuming the witness is right about the gunfire coming from behind the house."

Varno looked at him for several seconds, then nodded.

"Good thinking," he said. "You'd make a decent detective if it wasn't for luxury mansion explosions coming with the package."

Callen stood up, letting that comment pass too.

"Is there anything else?" he asked.

"About the bodies or what the teen heard?"

"Anything relevant."

Varno looked at him.

"The bedroom," he said.

"What about it?"

Varno nodded past the dining room table.

"You'll want to take a peek for yourself," he said, and turned to lead him deeper into the house.

* * *

"Hell of a thing," Sam said. He was standing out near the bougainvillea hedge on the north side of the property, watching the crime scene photographer take pictures of the dead dog.

A thirtyish woman of Asian descent, she had short, spiky black hair, and wore jeans and a blue County Sheriff's windbreaker.

"Yes," she said. "For the dog *and* master."

"I've got a question, Ms...." He read her nametag. "Omura."

"Emily," she said. "Em's fine." She lowered her camera. "I saw you pull up in that Challenger. The best muscle car on wheels... and *not* your typical detective car."

"That's 'cause I'm not your typical detective." He grinned. "Em... you see a picture here worth that thousand words I'm always hearing about?"

She motioned at the dog with her chin. "You tell me."

Sam crouched over the animal's remains. It was stretched out parallel to the back of the house, its head almost in the shrubbery, and its hindquarters pointing out into the yard.

"There are multiple entrance wounds," he said, his gloved hand carefully pulling the sticky, blood-soaked fur away from its chest. "This is a tight grouping... whoever did it knows how to handle a gun."

"And bear in mind the dog made a low target," Em said. "He—it's a male, I checked—would have stood two feet tall, max, and isn't very broad from shoulder to shoulder."

Sam grunted. "I didn't notice any footprints out here," he said. "You?"

The photographer shook her head slightly.

"No," she said. "Human or canine. But the lawn is in good shape…"

"And healthy, watered grass pops up fast after you step on it."

"Exactly." She wobbled the camera in both hands. "I've photographed every inch of the yard. But there are no shoe impressions, nothing to tell us where anyone might have walked."

Sam studied the dog's position on the ground. "It couldn't have been standing, or laying, this way when it was killed," he said. "If it was facing the bushes, it would've been shot in the side, not the chest."

She nodded. "Take a close look around his body."

Sam did, his eyes intent. After a moment he noticed the tiny spots of blood in the grass between the animal and the house.

"Sonofagun," he said, motioning to the blood specks. "This is forward spatter…"

"And the spray goes in the direction of the veranda doors," Em said.

He nodded, shifted his gaze to the bushes, and saw larger bloodstains on the smooth green bougainvillea leaves.

"These drops are bigger," he said.

"Right. And see how they kind of arc?"

Sam gave another nod. Some of the spatters were spherical, others teardrop shaped. But they all looked as if they'd been swiped across the hedge by a paint brush.

"They're castoffs and transfers," he said. "The dog thrashed around in a circle after it was shot, shook blood off onto the bushes. Then he must've made contact with them and smeared more onto the leaves."

"Right," she said. "That accounts for the distorted droplets." She squatted alongside him and pointed at one of the bushes. "Also see how several of the flowers look like they were ripped off the branches here?"

Sam shifted his eyes to the animal. There were little pink petals in the thick, curly fur on its flank and tail, confirming that its violent death throes sent it twisting into the bushes.

"The dog's hanging out in the yard, sees something... someone... in the house, turns to look, and gets blown away by that someone."

"Like his master," Em said. "It's even plainer with Sutton. He fell straight back, probably died before he hit the ground."

He let that sink in, glancing over at the dead man sprawled in the late day shadows across the yard. How many people owed him their lives? Almost two hundred shiploads of U.N. troops were evacuated at Inchon... about a hundred thousand soldiers in all, most of them American. Plus the fifteen thousand defenseless South Korean men, women, and children who'd faced cold-blooded slaughter from the Red Chinese invaders that overran them. If the Russian subs lurking in the Yellow Sea had managed to cut off the armada from shore, it would have doomed the entire rescue operation. And Sutton's leadership and actions were all that prevented it.

How many people?

Sam turned his back to the house, folded his arms across his chest, and gazed downhill for a while. Far below, down the gentle green slope of the hill, a band of tangerine sunlight was reflecting off the Santa Barbara Channel where it met the wide, sandy curve of East Beach.

It struck him that Sutton must have stood admiring the view countless times. Hadn't he once been the commander at Port Hueneme?

He expelled a breath and looked over at Emily Omura. She'd stood up, brushing off the knees of her jeans.

"Is photography your only specialty?" he asked.

She shook her head. "You're talking to the world's worst photographer," she said. "The Santa Barbara Sheriff's Office isn't LAPD, and we all pitch in where we're needed." A pause. "I'm an entomologist by training and experience."

"You do insects?"

"I wouldn't quite put it that way," she said. "Though I *have* been involved with a couple of guys who arguably fit the description."

Sam saw she was smiling, and smiled back.

"My guess is the dog wasn't shot too long before Sutton," he said. "I'm wondering if it's possible to fix its time of death."

"Relative to Sutton's?"

"Yeah."

She thought a moment. "Both their bodies are pretty stiff," she said. "But there might be differences in the biological processes leading to rigor mortis in humans and animals."

"Differences in timing, for instance?"

A shrug. "I'd think a forensic veterinarian could tell you for sure," she said. "If you don't know one, I could recommend somebody."

Sam nodded. He wanted to return to the house and see how Callen was doing.

"You've been a big help out here," he said. "Think you could email me your pictures for my files?"

She smiled.

"Of course," she said. "Crappy as they may be."

* * *

Elias Sutton's bedroom was a disaster area.

Following Detective Varno through the entryway, Callen was confronted with open dresser drawers with clothes spilling out of them, overturned storage boxes, papers scattered about the plush wool carpet... even the bedding was stripped from the mattress and tossed into a loose, disorderly pile.

"This place is a total shambles," he said.

"Besides being turned inside out," Varno added.

Callen didn't comment, thinking he would not let himself get baited into another round of semantics, never mind that it would seemingly kill the detective's fun.

His eyes roamed the room. Somebody had rifled through it, throwing things wildly about, leaving them wherever they landed. He saw an open glass display case on the wall opposite Sutton's bed, a jumble of small, odd-looking tubular cardboard boxes on the floor beneath it, their labels blue, white, gold, and various other colors....

"They're Edison cylinder records," Varno said. "Well, the *containers*."

Callen turned to him. "Like for a gramophone?"

Varno nodded. "They're all empty," he said. "Could be the records were stolen out of them... I'm guessing they're what's most valuable. But, who knows, it could be Sutton just collected the tubes."

Callen went further into the room, knelt over the boxes for a closer look. He counted almost two dozen of them, nearly all with their lids off and lying nearby on the carpet.

There was a desk by the bay windows across from

him, its drawers pulled out, their contents strewn all over the floor—pens, pencils, erasers, mounds of paperclips, rubber bands, sticky note pads, mailing envelopes, and dozens of other items large and small.

"Nothing's broken, no blood," he said, standing up. "For all this mess, I don't see any signs of a struggle."

"My thoughts exactly, Mr. Holmes," Varno said.

Callen massaged his stubbled chin. A copy of the *Los Angeles Times* was on the floor near the record tubes, folded across its length atop some shirts.

He bent, picked it up, and glanced at the front page.

"This is today's paper," he said, showing it to Varno.

"So it is," the detective said. "What about it?"

"Look around," Callen said. "Everything else was dumped in a hurry. But it's nice and neat. With a crisp fold. There isn't a page out of place."

"Meaning?"

Callen shrugged. "It's like somebody was standing right here, holding it in his hands, and—" He let the paper slip from his fingers to the pile of shirts— "dropped it. Just let it fall straight down to the floor."

Varno looked at him but said nothing. A sheriff's deputy drifted in, saw the two standing there together in silence, and left without either of them paying attention to him.

They still hadn't budged when Sam Hanna came through the door a half minute later.

"Jeez," he said, stopping to look about. "This room's a shambles."

Varno jabbed a finger at him. "Well put," he said. "You're a good man."

Sam grinned. "Appreciate it," he said.

Oblivious to their exchange, Callen glanced

thoughtfully down at the newspaper again, then looked up at the expansive bay windows, and moved off in their direction. They offered a view of a lush, manicured flower garden on the east side of the property. Facing outward, Sutton's blond-wood desk seemed custom built for the alcove where the windows projected from the house.

Callen eyed them carefully. The center window was fixed, the ones to its left and right hinged so they opened from the side. There was nothing to suggest forced entry, but the latch on the right window was turned to the open position. He moved around the desk, pressing his hand against it.

The window pushed easily outward.

"Did your people dust these for prints?" he asked, looking at Varno.

"Not yet."

"Go over the flower garden for evidence?"

Varno shook his head. "All I've got here are two techs…"

"Let's get it done," Callen interrupted, and then shifted his attention to the computer on the desktop.

Sutton obviously hadn't replaced his equipment in quite a while. His processing unit was an older midsized tower, the monitor a basic flat panel that probably dated back to the early two-thousands.

Callen pushed the power button on the front of the case, turned on the monitor, and waited.

The manufacturer's logo and operating system appeared on the monitor and then gave way to a full blue screen.

"The dreaded blue screen of death," Sam said from over his shoulder. "Its hard drive didn't boot—we're just seeing what's on the motherboard."

"Do you even hear a hard drive cranking in there?" Callen asked him.

Sam shook his head.

"Come to think," he said, "I don't."

Callen frowned, tapped a random letter on the keyboard, and then listened with his ear close to the CPU.

Nothing happened. He didn't hear any of the usual whirring or clicking startup sounds.

He hit a different key, listened.

Still nothing.

"What do you make of it?" he asked.

"Dunno," Sam said. "How about we open this baby up and find out?"

Callen nodded. He slid the tower forward, turned it to access the back… and then straightened, his eyes meeting Sam's.

The thumbscrews attaching the processor's cover to its chassis were sticking straight out of their holes. They'd been twisted almost completely loose.

Reaching with both hands, he lifted up the cover.

"Well, well," he said.

"Well, well, well," Callen said.

"Is this a bromance exclusive, or can I look too?" Varno said, and stepped between them.

The three stood peering into the computer's open chassis.

"*Oops*," Varno said. "Appears somebody made off with the hard drive."

Callen glanced over at him.

"Can anything make you quit?" he said.

The detective grinned.

"I gotta admit," he said, "it takes a lot."

* * *

Erasmo Greer sat on the sofa in his single-bedroom Western Avenue flat with a can of cola in his hand and his laptop computer on his knees, the faint blue glow of its monitor playing across the lenses of his glasses. Surrounded by the cartons of old clocks and clock parts crowding every available inch of his tiny living room, he'd blocked out the shouts and crashes of the nightly battle royale in the adjacent apartment, and signed into his merchant's account on ShopNow!

Erasmo bent to set the cola down on the floor, the sofa cushion flipping up underneath him as he shifted his weight. An orange plaid convertible he'd snagged for fifteen dollars at a local Salvation Army store—the same place he got his clocks and movements by special arrangement with a staffer—it had a few obvious deficiencies. The armrests were greasy and smelled vaguely of beer and mayonnaise, the frayed, saggy cushions had little white bouquets of stuffing coming out of them, and the bedframe's creaky metal springs would corkscrew into his back and sides when it was pulled out. But it was functional enough, and suited Erasmo's needs.

He didn't care about material possessions. Why should he? Even without his sizeable inheritance, he'd earned riches galore as an elite hacker, more money than he could spend in a dozen lifetimes. He could buy anything he wanted, indulge in every luxury imaginable, own majestic homes around the world... homes that would make his current employer's mansion in the hills look like a cowshed.

What truly mattered to him, though, was the thrill of accomplishment and his deserved recognition among the hacker community. In that regard he was already living his dream, *un rêve dans un rêve...*

But soon he would have to move on, hide himself in a new lifestyle. And he supposed that in the big picture this grungy, decaying Los Angeles slum wasn't where he belonged. Perhaps it was time to enjoy what others considered the good life. European villas and beaches with tucked-away coves. Days of sun and frolic, nights of vintage wine and music, a parade of beautiful, suntanned women competing for his arm.

He supposed he would buy a couch of fine leather. A plush sectional built by an Italian designer. He would laugh and lounge on it to his heart's desire. It would be an experiment of sorts. Would his happiness thrive in his new surroundings? How might they change him?

There was a loud thump on the wall and Erasmo sighed—the pair next door were quite literally in full swing. Well, he had better things to do than listen to their rumpus. Typing and clicking on his keypad, he went to his seller's account page.

Un rêve dans un rêve…

A dream within a dream.

Erasmo was perfectly aware of his occasional partner's limited intellectual capacity. Unlike himself, Isaak Dorani was strictly smalltime, inseparable from his environment. Take a frog out of the pond, and it would miss the mud at its bottom. Isaak would die in the mud rather than leave it behind.

That, however, was not his concern. His major problem now was satisfying Jag Azarian—and the clock was admittedly within a few ticks of running out.

In hindsight, Erasmo supposed he shouldn't have exaggerated his progress to Azarian. That was his one mistake. A sin of hubris. But he'd felt confident he could make the deadline. At one point, it had seemed as if there was so much time.

Time, he thought.

His *other* stock in trade.

His face pinched with concentration, he got to work. In his alias as TickTockDude, a vender of rebuilt and refurbished clocks, he'd earned a hundred-percent positive customer feedback rating in the electronic fleamarket. The income from his business meant nothing to him, of course. But his Shopnow! store had another function, and a very useful one, as a covert channel of communication.

He scrolled down his item queue, eyeing his current listings. The first was a square battery-operated Roman numeral wall clock, the second a plain round indoor/outdoor model. The third listing was titled:

> *Retro Alarm Clock—Black w/White dial—*
> *Twin Bell—Bedside*

Its description read:

> *Blackouts in your neighborhood?*
> *Who needs electricity? Go with vintage windup!*
> *A GUARANTEED boss-pleaser!*
> *Works perfectly, new movement, hands, and glass dial cover.*
> *Like all our clocks it is tested for accuracy!*
> *Buy from TickTockDude and wake up on time!*

Erasmo decided somewhat randomly that this would be the listing whose photo he'd modify for tonight's update to his zealous contractor—his hidden message was always encoded in one of the first five items on his seller's listings. Regardless of his selection, the idea was not to fiddle too much with the image, so as to avoid attracting notice from ShopNow!—and more importantly from intelligence and law-enforcement agencies that might be monitoring the site for covert activity.

Clicking to the REVISE ITEM link now, Erasmo navigated to the CHANGE PHOTO option, and then highlighted the picture he'd originally uploaded.

"And away we go," he said under his breath, clicking the DELETE button. After a moment, he dragged his cursor to ADD PHOTOS, chose INSERT from the dropdown menu, and scrolled to the replacement picture on his hard drive.

Erasmo carefully scrutinized the picture before beginning his upload. It was superficially identical to the first, except for the time displayed on its face. Whereas the original photo read ten minutes past ten, the hands on his substitute showed three minutes to twelve.

There was, of course, a more significant difference between the two. But that was invisible, and would be deciphered only by his rather ideologically extreme contractor after he downloaded it to his computer.

Clicking on the replacement image now, Erasmo saw it appear in the listing and nodded with satisfaction. His modified image would remain online for the next three hours—the prearranged window—after which he would yank it and repost the original as a security precaution. But even if a third party caught on and downloaded the substitute, there was slim chance anyone besides his intended recipient could extract his coded message. Not without the correct decryption key.

Erasmo bent and reached for his soda. What was it Albert Einstein once said? *If only I had known, I should have become a watchmaker.*

"Or maybe a clockmaker," he said, chuckling.

Then he gulped down what was left in the can and tried to relax, the computer still resting on his lap.

* * *

Jag Azarian swam as if he were gliding like smoke through the heavens. He stroked with his arms, his breathing even and regular, his lean body gracefully extended, his muscular legs propelling him toward the mountain's edges.

Undeviating with his routine, he swam ten fifty-meter laps, three times a day—first in the early morning, when the pool ribboned off into the broad horizon, merging with the brightness and cloud billows. Then at dusk as the giant red ball of the sun sank below the mountains, seeming to set the water around him aflame, giving the illusion that he was diving through molten lava. And then again shortly before midnight.

Now he took his third swim beneath the stars, alone with his thoughts of the powerful forces he'd set in motion, and the tide of blood and fire that would stem from their explosive collision. His inherited wealth, his education, his American citizenship—it was all for a purpose. Nothing was an accident. Nothing was coincidental. Though it had taken him many years to grasp it, he knew now that he'd been chosen to mete out the collective vengeance of his people, and teach the world its crimes against them were unforgotten.

As Azarian completed his ninth lap, he glanced toward the curving glass wall of his living room, and saw Karik appear from deeper inside the house, a towel draped over one arm. Thin and wiry, his short, pointed goatee giving his face an almost bladelike appearance, he held out a small remote control unit and the wall retracted seamlessly on invisible tracks.

Emerging onto the patio, Karik crossed to the lip of the pool, and waited.

Two minutes later, Azarian climbed from the water. He stood facing the house, naked, his long, dark hair dripping wet, small puddles forming on the tiles under his feet.

"What is it?" He took the towel, catching his breath. "I can see from your face you have something to tell me."

"A message," Karik said. "On your computer. From the Ticktockman."

Azarian regarded him closely.

"All right," he said. "I'm going to my office."

"Yes."

"See that I'm not disturbed."

"Yes."

At his desk moments later, wearing a black robe and leather slippers, Azarian took several deep breaths, closing his eyes, inhaling the scent of jasmine incense in the ancient Turkish burner across the room. Sitting back, he pressed the tips of his forefingers together under his chin to form a steeple—the back of his right hand scarred and missing its thumb from a childhood incident.

Relaxed, he channeled his thoughts along precise, germane lines.

Even as the clock struck twelve, he knew a lasting midnight was soon to fall over America, one many would find far darker than any that came before.

He opened the message on his computer now, eager to check on its approach.

2

"G, you smell something funny?" Sam asked, crinkling his nose.

Callen sniffed.

"Now that you mention it," he said, "I do."

Sam looked at him. "So it isn't my imagination."

Callen's face had puckered up.

"No, man," he said. "*Phew*, it reeks in here."

They stood in the doorway, frowns creasing their foreheads, looking around and sniffing the air for the source of the miserable, offensive stench that had met their arrival a few moments before.

The odor really was downright stifling, which said a great deal about its potency given the room's spacious dimensions.

With its high Spanish archways, exposed ceiling beams, terracotta floor tiles, elaborate wrought-iron room dividers, and orbit of special agents' desks around its perimeter, the large ground-floor bullpen of the OSP's mission house headquarters was an eclectic mash of architectural styles, furnishings, ornaments, and hung photographs and artwork that not only reflected Operations Manager Hetty Lange's colorful, even enigmatic, background, but her strong encouragement of individuality within the team dynamic. She'd been around long enough to know that several good heads were better than one, and had handpicked the members of her elite undercover arm of the NCIS as much for their quirky differences, and diverse specialties, as the one very important quality they shared—which was that they were unsurpassed in their abilities, resourcefulness, and proven track records.

Put simply, they were the best of the best.

For all their combined expertise, though, Callen the former DEA and CIA man with deep familial roots in the U.S. intelligence community, and Hanna the former Navy SEAL and three-time war veteran, were presently at a loss to identify the awful smell clinging to the insides of their nostrils.

"I'd say there's a dead rodent around someplace—" Sam began.

"But that'd be an insult to rodents," Callen interjected.

"Dead *and* alive," Sam said.

Callen nodded, lifted his right foot off the floor to examine his shoe bottom, then did the same with his left shoe.

"Didn't bring anything in off the street," he reported.

Sam checked out *his* soles and heels. "Me neither."

"Then what's stinking up the place?"

"Animalics," Special Agent Kensi Blye said, approaching from her desk across the room.

Both agents regarded her quizzically.

Tall, lithe, and dark-haired, her left eye hazel, her right eye brown, her skin as tan as the sand on an Iberian beach, Kensi, who was sometimes thought to be of Spanish or Portuguese descent—and uncoincidentally spoke both languages like a native—was wearing skinny jeans, an oversized blue plaid shirt, and a sidearm holder with a SIG Sauer P229 pistol configured for .40 S&W ammo.

"Ani*what*?" Sam asked.

"Ani-*m-a-l-i-c-s*," Kensi said, spelling out the second part of the word. "Actually, animalic therapy. It's the beneficial use of fragrances obtained from animals."

Callen looked at her. "Like animal parts?"

"Right." She shrugged. "Also secretions, excretions, and, ah…" She looked at him. "The biologically correct term would be *ejections*."

Callen frowned, feeling almost like he was two hours and ninety miles back up the road with Detective Varno. Suddenly everyone he came across was a walking Roget's Thesaurus.

"Why do I smell Deeks behind this?" he asked.

"Could be because I've singlehandedly taken on the job of changing the atmosphere around here," offered none other than Detective Marty Deeks himself, his voice carrying across the room from the grand, sweeping staircase that led to the second floor Operations Center. "No pun intended."

Callen watched as he descended. "Stay where you are," he said, holding out both hands to wave him off. "Not a step closer."

"That won't help," Kensi said.

"What if I said, 'not an inch'?"

"Still won't."

Callen faced her. "*No*?"

She shook her head.

"He's rubbed those scents on everything in here," she said.

"You're kidding, right?"

"Wrong." Deeks hopped off the staircase to join

them. "But we really oughtta call them pheromones."

Here we go again, Callen thought. "Does Hetty know about this?"

"Yep," Deeks said.

"And what's she think?"

"You'd have to ask her." Deeks nodded back toward the stairs. "She's up in Ops."

"I can see why," Sam said, fanning the air in front of his face.

Dressed in a tee shirt and jeans, Deeks extended his wrists out to him.

"Go on, Sam. Sniff 'em."

"No thanks."

"Seriously."

"I *am* serious. I don't want any part of your animal odors."

"Pheromones."

"A stink by any other name." Sam scowled. "What's wrong with you, dude? I mean, you think it smells *good* in here?"

"It shouldn't smell good," Deeks said.

"You think it should smell bad?"

"I think it should smell natural." Deeks sighed. "Take the cavemen, f'rinstance. What'd they have around them that we don't?"

"Caves?"

Deeks shook his head, his tussled dirty blond hair brushing his shoulders.

"Besides that," he said.

Sam looked stumped.

"*Nature*," Deeks declared, sighing again. "As in plants and animals. Our ancestors smelled them everywhere. Trees, flowers, grass... they poured perfume and nectar into their environment. With animals it was musk, urine, and fecal droppings."

"Oh for the good old days," Kensi said, and grinned.

Deeks stared at her unhappily a moment, then turned back to Sam.

"Listen," he said, "when your diet's short on certain nutrients, don't you take vitamin supplements?"

Sam shrugged.

"Sometimes," he said. "But my multiples don't have poop in their ingredients."

"You're missing my point," Deeks said. "Vitamins keep your diet balanced. They help you stay healthy and bring harmony to your system. You function better when you've got proper nutrition."

Sam looked at Callen.

"What scares me's that I'm starting to get the gist of all this," he said.

Callen frowned, looking at Deeks. "So you're saying we need animal stink around us."

"To be at our sharpest," Deeks said, nodding. "If perfume's the magical medium that lets a plant send messages to the world, then the pungent smell of anal glands is a civet's soul song."

"A civet?"

"It's an ugly catlike animal with a skanky butt," Kensi said. "They live in Africa and Asia."

"Oh," Callen said.

"Ah," Sam said.

"The two of you should take a whiff," Deeks said, holding out his wrists again. "Civet musk's produced all around the world from their anal secretions. But I experimented with my own formula." He offered a proud smile. "Blended with pureed oak moss, it's very smooth and buttery."

Callen wrinkled his face.

"Maybe another time," he said.

"Stay the hell away from me," Sam said.

"In fairness, you guys did ask about it," Kensi said, grinning like the Cheshire Cat again.

Callen appeared as if he might say something, then suddenly angled his head to look upstairs. A moment later, Sam's eyes followed.

"Gotta go," Callen said, and faced him. "Ready, partner?"

"On my way," Sam said.

The two men stepped past Deeks toward the staircase, leaving him standing there with his wrists still extended.

Puzzled, he looked around at Kensi and realized she'd also turned toward the stairs.

"What's going on?" he asked.

Before she could answer, Hetty Lange's voice came from the second-floor landing.

"I need everyone on deck… including you and your terrific stink, Detective Deeks," she said. "Immediately."

Isaak Dorani didn't like being blindfolded, not one goddamn bit. And he liked it even less while rattling along in a crappy old dinosaur of a van, bumping up and down with every dip, crack, and pothole in the road. If the damn thing ever had shock absorbers, they'd probably worn out years ago.

The crazies. Those damn crazies. Isaak couldn't have cared less what reasons they gave for tying a rag over his eyes, or how big he stood to score from dealing with them. They were stone killers, the whole bunch. He'd seen firsthand what they could do. The old man, his housekeeper, even that poor stinking yapper of a dog...

He was right there in the house when they blew them away. Right there. Close enough to hear the housekeeper pleading for her life, hear every word, not that too many left her mouth before they took her out. But what she said at the end, begging them for the sake of her kids, the gun practically in her face...

Isaak got sick to his stomach whenever he thought about that. These people were freaks, no denying it. As far as he could tell, they would do anything to get what they wanted.

Bumping along now, up and down, up and down, feeling like he was on a wheeled trampoline, he suddenly found himself thinking of those ancient phonograph records in Sutton's bedroom. He hadn't gone there looking to score them. The crazies had told him to bring out laptop computers, tablets, storage disks, anything electronic. Erasmo was right about one thing: they were very clear about what they wanted.

But after all the bad stuff went down, Isaak had noticed the records and decided they could be his personal ticket out of both the frying pan *and* the fire. He still didn't know exactly what they were worth, but thought for sure it was a small fortune. They said "Edison Company" on them, for God's sake, as in *Thomas* Edison. The dates on some of their boxes said they were over a hundred years old.

Though Isaak didn't have a chance to grab them all, he *was* able to stuff a bunch into his carry bag, thinking Daggut was bound to be interested. The fence specialized in quality antiques, after all.

Erasmo could talk all he wanted about accepting the risks. It was easy to talk when he was anonymous, hiding behind his zillion and one IP proxies and secret messages. He wasn't the one putting himself at the mercy of these lunatics.

Isaak really didn't give a crap what they said to him. Bumping along in the rear of the windowless van now—key word, *windowless*—he saw no good reason for them tying a rag over his eyes.

None.

"I don't like it," he said, his voice almost drowned out by the racket inside the van. Besides the old junker needing shock absorbers, its air conditioner was huffing and puffing like it was about ready to croak, leaving it stiflingly warm in the back even with the damn thing running full blast. "Not one goddamn bit, Gaspar."

The driver swung into a turn. "Speak up," he said. "I can't hear you."

But Isaak could hear him just fine. His weird, high-pitched voice somehow cut right through the racket inside the van.

Gaspar the Friendly Ghost, he thought, and took a breath to fill his lungs.

"I said this blindfold *sucks*!" he shouted. "You hear me all right now?"

"Yes."

"So?"

"I've told you before," Gaspar replied. "Think of the blindfold as protection."

Isaak frowned, wiped the sweat off his brow with his arm. The sun was pouring through the windshield, overwhelming the clanking, decrepit air-conditioner.

"Come on, man," he said. "You got no worries. Somebody could waterboard me, I'd never admit I knew anything. I mean, you know, why would I talk?"

"I can think of some reasons."

"Like *what*? In case you didn't realize it, my ass is on the line too—"

"I can't hear you, Isaak."

Isaak frowned. "I was just saying you people aren't the only ones with a ton to lose by getting caught," he said at the top of his voice.

The van rattled and swayed as Gaspar took another turn, pushing the rattletrap up to a pretty high speed.

"Pay attention, Isaak," he said. "The blindfold is for your protection. Not ours."

"*Mine?*"

Gaspar nodded. "We can't afford to take chances," he said. "If we thought you knew the location of our safehouse, we would have to kill you."

Isaak opened his mouth, then shut it. He'd heard all he cared to hear from Gaspar—enough to last him the rest of the drive, thank you very much.

He sat back, sweating heavily, rocking from side to side in his seat. While he didn't know exactly where they were, he figured it must be west of the city proper. Whether that also put him north or south of it, he couldn't tell. But with the intense heat and sun, he'd concluded he had to be driving through the Mojave, which stretched for hundreds of miles in both directions.

The van rolled on for another fifteen or twenty minutes, creaking and shaking on its rusty suspension. Then, finally, it lurched to an abrupt halt.

Gaspar got out, his feet crunching on gravel as he came around and swung open the rear doors.

"We're here," he said, taking hold of Isaak's arm.

"No shit," Isaak said. "You got my bag?"

"Yes," Gaspar said, handing it to him by the strap.

He slung the small black satchel over his arm. Its contents were worth twenty large, earning him four thousand in commission, a nice pile of cash considering he was just the middleman. For that kind of haul, he was prepared to do almost anything.

Isaak let Gaspar help him out of the van and then guide him up the path to the safehouse, his hand around his elbow.

He hadn't walked two or three steps before the screeching birds jolted him up straight. He'd heard their shrill, blood-curdling cries, coupled with the loud flap of their wings overhead, every time he came out here, and they never failed to make his skin crawl.

"Come on," Gaspar said, feeling him stiffen. "The door's straight ahead."

Isaak nodded and quickened his pace. Those birds almost sounded prehistoric, conjuring up a mental image of reptilian scales on their bodies instead of feathers. Whatever the hell they were, he was sure there was nothing like them in East Los.

He walked another few feet, then heard Gaspar hit his fist against a door.

It opened and they went inside.

"All right," Gaspar said behind him. "You can stop now."

Isaak stood still as he undid the blindfold. Although there was no air-conditioning in here, and it seemed to him the windows were always shut, he was glad to be out of the burning sun.

A moment later the cloth came off his face.

He blinked. Blinked again.

When his vision cleared he was looking at a tall, dark-skinned man in his late twenties, his shirttails hanging out over his waist, his long, full, shaggy beard resembling the kind worn by every lame-ass hipster Isaak would see hanging around the USC campus at

University Park. Pass him on the street, you might think he was a grad student getting a higher education in Chinese pottery, Native American weaving, or some other useless, artsy shit.

Though, naturally, Isaak knew better.

"Matous, dude," he said. "Whassup?"

The bearded man looked at him.

"We're not friends," he said, in his faintly accented English. "Don't pretend we are. For your own good."

Isaak didn't answer. To hear these people talk, you'd think they were more concerned about his welfare than his own mother.

Which really wasn't saying much, since she'd dumped him off at an orphanage when he was still a punk.

"Friend?" he said at last. "What friend? Who mentioned *friends*?" He cleared his throat. "Mister Business, that's me."

Matous just stared at him coldly. Then gestured at the satchel with his chin.

"You brought the items?"

Isaak nodded, blinking more fuzziness from his eyes. This was the only room here he'd ever been allowed in. It contained no furniture except for some scattered chairs and a large wooden dining table. Besides Gaspar and Matous, there were five other people present—two of Matous's usual bookends standing nearby looking watchful, a woman and two men seated at the table.

He'd never seen those three in the flesh before, but recognized them at once. Their faces were on the forged IDs in his bag.

He unzipped it and produced a large brown clasp envelope.

"Here," he said, handing the envelope to Matous. "These are top flight."

Matous opened it and took out one of the driver's licenses.

"They've got the new security features down to the last detail," Isaak said. "Put them under ultraviolet light, you'll see a smaller photo of the driver."

Matous carefully examined the license, ran his thumb over the signature, and nodded in silent approval as he felt its raised laser engraving. Then he reached into his pocket for his smartphone and thumbed on its flashlight.

Isaak watched him bring the flash up to the back of the license while looking at the front for the outline of the California bear. After a moment he nodded again.

"They got that grizzly down perfect," Isaak said, noting his obvious satisfaction. "I told you. These cards are the best."

Matous studied the license another minute, then put away the phone and looked up at him.

"What about the hard drive?" he said. "When can we expect the files?"

Isaak could hardly believe his ears. It was, what, eighteen hours since he'd pulled the drive from Sutton's computer? Eighteen, tops. Did it look like he was wearing a secret decoder ring or something? Plus, why ask *him* about this shit? Erasmo was supposed to have sent Matous's boss a message last night.

"That'll take a little longer," he said, staying cool. "The old man knew how to hide things. You can't do stuff like that overnight."

Matous kept looking at him.

"When?" he repeated.

"A couple of days—at least a couple," Isaak said,

thinking again that he was the wrong person to ask. "That's my best guess."

Matous's eyes continued to rest on his face. "It can't take any longer," he said, and smiled. "You'll see for us that it doesn't."

Isaak was quiet. The meaning of that smile was unmistakable. Matous hadn't been making a request.

He stood listening to the birds shriek away outside, carrying on like Halloween goblins at the stroke of midnight, thinking he could hardly wait to get paid and split.

"Look," he said. "The sooner I get back to town, the easier it is for me to grease the wheels, you know what I'm sayin'?"

Matous eyed him for what felt like a hundred years. Then he nodded.

"All right," he said, and glanced over at one of his bookends. "*Vcharel non*. Give him his money, Narem."

A short, broad-chested man in cargo pants and sneakers, Narem disappeared from sight, returning a minute later with a leather briefcase. He gave it to Isaak without a word, then returned to where he'd stood across the room.

"You'll get ten thousand now," Matous said. "The other half along with our payment for the data."

Isaak's eyes widened. "Wait," he said. "This was a rush job. My guys were expecting the full twenty thou."

"They were wrong," Matous said. "We're paying for a total package. The IDs are worthless to us without the information."

"But the people who knocked out the cards... I'm telling you... they don't even know about the hard drive. They're going to want their—"

Matous looked at him sharply.

"What they want doesn't concern me," he interrupted. "Take the money, Isaak. And call me tonight. I need to know when I'll see the contents of the drive."

Isaak stared at him. He was thinking the Russians that made up the cards would be beyond furious when they learned they'd been shortchanged. And they were not the sort of people anybody would choose to mess with.

On the other hand, he thought, the same could be said for his present company. He glanced at the three sitting around the table, saw them watching him closely, and felt the tiny hairs at the back of his neck prickle. Something about their expressions—about the stone-cold look in their eyes—almost made him freak. He didn't need a stronger hint that it was not in his best interest to put up an argument.

"Okay," he said, suddenly wishing he could leap into a time machine and give his ignoramus self of three or four months ago some choice words of advice about ever becoming involved with these crazies. "I hear you. I'll deliver the message. *Messages*, I mean. Hey, like my mama used to say... what's a lousy ten thousand bucks give or take?"

Matous gave him another telling smile.

"It depends what else is given to you, Isaak," he said. "Or taken."

Although diminutive in physical stature, Henrietta Lange encompassed worlds.

According to her NCIS biography and background check forms, she had lived several epic lifetimes in her six plus decades on earth. Reading her personnel file, one might have concluded that her arrival from the womb on February 29, 1949—a leap day, exceptional by definition—made the very firmament tremble, setting off cosmological upheavals and auroral displays. Surely a virtuoso artist must have painted his masterpiece on that same date, an author penned his greatest literary work, a composer his magnum opus. Oceans doubtless swelled as architectural wonders rose and fell. An enduring mystery of mankind must have unraveled, and another come into being.

Worlds.

Once upon a time, before her entry into the intersecting fields of covert intelligence and law enforcement, Hetty had enjoyed stellar careers in motion picture and stage costuming, celebrity realty, and boutique stock brokerage. Rumor had it that she shared more than wine with Sinatra, enjoyed a private weekend audience with Elvis at Graceland, and whirled through an intimate starlit pavane with George Hamilton on his lavish motor yacht.

It was said that the immortal Luciano Pavarotti dedicated his most tortured, impassioned performance of "Nessun Dorma," from the romantic opera *Turandot*, to Hetty while she watched contemplatively from his personal box seat in Milan's Teatro Alla Scala.

"Ed el mio bacio scogliera il silenzio, che ti fa mia!" he'd intoned as he'd sunk to one knee, his hands grasping out in her direction.

"And my kiss will break the silence that makes you mine."

Those in the first rows of the orchestra would later agree his cheeks were glistening with tears.

Worlds.

At various points along the line, Hetty earned a Master of Fine Arts degree at the Sorbonne, studied

ashion at the esteemed Ecole de Chambre
tale de la Couture Parisienne, and honed her
linguistic abilities at the Defense Language Institute
in Monterey, California, gaining fluency in Russian,
German, Mandarin, Spanish, Czech, Romanian,
Aramaic, Hebrew, Magyar, and Pashtun. She became
adept at the circular Korean martial art of Hapkido,
the combined sportfighting techniques of Chinese
Wushu, and the Filipino stick sword and knife
combat discipline known as Eskrima. Always good
with firearms, she would be the only woman ever to
earn the bronze in the smallbore rifle category of the
1964 Olympics.

Many years later, Hetty would break the senior
women's record for the ascent of K2, the second highest
mountain in the world. She earned a commercial
instructor rating for multiengine jet aircraft, and
wrote three published novels of some critical and
popular acclaim. She accumulated several decorations
with the Defense Intelligence Agency, won the CIA's
Intelligence Star for courage under conditions of grave
risk, and was admitted into the chivalric Dutch Order
of Orange-Nassau.

Worlds… and colossal worlds at that.

And Hetty was not yet finished setting high water
marks. Since becoming an Operations Manager with
NCIS in 2009, her clearance rate—the percentage of
cases her office solved—was consistently ranked among
the highest of anyone who'd ever held the position.

Yet in spite of it all, she was an unassuming woman.
Accustomed to keeping a stoic façade, sworn to the
highest levels of government secrecy, Hetty possessed
a quiet reserve that was deeply encoded in her
makeup, making it no likelier she would parade out

her accomplishments than her emotions.

Unless that accomplishment was brewing a perfect cup of tea. Then, and only then, would her features betray a flash of overt pride.

The gratified look on her face right now being an example. Standing at the entrance to Ops, she looked immodest indeed sipping her morning Zhen Mei, or Precious Eyebrows, the splendid green leaf variety prized by connoisseurs.

"I'm glad we're all finally together," she said as her agents entered from the stairs. Detective Deeks led the way, followed by Blye, Hanna, and Callen.

She eyed Deeks as he passed through the door.

"I will remind you to stay back from me."

He paused in front of her and started to say something, but she motioned him off.

"Back," she ordered.

He frowned, took a step in reverse. "This okay?"

"One more," she said.

He obliged.

"Thank you, Detective," she said, gesturing for him to halt. "I'll ask you to be mindful of keeping the proper distance next time."

He looked at her. "You told me you were into my animal aromatherapy."

"I told you I was willing to let you explore its benefits," she said. "Personally, I find the idea repugnant."

Deeks frowned.

"Wow," he said. "That stopped me cold."

"I take it that means you'll stay where you are?"

He shrugged. "I guess."

"Then it's a good thing." Hetty dipped the mesh tea temple in her cup, then looked around the room at her assembled team. "All right, let's get this briefing underway."

They waited silently, bathed in the room's low-glare cobalt light. With its state-of-the-art computer consoles, LCD interactive conference table, enormous touchscreen plasma display, and sound-baffling wall, ceiling and floor tiles, the Operations Center looked vastly different from the downstairs common area and bullpen. There were no decorative touches, no personal articles and ornaments... everything was clean and functional. Ops was the Office of Special Projects' digital eyes, ears, and brain center—and its technology rivaled or exceeded that of any other intelligence and surveillance facility on earth.

On the big screen now were four images. Its upper half showed a recent color portrait photograph of Elias Sutton on the left, juxtaposed with a black-and-white official U.S. Navy photo of a much younger, uniformed Sutton on the right. Beneath those shots were similar old-young images of another man—but while he was elderly and white-haired in the latter day photo, and looked like he'd been in his mid twenties when the black-and-white photo was snapped, both showed him to be impeccably dressed in a tailored sportcoat and wide-brimmed fedora.

"I know the man on top," Sam said, studying the screen. "But who's the dude in Brioni and Borsellino?"

Hetty glanced at him. "You have an eye for good clothes," she said.

He motioned toward the newer photograph. "Those threads leave good in the dust," he said. "That jacket must've cost four, five grand. The hat's a center pinch Como... I'm guessing it set him back a paltry four hundred bucks by comparison."

Hetty continued to regard him.

"I am duly impressed, Mr. Hanna," she said, dipping her teabag. "But a careful look tells me the sportcoat would sell for upwards of ten thousand dollars. It's *su misura*, as the Italians say. We call it bespoke in this country…"

"Custom made by a master tailor," Sam said. "That's style."

"And money," Callen said. "Why does he look familiar to me?"

Hetty turned to him. "His name is Holloway," she said. "Theodore 'Tip' Holloway."

"The CIA man?"

"Yes," Hetty said. "And before that CIG and OSS."

He met her gaze. In sorting through the tangled threads of his past, Grisha Aleksandrovich Nikolaev Callen, as he was named at birth, had learned his grandfather was an Office of Strategic Services operative stationed in Eastern Europe, and that his mother was brought up there and recruited by the CIA after moving to the United States. Callen had also discovered that his mother's handler—the person who sent her back overseas on the undercover assignment that led to her death—was Hetty Lange herself.

He knew all about the OSS, and how it was established to conduct espionage activities behind German lines during World War Two. Holloway had been one of the early intelligence officers with ties to William "Wild Bill" Donovan, a legendary figure who headed the organization through the nineteen-forties, and guided its transformation into the Cold War spy agency that would later become the CIA.

"Tip Holloway was a shadow's shadow," he said now. "From what I heard, he floated around some of the early special access programs, the kind with waived status."

"Whoa," Deeks said. "I'm pressing One on my touchtone keypad for English."

Callen looked at him. "Special access programs are highly classified. But a waived SAP is even more sensitive," he said. "It isn't listed in official breakdowns of government expenses. Oversight is limited to a handful of people in the Defense Department, and the funding's all black budget. The designation wasn't around when the OSS was in business, but off-budget projects were—and so was Holloway."

"If nobody minds my asking," Sam said, and motioned toward the upper half of the screen. "What's this got to do with Admiral Sutton? Or his murder?"

Hetty gingerly sampled her tea, let its flavor settle on her tongue a moment, then went back to dipping the bag in the cup.

"Patience, Mr. Hanna," she said. "I called everyone in here for a reason." She glanced over at the slight, spike-haired redhead standing behind one of the consoles, a tablet computer in her hands. "Nell, do you have the Deep Dive file ready?"

The analyst gave a pert nod. "I'm tossing it up on the big screen now," she said.

And almost as the words left her mouth, it appeared in its own overlay window. The document was typewritten, its first page stamped in ink with the designations CLASSIFIED TOP SECRET and EYES ONLY.

The heading read:

ISSUED BY THE OFFICE OF STRATEGIC SERVICES
INTELLIGENCE REPORT INDEX GUIDE 13-43549

SUBJECT: Deep Dive
SECRET GERMAN-JAPANESE U-BOAT
TRANSFERS OF ARMS, SCIENTIFIC PERSONNEL
AND TECHNICAL PLANS
1943-1945
FROM: Theodore P. Holloway, Project Director,
25 May 1945, Port Hueneme, California

"Port Hueneme's part of Naval Base Ventura County, isn't it?" Callen asked.

"It has been since it merged with Point Mogu, the adjoining air station," Hetty said. "But until the year two-thousand or so, it was an entirely separate facility."

"The Naval Construction Battalion Center," Sam said. "Admiral Sutton was its commander during World War Two."

"*Lieutenant* Sutton at the time," Hetty said with a crisp nod. "He was, in fact, assigned to the post in 'forty-three, and remained in charge until the end of the war."

"And I'm guessing they built ships over there?" Deeks asked.

Hetty shook her head. "The name is actually a bit misleading," she said. "Before Pearl Harbor, the United States had very few air and naval bases in Asia. But when hostilities broke out, we needed to quickly extend our reach—and the Port Hueneme facility was ideally situated on the West Coast. Contractors around the country would transport, store, assemble, and test the equipment for advance base construction there, then crate it for shipping to the Pacific theater of operations."

"You can still see some of the old buildings," Sam

said. "That storage area was pretty big."

Hetty nodded. "There were thirty warehouses… according to historical records."

Deeks looked at her. "Your pregnant pause tells me we're about to hear they were fudged."

She lifted her eyes to his face.

"Those horrid animalic odors do seem to have sharpened your deductive abilities," she said. "A thirty-first warehouse was built near the railhead. It headquartered a highly secret OSS program. And that was Deep Dive."

"So we're back to conversing in Spookese, huh?" Deeks said.

Hetty nodded, took another small sip of her tea. This time she looked satisfied.

"Yes," she said. "We are."

Sam looked thoughtful.

"One sec," he said. "This program… was the Navy involved? Or just playing the polite host?"

"I don't have a clear-cut answer. Lieutenant Sutton was the base CO. As you'll learn in a moment, the OSS would have needed his cooperation. He may well have had full knowledge of their activities."

Deeks looked at her.

"Were they, like, awful?" he said.

"I don't have enough information to judge," Hetty said. "I do know the Allies had grave concerns about German subs conveying dangerous new weapons to the Far East, and that those fears escalated toward the end of the war. The Kriegsmarine was adamantly opposed to using U-boats as transports—but Hitler had the final say."

"And he was a serious *heil*-me-or-else kinda dude," Deeks said.

Hetty appeared as if she might respond, then changed her mind and swung her attention around the room.

"I'm wondering if any of you have heard of *Speermädchen*?"

Callen nodded his head. "It's German for Spear Maiden—Hitler's plan to arm the Japanese with an atom bomb," he said.

Now Hetty was nodding too. "We've come to believe Tokyo had the centrifuge required for the nuclear refinement process," she said. "The Reich could provide rocket technology for a long range delivery system, and the most essential element of all—"

"Uranium," Sam said.

"Exactly," she said. "Their mines in Poland, Czechoslovakia, and elsewhere had produced large caches of ore—hundreds of tons."

Kensi's eyes widened. "Were they shipping it to Japan aboard submarines?"

"That's up for debate... from our contemporary perspective." Hetty shrugged. "Some historians insist there is evidence that *Speermädchen* boats carried stolen art, gold bullion, and fugitive Nazi war criminals to places of safety—besides providing the Japanese with superweapons and uranium oxide. Whatever the truth, the OSS needed to deal with the program."

"And they created one of their own to counter it," Callen said. "Deep Dive."

"That's the game. Check and mate."

"How'd they gather their information?"

"I was coming to that. We cracked the German Enigma code, and could intercept radio transmissions to and from their U-boats. The OSS and MI-6 also had spies imbedded as shipyard workers in the harbors where the subs went for refueling and resupply—and were loaded with cargo for their special tasks."

"I bet their manifests were falsified," Sam said with a shrug. "They could write anything they wanted on those pieces of paper—and would've done it to throw the Allies a curve."

Hetty gave a nod.

"Our spies and radio eavesdroppers knew they couldn't rely on cargo lists," she said. "Human intelligence was essential. A German submarine base might have several boats in port at a given time…"

"And while they were serviced, their crews would go on shore leave," Sam said. "Hang out at the beer hall, toss down a few, swap scuttlebutt. Stories would bounce around from one boat to the next like in every navy."

"Yes," Hetty said. "Captured submariners could tell us much more than the shipping forms, especially the officers and nonregulars."

Kensi's eyes narrowed with interest. "Nonregulars being…?"

"Scientists, engineers, and spies. Among other covert personnel."

"Leave your secret cargo off the manifest," Sam said. "Leave your secret passengers off the crew list."

"Indeed. In the last three years of the war, America and England sunk numerous Nazi submarines," she said. "They captured very few, though. Once Deep Dive was established at Hueneme, several of the boats and their crews were brought to the base for processing."

"'Processing,' huh?" Deeks said. "Spooky word."

"Its meaning in this case is fairly mundane,"

Hetty said. "There were between fifty and seventy-five prisoners of war for each sub—too many for the base to handle. My understanding is they were sorted out according to rank, status, and other criteria and then moved to various other facilities for interrogation."

"And Trip Holloway ran the show," Deeks said.

"Tip," Hetty said.

"Huh?"

"His nickname was Tip."

"Sorry," Deeks said. "Tip."

"Yes."

"*Not* Trip."

"That's correct."

"Ran the show."

"Yes."

"And wasn't gentle about it."

She looked at him but said nothing this time.

Deeks scratched thoughtfully under his chin.

"Okay, fellow Jedis," he said. "I figure Holloway, past tense, would have had regular contact with the grainy black-and-white version of Elias Sutton, our Santa Barbara homicide victim." He motioned toward the lower half of the monitor. "Can we safely assume there's also a connection between their present-tense color versions?"

Hetty's eyes held the faintest hint of amusement. She turned, stepped over to Nell's workstation, and gingerly set her cup and saucer down on a corner of the desktop.

"Nell," she said, "would you please let everyone see the document Eric was able to, ah, extract from the LAPD's database."

The analyst swiped a finger across her tablet, and

another overlay window appeared on the wall screen. The document *inside* the window read:

LOS ANGELES POLICE DEPARTMENT/DETECTIVE BUREAU
Robbery-Homicide Division
Special Investigation Section
Los Angeles, California 90012

INCIDENT REPORT #957237

Report Entered: January 7 14:23:35

STATUS: CONFIDENTIAL AND SEALED

REPORTING OFFICER:

Detective III Joshua Knowles

DATE/TIME REPORTED: January 7 12:07:28

ADDRESS: Bel Air Palms Senior Living

3462 Ocean Vista Road,

Los Angeles, California 90077

Subject: INVESTIGATOR'S PRELIMINARY ASSESSMENT AND RECOMMENDATION REGARDING MISSING PERSON/BURGLARY THEODORE PHILLIP HOLLOWAY

NARRATIVE:

On April 2, 2016, at approximately seven minutes past noon, Detective I Brad Matthews and Detective I Alberto Juarez arrived at the scene of a reported break-in at the above address, a 2-bedroom assisted-living condominium owned by Mr. Holloway, aged 93, in response to a 911 call. They were preceded by two patrol vehicles. The caller identified himself as John Murphy, aged 67, Holloway's home caregiver. Mr. Murphy was visibly distraught when he met the officers outside the residence, which he said had been "broken into and turned upside down." Mr.

Murphy stated that he had arrived at approx. 11:30 AM for a scheduled daily visit and found the front door wide open. Upon entry, he saw no sign of Holloway and proceeded to search the interior of the MP's home, conducting a room by room search for him. When it became clear he was not on the premises, he became worried and immediately contacted the police on his cellphone. The uniformed officers arrived within five minutes and conducted their own preliminary search of the dwelling.

It was then that they radioed for assistance. A short while afterward, Det. Matthews and Det. Juarez arrived and assumed control of the possible crime scene as investigators-in-charge.

Although there was no indication of forced entry or conclusive evidence of a struggle (pending forensics), the detectives found that the MP's drawers and closets had been emptied, and that clothing and other items were scattered throughout the apartment. Mr. Murphy pointed out that a laptop computer Mr. Holloway typically keeps on his desk was gone, along with a storage unit for data CDs and a backup drive. According to the caretaker, he is a very active computer user and often spends hours working on it.

It is <u>critical</u> to note that remote Internet monitoring of Mr. Holloway's premises by WEST COAST HEALTHAID, a provider of state-of-the-art health monitoring technology, <u>underwent a system-wide network failure one hour prior to Mr. Murphy's arrival</u>. Web-based surveillance cameras, motion sensors, and other devices either dropped offline or provided erroneous information about the victim's whereabouts. While the cause of the failure remains undetermined, it is my opinion that it is highly suspicious and warrants thorough follow-up investigation.

At this time, Mr. Holloway's whereabouts are unknown. His status has been listed as MISSING. The case remains

ACTIVE and coordination and communication within the
Department is essential.

Pg. 1 of 12 (w/attachments)

"Whoa, whoa. Hold up."

This was from Deeks, who had turned from the
screen to face the others.

"Yes?" Hetty asked.

"What I don't understand is how a remote
monitoring system goes into complete shutdown
without anybody noticing it," Deeks said. "There
must be alerts at the operator's end."

"You'd *think*," Kensi said. "I also wonder about
devices providing 'erroneous information.'"

"Like what devices, exactly?" he said. "Wristband
monitors? Video cameras? How does *all* the
hardware go wonky at the same time?"

"A system crash is one thing," Kensi said. "But
this almost makes me think someone manipulated
the network."

"Which means a hack," Deeks said. "That's
pretty sophisticated for stealing a senior's laptop
and disks."

"There may have been something of value to give
the burglars incentive," Hetty said. "Mr. Holloway
comes from a very prominent family, and one that's
amassed a sizeable fortune."

Deeks looked at her. "The *railroad* Holloways?"

"The same," she said. "They were giants in the
shipping industry. Back in the nineteen-twenties,
Caleb Holloway built more new lines than anyone
connecting the West Coast to the middle part of the
country. Not even the Vanderbilts had his success."

There was a thoughtful silence. Callen's eyes went to the wartime report. "Track fifty-seven," he said, reading the words from the top of the page. "Do you know what that means?"

"No," she said. "But I'm looking into it."

Callen nodded. "We can't blow off the idea that somebody wanted Holloway's computer," he put in after a moment. "Or information *on* the computer."

"Bearing in mind that whoever killed Admiral Sutton and his housekeeper took the hard drive right out of *his* PC," Sam said.

"Let's back up a sec," Callen said. "We have Elias Sutton and Tip Holloway. A couple of men in their nineties who knew each other during World War Two."

"And were stationed at the same *base*," Sam said. "Both in positions of command."

Deeks was back to rubbing his chin. "About two months ago, Holloway's condo gets burglarized—"

"And somebody makes off with his computer," Callen said.

"And he disappears," Kensi said. "Then, today, *Sutton's* home is tumbled—"

"And somebody makes off with *his* hard drive," Sam said.

"And he's killed," Deeks said.

"Anybody here who thinks this is all coincidental, raise your hand," Callen said, glancing around the room.

They were all quiet again.

"Two questions," Sam said. He'd turned toward Hetty. "Did Sutton and Holloway have any sorta connection after the war? Go into business together, socialize... whatever?"

She shook her head. "Not that I'm yet aware," she said.

"Then how'd you know to pull up that Deep Dive file linking them together? Before G and I even got back from Santa Barbara? I've read everything that's been written about Admiral Sutton and never heard about the OSS at Hueneme. Plus, the file's still classified. If it was *de*classified, it would be stamped right on the first page. And I'm wondering how come it isn't after seventy years."

Hetty looked at him.

"There's a story," she said.

Sam raised an eyebrow in a way that said they both knew she wouldn't divulge it until she was good and ready; everyone in the room knew there was nothing to do but wait when she was being deliberately elusive.

"Next question," he said with her reply, or non-reply, hanging in the air between them. "The police always ask the media for help in missing persons cases. They want the public on the lookout for the MP. And being that Tip Holloway is one of *the* Holloways, you'd especially think his disappearance would've been all over the news. But the LAPD's report on Holloway is marked confidential... making both files you threw onscreen secret."

Hetty looked at him.

"I believe you've well exceeded your two questions," she said.

"Maybe," he said, thinking that, if so, she hadn't yet given him a single answer.

Hetty kept looking at him.

"There's another story," she said.

Sam sighed. There she went again...

"Holloway was found two days after he was reported missing," Hetty said, catching him by surprise. "He was evidently in rough shape... though his hospital files were sealed, and we don't yet know his exact injuries. But he pulled strings within the department and arranged for the investigation to be closed."

Everyone in the room stared at her.

"Why on earth would anybody do that?" Callen asked.

She shook her head.

"That's part of the story I don't know," she said. "And that we need to find out."

3

"My God, is that stink coming from outside?" said a queasy-looking Detective Alberto Juarez, turning his gaze out the window at Spring Street.

Deeks and Kensi exchanged glances. It was now nine o'clock in the morning, and they had shown up unannounced at the LAPD's Robbery-Homicide Division headquarters, asking to speak with Juarez, one of the two detectives who responded to the break-in at Theodore Holloway's senior living condominium.

"Umm... I don't really notice it," Deeks said. "What kinda stink do you mean?"

"Like a sewer backup or something," Juarez said. A short, neat man of about forty in a navy business suit, white shirt, and blue-and-gray striped necktie, he stood sniffing the air where he'd met them in the reception area. "You sure you didn't see anything on the street?"

"No, nothing," Deeks said.

Juarez looked at Kensi. "How about you?"

She shrugged. "Well," she said, "we might've passed a garbage truck out front."

Deeks gave her a wounded look. "I don't think so," he said. "In fact, I'm sure we didn't."

Juarez was shaking his head. "This is worse than any garbage I ever smelled in my life," he said. "Seriously, it makes me want to lose my breakfast. And I didn't *eat* breakfast yet."

Neither of them commented.

Juarez turned to the receptionist at the desk behind him. "Barbara," he said. "Is it my imagination? Or are you being stunk out too?"

The receptionist screwed up her face.

"Stunk out," she said. "Big time."

The detective looked at the two agents. "There you go," he said. "Case closed."

Deeks cleared his throat, suddenly feeling defensive about the undiluted Siberian deer musk he'd dabbed on after his morning shower.

"You know," he said after a moment. "I read something recently about certain unusual aromas being good for you."

Juarez looked at him. "Oh?" he said. "How's that?"

Deeks shrugged. "They call it animalics," he said. "The idea that humans in the wild had animal *and* plant scents around them all the time, making it a natural part of our environment that we've lost in our civilized world."

Juarez looked at him. "First, 'animalic' isn't a real word," he said.

"Actually it is…"

"No it isn't," Juarez said. "*Animal* is a word. *Animalistic* is a word. Even *animallike* is a word since maybe a hundred years ago. And then there's *animism*, which is also a word, but doesn't have anything to do with animals per se." He paused. "*Animalic* is what you call a blend. Or a protologism if you want to sound brainy. Something that somebody who obviously thought he was smarter than the rest of us made up, and would like to *turn* into a word, I *guess* because the million plus real words in the English language weren't enough of an outlet for his precious self-expression."

Deeks scratched his head, thinking he hadn't wanted to start off on a bad note with the detective.

"And second?" he said, figuring he'd give him a chance to get the rest off his chest.

"What?"

"You said that was *first*," he said, and smiled. "What's second?"

"Thanks for reminding me. Second, what I'm smelling isn't what I'd call *unusual*... or an aroma," Juarez said, still looking around. "It's the kind of blast I figure you get in hell after the Devil eats his three-bean chili too close to bedtime."

Deeks and Kensi stood there as other detectives strode past on this typically busy morning at police headquarters in the heart of America's second busiest metropolis, over three hundred-fifty thousand people riding the rails to work every day here in downtown Los Angeles.

"That's gross," Kensi said. "Funny, but gross."

Juarez smiled.

"Should I tell you I'm sorry before or after you two tell me why you're here?" he asked.

She smiled back at him.

"You don't have to apologize," she said.

"No?"

"Nope," she said. Her grin broadened, all pleasantness and sparkling white teeth. "But we would appreciate you telling us about Theodore Holloway's missing person case file."

Juarez's grin evaporated, surprise overspreading his expression.

"What about it?" he asked.

"The reason it *automagically* disappeared in your department's computer system—or was buried, to put it another way—couple of days after he turned up alive," Deeks said. "For openers."

Juarez looked at the two of them for a long moment. Finally, he nodded.

"I think we better discuss this in my office," he said, his voice a near whisper. "Off the record, understood?"

He turned to lead the way, momentarily halting at the reception desk to glance over his shoulder at Kensi.

"It's Mr. Animalic here killing my nose with that smell, isn't it?" he asked.

She smiled crookedly. "It isn't me," she said. "That's all I can tell you."

"Will I need to fumigate this place?"

Kensi shrugged, shot Deeks a sidewise glance.

"Speaking from experience," she said, "it kind of grows on you after a while."

"So," Detective Juarez said, sliding his window open, "I'm assuming you two intend to let me know up top how Navy got hold of a sealed investigator's report."

Deeks and Kensi pulled a couple of chairs up to the desk and sat down to wait in silence.

Juarez took a long, deep breath. Then he turned, lifted a green potted plant off one corner of the desk, carried it over to the windows, and carefully placed it on the sill.

"I figure the fresh air might keep it from wilting away," he said, looking over at Deeks. "No insult implied."

Deeks offered him an innocent smile, his right ankle balanced on his left knee.

"Wouldn't think it in a million years," he said. "But I don't think Captain Philodendron has a problem."

"Oh no?"

"Plants absorb carbon monoxide during the day, and *produce* oxygen at night," he said. "So he'd be cool with a smell that's a little outside his comfort zone."

Juarez shrugged, rolled his chair back from under the desk, and lowered himself into it.

"I hear good things about you people," he said to Kensi. "That you can be trusted."

"If you mean about our talk here staying confidential, then, yes," she said. "We gave our word."

"And I'm actually '*you people*,'" Deeks said, reaching under his shirt to pull out his LAPD badge. His face was serious. "A department liaison officer attached to NCIS."

Juarez considered the tin for a full thirty seconds. Then he leaned forward. "This isn't about marking turf. I'm putting my career on the line."

"Just talking to us?" Kensi said.

He nodded. Opened his mouth as if to speak, closed it. Then nodded again.

"Yeah," he said finally. "Just talking. I need to know what got you interested in the Holloway case?"

Deeks and Kensi made brief eye contact, silently debating whether to open up to him. After everything they'd been through together, on the job, as friends, and then as lovers, there were questions that could be asked and answered without a word being spoken between them.

After a while, Deeks nodded.

"There was a double homicide in Santa Barbara

yesterday," he said. "You probably know about it."

"I only had to watch the news for that," Juarez said. "The Sutton murder's the headline everywhere. Frank Varno's handling the case down there. He's a solid detective—and *mi cuate*."

"Homies, huh?" Kensi said.

"*Si, hermana*."

Kensi smiled.

"Near the end of World War Two, Holloway and Sutton were both stationed at Port Hueneme," she said. "Sutton was a Navy officer, Holloway OSS."

"OSS doing what?" Juarez said. "I thought they built Quonset huts down there."

"Holloway was in charge of something called Project Deep Dive," she said. "Ever hear of it?"

He shook his head.

"It involved the processing of German naval POWs," she said. "The crews from aboard captured U-boats."

Juarez nodded. "Okay," he said. "What else?"

"Sutton's home appears to have been searched and burglarized," she replied. "But not for the typical valuables."

The detective's pupils widened slightly. "Was his computer missing?"

"Only its hard drive," she said. "He owned a desktop model."

Deeks carefully watched Juarez's face as that information sank in.

Then he lifted his foot off his knee and sat forward a little, taking the ball from Kensi.

"Santa Barbara's sending us the preliminary forensics when they come in," he said. "Meanwhile, we don't have any leads to the killer—"

"But you figure, two break-ins, two computers targeted, it isn't a fluke."

Deeks nodded.

"Like me figuring it's no coincidence you and that animal funk drifted into headquarters at the same time," Juarez said, and flashed a smile.

"Ha, ha," Deeks said dryly. "I'm overflowing with laughter inside."

"Any time," Juarez said, holding his grin another second or two before his expression turned serious again. "So how do you think these incidents are linked?"

Deeks glanced at Kensi, lobbing the ball back to her now.

"That's exactly what we came to ask you," she said. "But there's something besides the computers."

"Tying them together, you mean?"

"In a way," she answered, and took a second to formulate her question. "Your report says Holloway was missing from his condo... but it doesn't mention him turning up a couple of days later. Or say anything about his condition."

"They locked up his medical reports right away," Juarez said, and sighed. "You two *do* have your sources, huh? Makes me wonder if you really need an assist."

"If we didn't we wouldn't be here," Deeks said. "What exactly happened to him?"

Juarez meshed his fingers together on the desk and stared down at them. Then he shrugged and raised his eyes to Deeks's face.

"It's ugly," he said. "There were contusions all over his body, welts on his back and legs. You could tell he'd been slapped around from the bruises on his face."

"He's in his *nineties*," Kensi said. "That's beyond sick."

"There's more," Juarez said. "The old bird was pretty confused when he was found. Doctors at the hospital thought dehydration might have played into it… and it could have. But he also had slurred speech, memory loss, other symptoms that could have been caused by a stroke or head injury."

"Were they?"

Juarez shook his head. "His blood tests showed somebody dosed him with Trapanal," he said. "In the old days they called it—"

"Truth serum?" Kensi said. "This gets crazier and crazier."

"Yeah," Juarez said. "You ask me, Holloway was interrogated. That might sound dramatic, but I don't know how else to put it."

Deeks's eyebrows arched.

"Let's back up a sec," he said. "You talked about *when* he was found. But how about telling us *where*? And if you have any leads on a suspect."

Juarez took a breath.

"Holloway was in a rain ditch off route one-oh-eight out in Lancaster County," he said. "A cattle rancher driving a pickup spotted him out near Saddleback Butte Park."

"The middle of nowhere," Deeks said.

"All sand, Joshua trees, and abandoned properties from the development boom," Juarez said. "The area still hasn't bounced back."

Deeks nodded thoughtfully.

"It's been in the news a whole lot recently," he said. "I hear there're all kinds of problems with squatters."

"Yeah, the adverse possession laws in California are a mess," Juarez said. "When you've got blocks and blocks of empty homes out in the valley, and eighty thousand homeless Los Angelinos desperate to put roofs over their heads, it's a recipe for trouble." He paused, shrugged. "Back to Holloway... when the rancher and his wife spot him, they figure he's dead. Then the rancher stops his truck, gets out for a closer look, realizes he isn't, and calls the local cops. Holloway's conscious, and identifies himself when they arrive."

"How soon before you found out?"

"It must've been within the hour," Juarez said. "He was Medevaced to Antelope Valley Hospital, and my partner and I drove right out to see him. He was weak, banged up, and disoriented, like I told you. But he was lucid."

"Able to answer questions?" Kensi asked.

"Absolutely," the detective replied. "He's one tough geezer."

"Did he explain how he wound up in that ditch?"

Juarez shook his head.

"Tell you how he sustained his injuries?"

He shook his head again.

"How about later? When he left the hospital?"

"No," he said, sighing. "Never."

Kensi gave him a questioning look. "You think the drug affected Holloway's memory of what happened to him?"

Juarez spread his hands. "In my opinion he knows," he said. "Maybe not everything, but enough. For whatever reason, he just refuses to talk."

"How about witnesses?" Deeks asked. "Maybe at the assisted care facility when he disappeared? Or on the road? Or to the couple that rescued him? He didn't beam from his living room to the place where he was found. He was snatched from the condo, driven out to the desert, and left on the roadside for a goner."

"Or held prisoner a short distance from there and escaped," Juarez said.

"Either way," Kensi said, "you'd think somebody would see something along the way."

Juarez produced another sigh. "About the condo... Detective Knowles is my commander and you read his report. There was no one around to see anything. The people who run the place depend on a computerized monitoring system, and it crashed."

"Knowles called that suspicious," Deeks said. "You agree with him?"

"Don't *you*?" Juarez looked at him. "Listen, if I had my druthers, we would've checked into how that system failed. Combed the valley for twenty square miles around that road where the old man turned up. Knocked on doors, hit service plazas, circulated flyers. Except our probe was shut down. They told us to stop actively investigating it. And we did."

"Did the order come from Knowles?"

"He was the messenger," Juarez said. "But something like that has to come from higher up. Knowles wouldn't deep six a case unless he was getting major pressure. Even if he wanted to, he doesn't have that kind of authority."

"Any idea who might've wanted it closed?" Kensi asked.

Juarez said nothing for a long moment. Then he stood up, walked to the door, opened it partway, and peered out into the hall, glancing carefully left and right. A second later he shut the door again, went back around his desk, and returned to his chair.

"Coast clear?" Kensi said.

He shrugged, looking at both of his visitors.

"You asked me a question," he said. "I'll tell you two what I think. Just my gut feeling, okay?"

They nodded their heads.

"I think it was Holloway himself," he said. "I don't care if he's a relic. He's a CIA good ol' boy who knows the right people. And he's used to putting things away in dark places."

"Why would he protect his abductors?" Kensi said. "I don't get it."

"Me neither," Juarez said. "But you wanted to know what I think, and there it is."

There was silence in the room. Then Deeks sat forward again.

"A minute ago you told us you dropped your active investigation," he said at last. "What's that mean, exactly?"

Juarez smiled a little. "You're some kind of stinker, Deeks," he said.

Deeks shrugged.

Juarez continued to smile, but his eyes were serious.

"Look, something like this happens, it isn't only me and Matthews on the case," he said. "This is the Los Angeles Police Department. There's crime scene techs, an evidence analysis. It isn't easy to put the brakes on their tests—" He snapped his fingers "—just like that."

Deeks's eyes went to his. "You got hold of the forensics on the sly."

Juarez nodded. "Some of them," he said. "I have my contacts."

"What should we know about the results?" Kensi asked.

Juarez looked at her. "When Holloway went missing we dusted his apartment for fingerprints," he said. "You know how it goes... it's routine, and not always useful. Most times they belong to friends, family members, caregivers—and the vic, of course.

But the techs took a few latents from the desk area, and came up with an IAFIS match to a known felon."

Deeks looked at him sharply. "So right about now's where the camera holds a closeup on our faces while we eagerly wait for you to drop a name on us."

Juarez smiled. "Isaak Dorani," he said. "Smalltime hustler, long rap sheet. Car theft, multiple petty larceny convictions, credit card fraud, numbers, gun-related offenses... on and on."

"An overachiever," Kensi said.

"And he isn't even thirty," Juarez said. "We lifted two clean prints from Holloway's desk, and they were, as they like to say nowadays, consistent with Dorani's to a high statistical probability."

"In other words," Deeks said, "beyond a sliver of doubt."

"You got it."

"Did you and your partner interview him?" Kensi asked.

"We couldn't," Juarez said, his fingers lacing together on the desk. "They reassigned us before we had a chance."

Her eyes widened in surprise. "Wait," she said. "You have a suspect in a burglary-kidnapping and there's *no* follow up?"

"That's right," Juarez said. And looked at her. "Actively."

Deeks cocked his head and pretended to listen to something. "I'm thinking I hear an echo in here."

Juarez wound his thumbs thoughtfully.

"An old man's abducted and brutalized... as detectives we're trained a certain way, you know? It wasn't anything we could let go," he said. "So we tailed Dorani for a while. On our own time."

"And?" Kensi said.

Juarez reached into his pants pocket for a key ring. He unlocked a drawer on the left side of his desk, took out a padded, wallet-sized black media holder, and slid it across to Kensi and Deeks.

"Here you go," he said in a low voice. "Take it."

Kensi lifted the case off the desk.

"You'll find a couple of gumstick memory drives inside," Juarez said. "They're identical copies of my private case file. My only copies. And now they're yours. Far as I'm concerned, they never existed."

Kensi looked at him. "Thank you," she said.

The detective inhaled deeply, then exhaled.

"Dorani's in over his head," he said. "Involved with some scary, dangerous people."

She nodded.

"I don't know how Holloway fits into the picture," Juarez said. "But something about him is damned unkosher."

Kensi slipped the holder into her purse.

"We'll find out," she said. "And keep you posted."

Juarez gave both of them a long look.

"Watch your backs," he said.

4

"G, you there?" Eric Beale said, his voice coming over the speakers of Callen's Benz.

"Yup," Callen said from behind the wheel.

About an hour after leaving headquarters, he and Sam were midway between Los Angeles and Santa Barbara on U.S. 101—the Pacific Ocean edging up against the beach to their left, the coastal chaparral shagging the hills to their right, the sky a clear, cloudless blue field spreading seamlessly overhead from horizon to horizon.

"Okay, Eric," Callen said. "What's up?"

"The timeframe," the tech said.

"For?"

"Elias Sutton's last hours on earth. Specifically where he was before his murder, and when he got home."

"I didn't think we were a hundred percent positive he went out that day," Callen said.

"Weren't before," Eric said. "Are now."

Callen's brow creased with interest. "Let's hear it," he said.

"After we linked the admiral and Holloway to

Port Hueneme, I poked around online for more biographical info about those two," Eric said. "I was hoping for something else about their wartime service. An added connection."

"In other words," Callen said, "you went fishing."

"There's all kinds of stuff floating in the water," Eric said. "Sometimes I like to toss my net over the side and see what turns up."

"So," Sam said as the Benz shot past a big, sluggish moving van. "You snag anything?"

"Yes," Eric said. "On Wikipedia."

Callen frowned. "Everyone's favorite go-to for wrongness."

"Hey, I did this last night on my own time," Eric said. "It was easy, convenient, and the pizza delivery guy was at the door."

"But you did use other sources to verify the information."

"Absolutely," Eric said. "After a couple of megacheese slices."

"And?"

"Sutton's late wife, Mara, was born Mara Wigham. As in her hometown, Wigham, Maryland. Born January twelfth, nineteen twenty-four. Died on yesterday's date five years ago."

"Wait," Callen said. "Sutton was murdered *exactly* five years after his wife's death?"

"To the day," Eric said. "Her ashes are at Palm Grove Cemetery in Santa Barbara—"

"Only a few miles from Sutton's home…"

"Five-point-three to be exact," Eric said. "Since it was nine, ten o'clock at night when I got that info, I waited until this morning to email the cemetery administrator's office."

"About reviewing yesterday's grounds security video."

"Right," Eric said. "There are special dates when people typically visit grave sites. Birthdays, holidays, and so on." He paused. "The anniversary of a loved one's death rates high on the list. And in case you're wondering there *is* a Facebook top five list."

"Naturally," Callen said dryly.

"Anyway," Eric said. "I wondered if Sutton might have gone to see Mara before he was killed."

"Did the administrator turn over the video?"

"Via email about ten minutes ago," Eric said. "It's a huge cemetery and there are *lots* of security zones. But my guy was very cooperative. He looked up the location of Mara Sutton's crypt and sent me the file."

Callen grunted. "And?"

"I didn't need to look at a ton of footage," Eric said. "It shows a black BMW sedan turning into a parking area behind the mausoleum. Then a couple of men get out."

"Sutton?"

"Yes, sir. He's with his driver."

"How long did he stay?" Callen said. "The surveillance video would have to show the car leaving."

"It drove out of the parking area at exactly three fifty-five."

Callen thought a moment, remembering Varno's teenage bicyclist.

"An earwitness heard gunshots coming from Sutton's place between four fifteen and four thirty…"

"And the cemetery's about a half hour from there by car," Sam said.

Callen did the quick math. "So Sutton got home

from visiting his wife's grave just in time to be killed."

"Not the sort of welcome I'd opt for," Eric said. "But to each his own."

"What happened to that car?" Callen asked, thinking aloud. "And the driver? Neither one was at the scene."

"Taking your questions in order, we're clueless and cluelesser," Eric said. "I *did* get screen captures of the BMW's license plate numbers and run them through the DMV's database. The car's registered to Sutton. He's owned it for three years."

"Nothing on the driver?"

"Not yet," Eric said. "I should be able to find stuff, though. There has to be bookkeeping if he was on payroll. Plus it would be a breeze getting my sticky fingers on his IRS filings—"

"We'd need a subpoena to make that legal," Sam interrupted. "Key word, *legal*. And the paperwork could take days."

"Bah," Eric said. "Sometimes I abhor the pesky details."

Callen thought a moment. If the BMW belonged to Sutton, where was it?

"Check the insurance records," he said. "They're public. Insurers like to know when a car's regular driver is someone besides the owner. And where it's usually parked."

"Aye aye, sir," Eric said. "Incidentally, I have another cool infobit for you."

"Is infobit even a *word*, Blackbeard?"

"If it ain't, it ought to be."

Callen grinned. "Funny," he said. "Okay, what is it?"

"When I read Mara Sutton's obituary on the Web, I noticed that her mother, Charity Wigham, was formerly Charity Reynolds," Eric said. "Going back another generation, I noticed *her* father was Benjamin Reynolds, whose mother—if you follow—was formerly Vivienne *Holloway*."

"Wait," Callen said. "Sutton's wife and Tip Holloway are *related*?"

"Yep, cousins once removed," Eric said. "Apparently the ties between the Suttons and Holloways go way back. What's more, Vivienne's the daughter of *Caleb* Holloway."

"The railroad baron Hetty mentioned?"

"None other," Eric said. "I already told Deeks and Kensi about the family connection, FYI."

Callen glanced over at Sam. "My head's spinning from all this," he said.

"Mine, too," Sam said.

Callen was silently wishing for a cup of coffee.

"Anything else?" he asked Eric.

"That's all for now. I'll look into those insurance records right away. Oh, and don't get too dizzy—you're on the freeway," Eric said, and hung up.

"I just had a thought," Sam said seconds later.

"Uh oh," Callen replied, his hands lightly resting on the steering wheel. "Extreme danger alert."

Sam pulled a face.

"Seriously," he said. "What Beale told you about Admiral Sutton getting killed on the same date his wife passed... you think that's a coincidence?"

"You know what Sherlock Holmes says about coincidences."

Sam shook his head. "No idea."

"Me neither," Callen said. "But I don't think it's a fluke." He scratched behind his ear thoughtfully. "I figure you can look at things two ways. One, someone murdered Sutton that day to make a statement..."

"A revenge killing?"

"Something like that," Callen said.

"But revenge for *what*?" Sam said. "His wife died of a coronary."

Callen shrugged. "Maybe somebody feels he put her under emotional stress. Or ignored the signs she was at risk. Or took her to a lousy cardiologist."

"Are you *serious*?"

"You never know. It gets funny when you start to play the blame game."

Sam shook his head.

"They were married sixty years," he said.

"You think longtime couples can't have skeletons in their closets?"

"I know they can," Sam said. "But we're talking about a man in his nineties whose wife's been gone half a decade. Those old, hidden skeletons gather dust after a while."

Callen shrugged again. "Doesn't mean they're forgotten," he said.

Sam frowned. "C'mon, G. You're reaching here. A grudge against Sutton doesn't explain his missing hard drive. Or Holloway's missing laptop."

Callen drove in silence, mulling that.

"Okay," he said. "Ready for my next thought?"

"Go on."

"Say whoever wanted Sutton's hard drive knew it was the anniversary of his wife's death. And that he would visit her at the cemetery yesterday…"

"And figured it was a perfect time to break into his house?"

"Exactly," Callen said. "Snatch the drive while he's out. But the admiral gets home sooner than expected—"

"And *bang*," Sam said.

"More than once," Callen said.

Sam stared thoughtfully out the window a minute.

"That makes more sense," he said. "But what about the maid? Wouldn't the thief—or *thieves*—figure she'd be at the house?"

"Maybe, maybe not," Callen said. "She could have surprised him. We don't know her routine. Could be it was her regular day off and she shuffled her schedule. There's all kinds of possibilities."

Sam was quiet again.

"Okay," he said. "Let's go with your hunch. Somebody close to Sutton plans the burglary for the date the wife passed away…"

"Or somebody who's *tipped* by somebody close to Sutton…"

"Right, right," Sam said. "My question is, who do you think would know it?"

Callen toed the gas, watching the roadside hills blur by. "It's no state secret. Anybody with a computer and an Internet connection could look it up. Same as Eric."

"Yeah… but knowing Sutton would visit the cemetery—and *what time of day*—you won't find that online."

"Right," Callen said.

"You'd have to be somebody pretty close to him."

"Like a friend or relative."

"Or relative of his *wife*."

Callen glanced over at Sam. "Holloway," he said. "That makes the most sense."

Sam reached into his pants pocket for his smartphone, thinking.

"Got a call to make, Sherlock," he said, and pressed in Kensi's number.

5

The Metroline commuter train arrived in a rush, sunlight glinting off its polished steel flanks.

Its pneumatic brakes hissed as it stopped at the platform. Waiting there under the old west hotel façade, a woman stepped out of the shade toward its cab car's open doors. She wore jeans, a tee-shirt, and a backpack.

Before getting aboard, she discreetly paused to snap some photos of the car with her smartphone, focusing her attention on the ladder climbing up its side to the cab.

"Good afternoon," the attendant greeted her cheerfully. In his early thirties, with an open, pleasant face, he leaned out the door as she entered. "Welcome aboard the A.V. Metroline."

The woman looked at him. "A.V.?"

"Antelope Valley," he said. "It's local parlance."

"Ah," she said. "I see."

He smiled, looked down the length of the train, and waved at the next car's attendant, indicating he was ready to close his doors.

The woman saw his hand signal repeated five more times. The train was six cars long, and there was one attendant per car, a greater number than most other low ridership lines.

She knew the reason for the added personnel. During her research she'd discovered that the explosion of gangs and methamphetamine producers in the high desert's squatter towns had turned the railroad into a rapid delivery system for narcotics and illegal firearms. More attendants aboard the trains, along with rolling spot checks and searches by L.A. County Sheriff's deputies, were an attempt to curtail the drug traffic.

It was something her team would have to contend with in short order, and a primary reason for this morning's trip.

"You have plenty of room to spread out," the attendant said, entering the train. "We're thin on passengers during off hours." He smiled again. "Upstairs is best for sightseeing. Gives some nice views of the desert."

She smiled back at him. "Thank you. I believe I'll take advantage of it."

"If you don't mind my asking… are you from Scotland?"

"Close," she said. "No prize, though. I was raised in northern England. Manchester."

That was close enough to the truth. She knew Manchester well, having spent the early stages of her life in the village of Knutsford, twenty miles to its south. This was before meeting Tomas, her first lover, on a college trip to London. Before she left with him for Syria, Lebanon and the training camps, where her past self melted away within the chrysalis of her rebirth, leaving only its useful memories.

"Here on a visit?" the attendant asked.

Her dark, steady gaze held on his. "A special history project."

The attendant nodded.

"Well, good having you aboard... enjoy the ride," he said, and walked off.

The woman stared at his back, a cold, narrow look coming into her eyes. She knew she could attract any man she wanted. It was an advantage, and an effective one. She practiced its use as she did any weapon in her arsenal.

After a minute she turned to look around the car.

Its modern, bi-level passenger compartment was cool and spacious, with high-backed rearward-facing seats, and a carpeted staircase at the front of the compartment leading to its upper deck. At the top of the stairs was the operator's cabin, hidden behind a steel door.

The woman focused on it a moment, thinking. Once the operator entered the cabin, the only way to reach him was to gain access to the emergency stairs. But the door locked automatically when the train was moving, as an anti-hijacking precaution, just like the door to the flight cabin on a plane.

She considered that as the train pulled away from Vincent Grade Station. Then she climbed to the upper deck and took a seat.

Looking out her window, she could see the wide open desert spreading out into the visible distance.

She closed her eyes and settled back for the ride into Los Angeles.

The Bel Air Palms Senior Living facility where Theodore Holloway owned an ocean view condo was, in fact, in Santa Monica, ten miles *southwest* of Bel Air in the foothills above and across Sunset Boulevard. This deceptive misnomer annoyed Marty Deeks to no end—something he was making vocally and abundantly clear to Kensi while riding shotgun in her silver Cadillac SRX.

"Seriously, the place ought to be called the *Santa Monica* Palms," he said for the third time. Or was it the fourth? "According to local fair-naming laws."

She shot him a skeptical look, driving in fits and starts through the thick noontime traffic.

"There are *fair-naming* laws in Los Angeles?"

"C'mon, Kens, this is the real world, whoever heard of anything like that? I'm just saying *if* laws like that were on the books."

She rolled her eyes. "Why on earth do I put up with you?"

"Maybe because women think funny guys are hot."

Kensi shrugged. "I suppose that *could* be…"

"And because of my rakish good looks—"

"You're pushing it, Deeks." She switched lanes. "Our exit's up ahead."

Deeks peered out the windshield. "Hope Holloway's around," he said. "Much as I'd like going for a joyride with you. Of the consenting adult variety."

Kensi ignored him, although she was thinking she would have liked it too despite—or, heaven help her, maybe *because* of—the eau de wildebeest, or whatever it was, emanating in furry animalic waves from his side of the car.

Not that he didn't have a serious point. They *could* have phoned ahead to make sure Holloway was in. But he'd already refused to tell the police what happened to him. After talking with Juarez, and hearing from Callen and Sam about the retired

OSS man's family connection to Sutton, she'd grown convinced they were better off catching him with his guard down.

"He's in his nineties," she said. "If he isn't there, I think we should wait around... daytrip's the buzzword for seniors. With any luck, he won't wander far from home."

"Or get kidnapped again," Deeks said. "At least until we talk to him."

Kensi was silent as she eased into the exit ramp. A short while later she pulled up to the gate of Bel Air Palms.

The uniformed security guard grew curious as he stood eyeing their identification.

"Federal agents," he said from his booth. "Is Mr. Holloway expecting you?"

"No," Deeks replied truthfully.

"Yes," Kensi lied simultaneously, wanting to give him a swift kick.

"Either of you want to tell me which it is?" the guard said.

Kensi said nothing, figuring that if Deeks wanted the ball, he could have it.

"Not really," he said, leaning across the seat. "Being that U.S. government agents trump civilian guards when it comes to accessing the property."

Kensi flashed the guard a smile. "What he said."

The guard frowned, passed their cardholders back through her lowered window, and then glanced down at his wristwatch.

"This is rec time. Meaning you'll find Holloway on the main lawn," he said. "You can hear the music coming from there."

Deeks listened. After a second he noticed energetic

Latin strains in the distance.

"That salsa?"

"Zumba," the guard said. "When I started here ten years ago it was just called aerobics." He winked. "The fountain's where they arrange their hookups."

"Their *what*?"

"You'll see. It's worse than a college campus around here. And Holloway's the biggest horndog— loves to brag about his conquests." He cocked a thumb over his shoulder. "Go straight up this drive to the fountain. Can't miss it."

Kensi smiled again. "Thanks," she said, and shifted the car into drive.

The facility was eye-pleasingly landscaped, its grass lawns and manicured gardens of cascading bougainvillea and native roses bordered by low evergreen shrubs, fig trees, and predictably, ubiquitous rows of tall, bushy topped royal palms. There were residents on the paths off to the left and right, many but not all accompanied by caregivers, some in wheelchairs and walkers.

"If I make it to a ripe old age," Kensi said, "this might be the kind of place to spend the last handful of them."

Deeks stared out his window. "Really?" he said without looking at her.

"Yup." She noted his uncertain tone. "Not for you, Marty?"

He gave a shrug.

"No surfing here," he said. "I like to surf."

She laughed. "I think that activity presents a distinct threat to your health when you hit old age."

Deeks turned to her. "Nobody dies of old age, Kens," he said. "Something always kills you."

Kensi tossed him a quick glance, saw that his face was unexpectedly glum, and drove along in puzzled silence.

After about a third of a mile she heard the music blaring up ahead, turned a tree-lined bend in the drive, and saw the fountain that the security man had mentioned, a voluminous column of water sparkling high in the air above its circular pool. Two high speaker columns stood on the lawn, a group of seniors in light summer outfits dancing energetically around it to Latin-flavored rhythms.

Holloway was instantly recognizable: tall, wiry, and dapper, he had on a white linen blazer with a dark-blue pocket square, a matching blue shirt, tan trousers, a straw Panama hat with a black band, and black-and-white two-tone boat shoes. His arms raised high above his head, snapping his fingers, he was in the middle of the group strutting to the music with a short, silver-haired woman, rolling his shoulders and swinging his hips as he moved up close to her.

"Once a dandy always a dandy," Kensi said.

"And a randy dandy," Deeks said. "Look at that dude *grind*. At his age it's gotta be as hazardous as falling off a board."

Kensi didn't answer, but noted that his odd, gloomy mood had lightened up.

Pulling to a halt at the edge of the drive, they exited the car, and started across the short-cropped grass toward the dancers near the fountain.

"Mr. Holloway?" Kensi said, raising her voice over the music.

Holloway kept dancing away, doing a tight, amazingly graceful spin on his toes.

"Could be he's hard of hearing," Deeks said.

"Don't bet on it," she said. After years with

criminal investigation, Kensi had approached enough suspects, hostile witnesses, and otherwise reluctant or uncooperative parties to know when they were only *pretending* to be oblivious, and she was sure Holloway heard her call out his name, never mind that he couldn't have missed seeing her car pull up to the lawn.

She slipped into the crowd of dancers, trying not to bump any of them, reminding herself these were geriatrics here, and that not all were as limber as Holloway. In fact, some looked pretty brittle.

"Mr. Holloway, sir." Deeks pulled out his identification, walking briskly alongside her. "We'd like a word with you."

Holloway continued to act as if he didn't see the agents. Bowing gallantly to his partner, he again whirled around in a circle, but this time decided to try and pull a hasty retreat, though Kensi had no idea where he thought he was going. Spinning away now, he moved through the crowd as quickly as he could while clicking his fingers high in the air.

"*Baile, baile, baile, mi hermosa bebe!*"

This from a small, round old man who'd suddenly danced right in front of her, swaying his body from side to side, mouthing the words to the Zumba blasting from the speakers.

She tried to sidestep him, but his hands shot out and grabbed her arms.

"Sir…"

"You move over my dead body," he said, tightening his grip as if to restrain her.

"*What?*"

The little guy cleared his throat. "I'm Mr. Holloway's personal bodyguard," he said. "John Murphy, United States Secret Service. Retired." He abruptly looked around, his eyes wide. "Hey, crap... where'd your friend go?"

She assumed he was talking about Deeks, who had already hurried past her, caught up to Holloway from behind, and reached out to snag his elbow.

"Mr. Holloway," Deeks said, "if you don't mind, we need to talk."

Holloway turned, staring him in the eye a moment. Then he frowned and pulled his handkerchief from his lapel pocket.

"Do you know you reek like a dog that's just crawled out of a swamp?" he said, covering the bottom half of his face with the hanky.

Deeks grinned.

"I've heard comments to that effect," he said.

The woman straightened in her seat as the train nosed into the Los Angeles Transportation Center outside Union Station, a wide, one-hundred-thirty acre trench bordered by Mission Road on the north and the L.A. River on the south. Then she saw the attendant coming over from the top of the stairs.

"Piggyback Yard," he said. "That's what we call it. Not much to see, but it has quite a history."

"Really?" she asked, playing the role of interested tourist. "I wouldn't guess."

He nodded and motioned toward a row of parked container trucks off the track.

"It got its nickname because the trailers ride out of here on the backs of the freight trains," he said. "But Los Angeles went up on the back of this yard." He paused. "There were stockyards all along the river when cattle and horses were everything. Later on the machine shops went up—like the ones where my dad and grampa worked. They produced the locomotives for American Pacific right till the end of World War Two."

"And then what?" the woman asked.

"Everything changed," he said. "It started during the war. By 'forty-four or so American Pacific stopped producing steam locomotives and Caleb Holloway entered the picture. He laid the tracks you see around us, and the yard became a staging area."

"You seem to know a lot about it."

He laughed. "It's kind of my heritage. With the factories gone, Poppo—my grandad—and most everyone else who worked in them went to work laying rail for Holloway's outfit. His tracks went clear across the country to New England, and north through Oregon and Washington into Vancouver." He looked at her. "The last factory standing was run by the U.S. Navy—and *I* found out it wasn't even a true factory after a while."

"No?" she said. "What, then?"

"At this point hardly anyone knows this, but it became a holding area for enemy POWs toward the end of the war," the attendant replied. "I guess they started out making engine parts for battleships. Holloway built a special rail line up to Port Hueneme, so they could go straight from here to the base. But Poppo was a crew foreman at that time, and his boys maintained the line, and they all saw uniformed prisoners getting off the trains under guard on the return trips. And heard them speaking German when they were marched inside."

Her eyes steadied on his face. "Can we see the building from here?"

The attendant shook his head no.

"It would've been way at the far end of the yard,

and the truth is there isn't really much to look at anymore," he said. "The factory's long gone. What's left is on the surface just an average track siding, and maybe the corner of a transfer station."

She angled her head curiously.

"On the surface?"

He smiled. "You really *are* paying attention," he said. "People's eyes used to glaze over when I blabbed about this stuff. So I kind of stopped. Haven't mentioned it to a living soul in ages."

"Seriously? I think it's fascinating."

His smile broadened.

"Those words are music to my ears," he said. His voice lowered a notch. "Okay, here's another family secret. When I was maybe nine or ten, my dad took me over to the factory. It was about to be knocked down, and he wanted to show me one of the storage areas underneath the place. There were quite a few once upon a time."

The woman struggled to keep herself in tight control.

"Did you actually see them?"

"Better believe it," he said. "Most of 'em were walled off years before, and the room I saw was pretty well cleared out." He paused. "I'm Drew," he said. "Drew Sarver. I hope this isn't out of bounds, but if you're really interested, I'd love to give you a tour of the yard."

She studied him carefully. "My name is Milena, and I think that would be wonderful." She smiled. "Is there a time that works best for you?"

"I'm free most evenings," he said. And then paused a moment. "In fact, I have a brainstorm."

"Oh?"

He nodded. "Do you follow baseball?"

"A bit," she said. "Why?"

"Well, the rail series between the Dodgers and Angels is coming up. It's a total sellout, but I have tickets for tomorrow night's game down in Anaheim." He shrugged. "Anyway, I have the day off, so we could walk around Piggyback and go right up to the old factory area. After that we'll take the express line from Union Station to the stadium."

The woman breathed. She felt as if she was in the saddle of a charging, inexorable fate.

"Sounds like a wonderful plan to me," she said. "I can hardly wait."

The attendant grinned.

"That makes two of us," he said.

Although it was only a short distance from the fountain lawn, Kensi and Deeks gave Holloway a lift back to his condominium in the car, with Murphy coming along at his own insistence.

Holloway quickly led them inside, his front door opening to a bright, spacious living room with cream-colored furniture. A broad picture window opposite the door looked out on a little garden with a tidy hedge.

It was all tasteful, if plain, with two significant exceptions—an antique gramophone on a corner stand, and a vibrant orange-toned silkscreen of a tiger's face hanging on one wall.

Deeks noticed both as he entered the room. The phonograph was in perfect condition, its brass witch's hat horn polished and sparkling, the hand-painted flowers on the bell still bright. The print, he realized, was a signed and numbered Andy Warhol original.

He studied it a moment, his lips forming a silent "wow."

Holloway saw. "The 'Siberian Tiger,'" he said, stepping toward him. "It's part of a series from the nineteen eighties, the theme was our planet's fading species." He paused. "At ninety-four, I can relate."

Deeks smiled at that. But Holloway didn't strike him as faded at all.

"Can I fetch anyone a drink?" The old man turned to Kensi. "I can't tell if you look resolute or thirsty."

She shrugged her shoulders.

"I have some questions for you—and no thanks. I'd rather not waste time."

He gave her a small smile. "Now I can tell, at least," he said, motioning her toward the sofa.

She sat down, Deeks beside her. As Murphy drifted over to the window, Holloway lowered himself into a club chair opposite them.

"So," he said, "which of you is going to tell me why you're here?"

Kensi wasn't playing his game. "Actually, Mr. Holloway, I'd like to know why you tried to avoid us back at the fountain."

He shrugged.

"I assumed you came to discuss what happened to me two months ago," he said. "I prefer not to talk about it anymore."

"Is there a reason?"

"It's distressing to me. Highly traumatic. And I've already told the police everything I know."

"But we aren't the police."

"No matter," he said. "You were waving badges."

"Cards," Deeks said.

Holloway stared at him.

"We wave ID cards, not badges," Deeks said. "I try to be an accurate agent."

Holloway didn't seem amused.

"Sir," Kensi interjected, "I assume you know Elias Sutton was shot to death in his home yesterday."

"Of course. I read the news."

"The two of you go back most of your lives, isn't that so?"

"Yes. *All* our lives. That's no secret."

Kensi nodded. "In fact, weren't you related?"

He looked at her. She could see that surprised him.

"Distant cousins," he said. His eyes narrowed. "It isn't common knowledge. You would have to study every branch of our family tree to know."

She let that stand without comment. "If you'll forgive my saying so… you don't seem too upset."

He frowned. "Young lady, not that it's any of your concern, but I'm devastated. And I don't see why you would have any other impression."

"Well," she said, "you were kind of partying up a storm before."

"With a rascalish twinkle in your eye," Deeks added.

Holloway shook his head. "I like to dance," he said. "Is that problematic?"

"No," Kensi said. "But dancing isn't a typical reaction when you lose someone. Especially with the circumstances being so horrible."

His eyes held on her. "Tell me that in sixty years," he said. "Wait. That won't be possible, will it? I'm persistent and in decent shape. But a hundred-fifty and change? I hardly think I'll hang on that long."

She looked back at him. "And your point…?"

"Is that I value every moment, young lady," he snapped. "Zumba gets me out of these four walls. Is it better to sit here alone, wailing out my grief?" He looked at her. "Who are you to tell me how—and when—to express it?"

Kensi thought his irritation genuine and almost felt guilty. But she was remembering Callen's phone call.

"Sir, do you know yesterday was the anniversary of Mara Sutton's death?"

"Was it?" he answered quickly.

"Yes," she said. "So you *didn't* know?"

"No," he said. "I remember she passed around this time of year. I suppose if I thought about it, I might have recalled."

She nodded, watching his face.

"I didn't just ask out of curiosity," she said. "Mr. Sutton visited his wife's resting place every year on that date. We believe whoever killed him forced entry into his home while he was at the cemetery."

"Are you suggesting it was planned that way?"

Kensi continued to read his expression. It didn't change. But he was once a trained military interrogator for the OSS and CIA. How many spies and war prisoners would he have grilled in his career? Probably hundreds. He would know what she was looking for.

"He might have surprised them," she said after a moment. "There's evidence the purpose of the break-in was to steal something from the house. And that he walked in at the wrong time. Do you think it's possible?"

"I don't know," he said. "Why do you ask?"

"Because of your own experience," Deeks said, jumping in to keep him off balance. "When somebody did the same thing to you. Right here."

There was sudden movement across the room, where Murphy was standing at the window. Deeks turned to see him step toward the sofa.

"C'mon, that's enough," he said. "Mr. Holloway told you he's done talking about the incident."

Deeks flashed him a smile.

"You mean his *kidnapping*," he said. "Sorry. I'm just being compulsively accurate again."

Murphy glowered, his cheeks florid with anger.

"You think this is funny?" he said. "Mr. Holloway did more for our country than you'll ever know. He invites you into his home, you got no right to come in here and piss on that."

Deeks didn't say anything. Murphy looked about ready to hit him with a running tackle, and a knockdown, drag-out wrestling match with a retired old Secret Service agent would not earn him a whole lot of praise from Hetty or anyone else.

Holloway's hand came up in the nick of time.

"It's all right, John," he said. "I don't feel these agents mean any disrespect."

Holloway turned to Kensi. "Agent, if I may read meaning into your questions, do you believe *I* would have shared knowledge of Elias's cemetery visits with someone who planned to break into his home?"

She shrugged.

"I only asked," she said.

"But you thought it possible," Holloway pressed. "Or you *wouldn't* have fished for it."

She gave another shrug.

"Nobody's judging you," she said. "We all share information with people without knowing how they'll use it. Things slip out."

Holloway's posture stiffened. "Rest assured, I would remember if that bit of information *slipped out*." He motioned toward the gramophone. "I want you to know that isn't just an artifact, Agent. It's a family heirloom."

Kensi raised an interested eyebrow. "From Sutton?"

"Yes," he said. "He gifted it to me on my ninetieth birthday. It belonged to his parents and you won't see many like it. But it was special to him for other reasons besides."

She digested that a moment. "You two were close."

"Very," Holloway said. "I may be older than you and your partner put together. But I'm not careless, or a fool, and my memory works fine. The date of Mara Sutton's passing isn't something that normally comes up when I'm at the barbershop or the grocery. Nor is anything related to it. I would know if I discussed it with someone."

"And you'd have told us?" Deeks asked.

Holloway looked at him. "I just explained what Elias meant to me."

"Right," Deeks said. He scratched his head. "Pretty sure one's got nothing to do with the other."

Holloway said nothing.

Kensi watched him carefully. It seemed as though Deeks's question had bothered the old man. She thought about Detective Juarez's belief that it was Holloway himself who pulled the strings to shut down LAPD's probe into his abduction. And something else she and Deeks had gotten from Juarez also crossed her mind.

"Mr. Holloway, we won't disrupt your entire afternoon," she said. "But there is one other thing…"

"Oh?" Frowning.

"I think it's reasonable to wonder about a connection between the break-in at this residence, and the one that led to Mr. Sutton's murder," she said. "Don't you agree?"

He was silent for a long moment.

"You know the facts," he said finally. "I'm not an investigator."

"Fair enough," she said. "But on the surface the two crimes do appear similar. Don't you think?"

"On the surface, yes. I can't deny it."

"I want to show you something. Would that be okay?"

Holloway sat still.

Almost too still, she thought.

"Go ahead," he said. "I would like to be of help."

She produced her smartphone from her belt pouch, tapped the screen, and then held the phone out to him.

"This is a police booking photo," she said.

"A mugshot?"

"That's right," she said. "I'd like to know if you recognize the person."

He eyed the display. It showed a dark-complected man in his twenties with curly brown hair, deep-set green eyes, and a large, long chin.

"He doesn't look familiar," he said, shaking his head. "I don't think I've ever seen him before."

"His name is Isaak Dorani. Does that help?"

"No." He shook his head again. "Should it?"

Kensi watched him closely, seeing no physical sign that contradicted his denial. She briefly considered telling him Dorani's fingerprints were found on his desk after his abduction, wanting to see how he reacted, but her gut told her to hold off on that particular disclosure.

"Dorani's what the cops call a career smalltimer," she answered instead. "He has a long history of petty crimes."

Holloway lifted a silver eyebrow. "And?"

She shrugged, pulling the smartphone away from him.

"I was just curious," she said without further explanation.

He sat looking at her as she returned the phone to its pouch.

She rose off the sofa, Deeks standing up beside her.

"Sir," she said. "Before we go... is there anything you care to tell us?"

"About?"

"Whatever." She gave another shrug. "Whatever comes to mind."

He looked at the agents for a protracted moment, then shook his head.

"I'm sorry," he said. "I have nothing useful to offer."

She nodded, reached into her jeans for her wallet, and leaned forward to hold out her card.

"You'll let us know if that changes?"

Remaining seated, Holloway took the card from her hand.

"Of course," he said. And suddenly looked up at her. "Elias was the last of a breed. A warrior with courage and scruples. He deserved a better end to his life."

She nodded, saying nothing.

A moment later, Murphy came around to lead the agents toward the door.

Deeks paused behind Kensi as she stepped outside, turned to look over at the Warhol print.

"'On what wings dare he aspire? What the hand dare seize the fire,'" he said.

Murphy gave him a questioning glance, holding open the door.

"Blake," Deeks said with a huge smile. "'The Tyger.'"

Murphy nodded.

"Nice," he said. "But you still stink."

6

"Here we are... We call it Rusty Corners for reasons that should be obvious," said the young duty officer, spreading his arms to gesture at the collection of deteriorated structures around him. "It's officially designated Naval Construction Battalion, Area CRS-1."

Callen leaned back against the door of his Benz, Sam beside him, both men taking it all in. The officer, a straw-headed junior grade lieutenant named Harrison, had ridden out with them from the NCIS offices at Port Hueneme's main entrance.

"The CRS stand for Cargo Receiving and Storage?" Sam asked.

"Right, sir," Harrison said. "The numeral 'one' means it's the first development of its type to be put up after the base was established."

Sam nodded thoughtfully, his strong arms folded across his chest. Set about a mile behind the beach, harbor inlet, and naval wharves, the compound was overrun with seagulls, scores of them. The birds squawked and flapped overhead as they wheeled in the ocean breeze or squabbled over perches atop the one and two story utilitarian buildings. All the structures stood on crumbled concrete slabs, with low gable roofs, corrugated metal sides, and large sliding doors through which crates of supplies and materiel would have been moved in and out. Some had open vehicle bays and attached sheds, and many wore a coat of peeling blue paint spattered with bird droppings.

"These are the last buildings still standing from World War Two," Harrison said. "You couldn't have picked a better time to come see them."

"How's that?" Callen asked.

"Rusty Corners is scheduled for demolition," Harrison said. "It'll be gone in another few weeks, a month at the outside."

Callen regarded him through his sunglasses. "Somebody needed seventy-five years to decide it's an eyesore?"

Sam heard a gull shriek above him and looked up.

"Think you just dissed one of the residents."

The young lieutenant chuckled. "I can't tell you about the timing of the demo," he said. "I do know a preservation assessment *was* recently conducted. And that it was hundreds of pages long."

"You know who ordered it?"

"No, sir. But none of the prefabs met the government requirements for being added to the register of historic buildings."

"How's that make sense?" Sam said. "This base made the Quonset huts that quartered our troops in the Pacific theater. I figure that'd be enough."

Harrison simultaneously shrugged and shook his head.

"I wish I had greater knowledge of the evaluation process," he said. "You can get the details from the History and Heritage Command. Or we could drive out to see the curator at the Seabee Museum when we're finished here—it's right on base."

Callen looked over the forlorn development, thinking it was about the size of some small, middle-of-nowhere town, the kind with a single traffic light where its single street intersected with the only county road passing through it.

"Which of 'em is Building Thirty-One?" he asked after a moment.

Harrison gestured toward a long-neglected roadway that went curving past several of the structures in a northwesterly direction. It was pitted and scrawled with cracks, and there were tall, dry weeds spindling up through the asphalt.

"We can walk right up to it," he said. "It's the largest building... situated back near the old railroad tracks."

Sam crunched an eyebrow.

"I know Hueneme has a railroad connection," he said. "*Didn't* know it goes all the way out here."

"It hasn't since these buildings stopped being used," Harrison said. "But there was an industrial siding that served them for over two decades." He paused. "Want a look at it while I show you Thirty-One?"

"Sure," Callen said. "Might as well kill two birds with one stone."

Sam glanced up at the swooping gulls.

"Not so loud, man. You're upsetting the natives again," he said, and boosted himself off the side of the car.

Callen joined him, as Harrison turned to lead the way along the derelict road.

* * *

"Kens, is this the best or what?" Deeks said. He was in the passenger seat of her parked SRX, holding his smartphone up to the window, zooming its camera lens on the thin, dark-haired guy climbing the stairs of the shabby East Hollywood walkup across the street. "We pull into this spot and there he is. Which makes us two for two considering we had no trouble finding Holloway doing his lawn rumba—"

"*Zumba.*"

"Right, sorry."

She watched as the guy neared the second floor.

"I admit we're looking good," she said. "Let's check the face-rec results to be on the safe side."

Deeks nodded and tapped his phone's display. Though it paid to be cautious, he was certain it was Isaak Dorani on the building's outdoor stairs. They had, after all, driven here straight from Bel Air Palms, pulling his address out of Juarez's unofficial file.

Now Kensi checked the synched display on her dashboard as the federal NGI biometric system ran Deeks's camera image against its exhaustive database. After a few seconds it beeped to signal a match, bringing up a preexisting photo of their man.

They exchanged glances. No question, it was Dorani up on the stairs.

"Bingo," Deeks said.

"Bull's eye," Kensi said.

"Pin the tail on the donkey."

"You are *so* immature," Kensi said, ignoring his frown. She watched as Dorani reached the second-floor walkway and trotted up to his door, keys in hand. "He's sure in a big hurry," she said.

Deeks nodded, tapping his phone again to pull Dorani's rap sheet from the NGI.

A low whistle escaped his lips as it appeared on the dashboard screen.

"Talk about repeat offenders," he said. "Learning from his mistakes definitely *isn't* one of his favorite activities."

Kensi scanned the laundry list of criminal offenses. *Shoplifting, purchase of a handgun without safety certificate, petty theft, attempted burglary, possession and passing of counterfeit U.S. currency, resisting arrest, burglary in the second degree (automobile), grand theft person (pickpocketing), assault in the third degree…*

"Almost every one of those is a wobbler," Deeks said, using LAPD jargon for transgressions that could be prosecuted as felonies, misdemeanors, or even mere legal infractions at the prosecutor's discretion. "He's probably skated a bunch of times."

"Especially the *last* time," Kensi said. "That raised things to another level."

Deeks agreed. Back in his cop talk days, he would have labeled the break-in at Holloway's condo a hot prowl burglary, one where the victim was home when the intruder entered, and where kidnapping or murder was a possible intent. A conviction for a hot prowl easily meant a five-to-fifteen year stretch behind bars, maybe longer for someone with Dorani's prior criminal history. In the case of the Holloway burglary, the fact that he *was* abducted from his home, and that Dorani's fingerprints were lifted from his desk, would have virtually guaranteed he got the book thrown at him.

But the opposite happened.

Dorani didn't just receive leniency. Thanks to Holloway, he was given a free pass.

It only made sense to Deeks if Holloway had

something he wanted buried, and buried deep. *Or* if he was afraid of something.

Or both.

Now the agents watched Dorani push open his door and practically dive into his apartment, letting the door swing shut behind him.

Deeks looked at Kensi. "Think we should go knock?"

She thought about it a second, then tipped her head toward the apartment building.

"A low rent dump like that won't have a backdoor so he can tiptoe out on us," she replied. "I say we hold off. And maybe find out why he's in such a rush."

Deeks nodded.

"Know any other game calls while we wait?" he asked.

Kensi leaned back against her headrest, momentarily closed her eyes, and sighed.

"Oh, what fun to be nine again," she said.

Isaak took the cellphone from his pocket and checked the time. He had a half hour—well, twenty-seven minutes, to be exact—until his appointment. If he left here in the next five minutes, caught one of the bandit taxicabs that drove around in circles near the freeway entrance, and told the driver to put the pedal to the metal, he might, just *might*, make it to the hock shop with his swag.

Now he shot across his furnished apartment to the bedroom, almost tripping over his three cats as they took off after him at full speed, chasing him and each other down the hall.

The small, square room contained a single clothes closet, a plain metal bedframe and mattress, a wobbly old dresser, and a carpet that had been a stained, threadbare dust trap when he moved in four years ago, and now looked like something the city garbage collectors wouldn't want dirtying up the back of their truck. Opening the closet to an avalanche of junk and rumpled clothes, Dorani quickly knelt and reached for the cartons at the bottom. The one he'd come to fetch was pushed far toward the back, and he would need to shift the others around to rummage it out.

Sliding out the cardboard box, he propped it on his knees, and opened the flaps for a hasty look at the goods.

The Edison cylinders he took from Sutton's home were all inside, safely wrapped in newspaper. Fifty in their original tubes, with over half coming from the Blue Amberol 5000 series. From what he saw on the Web, the blues went for between five bills and a grand a piece, depending on where they fell in the series. It was plenty of getaway money even if Daggut nickel-and-dimed him to death.

But he couldn't stick around here calculating his take. If he knew anything with absolute certainty, it was that Daggut would pull his lockout routine if he was even a minute late.

He needed to move fast.

"Don't miss me too much," he said, looking down at the cats. They were wrestling on the floor now. "You'll eat when I get back."

They kept rolling around, biting and knocking the hell out of each other, and *damn* if they weren't ignoring him all of a sudden.

Dorani dashed back along the hall, through the front door, and out of the apartment, barely pausing to lock the door before he sprang downstairs to the sidewalk.

* * *

Across the street in her SUV, Kensi and Deeks watched him turn toward the corner up ahead and then race off in the general direction of the Hollywood Freeway.

"Well, wouldn't you know," Deeks said. "There's our guy again."

"Wonder wherefore he's bound."

"And what's in that box."

Kensi reached for the ignition key.

"Let's find out," she said.

The first thing Hanna and Callen noticed about Building 31 was its size. The shadow it cast in the midafternoon sun spread all the way across the wide cement lot it stood upon, covering it like a dark blanket.

"Wow," Sam said, walking up the pavement with Harrison. "You said the place was big. I didn't expect *humungous*."

The officer smiled. "I remember saying it was larger than the rest, sir," he explained. "Wasn't intending to quantify it."

"Yeah, well. You ever invite me for a light lunch, I'm gonna prep for an all-you-can-eat buffet."

"Dude, please, no stretch pants," Callen said from Harrison's opposite side. He glanced at the lieutenant. "You seriously *don't* want to see him in stretch pants."

Harrison laughed.

"I'll try to remember your warning, sir," he said.

They walked on under a shifting cloud of gulls toward the northern border of the lot, where the building stood against the sandy bluffs of Point Mugu State Park. With its double-gabled roof and solid metal hangar doors, it dwarfed the two galvanized steel Quonset huts shouldered up against its east and west sides.

"You know what this place was originally used for?" Callen asked.

"Yes," Harrison said. "It was designed as a cleaning and stripping center for aircraft. They'd hangar several planes at a time."

"And how about those huts?"

"They stored supplies used for the painting and stripping," he said. "Flammable chemicals and other hazardous materials."

Callen looked thoughtful. Shaped like upside-down U's, the long, low huts were almost immersed in the larger building's shadow.

"Anything inside them now?" Sam asked.

The lieutenant shook his head. "They were cleaned out to the bare walls years ago. But some of the old fixtures are in the museum."

"The one here on base?"

"Yessir," Harrison said. "The collection might even have artifacts from Project Deep Dive. Be worth a visit, since that's what you're interested in."

Callen gazed past the Quonsets into the middle distance. There, between the lot and ascending hills, something on the ground was catching the sunshine, throwing off brilliant, silvery glints of light.

Harrison saw him shift his attention.

"That's the rail siding," he said. "The ridge just out back is where they had the big cookout."

Callen turned to him. "What do you mean?"

"The CIA and Navy burned thousands of sensitive documents when they emptied Building Thirty-One," he said. "All authorized by Theodore Holloway... I thought you might be aware of it, since he was Project Director of Deep Dive."

Callen shook his head.

"No," he said. "I had no idea."

"Well, he was the man in charge."

"You telling us he came back to Hueneme for it?" Callen said.

Harrison nodded, meeting his gaze.

"Oversaw everything," he said. "As I understand."

Callen exchanged a quick glance with Sam. Something told him Harrison didn't miss it, though the lieutenant gave no sign one way or another.

"Come on," he said. "I'll give you that look at the tracks, and then we'll double back to Thirty-One."

The three men walked across the lot in the building's shadow. About three hundred yards up, the pavement's crumbling edges gave way to a broad strip of sand and rampant sagebrush. Harrison pushed through the tall, stiff shoots, leading the way to the remnants of a low gravel embankment on the other side.

The sun beating down on them now, their boots crunching on the gravel, they climbed the embankment and stepped onto the tracks. Callen turned to his left and saw the tracks running east for about a mile before they curved off to the south. A glance to the right revealed a corroded iron buffer stop only fifty feet away. There were faded but discernible letters painted in red on the crossbar:

DE D ND

"Dead end," Callen said. "Beyond here lies nothing."

Harrison motioned in the other direction, where the

track ran straight for about a half mile before curving southward.

"The siding ran back and forth from here to the harbor shipping wharves," he said. "The local rail spur was there long before the Navy came in. And it's still active."

"The base using it?" Callen asked.

"Yessir, to bring in supplies," Harrison said. "But this whole area's agricultural country. Oranges, beets, grain, you name it. Farmers truck their crops down to the spur, then load them aboard trains for Los Angeles, where the line connects with Western Pacific."

"At Union Station?" Sam asked.

"Right next door," Harrison said. "Piggyback Yard. From there the cargo can go anywhere in the United States on the flatbacks."

Callen considered that, squinting to look down the track in the sun's intense glare. Then he turned to Harrison.

"Lieutenant," he said, "do you wonder *why* we're here asking you about Deep Dive? A seventy-five year old government project? I mean, that's even before Agent Hanna was born."

Sam's frown made the young officer smile.

"Ask no questions, hear no lies," he said. "If I may be so bold, sir... as a liaison with NCIS, I've learned not to ask agents about their investigations."

Callen let that one slide, a thin smile tugging at his lips.

"But you heard of the project before today?"

"Of course, sir," Harrison said. "There aren't many written records. But it's no secret captured German U-boats came into this base toward the end of the war. That's when Building Thirty-One became a temporary holding facility for the sailors and payloads taken off the subs."

Callen regarded him closely. "Anything else?"

Harrison looked straight back at him. "I know Admiral Sutton was base commander when Deep Dive was initiated… and I know he was murdered yesterday," he said. "I figure you're here in connection with that."

Callen looked over at Sam.

"I really like him," he said.

"Me too," Sam said. "In fact, I'm positively *smitten*."

Harrison grinned.

"You ready to see Thirty-One now?" he asked.

Callen gestured down the embankment.

"After you, Lieutenant," he said.

Deeks raised his eyes from his tablet to look out the window of the SUV, his gaze going to the grimy Skid Row pawnshop Isaak Dorani had dashed into minutes earlier. He was once again thinking that, in an ideal world, they would have returned to headquarters and switched vehicles, gotten into some plain Jane Dodge sedan before tailing their guy to the shabbiest part of Los Angeles, America's undisputed capital of income inequality. The Cadillac wagon could not have been more conspicuous among the beaters lining the curb.

"Anything on the shop yet?" Kensi asked.

Deeks checked his screen. *Lo and behold*, he thought, noticing his search results had appeared at last. The L.A. county records database seemed woefully sluggish to him, but that was probably because he was spoiled by Beale's technical wizardry at uncovering information, coupled with the OSP's high-flying proprietary systems and search engines.

"This just in," he said in a mock newscaster tone. "The owner's name is Zory Daggut, and he enjoys playing in dirt and slime." He paused to skim his query results. "A year ago he was charged with failure to comply with city ordinances related to his store inventory and transactions."

"In other words, he's a fence."

"*Suspected* fence. The city has mandatory electronic reporting for pawnshops—brokers have to enter everything about the items they receive into a database for the cops. They're also supposed to take the customer's thumbprint and driver's license number." He read some more. "Looks like Daggut ignored those practices in connection to some local burglaries and was accused of pawning stolen goods. Also looks like his arrest came after several warnings."

"Suspected my foot," Kensi said. "How's he still in business?"

"The district attorney dropped all charges against him," Deeks said. "These records don't provide a reason."

"Meaning he cooperated with the investigation."

"Righteo."

"Which makes him a fence *and* a stoolie," Kensi said.

"Guess that qualifies him as a multitasker."

"And an uber-sleazoid," she said.

They were silent a little while. Out on the street, everyone and everything looked downtrodden and faded in the afternoon sun. The apartment buildings, the storefronts, the poor and homeless people staring vacantly from broken stoops while smoking cigarettes and drinking brown-bagged alcohol.

Deeks found himself wondering about the carton Dorani brought into the pawnshop. He'd dashed from his building to the intersection where he caught the gypsy cab, then almost tripped over a pile of trash bags dashing across the sidewalk. Why the crazed hurry?

He turned to Kensi just in time to see an old Dodge with a handwritten TAXI sign in its windshield drive slowly past them and pull up outside the hock shop.

Seconds later, Dorani left the building with a large brown paper sack.

"He must've called for a pickup," Kensi said. "Did you notice his box magically turned into a bag?"

Deeks nodded.

"Abracadabra," he said. "His box of tricks becomes a bag of cash."

"Yep, and I'm thinking he didn't come here to pawn an old set of silverware," Kensi said.

Deeks nodded again. "Should we take him now or later?"

She straightened.

"*Now*," she said, and pushed open her door.

Dorani realized he was in trouble the instant he spotted the man and woman exiting the vehicle. He would have pegged them as undercover cops, or something resembling cops, even if their ride wasn't a fancy Cadillac crossover in a neighborhood where you saw five times as many people pushing around shopping carts filled with their worldly possessions as motorists at the wheel.

Isaak had crossed paths with the law often enough to *smell* a bust in progress—especially when he was the luckless slob about to get busted.

He momentarily froze at the gypsy cab's wide-open backdoor, unsure what to do.

"*Hey! Federal agents! Stop right there!*" the guy from inside the SUV shouted at him, sprinting alongside the parked cars at the curb.

Dorani hesitated for another split second before he let go of the door handle, clasped the money pouch against his chest, turned back onto the sidewalk, and took off running in the opposite direction.

"Kens, *why* do I bother telling these guys to stop?" Deeks said, charging after Dorani. "They *never* stop!"

Her only response was to gesture toward the vehicles along the curb and split off toward the sidewalk, cutting between the parked and double-parked cars, then taking off after Dorani on the crowded pavement. There were heads poking from doors and windows, and people floating aimlessly around her, none of them bothering to get out of her way.

Deeks stuck to the street, breaking into an all-out run as he drew his Beretta sidearm, angling it downward in the low ready position.

Dorani very aptly ran like a thief, taking advantage of his head start. He bolted toward the corner, reaching it several seconds ahead of his pursuers, then swung left at the cross street to head east on Alameda Avenue.

Deeks plunged after him. Out the corner of his eye, he saw Kensi to his right, maneuvering through the zonked, bleary-eyed onlookers on the sidewalk. She gripped her SIG semiautomatic, pointing it down at a forty-five degree angle, following the same procedures he was.

Sweat pouring down his face, Deeks focused on

their man. He'd gained on him a little, his relatively clear path off the curb helping to shrink the distance between them. Meanwhile, Kensi was only a few steps back despite the people crowding the street around her.

Dorani snapped a glance over his shoulder, saw they'd gotten closer, put on a burst of speed to reach the corner—and then abruptly changed direction. Still clutching the pouch against his side, he veered off Almeda onto the sidestreet and momentarily disappeared from sight.

Afraid he might lose him if he ducked into a building or alleyway, Deeks pushed himself to run harder, staying off the curb, his chest heavy from breathing ozone-saturated air and car exhaust.

He was nearing the corner when he heard a high, shrill scream around the block, followed by a loud crashing noise. Sucking in a breath, he turned onto the sidestreet and realized Dorani had pushed over a homeless woman's overloaded shopping cart, scattering its shabby contents all across the middle of the sidewalk. There were dresses, shoes, bundled blankets, canned goods, water bottles, a radio, a bible, heaps of belongings strewn across the pavement, a sudden helter-skelter obstacle course Dorani had thrown across Kensi's path, allowing him to gain some separation from her.

As the woman fell to her hands and knees, shrieking away while frantically gathering up her possessions, Deeks hoofed past her toppled wagon and shot onto the sidewalk, pulling further ahead of Kensi now.

Meanwhile, Dorani was still laying down convenient hurdles. He knocked over a trash can outside a storefront, then another, a third, upending the whole row of them as he ran on up the block. They rolled and clattered on the sidewalk with their lids knocked off, pouring out mounds of rubbish.

Deeks kept running, dodging the cans, wading through their disgorged trash. He felt a cardboard container crumple underfoot and nearly tripped on something wet and slippery, but somehow managed to stay close to his target, thinking he'd seriously had enough of the guy.

Dorani must have thought something similar at the same moment. As Deeks sprinted past the barrier of toppled garbage cans, he saw him reach around his back with his right hand, then slide it up under his flapping, untucked shirt.

Deeks had chased enough bad guys in his day to know he was going for a weapon—most likely a gun. He also knew there were civilians all around them. Getting into a shootout under those circumstances would be a sure and total disaster.

They needed to end the chase before Dorani pulled the weapon from under his shirt.

The idea hit him in a flash.

Abracadabra.

"Give us the funny money!" he shouted. *"It's all we want!"*

About five yards up ahead, Dorani stopped dead in his tracks.

"Funny money?" he said. He turned his head halfway around, his back still toward Deeks. *"What* the hell are you talking about?"

"The counterfeit cash in that pouch," Deeks said. He'd also come to a halt, gripping his gun in both hands now, aiming straight at Dorani. "Turn it over to us."

Dorani stood motionless, his hand lingering under his shirt.

"This is nuts," he said. "I got no idea—"

"Don't act stupid," Deeks said. "We've been on Daggut for months."

"*Daggut?*"

"Right. You're just an accessory."

"Huh? Accessory to *what*?"

"Circulating counterfeit bills," Deeks said. "Nobody prints them like he does without getting our attention."

Dorani's posture stiffened.

"Wait," he said. "Who the hell *are* you?"

"U.S. Treasury Enforcement," Deeks said, figuring that sounded as good as anything. "Now turn over the bills."

Dorani didn't answer. He remained perfectly still, his hand tucked under his shirt.

Meanwhile, Kensi had jogged up beside Deeks. He shot her a glance, saw her acknowledge it with a slight nod.

"We have two guns to your one," she said. "I suggest you drop yours."

Dorani stood there another few seconds without budging, making Deeks wonder if his ploy was really going to work. Then he pulled the weapon from under his shirt and let it slip from his hand to the pavement.

It hit the concrete with an odd clatter, sounding much too *thin* for metal. Nor was the gun a plastic toy, though. The agents would have identified one of those in a second.

Kensi traded another look with Deeks, scrambled to retrieve it. The surprised expression on her face as she picked it up reinforced what he already knew. It definitely wasn't the sort of weapon carried by your average street thief.

She rose from her crouch, slipping it under her waistband.

"All right," she said behind Dorani. "Now hand me the pouch."

He hesitated a second.

"Fake money," he said. "You're saying Daggut gave me a pouch of worthless phoney bills?"

"As if you didn't know," Kensi said. "Come on. Let's have it. Then keep your hands behind your back where we can see them."

Dorani produced a long sigh of resignation. Then he held the pouch out for her to take.

She tossed it back to Deeks, patted him down, slapped on the cuffs.

"Okay, Isaak," she said. "We want to have a little talk with you."

He expelled another breath.

"Why not talk to that fat, counterfeiting bastard *Daggut*?"

Kensi grabbed his elbow, getting ready to walk him back to the car.

"No need to call people names," she said.

7

The curator of the Seabee Museum greeted Callen, Sam, and Lieutenant Harrison inside its front entrance as they arrived from across the base.

"Warren Alders," he said, extending his hand to Callen. A tall, fit man in his thirties, he wore a crisp white shirt with carefully rolled up sleeves. "It's a pleasure to meet you. I'm glad I was here when the lieutenant called. We usually close our doors at four o'clock, but I had some admin to finish today."

Callen smiled as they shook, noticing his strong, firm grip. It was now almost four-thirty in the afternoon, and the museum was deserted aside from the small group and their host. Harrison had phoned Alders from Rusty Corners after guiding the agents on their walkthrough of Building 31, where they observed little of consequence. Stiflingly hot inside, its furnishings and equipment long since removed, the main structure was a huge, vacant shell, with discolored metal walls, sand-caked windows, and a pitted floor with loose divots of concrete that shifted under the men's feet as they looked around.

Now Alders turned to exchange a handshake with

Sam, whose eye immediately went to a small gold tattoo on his forearm. It showed the prow of a ship breaking through a wave, with a crossed saber and flintlock pistol behind it.

"You a Swick?" he asked.

Alders nodded. "That's right. On time, on target—"

"Never quit," Sam said. "What unit?"

"SBT Twelve," Alders said. "Split a couple tours between the Gulf and West Africa."

Sam grinned. "I'm a former SEAL. Did lots of VBSS ops during Iraqi Freedom… deployed with the USS *Chosin*."

"Ah, fellas… hate to interrupt," Callen said. "But can we do this in English?"

Sam inclined his head toward Alders.

"He was a Special Warfare Combatant-craft Crewman," he said. "One of the boat operators who'd insert us and extract us from our missions. Without those aces, we weren't going anywhere."

Alders smiled. "Most boys grow up wanting to drive fast cars," he said. "My childhood fantasy was piloting fastboats and Zodiacs."

"Living the dream," Callen said. "How long've you been at the museum?"

"Eight years next month," Alders said. "I got my honorable discharge thanks to running into a bomb in Afghanistan—long story, as they say—and used the GI bill to earn a Masters in history. Six years after the museum hired me as a cataloguer, the previous curator retired and I got chosen to replace him." He shrugged. "Guess I got lucky."

"*We're* the lucky ones," Harrison said, and motioned down the sunlit entry hall. Beyond the framed movie and recruiting posters lining the walls, a gallery of uniformed mannequins and dioramas showed the construction battalions at work. "Before Mr. Alders came along, the museum's collection was mostly crammed away in storage rooms. He pulled in the grants so things could be on display."

"Typical boat boy," Sam said. "They'd risk their lives to pull your ass outta the middle of hell, insist it was all in a day's work." ˙

Alders stood there looking uncomfortable. Meanwhile, Harrison checked his wristwatch.

"I should really head back to my office," he said, and turned to the agents. "You can reach me on the phone later."

Sam and Callen thanked him for his help, and waited as Alders unlocked the museum's wide glass doors to let him out. A minute later he rejoined them.

"So... I hear you came here to look at Area CRS-1," he said. "Building Thirty-One in particular."

Callen nodded. "Lieutenant Harrison mentioned the compound was slated for demolition," he said. "How's that possible?"

"By that, do you mean, 'How come it wasn't given protection as a historical site?'"

"Yes."

"I fought hard to save it," he said. "Hueneme has quite a few historical buildings. But the preservation committee made the distinction that CRS-1 was only an infrastructure facility used in support of the base's operations. That its buildings had no direct connection to a significant technological development, event, or person."

"Wait," Sam said. "How's Project Deep Dive not *significant*? It wasn't every day we brought in sailors from German submarines."

"That was the heart of my case," Alders said. "For all the good it did me."

"What was the committee's reason for rejecting it?"

Alders shrugged.

"I didn't exactly get one," he said. "There was talk of using the entire plot of land Rusty Corners and the rail siding occupies for a modern storage facility, or a housing adjunct for the Seabees. But we've had so many budget cuts and personnel reductions over the past few years, I don't see either happening." He produced a sigh of resignation. "The battle was over when Elias Sutton, God rest his soul, declared himself in favor of tearing down the complex."

Sam's eyebrow went up. "He really do that?"

"Yes, in a ten-page recommendation to the committee. Even after his retirement, the admiral carried a lot of influence with the Navy and Congress. And of course he's a legend around Hueneme."

"And *his* reasons?"

"Modernization, in a word," Alders said. "He felt we should be proactive, and clear the land for when expansion funds become available." Another shrug. "I admit it's a big chunk of real estate."

"Did he have anything to say about CRS-1 and Deep Dive specifically?" Callen asked.

"Only that in his view the building was just a waystation for German prisoners en route to longer-term internment camps," Alder said. "His contention was that we had almost seven hundred POW camps in our country during the war, and that no one made a fuss about preserving them."

"And by that logic, it followed that Rusty Corners shouldn't be an exception."

"Right," Alders said. "But with all due respect to

the admiral—do you know how many U-boats we captured during World War Two?"

"Wild guess," Sam said, "I'd say maybe a dozen."

"Seven," Alders said. "Four of the subs were escorted into Hueneme." He paused. "One of those—U-437—was the only Type IXD2 boat ever brought to our homeland."

"There something special about it?" Sam asked.

Alders nodded.

"We'd probably need three hours just so I could scratch the surface," he said. "And I promised to take my kids to the movies tonight."

Callen turned to him. "Mr. Alders—"

"Warren, please."

"Warren… how about you give us the for-dummies edition? That's pretty much my speed anyway."

Alders looked at him a moment, then gave a small smile.

"Okay, let's see," he said, massaging the back of his neck. "U-437 is *inherently* unique because she was a longrunner. Designed to stay at sea for months without having to refuel. Only thirty German IXD2 boats were commissioned as combat vessels, and in the last years of the war a handful were converted into long-range transports. With their torpedo tubes removed for extra cargo space, they could carry over two hundred tons of freight."

"What sorta freight?" Sam asked. "And where were they taking it?"

"The Far East," Alders said. "Japan, and Japanese naval bases in Malaysia." He looked at Sam. "Tokyo desperately needed certain materials for its war machine. Mercury, rubber, other resources. It also wanted secret German aircraft and rocket technology."

"So what did the Nazis stand to gain by sharing it?"

"A fortune in yen, gold, and jewels," Alders said. "But finances weren't at the heart of Hitler's plan. He was hoping a strengthened Japan could distract America from the European campaign. In his mind, if our forces in the Pacific took a major beating, we'd have to redeploy manpower there to offset our losses."

"And leave poor, helpless Berlin alone," Sam said.

"Something like that." Alders inhaled, gathering his thoughts. "Anyway, it's late May, 'forty-five. U-437 is en route to Japan with a full hold of goods, when a couple of our destroyers, the USS *Linette* and USS *Phillips*, pick her up in the Malacca Strait. There's no fight—Germany surrendered earlier in the month, and the grand admiral has ordered all U-boats at sea to surface and capitulate to Allied vessels." He paused again. "Right before they bring her into Hueneme, every American sailor on the destroyers is required to sign an oath of secrecy about the submarine's capture. Violating it could result in court martial and even a death sentence."

"Was that SOP?" Sam asked.

Alders wobbled his hand in an equivocal gesture.

"It was done earlier in the war when other subs were captured, because U.S. intelligence didn't want the enemy to know we had their Enigma code machines," he said. "But in every other instance the sailors were released from their oaths after Germany's surrender."

"And the war was already *over* when U-437 was netted."

"That's right."

"So, what were we still trying to protect?" Callen asked.

The curator's expression underwent a marked

change. He stood pensively a few seconds, then gave the agents a long, confidential look.

"I think it depends on your definition of 'we,'" he said at last.

"You have something to tell us?" Callen asked.

Alders was still looking straight at them.

"Better," he said. "I have something to *show* you."

The museum's collection room was hidden away behind a large exhibit hall, where restored tractors, bulldozers, trucks, and jeeps from the Naval Construction Battalion's past were displayed alongside modern armored construction and ordnance-clearing vehicles.

After guiding Sam and Callen through the hall to a locked steel door, Alders swiped his ID card through a reader, then tapped his security code into its keypad and led them inside.

Calling the space a *room* was something of a misnomer. It was actually a series of branching, climate-controlled corridors, illuminated by cool LED ceiling panels, and walled by tall, upright shelves with alphanumerically labeled cabinets.

"We have over five thousand artifacts back here," Alders said. He gestured toward a shelf of black storage boxes. "Everything from the documents in those boxes to what you'll see around the corner."

The agents followed him into another corridor lined with shelves and cabinets. Ahead of them was a mannequin in antiquated deepwater diving gear, with a huge copper-and-brass helmet, brass corselet, twill suit, and weighted shoes.

Sam noticed something besides painted blue eyes staring out of the helmet, stepped up to the round front port, and saw a rubber fish jammed inside, the diver's nose in its open mouth.

He looked around at Alders.

"This how curators entertain themselves?" he asked.

"Some of them," Alders said, turning a bend. "Come on, my office is in here."

Again it was really just an extension of the corridor. One side was occupied by a large worktable with several flexible LED magnifier lamps clamped to its edges, drawers underneath its heavy oak surface, and some straightbacked chairs around it. The other wall was lined by more storage units. There was clutter everywhere.

Alders went over to a wall safe just beyond the table.

"This was installed by Vance Coriell, the curator who preceded me," he said, reaching for the combination dial. "He started here in the early nineteen-sixties, held his position till he was over seventy years old."

The agents waited as he turned the dial, then took hold of the handle and opened the door.

"When I first started cataloguing for Vance, I would often come back here to ask him a question, and find him examining some item or other with his magnifying glass," he said, pointing his chin at the worktable. "Everything looked the same as it does now, except he used standard incandescents rather than LEDs." He reached into the safe and produced a white cardboard box shaped something like a hardcover book. "If it was late in the day, and he was finished with the museum's official work, he'd be studying what's in this box."

Alders carried it over to the table, shuffled some papers around to clear a space, and set down the box.

Then he pulled two pairs of blue latex gloves from a dispenser, handed them to Sam and Callen.

"Vance was curator while the Cold War was at its chilliest," he said. "At that time, CRS-1's buildings had been sitting untouched for over a decade, since the end of World War Two. After the Cuban Missile Crisis, the Navy ramped up the number of bases overseas, and Hueneme's brass decided to put those buildings to use again."

"It wasn't Elias Sutton, right?" Sam said. "By then, he'd already fought in Korea."

"And become a rear admiral at the Pentagon," Alders said. "No, it wasn't Sutton who reopened Rusty Corners. A panel of officers made the decision, and I strongly doubt he was even aware of it." He turned on one of the flexible lamps, adjusting the neck so it shone over the box. "Vance knew there was a mother lode of artifacts in those buildings, and couldn't wait to get hold of them for the museum. When they began emptying out all the old fixtures and equipment, he would go out there and oversee everything." A pause. "Did Harrison take you over to the railroad tracks?"

"Matter of fact, he did," Sam said. "Told us it was out back by the ridges that they burned a lot of what was in the buildings."

Alders nodded.

"That occurred years earlier—after Project Deep Dive shut down and the OSS moved out of Building Thirty-One," he said. "Most of what was thrown into the burn barrels were sensitive paper documents." He chuckled. "Vance was leery of that practice. Called it a memory hole."

"Orwell," Sam said, nodding. "*Nineteen Eighty-Four*."

"Good old Vance," Alders continued. "He insisted

burning government records was better suited to the Ministry of Truth than the United States of America." He took another pair of gloves from the dispenser and slipped them on. "So while the Seabees were moving stuff from the buildings onto pickup trucks, Vance decided to walk out to the slopes and poke around. Did it a few times, I think. He had a sixth sense for uncovering the past, and figured it was worth a shot."

Callen peered at the box Alders had taken from the wall safe.

"Is that where he found whatever's in there?"

Alders nodded. He moved a chair out from under the table, shifting a heap of papers from it to the floor. Then he slid the chair toward the lamp, sat down, and lifted up the box.

"Here we are, gentlemen," he said, waving the agents over to him. "I think you should see this for yourselves."

As they approached the table, Alders opened the box with his gloved fingers, extracted a brown business-sized envelope, placed it on the tabletop, and then gingerly reached back in.

The charred leather binder he slid out now was small—six inches by five inches or so—and appeared handstitched, its spine, corners, and edges singed and blackened by flames.

"I told you Deep Dive's classified papers went into burn barrels, but the men who cleared the building couldn't fit everything into them," he said. "This little item was apparently jammed between the interior trays of a trunk or footlocker they set on fire."

Sam stood looking over the curator's right shoulder, saw a pair of ideographs etched into the middle of the cover:

日記

"Is that Japanese?" he asked.

"*Kyujitai*," Alders said. "Traditional characters that were mostly used until World War Two. After the Occupation, it became more common to see *kanji*, a simplified form of writing."

"And I'm guessing Vance hurried to get it translated."

Alders smiled. "I can only imagine his excitement," he said. "What it says is *journal*. In the sense of a personal diary or notebook."

Callen leaned forward to inspect it. "Vance found this out by the ridge?"

"In the footlocker," Alders said. "For some reason it was just partially destroyed by the flames, and Vance assumed the Seabees hosed down and buried what remained of it. But when Tropical Storm Katherine hit in 'sixty-three heavy rains washed away the topsoil covering its metal hardware. He noticed a corner of it sticking out of the hillside, came back with a shovel, and dug it out."

The agents were quiet a moment. Then Sam nodded at the journal.

"What's inside?" he asked. "Anything legible?"

"Not much." Alders held the binder directly under the magnifier lens, opening it to show him its scorched, water-and-smoke-damaged flyleaf. "The ink on the pages smeared badly when they doused the trunk, and then the floodwaters compounded the damage."

Sam looked at the thick sheet of parchment paper through the lens.

"Something's written there," he said. "More Japanese kyujitai?"

Alders brought the light down nearer the page so they could look more closely at the smudged characters:

森春

"Vance explained it took him a while to decipher them," he said. "He could've contacted Japanese-speaking colleagues for an assist, but he was always cagey about his discoveries. More than usual in this instance because it was something the OSS tried to wipe out of existence." He paused. "As you can see, the last character's especially faded... almost illegible."

"But he got it figured out," Callen said, looking at him. "Or am I wrong?"

Alders lifted the envelope off his worktable, pulled out a folded sheet of paper, and opened it at the crease, pressing it flat on the table.

"I'm not sure how, or when, but he did it," he said. "Here's what he wrote."

森春男
Mori Haruo/Haruo Mori
June 5 1898-Jan. 17 1944

"Looks like a name," Callen said. "And dates, obviously."

Alders was nodding his head.

"The Japanese write their family names *before* their given names," he said. "If you're wondering about his transposition."

"Haruo Mori," Sam said, reading aloud. "Should it ring a bell?"

Alders looked at him. "It isn't exactly famous," he said. "But during the nineteen thirties and early forties he was one of Japan's leading physicists. Worked with Yukawa to model atomic nuclei."

Callen tugged his ear. "Those dates," he said. "Are they when Mori was born and died?"

"You got the first right," Alders said. "But the second is when he set sail aboard the U-437... the last captured Axis submarine to ever enter Hueneme... never to be seen or heard from again."

The Pacific Ocean, shiny and blue, spread out beyond the palm-studded strip of beach to Callen's left as he sped north on 101 toward Santa Barbara.

Following a curve of the freeway now, he glanced out across the water as cloud shadows scuttled across its surface, teasing him with a false glimpse of the past. In his imagination, the warships *Linette* and *Phillips* briefly appeared offshore, their dark shapes sailing down the channel with a third between them.

He turned his eyes back to the road, thinking about the captive U-437.

"G, you have that look on your face," Sam said from the passenger seat.

"What look?"

"The look that says we oughtta look into what we got from our look around the base," Sam said. "Unless you'd rather we see which of us knows more words that start with double-o."

Callen frowned and shook his head. "We're meeting Varno in a half hour," he said. "We can probably look forward to him doing that."

"Agreed," Sam said. "So we working our way forward in time or back?"

"Your call," Callen said. "I'm busy driving."

"For a change." Sam thought a moment. "Okay, you ready?"

"Shoot."

"Forward to back," Sam said. "About a year ago, the Navy orders a study on whether Rusty Corners should be flattened like a tamale or preserved as a historic site."

"Rusty Corners *and* the area out by the railroad tracks."

"Right, the area where Curator Vance found the footlocker with Haruo Mori's journal inside." Sam patted the archival box on the seat next to him. "And where the CIA held a secret document cookout about fifty years ago."

Callen nodded.

"If there's any thought given to saving the compound," he said, "Elias Sutton puts the kibosh on it."

"Insists it's got no historical value."

"Which is kinda ludicrous."

"*More* than kinda, you ask me," Sam said.

"And speaking of the cookout," Callen said, "that's actually a cutesy way of referring to a thorough housecleaning of Building Thirty-One."

"By Tip Holloway."

"Who was with the CIA."

"An agency that grew out of the OSS."

"Which Holloway worked for while he and Sutton were stationed at Hueneme near the end of World War Two," Callen said.

Sam nodded. "I dig your segue," he said.

"Thanks," Callen said. "Now I'm blushing."

Sam grinned. He'd kept his hand on the box Alders had entrusted to them.

"It's during this Cold War cookout that the footlocker is lugged over to the ridge and torched," he said. "As top cat, Holloway either would have ordered or approved of that…"

"Either way, he has to know…"

"But he probably *doesn't* know the Seabees who did the cleanup buried it afterward," Sam said. "And that it's still partly in one piece when they do."

Callen was momentarily quiet as the sun again fell behind the field of low, puffy stratus clouds rafting over the water.

"You know, Sam," he said, "I don't want to sound paranoid, but it just struck me that in the forty-eight hours since the Sutton killing, we've found out about three—no, four—possible attempts to conceal, suppress, cover up, or otherwise obfuscate information."

Sam nodded.

"I've been thinking about it too," he said, and began ticking them off on his fingers. "There's Tip Holloway using his clout to get the police off his kidnapping investigation a couple months ago…"

"And Elias Sutton advocating that the Navy knock down Building Thirty-One around the same time, which might or might not be coincidental…"

"And *Holloway* ordering the destruction of sensitive Deep Dive records and other stuff from *inside* the building back in the sixties…"

"Making it twice that he's been involved in keeping things quiet," Callen said.

"Right," Sam said. "Twice that we know."

"Or is it three times?" Callen said. "According to Alders, Mori's journal is among the stuff that's removed from the building at his command. This is sixteen years after it was secretly confiscated from U-437…"

"Back when Holloway *and* Sutton were calling the shots together at Camp Hueneme." Sam was still counting on his hand. "I'm at four definite or possible cover-up attempts so far."

Callen glanced over at him.

"I think we can up it to *five* if we accept what Alders says about the sub's irregular passengers," he said. "We *do* take his word for it, right?"

Sam nodded his head. "He's a no bullshit boat guy," he said. "We trust him."

"Then it's definitely five attempts to hide info," Callen said. "Because Alders has declassified British intercepts of radio cables between Tokyo and Berlin, naming Mori and three other Japanese scientists who were in Germany as advisors…"

"This is late nineteen forty-four…"

"Specifically, November 'forty-four," Callen said.

Sam nodded. "The cables involve Japan's request to have the scientists return to their country aboard a German cargo submarine…"

"One that's scheduled to sail out of Kiel in mid January nineteen forty-five, and secretly arrive in Kobe, Japan six to nine months later," Callen said. "Except the war ended *four* months later in *May* 'forty-five, and the sub…"

"U-437…"

"Surrendered to the Allies before it ever got there."

"Surrendered," Sam said, "and was brought to Hueneme."

Callen drove through the late afternoon traffic, coming up on a high white sound wall between the freeway's northbound and southbound lanes. It suddenly blocked the ocean from sight.

"Alders says every German sailor aboard the sub

was accounted for," he said. "But there's no record of Japanese passengers arriving at the base with them."

"No *public* record anyway, G," Sam said. "I read somewhere that maybe one percent of the military records from World War Two are still classified. Federal intelligence agencies are exempt from the Freedom of Information Act. They can turn down FOIA requests for reasons of national security…"

"So if the CIA wants to keep certain Deep Dive files under wraps, it's entitled," Callen said. "But why? You telling me that after seventy years, they're protecting our country from something?"

"Maybe," Sam said, "it *ain't* the country they're trying to protect."

"Then who?" Callen said, flicking him another glance. "Or what?"

Sam sat there a moment, then shrugged.

"Don't ask me," he said. "All I know is my hand just ran out of fingers."

8

"Simple question, okay?" Isaak Dorani said.

"Sure," Kensi said, which was not to guarantee he would get an answer.

"Where the hell *am* I?" he asked.

Kensi sat facing him across the table, a plain manila file folder in front of her. Although Dorani had no way of knowing it, his question really wasn't so simple at all.

Located at a small craft marina about a mile from headquarters on Los Angeles Harbor, the place she and her fellow NCIS agents called the Boatshed was, in fact, a genuine, honest to God boatshed, complete with burgee flags hanging from its rafters and an assortment of kayaks, canoes, oars, buoys, and fishing nets mounted on its bare wooden walls.

For the agents it was also a safe, secret location where they could bring endangered witnesses and hold their suspects for interrogation. When you were with the Office of Special Projects, and the evildoers you were investigating ranged from major narco-traffickers and arms dealers to terrorists of every stripe, it made sense not to bring the individuals you held in custody, or needed to protect from harm, to headquarters and risk exposing its location, putting them, your own personnel, and your entire covert operation in jeopardy.

At the same time, however, you needed to bring them *somewhere*.

And so the OSP had used its various resources and connections to procure the shed from its original yacht club owners and transform it into a home away from home. Well, actually, two interrogation rooms, an observation area, a main conference room with a homey little *kitchen*, and enough expensive technology to keep it fully linked to HQ... but why nitpick?

Bottom line, Kensi was hardly willing or able to give the caged, thieving little bird perched opposite her the answer to his question, simple or otherwise.

"I'll have to give that one a pass right now, Isaak," she said, folding her hands against the edge of the table. "If you don't mind."

Dorani frowned.

"And what if I *do*?" he said. "How is it that, all of a sudden, everybody and their mother thinks they can throw a blindfold over my eyes, then take me wherever they want afterward? Lemme tell you—"

"Everybody?"

"Figure of speech," he said.

"Oh?"

He shrugged. "Right," he said. "That's what it was."

His expression was not the least bit convincing. But she let it ride for the moment, wanting to get straight to the point.

"Isaak," she said. "Do you know someone named Theodore Holloway?"

He looked at her for a long moment.

"No," he said. "Should I?"

"How about *Tip* Holloway?" she said. "Does *that* name sound familiar?"

He shook his head. "Tip, Schmip, Blip, I never met anybody named Holiday—"

"Holloway."

"Whatever."

She inhaled, exhaled slowly.

"Have you ever been to the Bel Air Palms Senior Living facility?"

"No."

"You're sure?"

"Positive," he said. "Do I look like a freakin' senior citizen to you?"

"That has nothing to do with what I asked."

"Well, I ain't a fogey, and I don't know no fogies. And if I did know one, I wouldn't visit 'em in some stinking old age home."

"No? Why not?"

"Because old age homes depress me." He paused, rolling his shoulders. "Besides, what's any of this got to do with Daggut slipping me those junk bills?"

Kensi regarded him calmly.

"We'll get to that in a minute," she said.

"What's wrong with getting to it *now*?" He stuck his chin out at her. "You're supposed to be a Treasury agent, right? So how come you don't stick to the subject of me, an innocent customer at a hock shop, getting fleeced by its crooked owner." The chin went out further. "A guy hits hard times and has to sell all his worldly belongings, he'd like some honesty from the people who're buying them. Instead, it's like he's meat for the goddamn vultures."

Kensi waited until he stopped rambling and then pushed her folder across the table.

"I'll tell you what," she said. "You take a look at something for me here, and then maybe we can discuss the pawnshop."

Dorani frowned, glanced down at the folder, and flipped it open. His eyes widened. Inside was a fingerprint card with his police mugshot and basic personal data on the upper right-hand corner.

"These are latent prints," she said. "They were collected from a crime scene back in January."

He snapped his eyes up from the folder.

"Huh? What crime scene?"

"A burglary-kidnapping at Bel Air Palms," she said. "When they were input into the AFIS system, they drew a positive match with prints already on file for you."

Dorani was staring at her.

"I told you I never been to no old fogies' home."

"Then how do you explain what your fingerprints were doing there?" she asked, meeting his gaze. "Because they were found on the victim's desk."

He shrugged, pushing the card back across the table.

"Gotta be a mistake," he said. "Being I'm not a magician, my prints can't be where *I* never was."

Kensi held his gaze. The bird was experienced enough at this drill to keep his feathers unruffled, give him that.

"So you've never been in Theodore Holloway's condominium?"

"No," he said.

"Didn't leave those fingerprints on his desk."

"No."

"Never heard of him before."

"No," Dorani said, and cleared his throat. "Biff, Boff, whatever his name is, I'm telling you I never did. For the second time. Or is it the third? I'm getting *hoarse* here for Chrissakes."

Kensi sat quietly a second, thinking about the perfectly maintained gramophone she and Deeks noticed in Holloway's apartment, which he'd told them was a prized family keepsake given to him by Elias Sutton.

"Okay," she said. "Let's get to the hock shop."

Dorani looked heavenward.

"*Finally*," he said.

"Can you tell me what you went there to pawn?"

He hesitated for the briefest instant.

"Mr. Dorani…?"

"Rare coins," he said, then, "Silver dollars."

Kensi's eyes narrowed on his face. "That's what you gave Zory Daggut."

Dorani pursed his lips in disgust. "You must get off on makin' me repeat myself," he said. "Yeah, I brought him coins, and valuable ones too. What's the problem… Daggut tell you it was something else?"

She shrugged.

"Right now I'm just interested in what *you* tell me," she said. "And while we're on the subject, whatever happened to your pawn ticket?"

He looked at her. She waited.

"Who knows?" he said. "Guess I lost it."

"How?"

"How *what*? What'dya mean by 'how'?"

"How did you lose your ticket?"

"No clue," he said. "Wild guess, it could've dropped outta my pocket while you and your friend were chasing me down the street."

Kensi nodded. "Like when you reached for your machine pistol?"

He stared at her again. "Gimme a break," he said. "I didn't reach for nothing."

She smiled thinly.

"That's a very interesting statement."

"Yeah? Why?"

"Because, in case you don't recall, I was directly behind you," she said, "and saw you reach for the gun."

Dorani shrugged.

"Eye of the beholder," he said. "Truth is, it was falling down my pants. And I tried to stop it."

"Oh?"

"Right," he said. "Didn't want to shoot myself in the leg. Or someplace worse. And by the way, you can forget about trying to pin an illegal firearm rap on me."

"You're sure?"

"Positive," he said. "Don't pretend you don't know why, either."

"I'd hate to put words in your mouth," she said. "So how about telling me?"

"It's a three-D printed gun," he said. "I downloaded it from the Internet, put it together myself." He shrugged. "Ain't no law against that."

She sighed. "You're right," she said. "But there *are* laws against carrying a concealed weapon. And threatening an officer with one."

Dorani shook his head. "I just told you I didn't pull it on nobody," he said. "Besides, the only reason I brought it along was for protection."

"Really? Against who?"

"Criminals on the street," he said. "Figured I'd leave the pawnshop with big money for my coins." He spread his hands. "Who knew it'd all be counterfeit?"

Kensi sat there quietly a moment. She was not inclined to mention that his printed semiautomatic looked nothing like any other weapon of its type she'd ever seen, and that the same went for its ammunition.

While these things did not make either illegal, they *did* raise certain questions in her mind, and she wanted to run some tests on the gun before asking them.

"Isaak, I won't deny you brought your 'A' game today," she said. "But you still haven't explained your fingerprints at Theodore Holloway's apartment." She paused. "Among other things."

"Oh yeah?" he said.

She smiled at him.

"*What* other things?" he said.

She kept smiling.

"Come on," Dorani said. "You're not foolin' me for a second."

"No?" she said.

He shook his head, smiling back at her now.

"If you had anything else, you'd tell me," he said, his smile expanding. "Besides, LAPD *closed* that case."

Gotcha.

"Oh?" she said. "How do you know?"

Dorani abruptly stopped smiling.

"I thought you never heard of Mr. Holloway before," she said. "That *is* what you told me a minute ago, right?"

It was his turn to stay silent. He crossed his arms over his chest, staring across the table at her.

"I'll ask you again," she said. "If you've never *heard* of Holloway, how do you know the police investigation into his kidnapping was shut down?"

Dorani sat there with his arms folded. Opened his mouth, closed it.

"I want me a lawyer," he said at last.

Kensi stood up.

"Famous last words," she said, and turned toward the door.

* * *

Driving through Santa Barbara on East Figueroa Street, Sam quietly watching the scenery beside him, Callen saw a large chocolate Labrador stretched out under a Moreton Bay fig in someone's front yard. The dog raised its head lazily as he waved out his window, regarded him with mild, fleeting interest, then settled back down on the grass.

"Canines," he said. "I hold them spellbound."

"Noticeably," Sam said.

Callen went on past a string of private residences with stucco porches and neat green lawns. Its wide, clean sidewalks shaded by palms, jacarandas and fig trees, the street rolled gently up and down for a while before beginning a steadier climb toward the Santa Ynez range in the distance.

Low and whitewashed with a red tile roof and arched entryway, the Santa Barbara Police Department was one of several neo-Spanish municipal buildings concentrated in the town center, about a mile from the highway exit.

Callen was pulling into the parking lot when his smartphone rang through his car's stereo speakers. He answered the call over the Bluetooth.

"Beale?"

"Guys, I have a name for you," Eric said.

"Grand Sorcerer?" Callen said, swinging into a spot. "I'd like to be called 'Grand Sorcerer' at least once in my life."

"Call me the Wizard of Ops and I might consider it," Eric said flatly. "The name belongs to Elias Sutton's personal driver."

"Let's hear it," Callen said.

"Ronald T. Valli," Eric said. "He's listed as an

employee on Sutton's tax forms, and named as a 'frequent driver' on his auto insurance policy."

"You got an address?"

"Yeah… he lives in Carpinteria with his wife and child. And there's more."

Callen exchanged glances with Sam.

"Go on," he said. "We're listening."

"I did some cross-indexing," Eric said. "Valli has two felony convictions, both for home burglaries. His last got him five years at CSP-Sacramento, although he gained early parole for good conduct."

"When was this?" Sam said.

"A little over three years ago."

"He clean since?"

"There's no record of legal trouble since his release. Not even a traffic summons. "

Sam looked thoughtful.

"Sutton was a major booster of prison reform in the Senate," he said. "He talks a lot about second chances in his book."

"Then I can see how he'd have a soft spot for Mr. Valli," Eric said.

Callen cut the Benz's ignition. "How's that?"

"Valli's former Navy," Eric said. "He received an honorable discharge after eight years of service."

"And then gets into robbing homes," Callen said. "How's that happen?"

"It isn't easy to adapt after service life," Sam said. "A person can lose himself… doesn't matter if you're a seaman or an admiral." He paused. "Sutton understood."

Callen digested that a minute.

"You have a photo of him, Eric?"

"Several," Beale said. "Off his military and prison files."

"Cool, shoot 'em over to us."

"Already done—you need to check your email more often," Eric said. "I'll let you know if anything else turns up."

And with that the tech disconnected.

Sam looked at Callen, exiting the car. "Next stop Carpinteria, huh?"

"Right," Callen said.

Sam frowned, reached for his door handle. "I was kinda hoping to grab a pizza after we leave here."

"Justice never eats," Callen said.

Detective Frank Varno was sitting with his feet crossed on his large oak desk when his receptionist showed Sam and Callen into his office.

"*Hola*," he said without budging. "Make yourselves halfway comfortable, why don't you?"

They sat down in the chairs opposite him and waited. His office was clean, spacious, and tidy, the only decoration a smattering of golf memorabilia. Behind Varno, a large bay window offered a charming view of the employee parking lot.

"Want something to drink?" Varno asked, nodding at a mini fridge against one wall.

"What've you got?" Callen said.

"Sparkling mineral water, cola, ice coffee… and ice tea." Varno grinned at him. "It's regular tea, so you know. Nothing fancy like *oo*long."

Callen gave Sam a quick I-told-you-so look.

"I can use a little sparkle right now," he said.

"Same here," Sam said.

Varno swung his legs off his desk, rolled his chair over to the fridge, grabbed two bottles of mineral water, and lobbed them to the agents.

"So," he said. "You guys couldn't stay away because you missed me, right?"

Callen unscrewed his bottle cap. "You're the last person I think about every night," he said.

"And the first one I think about when day breaks," Sam said.

"Although we *would* kind of appreciate another look around Elias Sutton's place," Callen said.

"Being we're in the neighborhood anyway," Sam said.

Varno rubbed his jaw as if he'd been punched.

"*Oof*," he said. "Pick me up, knock me right down." He smoothed a finger across his bristly white mustache. "You know, I've been all the rage in SoCal these last couple days."

"Aren't you always?" Callen said.

"In a word," Varno said, "no."

Callen took a sip of the fizzy water, imagining the detective putting balls across the floor while the cars came and went outside.

"Your sudden popularity have something to do with the Sutton case?"

"Smart guy," Varno said. He sank back in his chair, folding his hands across his middle. "First thing this morning, I get a phone call from Josh Knowles. He's a commander with Robbery-Homicide in L.A."

"He been missing the hell outta you too?" Sam asked.

"Hilarious," Varno said. "Knowles is a good one. I like him. But I don't like somebody thinking he can throw his weight around. Ranking detective or not."

"What'd he want?"

"Everything I have on the Sutton homicide,"

he said. "Evidence, reports, the whole nine yards. Claimed it was because LAPD was better equipped to handle the case."

Callen raised an eyebrow. "That's all pretty irregular."

"A senator getting *murdered* is pretty irregular," Varno said. "So's you NCIS heroes showing up at the crime scene."

"*We* didn't try to cut you out of the picture."

"Which is why you two are here enjoying my fizzy H2O and Knowles isn't," Varno said. "It's one thing to offer an assist. Or ask me to share. Another to steamroll me."

"I'm guessing you didn't let him," Sam said.

"You agents really *are* sharpies," Varno said. "I kept it professional. It isn't enough to call Sutton a VIP. The man was in his own league, and I figured Knowles might be getting squeezed by his bosses to find his killer—maybe even the feebs." He shrugged. "There's no chance an investigation this major is gonna stay totally in my hands anyway. So I promised I'd think about it."

"Did you?" Callen said.

"Some," Varno said. "Al Juarez is a Detective First Class in Knowles's department. Close friend of mine. I decided it wouldn't hurt to give him a ring."

Sam scratched his head. *Knowles. Juarez.* The names sounded familiar.

"Turns out two people from your office came by to see Al today," Varno said. "None other than Blye and Deeks. Al felt they were straight shooters. Told me they needed some information, and requested it nice and polite."

Listening, Sam straightened in his chair. He'd suddenly realized what had set all the bells ringing.

"The Theodore Holloway kidnapping," he said.

"Juarez was lead investigator, and Knowles the chief who signed the case report. Am I right?"

Varno nodded. He was back to rubbing his mustache.

"I'm not privy to everything about that hot mess," he said. "But I know a little." He paused. "Al says he made sure your friends left his office happy, and I think maybe I'll follow his lead."

"Happy is good," Callen said.

"Beats sad and blue," Sam said.

Varno leaned forward, pressed a button on his intercom.

"*Yes?*" a woman answered.

"Hey, hey," Varno said. "I'm wondering if you could free yourself up a minute."

"*Sure... what's it about?*"

"The Sutton case," Varno said. "We have a couple visitors in my office."

"*Okay. Be right with you.*"

"Great," Varno said. "We'll want to discuss the trace evidence. Especially the latents."

"I didn't know you recovered fingerprints," Callen said.

"Well, now you do," Varno said. "Remember those old phonograph records at Sutton's house?"

Callen nodded. "That pile on the bedroom floor."

"Right," Varno said. "Except the prints came off a cylinder we recovered *behind* the house. Or what was left of the cylinder—it was pretty busted up."

Callen furrowed his brow. "You find a match?"

Varno had no sooner opened his mouth to answer than the tech appeared in the office entrance. Wearing a lab smock and cap, she carried a tablet computer in her hand.

The agents rose and turned toward the door.

"Emily the entomologist," Sam said. "Good to see you."

"Sam from NCIS," she said, and smiled. "Likewise."

Varno sighed heavily. "What a heartwarming crime scene reunion... the world is a beautiful place," he said. "Back to your question, Callen, we not only found prints, but got a strong set." He looked over at the tech. "Feel free to jump in."

She entered the room, tapping her device screen.

"Give me a second," she said. "I have a picture to show you—a recent mugshot of the person associated with the latents."

Sam and Callen studied the photo on her display. It showed a man of about twenty-five with dark eyes, curly hair, and a narrow face that widened disproportionately at the chin, giving it an anvil-shaped appearance.

"This guy have a history?" Sam asked, glancing up at her.

She tapped her screen again to bring up his file.

"Smalltime crook, lengthy record," she said with a nod. "His name is Isaak Dorani."

Kensi received Callen's call on her cell right after getting off the phone with the Public Defender's Office. A minute or so later, she reentered the interrogation room and sat back down opposite Dorani.

"Counsel's on the way," she said.

"Peachy," he said. He leaned back in his chair, a stubborn expression on his face. "Now could you do me a favor till the lawyer shows up?"

"What is it?"

"Leave me the hell alone."

Kensi shrugged philosophically.

"Sure," she said. "It isn't like I can ask you questions in the meantime."

"A shame, huh?"

"It's okay, they can wait," she said. "Although I'm itching to ask about the latest set of crime-scene fingerprints that match yours."

Dorani blinked. "Mine?"

She nodded.

"Come on," he said. "Do I look dumb to you?"

She smiled, saying nothing.

Watching his face.

"I mean, you think I'm taking that bait?" he said.

She kept her eyes on his face. A nervous curiosity had crept into it.

"Honestly," she said. "We shouldn't be talking to each other right now."

Dorani looked at her. "Make up your mind, lady," he said. "You just told me—"

"That I can hardly wait to ask about the prints found at the home of Elias Sutton," she said. "But I *will* wait. Because I want things done by the book. With a defense attorney present. So you have no wiggle room when we charge you for the murders of Sutton and his housekeeper."

Dorani sat up in his chair, crossing his arms.

"Who's Elijah Sutton?" he asked.

"Elias," she said. "The famous military hero. And former United States senator."

He jutted out his chin, his arms tightly folded. Kensi saw something new in his eyes now—a glint of fear.

"I thought this was about counterfeit money."

She shrugged.

"Things change," she said. "Nobody could have predicted we'd find those prints on an antique phonograph record at Elias Sutton's house. A record exactly like the ones you brought Daggut…"

"Wait a second, I gave him *coins*—"

Kensi held up a hand.

"Really," she said. "Don't talk. It's for the best."

"Who's talking?" he said. "I definitely ain't talking—"

"Good," she said. "Because your lawyer ought to be here any minute. Then we can discuss those cylinder records. And the fact that Theodore Holloway had the same kind of records in his home. Where it happens your fingerprints were also discovered."

Dorani was suddenly shaking his head. "Something's wrong with this setup," he said. "You gave me all kinds of bull about fake cash. But that ain't really why I'm here, is it?"

She kept her expression neutral, didn't answer.

"I bet you and the human skunk aren't even goddamn Treasury agents," he said.

She shrugged, letting him rattle on.

"Listen," he said angrily. "I don't like being busted under false pretenses. And I'm thinking I'll want an explanation before I walk outta this place."

She stood up, and grabbed the doorknob.

"I have a hunch you'll be stuck here for a while, Isaak," she said. "Hope you have somebody to feed your cat in the meantime."

He jerked as if at a loud, sudden noise.

"Hang on," he said. "What cat?"

"I'm sorry," she said. "Did I say 'cat'?"

"Unless I'm hearing things, that's *exactly* wha—"

"I meant *cats*, plural," she interrupted. "A red longhair and a gray tabby. And a white one with itchy ears."

Dorani stared at her.

"I want to know where you got all this stuff about cats," he insisted.

"We really shouldn't discuss it right now," Kensi said. "Since you *are* still waiting for your attorney…"

"The shyster's for when you ask me questions," he said. "This ain't *about* questions."

"No?"

"No," Dorani said. "It's about you telling me what the hell these cats have to do with anything."

"Well," she said. "I suppose it won't hurt for you to know their fur, and some dead ear mites, were found inside and outside Elias Sutton's home."

Which was true, based on what Callen told her of the Santa Barbara crime lab's findings.

"And on the box of cylinder records we took from Daggut's shop," she added.

Which was not true, at least not yet. Although she and Deeks had confiscated the box from the pawnbroker, and delivered it to the OSP's own forensic laboratory for testing.

Dorani was still staring at her.

"I told you I brought *coins* to that pawnshop," he said. "But let's say for the sake of argument they were records, and they *did* come from some famous general's house…"

"He was a naval officer," Kensi said. "Admiral Elias Sutton."

"Admiral, general, Indian chief, I still never heard of him," Dorani said. "*Again*, though, if you'll let me finish… say I brought Daggut records and not coins. Could be I got them secondhand without knowing where they came from. Like, for example, from some neighborhood kid who told me they belonged to his flaky grandma."

Kensi looked at him.

"When you put it that way," she said, "it sounds almost plausible."

"Hail Mary," Dorani said, pressing his palms together as if in prayer.

"Except it wouldn't account for your fingerprints being plastered all over Elias Sutton's premises," she said.

Which was of course an exaggeration. But the last she'd checked there was nothing unconstitutional about speaking figuratively in what was, after all, not yet an official interrogation.

Dorani dropped his hands to the table and sat there staring at her.

"Where's my lawyer already?" he said. "I'm tired of waiting for that dragass to get here."

"Relax," she said, opening the door a crack. "It isn't like you're going anywhere for a while."

He frowned, hesitated.

"Listen," he said. "Before you take a walk..."

"Yes?"

She waited.

"Say there *are* a few cats in my apartment... Say there are, it don't necessarily mean they belong to me. For all I know they could've crawled in my window. Come right up the front stairs or something."

"The stairs."

"Right," he said. "Or maybe climbed the wall from the alley." He shrugged. "I swear those cats are like Spider-Man. There're strays everywhere these days, it's a cryin' shame, you want my honest opinion."

Kensi sighed. "Okay, Isaak," she said. "What's your question?"

"My question, if you'd stop interrupting me, is what if I *do* get hung up here?" he asked. "That happens, who'd take care of those stinking animals?" He swallowed hard. "They would die of hunger and thirst."

Kensi stood with her hand around the doorknob. He looked suddenly worried.

She regarded him a long moment, and then finally sighed.

"I'm thinking we can probably make some arrangements," she said.

Callen was strapping himself into the Benz when his cell rang. Having just gotten off the phone with Kensi minutes earlier, he figured she might be following up with a question about the Santa Barbara crime lab reports. But the Caller ID told him it was Beale again. He switched over to Bluetooth so Sam could hear.

"Do you ever go home?" he asked, glancing at the dashboard clock to see it was now a quarter to six. "Eat and sleep like a normal flesh and blood human?"

"Actually, Nell and I are making an artichoke pizza for dinner here at HQ."

"Really? From scratch?"

"How else?" Nell answered for herself on the speakerphone. "He bought the frozen pizza, I topped it with canned artichokes."

Sam rolled his eyes.

"Two world class chefs in the making," he said. "Don't blow all your culinary secrets at once."

Callen reached for the ignition key, eager to get on the road.

"Okay," he said. "What've you got for us?"

"A quick hit," Eric said. "Remember when I told you Sutton's driver, Ronald Valli, did time in the Sacramento State Pen?"

"Right."

"Well, Nell pulled his incarceration record from the State database…"

"And it turns out Valli and Isaak Dorani were cellmates," she said, finishing Beale's sentence. "For almost three years."

Callen and Sam traded looks.

"Is this the one-and-the-same Isaak Dorani whose fingerprints were in Sutton's bedroom?" Sam said.

"Right. Holloway's too, according to Kensi and Deeks," Nell said. "Also the Isaak Dorani who tried to pawn a box load of Edison phonograph records that were almost certainly stolen from Sutton."

"And who we have at the Boatshed for questioning," Callen said.

"Exactly."

Callen started up the car.

"Thanks pizza guys," he said. "Carpinteria, here we come."

9

Ronald Valli lived a ten or twelve mile drive back toward Port Hueneme from Detective Varno's stirringly impressive parking lot-view office.

A modest 1960s Cape Cod home, it stood on a small lawn with a low corral fence and lilac hedges. The lime-green Ford hatchback in a carport beside the house sported a BABY ON BOARD sticker on its tailgate.

Callen pulled up behind it, Sam peering at the car through the rear window.

"Eric mentioned Valli had a kid, right?"

Callen nodded.

"There's a child safety seat in back," Sam said. "Plus that bumper sticker."

"Adds up to a kid," Callen said, cutting the engine. "Let's go."

Outside the front door, the agents rang the bell, and waited.

No answer.

Callen rang a second time. Still no answer. Sam bent his head, listened, heard the sound of an infant crying inside the house.

"You hear that?" he said.

"More kid evidence," Callen said.

"We are *good*," Sam said.

Callen pressed the buzzer again and held it down. The sound of the wailing baby got closer. Then the door finally opened.

The woman that appeared in the entryway was somewhere in her early thirties with long, wavy brown hair. She wore frayed denim cutoffs and open-toed sandals and had a plump, bawling infant slung over her shoulder.

"Mrs. Valli?" Callen said.

She nodded, adjusting the baby in her arms. Callen noticed the front of the little girl's shirt read:

I ♥ DADDY

"Do you mind my asking who you are?" she said.

Sam pulled out his ID.

"Federal agents," he said. "We'd like a word with your husband Ron."

The woman looked at him a moment. Shifted her eyes to Callen. Then just stood there and held the baby tightly in her arms.

Callen was thinking she looked upset. But maybe she was just tired from dealing with a cranky infant.

"Ma'am?" he said. "Are you all right?"

She nodded, opened her mouth to answer, closed it as if abruptly changing her mind.

And burst into tears.

Erasmo Greer stared at the notebook computer resting on his lap, shaking his head in astonished disbelief. He hadn't slept in... how long was it now? Eighteen hours?

Twenty? Since sometime the day before.

He wondered if he could be seeing things in his fatigue.

Blinking rapidly, he took off his glasses, rubbed their lenses on his shirt, and set them back on the bridge of his nose. Then he returned his eyes to the computer.

He wasn't delusional. The open .pdf file on Sutton's hard drive was still right in front of him. Right there on his screen.

Sitting up straight on the couch, Erasmo clicked a key to save the read-only file to his own computer, importing it from the stolen drive balanced on his armrest in a wireless SATA enclosure.

He had gotten sidetracked, and badly, but supposed it could be attributed to his mental and physical exhaustion. With his final deadline having come and gone, he'd pushed himself to the brink, knowing he was out of excuses, his back pressed against the metaphorical wall.

Azarian was clear about what would happen if he failed to make good on his promise. In fact, he could not have been any clearer.

Erasmo steadied his gaze on the screen now, thinking.

Deep in the tracks.

When Holloway blathered those words under narocsynthesis, he'd assumed they had a double meaning. That they not only referred to a railroad track, but a track on the hard disk where old man Sutton might have secreted his information.

All that made perfect sense, but there was a *third* association that had completely slipped past him.

It could not have been more infuriating given the stakes.

Erasmo shook his head. He'd been deked. Led on a wild goose chase by the ghost of old man Sutton.

Or was it *really* Sutton?

Erasmo wondered if the old man could have possessed the technical knowledge needed to pull it off.

Deep in the tracks. He had taken the phrase literally, launching his digital treasure hunt in a systematic fashion.

Sutton had used Level 3 full-disk encryption software on his hard drive, which was strong enough to thwart most trespassers. But Erasmo wasn't *most*. His first steps were to find a backdoor in, and then sort through every byte of recorded data on the drive.

When nothing turned up, he'd searched for a hidden partition—and quickly found one.

That was also easy enough. Although its file extension was masked, Erasmo had run a scan of the hard drive's service area—and noticed a large amount of its allocated space was mysteriously unavailable. For someone like him, it was a telltale sign the memory was being used for stealth storage.

The hidden partition was essentially a virtual drive, something people used to conceal their most valuable and secret data, and Erasmo had been sure the map would be there. But after mounting and decrypting it, he again came up cold. He found several versions of the manuscript for the old man's published memoirs, fragments of a second work in progress, a great many speeches and committee reports from his years in the Senate, and assorted personal and financial documents.

But there was nothing at all related to what he was looking for.

That seeming dead end left Erasmo stumped.

The files on the hidden partition would have been important to Sutton, yes. But they were fairly unremarkable. Why bother stashing them on a hidden drive after having already encrypted the primary, physical drive? The added trouble didn't seem warranted.

After that proved a waste of time, Erasmo went rooting for passwords to a cloud vault. If the info wasn't on the computer, he had reasoned, it must be stored in an outside host.

In hindsight, that was his biggest misstep. Sutton's browsing and download history indicated he used the Internet mostly for routine email, reading the news, and occasionally streaming movies. Though several of the programs installed on his machine offered cloud backups, he'd never taken advantage of them.

That brought Erasmo back to square one.

The information had to be on the drive. But where?

His frustration had only intensified as he tried to make sense of it. He racked his brain throughout the night, probing the drive's registry and directories, sifting through every bit of data, drinking one Red Bull after another to stay awake.

But nothing worked.

Dawn crept through his window blinds along with a feeling of hopeless futility, and by afternoon he was wearing down.

It was desperation more than anything else that prompted him to check the hard drive's controller— the flash chip and circuitry that communicated with the CPU, and functioned as the drive's own miniature operating system. Like the disk's service area, the controller had a small allocation of ROM memory, possibly two or three megabytes, most of which would be reserved for hardwired command codes. Theoretically, however, some of it would still be available for data storage.

Erasmo had known this was a longshot. The drive controller's tiny memory was not intended to hold user data. Its resident code normally remained unaltered through software updates, disk encryption, even a complete disk wipe. Writing information into the controller's memory required commands that would be highly guarded by the hard drive's manufacturer. And while the CIA and NSA had developed sophisticated ways of doing it for espionage purposes, their methods were far beyond a limping relic from the vacuum-tube era like Elias Sutton.

Still, Erasmo decided to play his hunch. The old man was well connected. If a third party helped him bury his map on his computer, the full hard-disk encryption could have been a deliberate blind, something to draw attention from the actual hiding place. It was a devious, *ingenious* trick…

For most of the afternoon, Erasmo had worked to access the controller's flash chip and examine its memory layout. He didn't need long to identify binary strings that were uncharacteristic of hard drive firmware and looked suspiciously like custom code.

A little more analysis told him he'd found a hidden cubbyhole in the closet, one containing a single data bag, a ciphertext file conspicuously protected by an entirely different form of encryption than the rest of the hard drive's information.

That was two hours ago.

Ten *minutes* ago, his head pulsating from stress and exhaustion, he had finally decrypted the file…

And realized it was a list.

A *list*.

When he read it, he was rocked to his core.

Erasmo looked at the clock on his computer now, his eyes stinging and bloodshot. He needed to bring himself into focus, needed to *think*. It was almost six-thirty. Late, very late in the day. He had repeatedly called and messaged Azarian, but gotten no answer.

That wasn't a good sign. He'd blown his deadline, left it shattered to bits and pieces behind him. Which would not go down well with his employer. Azarian had no idea of the difficulties he'd faced completing his task.

And he wouldn't care, of course.

Men like him…

They made their own rules.

And dealt out their own punishments for breaking them.

Erasmo could only hope he was pleased enough with his findings to let him live.

"May I?" Sam asked, and held out his hands. "I have two of my own… a boy and a girl."

Karyn Valli sat on the living room sofa, Callen and Sam opposite her in matching gray armchairs. She was weeping uncontrollably, the baby also still crying in her arms.

"You're sure?" she said.

He nodded and rose from his chair. "What's her name?"

"Lila."

"Sweet Lila," he said, taking the little girl from her. "One part honey in a cup, two parts angel powder."

"A baby from scratch?" Callen said.

Sam grinned.

"That's the classic recipe."

He settled back into the chair, felt the baby squirm against his chest, and lifted her so her chin was resting on his shoulder.

"What's the matter, hon?" he said. Rubbing her back, his large hand as wide as she was. "I'm guessing you just need to get rid of some gas."

The baby squirmed against him some more, but quieted a little.

Callen watched him a moment, wondering how he could miss something he'd never had. Then he reached into his pants pocket for a pack of tissues and silently held it out to Karyn.

"Thank you." She took a couple from the pack and dabbed her face, wiping mascara off her cheeks. "I'm really sorry I started to cry... but..."

She hitched in a breath and broke down in tears again.

He sat there a minute feeling awkward. In the seat beside him, meanwhile, Sam had shifted Lila to his lap, where she was now making happy baby noises.

"Doll face," Sam clucked. "You have a *honey doll* face."

Callen cleared his throat. "Mrs. Valli..."

"Karyn," she said. "Please."

He nodded.

"Karyn, we came here to speak with your husband..."

"I don't know where Ron is," she said, sniffling. "He left this morning without letting me know."

"Didn't say anything?" Callen asked. "Write you a note?"

"No," she said. "I was up with the baby at five, six in the morning, and fell asleep. When I woke up, he was gone."

"And when did you last see him?"

"Right around the time I got back to the bedroom."

"After being up with Lila."

She nodded.

"Has he ever done anything like this before?"

"Never. He's a very responsible man."

"So what could make him do it now?"

She shook her head, her eyes red, her cheeks wet from tears.

"I don't know," she said, and then lowered her gaze. "I wish I could tell you."

Callen watched her closely, thinking she knew more than she wanted to divulge.

"Karyn," he said, "I assume you know what happened to Elias Sutton."

"Of course," she said. "Ron is… *was*… his driver."

"Can you tell me how long he worked for him?"

"Three years… it would have been four next December," she said. "Ronnie and I started dating about a month after he was hired."

"And, as far as you know, there were no problems between him and the senator?"

She looked back up at him, swabbing her eyes.

"Do you think my husband did something to hurt him?"

"I don't know," Callen said. "Do you?"

She kept looking at him, the tissues bunched up in her hand.

"Ronnie loved him like a father," she said, her voice suddenly firm and defiant. "Admiral Sutton…" Her voice fell off, the tears flowing again. "Ron always used the title *Admiral*… He gave him a chance when no one else would."

"After his parole, you mean," Callen said, laying it right out there for her.

Karyn didn't answer immediately. Callen waited, listening to Sam and the baby coo at each other.

"Ron's... mistakes... were all a long time ago," she said at last. "He told me about his past before we were married. Never hid anything from me."

Callen nodded, waiting.

"When he got out of prison, Ronnie could barely get a job washing dishes," she said. "He didn't think he had a shot when a prisoner reentry counselor sent him to interview with Admiral Sutton. A former United States senator hiring a two-time felon as his personal driver... who would expect it?"

"But he got the job."

"Yes," she said. "Elias Sutton didn't just talk about people having the ability to change their lives. He *believed* it in his heart and soul."

Callen took a deep breath. "Karyn, a few hours before Mr. Sutton and his housekeeper were killed, Ron drove him to the cemetery where his wife is interred..."

"I know," she said. "Yesterday was the anniversary of her death. He went every year."

"We think the murders took place minutes after he got home," he said. "Your husband would've dropped him off, which probably makes him the last person to see him alive."

"Yes..."

Her voice caught, her eyes dropping back to her lap.

Callen suddenly wondered about something.

"Karyn... was Ron in the house *after* the murders?"

She was weeping outright again, breathing in moist, ragged snatches.

"He brought the car for gas," she said. "Admiral Sutton read the paper every day, and Ron picked it up at the station." She took a fresh tissue from the pack and blotted her face again. "When he got back to the house... he... found the side door open, went inside... and saw what happened there."

Callen looked at her. "Can you tell me why he took off instead of coming forward?"

Karyn's shoulders were trembling. "I... I think Ronnie was afraid he would be an automatic suspect," she said.

"Because of his record."

"Yes. He didn't admit he felt that way, but I knew."

"Did he say anything about wanting to contact the police?"

"He told me he'd already done it. That they told him they'd be in touch."

"And you believed him."

She nodded. "He didn't sleep all night. I could see he was worried and upset. But who wouldn't be?"

There was a long silence.

Sam stood up with Lila back in his arms. She was falling asleep, her cheek against his shoulder, his hand supporting the back of her head.

"Would you like me to put her in her crib?" he whispered to Karyn.

"That's okay," she said, smiling through her tears. "You don't have to bother..."

"It's no bother," he said. "Just show me where to go."

She motioned toward the hall. "If you turn right, it's the first door," she said quietly. "And thank you."

He nodded and left the room.

After a minute, Callen turned back toward Karyn. There was one last subject he needed to bring up.

"I know this was before you met him... but when Ron was in CSP-Sacramento, he shared a cell with someone named Isaak Dorani," he said. "I wonder if you—"

She snapped her eyes to his face, then averted them.

"Karyn," he said. "Is the name familiar?"

She didn't answer.

Callen sat forward in his chair. "I didn't come here to rack up a parole violation for Ron," he said. "This isn't about him associating with a felon."

She remained silent another few seconds. Her crying had subsided enough that she could stop wiping her face. Finally she took a long, deep breath.

"Isaak's my husband's pet project," she said. "He gets into hot water, Ronnie helps pull him out." She paused. "He remembers the difference it made when Admiral Sutton believed in him, and wants to do the same by believing in someone else."

"Sounds like you aren't sure he picked the right guy."

Karyn gave him a downbeat smile.

"Isaak's a character," she said. "He's sweet in his own weird way. The original mixed-up kid… you have to know him to love him."

"Have they been in touch lately?"

She nodded.

"He phoned last night," she said. "Around midnight."

"Odd hour," Callen said. "Does he usually call that late?"

She shook her head.

"Never," she said. "Ron told me it was because he heard about Admiral Sutton in the news."

The room was silent. Callen heard the low creak of wooden floorboards under the carpet, glanced over his shoulder, and saw Sam returning. Rather than sit down, he stood behind his chair with his hands on the back of it.

"Lila's in dreamland," he said. "She hardly budged

when I laid her down in the crib."

Karyn smiled. "She takes after her mom."

More silence. Callen lifted his eyes to Sam's, nodded, and looked back at Karyn.

"Thanks for your time," he said to her. "If Ron contacts you, please tell him we only want to talk. And if you have any idea where he might be…"

She suddenly met his gaze. Held it. Filled her lungs with air, released the breath, then inhaled and exhaled again…

"I think I know," she said at last.

10

Daylight was well on the wane at seven P.M. when the white Porsche Panamera slid up to the decrepit tenement on Hollywood Boulevard and Western, the lavish German sedan an incongruous sight amid the tired watering holes and adult novelty shops that shared the street.

Karik left the car first, sliding out the front passenger door. Then he went around to the rear door and opened it. His eyes were watchful.

The slender, athletic man who exited from the backseat was wearing a light tan sport coat, black jeans, and black ankle boots. Polished to a soft, even shine, the boots were lace-up chukkas made of supple, handsewn peccary leather. His long, dark hair was slicked straight back and fell several inches below the collar of the tailored jacket. Underneath the jacket, in a sheath on the left side of his belt, was a spiked titanium kubotan customized for his grip.

There were only a few scattered people on the avenue—a couple of teenaged bangers in sagging jeans, a woman with a gaggle of kids and a stroller, a gaunt, pale drag queen smoking a cigarette outside a vacant, fenced-off lot.

None of them gave the car, or the men who got out of it, a direct look. In this west Los Angeles slum, a wrong look at the wrong time could easily get you shot or stabbed, and people knew when to mind their business.

The Porsche's tinted window slid halfway down, and the long-haired man leaned over to speak to his driver. After a few brief words, he straightened and turned toward the tenement.

Karik shut the door and followed slightly behind him. The Porsche pulled from the curb and drove off.

The two men pushed through the partially boarded-up outer doors of the apartment building, Karik stepping over to the double row of buzzers in its vestibule. He quickly found the name and apartment number he was seeking.

He moved toward the inner door without ringing the bell. Pressing his palm against the lockplate, he applied his shoulder to its flyspecked glass and pushed hard.

The door rattled a little and swung open.

The lobby was large and dim, its light fixtures broken, its tiled floor covered with cigarette butts, candy wrappers, and other assorted trash. Someone had left a furry pink slipper just inside the doorway.

Karik pushed it aside with the toe of his shoe, holding the door for the long-haired man.

"Remember what I told you," the man said in a quiet voice.

Karik nodded, letting the door swing shut.

Then he once again fell in behind Azarian as they climbed the stairs.

* * *

The practice range was in a shallow gully about a quarter mile from the safehouse. Hidden under an overhang of rock and thick, thorny scrub, its wooden target stands, obstacles, and mockups could be dismantled at a moment's notice.

Alysha thought it reminiscent of the Hama al Riyaah training camp, where she had lived with Tomas and the mujahideen of the Marwan Hadid Brigade. At the facility she had combat conditioned her body, learned how to use a handgun and assault weapon, and eventually honed her skills with a sniper rifle.

It was after almost a year there as Tomas's lover that her attentions drifted to a powerful, charismatic al-Qaeda soldier named Umar, with whom she would steal off to Iraq, three hundred miles to the south.

At the Al Karar camp, in Tigris province, she became schooled in the arts of stealth combat, took training in water and forests, and became expert in the making of improvised bombs.

Her goal was to become the perfect killer.

At first, she thought it was because her killing ability impressed Umar. But later she would see her time in Iraq as another stage in her Emergence.

When the Syrian civil war erupted, she and Umar returned there to join al-Qaeda's Jabhat al-Nusra front in its rebellion against the Assad government. But a group of the insurgents would soon attack the ethnic Karikian town of Kessab, setting fire to churches, looting homes, abducting and torturing villagers of Armenian origin.

Umar and Alysha were elsewhere in Syria when the massacre occurred. Sickened by it, Alysha had decided she was moving on. With or without Umar.

They were at Hama al Riyaah to pick up weapons

and ammunition when she again met Tomas. She'd thought then that he would try to kill her as payback for her infidelity. But in hindsight, she realized his loyalty to the cause always exceeded his passions.

Tomas was recruiting again, only for a new leader rising in America. His name, he told her, was Azarian…

They would soon leave Syria together, fugitives from both al-Nusra's mujahideen and their enemies. Using money and other bribes—including ancient temple relics—to make their way through the dangerous smugglers' routes that led back toward Europe.

Now she carried her ghost gun to the shooting range, where Tomas and Yuri were practicing. Like her, and Matous's team at the far end of the ravine, they were dressed in desert camos.

A pair of binoculars strapped around his neck, Tomas acknowledged her with a slight, silent nod as she stopped at his side. Then he aimed his own weapon at the target sheet fifty yards in front of him, emptying its magazine with a series of three-round bursts.

The cardboard sheet trembled as his fire passed through its near life-sized human silhouette.

Yuri checked his wristwatch.

"Twenty seconds," he said.

Tomas examined the results through his binoculars, then handed them over to Alysha.

She raised the goggles to her eyes. His bullets had all struck the target's chest area.

"So?" he said in a satisfied tone. "What do you think?"

She lowered the glasses.

"You score well," she said. "Standing still."

He did not comment.

She gazed off to the right. About thirty feet from

the firing range, a plywood mockup of a Metroline train's locomotive stood near the wall of the ravine. Assembled to its precise specifications, with openings for the windows and doors, it had a ladder climbing up its side to the control cabin. Another human silhouette target at the top of the ladder represented the train operator preparing to enter the cabin door.

"Let's see how I do," she said.

She turned, walked back to the spray-painted hundred yard line, and took her position directly behind it.

"Yuri?" she said, nodding her readiness.

He set his stopwatch.

"*Now!*"

Raising the weapon in a two-handed grip, she dropped to a high crouch and triggered a burst at her target, then bent to a low crouch and discharged another salvo. Without pausing, she sank to her right knee, fired again, went down on both knees, fired, went down to her stomach, fired prone from the ground. Then rolling onto her back, firing with the rifle upside down. Next she maneuvered in reverse: prone, firing, knees, firing, one knee, low crouch, high crouch, firing, firing, firing until she was standing straight up again.

Alysha repeated the entire drill from start to finish, down and up with the gun spitting in her hand. And then, fluidly, she scrambled toward the mockup locomotive, stopping midway between the fifty and hundred foot lines, aiming at the operator's figure high on the ladder.

Firing.

The figure was knocked off the rungs, a gaping hole in its upper torso.

Seconds passed. A dead hush fell over the ravine.

Alysha lowered the ghost gun to her side, dusted off her clothes, and strode back to the firing line. Tomas was looking at the targets through his binoculars.

"So," she said. "What do you think?"

He held the glasses out to her. "You do well on the move," he said. "See for yourself."

Alysha shook her head.

"No need," she said flatly. "I'm going back to the safehouse. Would you like to come with me?"

He looked at her as gunfire once again began reverberating inside the gully walls. Yuri was taking his turn at the line.

"My answer hasn't changed since London an eternity ago," Tomas said.

He fell in beside her as she turned toward the pass leading up the slopes.

Erasmo heard the knocks at his front door and jolted up straight on the couch. He never invited anyone to his apartment. No one ever knocked but deliverymen with Chinese takeout or pizza, and he hadn't called to order any food.

He sat there quietly with his computer on his lap, facing the door across his cramped, cluttered living room. It was probably better not to answer. Chances were somebody was at the wrong apartment. Surely, that was the case. He did not appreciate being disturbed, not at any time. But it was especially unwelcome after the long, draining twenty-four hours he'd been through...

Whoever was out there knocked again. *Hard.*

Erasmo's entire body stiffened, his heart racing, his

computer nearly falling off his lap.

He checked the time on his watch. It was just after seven. Who could it be?

Frowning, he shifted the computer from his knees to the sofa. Then he rose and wound his way toward the door between stacked cartons of clocks and clock parts.

The third set of knocks was the loudest yet.

"Answer the door, Mr. Greer."

Erasmo shivered. The voice belonged to Jag Azarian's assistant. The servile parasite who always answered his phone.

Karik.

He stood perfectly still, not making a sound, hoping his unwanted visitor might think he wasn't at home, turn around, and leave...

More knocks. Loud, rapid, and hard enough to rattle the door in its frame.

"Open the door," Karik said. "I won't ask again."

Erasmo took a deep breath. Karik clearly wasn't going anywhere.

This was not a good thing. No, not at all.

He turned the latch and opened the door a crack, leaving the security chain on.

"Yes?" he said, and pushed his face into the opening. "What is it?"

"Enough," a second voice said. "Let us in. Or we'll do it ourselves."

Erasmo felt his heart kick against his ribcage.

The voice belonged to Azarian himself.

He felt utter astonishment. Until now he had only seen Azarian once, in a single video conference soon after their initial hookup over the Darknet.

But they had never met in the flesh. For Azarian to come here...

He reached up, slid back the chain, and opened the door.

The two men pushed past him into the apartment. He stumbled backward off balance, the doorknob tearing free of his hand, the door slamming shut behind them.

Azarian stood between him and the door, Karik stepping slightly to one side. He was well over six feet tall. Taller than Erasmo had imagined. His eyes strikingly dark.

"So," he said, looking around. "This is your home."

Erasmo nodded. "Small, but efficient, as they say…"

"It's a filthy sty," Azarian said. "My skin crawls having to stand here."

Erasmo felt indignation claw through his fear. He had worked hard for weeks—worked day and night. Yes, he'd stretched the truth a bit when it came to his progress. But it was only to buy the time to do his job properly.

And he'd succeeded, hadn't he? He had found the goods. The exact thing Azarian hired him to do.

It struck him that he should not have to stand here cringing in front of his employer. That he might benefit from peppering his entrée with a little self-assertion. He deserved some respect.

"'If a cluttered desk is a sign of a cluttered mind, of what, then, is an empty desk a sign?'" he said.

Azarian's dark eyes flashed.

"Einstein," he said.

Erasmo nodded.

"He was the man," he said. "Smartest dude ever. Smart is *au courant*."

Azarian stared, Karik waiting silently beside him.

Something in their expressions made Erasmo decide to step up his pace.

"All right," he said. "Before the wheels fall off our bicycle-built-for-three, you'll want to hear me out."

"Meaning?"

"Meaning the last time we spoke, I told you I was close to finding the glow dust."

"And?"

"And what if I told you I found it?" he said. "Well, basically."

Azarian kept staring.

"All right," he said. "Talk."

"It goes back to Holloway," he said. "When he blathered that the vault's location was on Sutton's computer—told your people it was deep in the tracks—they misconstrued what he was saying. They assumed he meant the *railroad map* we've been seeking was on the hard drive. But that was wrong. A big, bad logical overextension."

Azarian waited.

"Sutton owned a large collection of old Edison wax cylinder records," Erasmo said. "The old man catalogued their titles, artists, release dates, and was meticulous about it." He took off his glasses, rubbed the lenses on his shirtsleeve. "I turned up the list of records on his hard drive. A document file." He rubbed his lenses some more. "All along, I'd been searching the disk for information about the map. That's where data is supposed to be recorded. But it wasn't there. So I looked in a flash memory chip on its circuit board. Where data *isn't* supposed to be recorded… and there it was."

Azarian edged closer to where he stood amid the packages of clockwork.

"I paid you to find something specific. Explain what all this has to do with it."

"All right, Gramophones One-Oh-One," Erasmo said. "The early ones recorded as well as played, and could be used for dictation. When a person recorded, he would crank the cylinder around and talk into the horn. The cylinder turned against a needle, and the needle cut grooves into the wax, vibrating up and down with the sound of his voice, making deeper and shallower cuts as it got softer and louder." He paused. "On playback, the process was reversed. The needle *tracked* its way through those cuts in the record's grooves. That's how individual songs on an album came to be known as tracks."

Azarian gave an almost indiscernible nod. "You're telling me Sutton left the information about the cache in a voice recording," he said. "That the map is his spoken word."

Erasmo put his glasses back on, the thick lenses making his eyes look huge.

"A hot, *hot* track," he said. "But wouldn't it be entertaining if he waggishly *sang* the coordinates?"

Erasmo could see the eagerness on Azarian's face— and why would he even bother concealing it? He wanted the stockpile. Nothing else could bring him down from his mansion in the hills.

"When did you find all this out?" he said.

"Tonight, not an hour ago," Erasmo said. "I tried to contact you."

"And you have the list."

Erasmo nodded back to where he'd left his computer on the couch.

"Yes," he said. "Saved to my hard drive."

"Anywhere else?"

"I didn't have a chance to copy it, if that's what you mean."

Azarian exchanged a quick glance with Karik, then returned his attention to Erasmo.

"The recording," he said. "How will we know which one it is?"

"Sutton catalogued it as two-three-two on his list. Just the number," Erasmo said. "That name would match the one on its tube container."

"And do we know where he kept it?"

"*I* know it was in his home the day he left this mortal coil," Erasmo said. "Our mutual associate Isaak Dorani expropriated a box load."

"Expropriated."

"Stole, in other words."

"Tell me about that."

"Isaak said they were his insurance," Erasmo explained. "I don't know what he meant, and I didn't bother asking him. But he told me he was bringing them to a fence."

Azarian's expression altered in the smallest way.

"Do you know where this fence is?"

"Downtown, in Skid Row," Erasmo said. "He mentioned a name. Dagger. Or Duggat. Something like that."

A long silence. Erasmo saw Azarian's hand slip under his sport coat and suddenly grew very uncomfortable again.

"There is a historical figure I've always admired... as you do Einstein the scientific genius," Azarian said at last. "He is Genghis Khan, the world conqueror."

Erasmo wondered nervously what he was reaching for under his jacket.

"It is ironic that he embraced the Turks, the eventual

slaughterers of my people, as allies of convenience," Azarian said. "But we are, all of us, imperfect beings."

He took a step closer to Erasmo. His hand moving slightly under the jacket's lightweight fabric.

"Like your scientist, the Great Khan left many words to be remembered by future generations," he said. "Would you like to hear my favorites?"

Erasmo was thinking he would be perfectly fine without that. But it didn't sound as if he had a real choice.

"Do tell," he said, hating the tightness in his voice. "I—"

A bony hand clamped over his mouth, muffling the words. Reflexively trying to pry it loose, the muscles of his throat bulging with the effort, he realized it was Karik. The wiry little man had stolen up behind him while he was focused on Azarian, and he was stronger than he looked. Erasmo gagged helplessly.

Then Azarian's fist appeared from under the jacket, something shiny and metallic clenched inside it. Erasmo thought at first it was a knife, but quickly realized it was some kind of rod or baton.

He kept struggling to break free of Karik's hand, but it remained locked over his face, pressing against his lips and teeth.

Azarian took a large step closer, raising the metal object in his hand.

"'I am the punishment of God,'" he said in a chest-deep voice. "'If you had not committed great sins, God would not have sent a punishment like me upon you.'"

Erasmo gaped up at the object from behind his glasses, then saw it come flashing down at him.

And felt the punishment.

* * *

"Hello, Drew?"

"Milena, hi… I was just thinking about you!"

"Like minds," she said.

"Guess so," he said. "How's it going?"

"Great," she said. "It's been a wonderful day."

"Same here…"

"Starting with you being so kind to me on the train."

"I was about to say starting with when we *met* on it."

She laughed. "Here we go again."

"Yeah."

"It's true, though," she said. "You made the ride a pleasure. And gave me a fascinating history lesson."

"Well, I won't turn down the compliment." A pause. "We're still on tomorrow, right?"

"Without fail," she said. "That's the reason I called. I can't talk for more than a minute—there's a lecture on campus. But I wanted to tell you how much I'm looking forward to it."

"It'll be lots of fun," he said. "There *is* one thing I have to ask, though, before I take you on that Piggyback Yard tour."

"Oh…?"

"Right," he said. "About your allegiance to the cause."

She froze a moment. "I don't understand…"

"The question's whether you'll be wearing a Dodgers or Angels cap."

She was quiet a second. Then she laughed.

"You had me there a second, Drew."

"Sorry, couldn't resist," he said, chuckling. "You should know I bleed Dodger blue. But I did want to find out. In case I pick one up for you."

"I'll tell you what, being from England, my baseball loyalty is up for grabs."

"You sure?"

"Positive. I am a Dodgers fan."

He laughed again.

"You know," he said. "I don't want to embarrass myself... but I almost feel we were meant to cross paths today."

"I was thinking the same, Drew."

More silence. He cleared his throat.

"Well, then," he said. "I don't want to keep you from your lecture."

"Thank you."

"See you when I get off work tomorrow?"

"At the station," she said. "Six on the dot."

"G'night, Milena."

"Until then," she said, and disconnected.

Tomas came up behind her in the bare living room. Outside the safehouse, the faint sound of semiautomatic fire shivered in the air. They were still drilling at the practice range.

"You're good," he said. "If I didn't know better, I would think I heard your heart pattering away."

Alysha gave a cold smile.

"It's only the guns you hear," she said. "Make no mistake."

She dropped the burner phone into a trash receptacle.

"What if your windup trainman calls with a change of plans?" he said.

"He won't," she said. "You can be sure of that."

She stood a moment, noticing his eyes on her.

"What are you looking at?"

He shrugged. "Nothing," he said. "I was remembering."

The guns continued to rattle in the distance.

"It's likely we'll die tomorrow," she said.

"Yes."

She stepped closer to him, put a hand lightly on his chest.

"So?" she said. Her eyes on his. "Will you stand there with your old memories for comfort?"

"Or what?"

Her hand slid down the front of his shirt.

"You know what," she said. "Yes or no?"

He swallowed, his breath suddenly short.

"Yes," he rasped, and pulled her into his arms.

Zory Daggut was just getting ready to close out his register when the doorbell rang at a quarter past eight. Frowning, he peered out the storefront window from behind his counter.

The man at the door was short, thin, and neatly dressed in a dark blue sport jacket, with black hair and a pointed goatee that gave his face a sharply triangular, almost devilish appearance. Daggut pegged the guy as the type of hardcore squeaker who had a wallet full of money to spend, but would go poking around the worst sump holes in Los Angeles to save himself a dime. Somebody who'd want to pick up two sets of hocked diamond earrings for the price of one, so he could keep his wife *and* mistress happy, and maybe even pick up a *third* shiny little trinket for mom's birthday in the bargain.

The guy outside hit the bell again.

Daggut was tempted to make believe he hadn't

heard it. He was open from 8:30 A.M. till 8:30 P.M., six days a week, and really didn't want to be stuck here an extra minute tonight. Customers like this guy could absolutely mean a nice sale despite their miserliness. But they usually took forever making up their minds, asking endless questions, wanting to see every item ten times before making a decision, then asking *again* right when you put it back in the case... and it had already been a long, aggravating day.

Unfortunately, Daggut thought, it was also a day when he'd found himself out three thousand bucks thanks to that compulsive bullshitter Isaak Dorani, and those federal agents who'd come through his door a few minutes after Isaak left the shop.

He scratched the snake and skull tat on his arm, a recent addition that itched like hell.

The bell rang a third time.

Daggut frowned. Three thou was a huge goddamn number in the minus column. Sickeningly huge, in fact. Maybe it wouldn't hurt to see what that clown outside wanted. If the guy started in with a cheapskate show-and-tell routine, he would tell him to come back another day.

Sighing, he went to the front door, turned the latch, and moved aside to let him in.

"How you doin'?" he asked. "Need some help?"

Little Mephistopheles stood there a second as the door swung heavily shut, its chimes tinkling behind him.

"Yes, thank you," he said, his gaze going past Daggut to the back counter. "Would you be kind enough to let me see your jewelry case?"

Daggut almost burst out laughing. Nobody could ever say he didn't know his customers.

"Sure," he said. "Follow me."

He led him toward the display case, went around behind it. "You looking for something special?"

The guy leaned over the counter, not even glancing inside. He flicked his eyes quickly left and right, as if to see if there were any other customers in the shop with him. Then he lifted them up to Daggut's.

"Yes, Mr. Daggut," he said in a low voice. "I've come here for the Edison cylinders."

Daggut looked at him.

"Cylinders?" he said, struggling to cover up his surprise. "I dunno what you're talking ab—"

The little man drew the gun from under his jacket before he could finish his sentence, pointing it straight across the counter.

His eyes widening in dismay, Daggut saw it was a Glock 41 longbarrel, a cannon that fired forty-five caliber slugs and would blow a hole in him so wide you could drive a moving van through it.

"Sir, I don't intend to play games," the man said, angling the gun up at his chest. "Sometime earlier today, a common thief named Isaak Dorani brought you a box—a rather *large* box—of thirty or forty rare cylinder records. I will not ask if you knew they were stolen property. Indeed, I will ask no questions whatsoever. I will simply, and politely, request that you turn them over to me right now. And then I will leave here without further disruptions."

Daggut returned his stare. He'd had guys come in and stick him up plenty of times. Never anyone dressed like Little Mephistopheles here—most were junkie gangbangers with colored rags hanging off them and so many piercings in their faces they looked like human pincushions. But that happened enough, you knew the ones who'd hesitate before pulling the trigger. When somebody seemed even the slightest bit indecisive, he would get the tire iron from under the counter and turn his head into brain pudding.

This guy's eyes were telling him he was a stone cold killer. He needed to be straight with him.

"Listen," he said, unconsciously scratching his arm. "I'd give you the records in a second. But I don't have them."

Little Mephisto stared at him. The gun looked outrageously large in his thin, almost dainty hand.

It also looked very steady there.

"Mr. Daggut, are you claiming you did not receive the cylinders?" he asked.

Daggut shook his head, trying not to look stunned. How did the guy know his name?

"I bought them," he said. "Set myself back three thou. But Isaak isn't gone twenty minutes when this guy comes in here flashing his ID, says he's a federal agent—"

"What do you mean 'agent'? Was he with the FBI?"

Daggut shook his head.

"That's what I wondered," he said. "He smelled ripe, let me tell you. Like he wouldn've known a shower stall from an outhouse. I didn't believe the *agent* line, figured he might be mental, you get all kinds around here. But when I asked, he explained he was Naval Intelligence. And that's what his card said. NCIS."

"What happened next?"

"He asked about the cylinders, same as you. Asked what I knew about 'em."

"And then?"

"I told the truth. That I got them from Isaak. And that Isaak said *he* inherited 'em from his loco grandma. Or somebody else's fruitcake grannie. Something like that."

"Go on."

"He told me I had to turn them over to him. That they were evidence in an investigation."

"And?"

"That's exactly what I did," Daggut said. "Went into my back room for the carton and put it in his hands."

"What else?"

"That's it," Daggut said. "He tells me he'll probably have some more questions later on, and then leaves here with the box."

The man angled his chin up slightly. An instant later, Daggut saw an even slighter twitch at the hinge of his jaw.

"Questions," he said.

Daggut was suddenly thinking he'd made a stupid mistake. That he should have kept that particular detail to himself.

"I told him everything I know… just about Isaak and his grandma," he said. Then added, "He can talk to me another ten times, a hundred, I got nothing more for him."

Little Mephistopheles stared over the top of the gun.

"That's all? You're certain no more was said between you?"

"Not a word," Daggut said. "Agent Stinkbomb takes the box from my hands, and two seconds later he's out the door. And I'm out my Edison swag and the three thou."

The man looked at him for a long moment, his jaw muscle again moving almost imperceptibly.

"Thank you," he said. "You've been most helpful."

Daggut felt a speck of relief. He inhaled and stopped scratching.

"Anything else I can do for you?" he said.

Little Mephistopheles shook his head.

"No," he said. "There will be no more questions, Mr. Daggut."

Daggut furrowed his broad forehead, wondering if he'd heard an edge of sarcasm in his voice.

Then the gun roared hotly in his face, giving a loud and clear answer.

11

It was nine o'clock at night in the Boatshed, where two Navy masters-at-arms were guarding an increasingly irate and impatient Isaak Dorani, who was still awaiting the arrival of his attorney from the Public Defender's Office. As for the lawyer, a woman named Lauren Scardella, she was inexplicably missing in action, having last phoned in over an hour ago from the thick of a freeway traffic jam somewhere near the downtown area. At the time, she'd optimistically given her assurances that she was no more than fifteen minutes away.

Not far away at OSP headquarters, meanwhile, Kensi Blye and Nell Jones were about to give Dorani's highly unusual ghost gun a workout in the forensic shooting range. Both were at the firing line, their earmuffs down around their necks. Its steel walls covered with ballistic rubber tiles, the long, sound-baffled room was quiet except for the murmur of sterile HEPA-filtered air flowing from the vents.

Kensi inspected the gun's loaded fifteen-round magazine, slapping it into the well with her palm, then racking the slide to chamber a round.

"Thanks for hanging out late to meet me," Kensi

said. "I wanted to get this done before Dorani's lawyer shows. Assuming that happens."

Nell smiled.

"Technically, I stuck around with Eric," she said, "to make artichoke pizza."

"Oh?"

Nell nodded. "We're experimenting," she said. "When you called, I just went up and got the gun up from Evidence. And here you were."

Kensi looked at her, intent on a little mischief, being that nobody was exactly sure what was going on between the two techs after hours.

"So… how'd your experimentation go?" she asked.

"You mean with the pizza?"

Kensi shrugged. "Pizza, Eric, whatever."

Nell looked slightly flustered.

"I'd suppose I'd call it, uh… delightful," she said.

Kensi decided to press a little. "And by that you mean…?"

"Well, I'm crazy about artichokes," she said.

"Uh huh."

"Eric is too."

"Uh huh."

"We can't resist them when we're together," Nell said, a suddenly distant look in her eyes. "They're so very hard on the outside…"

Kensi felt her cheeks flush with warmth, thinking she regretted having gotten this whole thing started.

"Ah, Nell—"

"So succulent inside…"

"Nell."

"I love sliding the fleshy part over the edge of my teeth," she said, still staring off into space. "Then onto my tongue and—"

"Nell!"

The tech blinked as if abruptly shaken from a trance.

"Oh," she said, clearing her throat. "Sorry."

Kensi took a deep breath.

"The gun," she said.

"Right."

"I want to see how it fires."

"Right." Clearing her throat again. "So do I." Smoothing her purple floral dress. "I mean, what makes it extraordinary is that it has no metal components." She formed an O with her thumb and forefinger. "I mean, *zero*."

Kensi nodded, raising the muffs over her ears.

"Typically on printed plastic guns the lower receiver is still metal," Nell said, doing the same with her ear protectors. "Other parts too. Like the trigger assembly."

Kensi turned to face the target downrange, getting into her stance. Her fingers wrapped around the weapon, legs slightly spread for balance.

"The only printed plastic guns that ever worked effectively were single shot models," Nell said. "On a semiautomatic pistol or carbine set for burst fire, the heat and pressure of the powder gas, and the kinetic force of the explosion, would melt the muzzle and break the rest of a gun apart."

Kensi sighted over the nub at the end of the gun barrel and repeatedly squeezed its trigger, the weapon jolting in her hands as she ran off its clip into the target's chest area. Then she pulled the muffs from her ears and looked it over, turning it from side to side.

"There's no damage," she said, holding it out. "How's that possible?"

Nell took the gun for a closer look.

"My lab work tells us it's made of a superpolymerceramic composite material we've never seen before. It's much stronger than either one separately," she said, hefting it in her hand. "And really light."

"And this new composite first turns up in the hands of a hopeless schnook like Isaak Dorani?" Kensi said. "That seems kind of odd to m—"

She looked up, seeing hallway light spill into the room as the door unexpectedly opened.

An instant later Henrietta Lange stepped through.

"Hetty," Kensi said. "I didn't realize you were here this late."

"I wasn't," Hetty said soberly. "But it's turning into an eventful night."

"What's going on?" Kensi asked.

Hetty frowned.

"Murders," she said. "Two of them."

The hundred mile drive from Carpinteria to Big Santa Anita Canyon took Callen and Sam over two hours on the Foothill Freeway, most of it over dark, rolling stretches of blacktop with scant town lights along the way, intermittent reflective lane dividers, and the tree-clad mountain shoulders pressing in on both sides.

Now Callen turned a bend in the road and saw the rectangular outline of a hand-carved wooden sign up ahead. He leaned forward as his highbeams splashed it:

Tanly Flat
RECREATION AREA

ANGELES
National Forest

"Oh, my stars and garters," he said. "We're almost there."

Sam stretched beside him. "Finally, man," he said. "My body aches in places I didn't know could ache."

Callen pulled a face.

"Don't get graphic," he said, reaching for the coffee in his cup holder. "I'm too whacked from driving all day to handle it."

"Hey," Sam said. "Didn't I offer to take over?"

Callen drank some coffee, frowned. It was already tepid when he'd picked it up at a gas station about fifty miles down the road.

"Your eyes being shut made it kind of hard to take you seriously," he said.

Sam yawned and held a hand out.

"Fusspot," he said, taking the cup from him. "Let's just hope Karyn guessed right about hubby coming here."

Callen rode his brakes, peering out the windshield. After a minute or two he saw a low, wood-frame structure about a hundred yards up the road to the left. There were saddles, leather harnesses, and thick coils of rope hanging from its wide front porch.

"That's the pack station," he said, pointing to a window. "See the nice donkey?"

Sam looked out and saw a long, horse-like head framed inside it.

"Wonder if he smells anything like Deeks?" he said, puckering his face as he sipped from the coffee cup. "This wastewater just took a year off my life, by the way."

Callen pulled behind the building into its gravel-and-dirt parking area. It was large, pitch dark and surrounded by soaring alders and pines. Cruising slowly around its uneven borders, they could make out eight or ten vehicles—mostly pickups and SUVs—in the spill of the Benz's headlights.

Sam suddenly pointed out his window.

"Stop the show," he said. "Look over there."

Callen did. Parked under a shelf of overhanging branches, the BMW sedan was a conspicuous sight in the backcountry lot.

He came to a halt behind it, leaving his headlights on. Then he took a Maglite from his glove box and they both got out.

Sam was walking toward the rear of the BMW when he abruptly stopped in his tracks.

"G," he said. "Don't step on the rattlesnake."

Callen made a disbelieving face. "You seriously think I'm falling for that?"

"Falling for what?"

"For a stunt that wouldn't sucker a gullible nine year old."

Sam spread his hands. "Listen, man, I'm just trying to—"

The rattling noise silenced him at once.

Callen looked at Sam's face a second, then glanced down.

The snake was coiled in a loose S between them and the rear of the BMW, its wedge-shaped head rearing off the ground, its tail pointed straight up and quivering in the air.

"Okay," he said, looking back up at Sam. "I believe you."

Sam frowned. "Some people can't find it in their hearts to trust."

The snake shook its tail again.

"Hey, I said I *believed* him," he said, staring at it.

"They like sleeping on rocks and gravel during the day," Sam said. "Night's when they hunt for prey."

"Fascinating," Callen said. "So now what?"

"Move off its turf... slow," Sam said in a quiet voice. "Rattlers are shy. He doesn't want to mess with you any more than you want to mess with him."

Callen took a measured step away from it, another, then stopped, Sam doing the same on the opposite side. After a few seconds the rattler went slithering off into the darkness.

"Next time, warn me," Callen said.

"I'll try to remember," Sam said.

They turned back to the sedan. Callen knelt to shine his flash directly on its license plate, Sam checking his smartphone to confirm the obvious.

"The tag number matches Sutton's," he said. "This is his BMW."

Callen stood up. Looking around the parking area, he spotted the trailhead off to his right amid the trees. Barely discernible in the pale yellow throw of his headlights, it was wide enough for a loaded pack mule to negotiate.

"Ready for a moonlight hike?" he said.

Sam glanced up at the pitch-black sky. "There's no moon," he said.

"So what's wrong with using your imagination?"

Sam made a face. "All right, Boy Scout," he said. "But try not to wake any more wildlife."

Callen grinned.

"Valli-deri, Valli-dera," he said, turning toward the trail.

* * *

The mule trail wound downhill at a gradual pitch, leading Sam and Callen under dense stands of juniper, alder, and other forest brush. It was a dry, pleasant night, the air sweet with leafy, resinous smells.

They had walked for about twenty minutes when they emerged from the trees into a level, shallow basin. A crisp breeze blew in their direction, pushing off the heat of the day.

Callen stopped, his feet planted on the trail. Only the chirping of the crickets could be heard in the stillness of the night. To his left and right, patches of curling mountain fern rose waist-high from the bare rocks, rustling softly in the steady breeze.

He could see the glow of electric lights on the far side of the depression.

"That's gotta be the cabin," he said quietly. "According to Karyn there's nothing else close by."

Sam stood close beside him.

"What next?" he said. "If Valli sees us coming he's bound to take off."

"Plan A," Callen said, "we don't let him see us coming."

"This is why I insist on you as my partner," Sam said.

They stepped off the trail into the screening ferns. Soon they could make out the log cabin's dark, squat outline against the hillside. The light pouring from its front windows showed nothing outside but a small attached toolshed, and a woodpile with a plastic tarpaulin over it.

They inched closer, coming within fifteen or twenty yards of the place. Sam peered up ahead and tapped Callen's shoulder. The window blinds were raised, and he'd spotted someone moving around inside.

A man.

Callen nodded, seeing him too.

He thumbed off the Maglite and they pushed on through the bushy ferns.

After a few yards, Sam paused again. The breeze in his face.

He sniffed. Frowned. Took a deeper breath through his nose. Then turned to Callen.

"You smell that?" he said.

Callen nodded.

"Gas," he said. "It's pretty strong."

Callen could still see the man through the window, and was now close enough to discern that he was in the kitchen. There was a refrigerator, a sink, a counter with food spread out on it...

The stove.

He was turned toward the stove.

Callen felt his heart jump, looked at Sam, saw the concern on his face.

"We better hurry," he said.

"Ron!" Callen banged his fist on the cabin door. "Ronald Valli, *open up*!"

There was no answer. No time to waste, either. The propane stench leaking from the cabin was sickening. Even out here in the open with plenty of fresh air to dilute it.

Inside...

Callen looked at Sam, nodded, then stepped away.

Inside, the man standing at the stove whipped his head toward the entryway.

The agents saw the box of matches in his hand, his other hand holding the matchstick against it, both hands frozen now as he stood there gaping at them in stunned surprise...

"Ron, don't do it."

This was Sam now. Instantly grasping the situation. The kitchen flooded with gas, Valli holding a book of matches, it didn't take a genius to figure out what was happening.

Valli looked at him, a woozy, confounded look on his face.

The match against the striker.

"Who are you?" he said. "What do you want?"

Sam just looked at him, his large frame filling the doorway.

"Put away the matches," he said. Holding out his hands. "C'mon, Ron. Listen to me."

Valli shook his head.

"Are you with the police?" he asked.

"No, no. We aren't cops..."

"Then tell me who you are."

Sam took a breath. His stomach was turning from the fumes.

"We're from the Naval Criminal Investigative Service," he said. "We spoke to your wife—"

"Karyn?" Valli's hands started shaking. "Where?"

"At your home," Sam said. "She's worried sick."

Valli stared at him with his clouded eyes.

"Ron," Sam said. His tone leveled. "Drop the matches."

Valli shook his head again.

"I want to know what you're doing here," he said. "Make it quick."

Sam knew he had to tell the complete truth. Valli was desperate, scared, and disjointed from the gas. One false note in his voice, and it might be over.

"We need your help finding whoever killed Admiral Sutton," he said. "Bottom line, man. We need your help."

Valli's eyes went to Callen, who'd moved up close behind Sam now.

"You," he said. "Who gave you the idea I'd be here? Was it Karyn?"

"It's like my partner told you," Callen replied. "She's worried."

Valli's hands were shaking uncontrollably.

The match still held to the flint strip.

"Get out of here," he said. "Both of you. Go away."

Sam shook his head.

"No."

Valli raised the match and matchbox to his chest.

"*Go away*," he said. "I mean it."

Sam shook his head again.

"Ron, listen," he said. "You do this, it's blowing the roof clear off the place. You'll be taking us with you."

Valli was silent again. His gaze roaming from Sam to Callen.

And then the dam burst. Tears brewed from his eyes, huge droplets, gushing down his face.

"I'm no good," he said. His voice breaking. The words harsh, guttural, like a groan of pain wrenched from his throat. "No good to anyone."

Sam knew better than to press for an explanation. The man was already overwhelmed, and if he tried that, he would lose him. But it occurred to him that whatever feelings of guilt had driven Valli to the brink were not those of someone who would have deliberately harmed Elias Sutton.

He didn't think about what he said next, trusting himself, going with his instincts.

"That isn't true," he said. "I know for a fact. Saw with my own eyes."

Valli spoke through his tears. "What are you talking about?"

"Not what," he said. "Who." He paused. "I meant your daughter. *Lila*. When I saw her, she was wearing her 'I Love Dad' pajama top. Big pink heart in the middle..."

"Shut up." Breathing hard. "You don't know anything."

Sam shook his head.

Don't lose him, he thought. *Just don't lose him.*

"I know a happy kid when I see one, Ron," he said. "I have a couple of my own. Boy and a girl. I know." He paused. "They don't get happy on their own."

Valli looked at him, tears pulsing down his face. His cheeks and lips wet with them.

His hands shaking hard, match still to the flint.

"I'm sorry," he said, his eyes steady on Sam's. "I... am... really sorry."

Sam's heart stroked against his ribcage. He sensed Callen bracing behind him.

Valli hitched in a breath, suddenly turning away from the agents.

Then his fingers opened wide and he dropped the matches to the floor, sinking to his knees, wrapping his arms around his middle, dissolving into anguished, fitful sobs.

Sam and Callen came racing into the cabin a heartbeat afterward.

12

Lauren Scardella, the lawyer from the Public Defender's Office, finally arrived at the Boatshed around a quarter to ten, frazzled and drained after enduring almost two hours of being trapped in the bottlenecked, closure-ridden hell on earth that was the metropolitan Los Angeles freeway system.

"Sorry for falling victim to Carmageddon," she said to Kensi and Deeks in the observation room. "I'd sign away ten years of my life for a teleporter. Right now, on the dotted line. Ten years for a *refurbished* model."

"Animalics might be a more realistic option," Deeks said.

"Ani… *huh*?"

"That's pretty much the standard response," Kensi said. "It's a form of aromatherapy. Except using ground Himalayan yak gonads instead of lavender."

Scardella sniffed the air. "You know," she said. "I *did* notice a yakky, gonady thing going on here."

"Actually, it's a civet's anal glands," Deeks said.

She clapped her hands to her temples.

"Of course!" she said. "How could I not tell the difference?"

"So what do you think?" he asked.

Scardella sniffed again.

"Well," she said. "It's… it's sort of *intriguing*, now that you mention it."

He nodded.

"It won't get you through traffic any faster," he said. "But you'll be calmer while you're stranded."

"Your client's waiting in the interrogation room," Kensi said, and nodded toward the door. "We assume you'll want to confer with him."

"And may I ask why he's in custody?"

"He's here because we plan to book him for complicity in the murder of Elias Sutton, the kidnapping of Theodore Holloway, and about a dozen other related felonies," Kensi said. "For starters."

Scardella gave her a wry glance. A smartly dressed brunette in her mid thirties, she appeared fully alert despite her long drive.

"That's all?" she said. "No JFK or Hoffa assassination theories in the mix?"

Kensi met her gaze.

"I'm going to tell you something as a courtesy," she said. "We plan to share some developing information with your client. In an effort to persuade him to cooperate."

"'Developing' as in…?"

"Two of Mr. Dorani's crooked playmates were murdered tonight," she said. "We're thinking he'd have been number three if we hadn't brought him here."

Scardella gave her a sharp look.

"Can you give me the names of the victims?"

"I'll fill you in before we get started," Kensi said. "In the meantime, would you care to see our lab reports?"

Scardella produced a weary, fatalistic sigh.

"Yes, Agent," she said. "I think I'd better."

Tomas turned his head on the pillow, glancing over at Alysha. She lay with her back to him, sleeping.

He looked at her now in the darkness. There had been an urgency to their passion tonight, almost a mutual greed. Was it because they both knew this time likely would be their last?

He supposed that very well could be.

In England, he had believed he was recruiting her. That was his mission, and she seemed a perfect candidate. Restless, questing, a bit naïve, seeking more than her modest suburban existence could give her.

Later, he came to feel she had always looked to free herself from that sheltered life. That she'd simply awaited the right chance. That in a sense, *she* recruited *him*.

Propping himself on an elbow now, Tomas reached over to touch her naked shoulder. But his hand froze above it in the darkness, then withdrew, falling to his side on the bed.

He remembered, from the first, thinking his purpose to her would expire. She could be arrogant, but not selfish, and he'd never felt she consciously used him. His pride would never have let him accept that. But he always knew she was in the process of moving on.

Knew… and accepted, even in their moments of greatest intimacy. If she could be his at those times, if he could share those passing moments with her, then he would live with the terrible certainty that she would someday leave him behind. For whatever, whomever, did not matter.

When she took up with the mujahid Umar, went to train with him at the Al Karar camp, it was no surprise. Tomas had often forced himself to imagine the day, as if to build up scar tissue, and dull the eventual sting.

But he had learned a steady, lasting pain was worse than the sharpest cut.

By far.

He slid closer to her under the sheets, keeping his hand down at his side. Her advances at the practice range were unexpected. Even after they fled the carnage of Syria, returning to Europe amid the hordes of immigrants fleeing ISIS, he'd never believed they would be lovers again. Their revived connection was built on necessity. Azarian had begun to make his plans, and Alysha's unsurpassed skills as a fighter and infiltrator fit right into them.

She thought him a fervent devotee, his heart burning for the cause, and she was not mistaken in her belief. But in the secret depths of his heart, nothing about the mission meant more than its reward of final oblivion.

When it was done there would be no more goodbyes. No more moving on in separate directions. No more pain for him.

"Are you awake?" he asked.

"Yes," she said, without facing him.

His breath short, he raised his hand from the mattress, then lowered it slowly, almost hesitantly to the side of her head, as if against some invisible pocket of resistance.

"I love you," he said, and stroked her hair. "I have always loved you."

Silence. He waited.

"I know," she said, without turning her head.

Distanced from him.

Looking somewhere *beyond*.

Tomas wished he could have died then and there.

But he was thinking tomorrow would be soon enough.

"Wait," Isaak said. "*What* about Daggut?"

"He was shot to death tonight," Kensi said. "In his pawnshop."

Isaak stared at her, a disbelieving expression on his face.

She was back in the interrogation room, a tablet in front of her. Opposite Kensi, Scardella sat with her briefcase slung over the back of her seat. A pad, pencil, and requisite tablet in front of *her*, she was paying close attention to Kensi's every word.

"She's yankin' me here," Isaak said, turning to the attorney before Kensi could answer. "This is some kinda trick, right?"

Scardella shook her head.

"I'm afraid it's true," she said. And then glanced pointedly at Kensi. "But I'm also not sure it has any bearing on why Mr. Dorani is in custody."

Kensi smiled thinly.

"Well, then, maybe I can explain," she said. "The late Zory Daggut, who I might stress was shot multiple times in the *face*, was a known fence. And it so happens that just this afternoon he accepted hot items from your client. Antique Edison cylinder records burglarized from the home of Elias Sutton—"

"Or so you allege," Scardella said.

"Or so the lab reports reveal," Kensi said, firing a look right back at her. "But, fine, if you want to change the subject, we can move on to the murder of Erasmo Greer."

Isaak straightened up in his chair, blinking rapidly, the color draining from his face. "Who?"

"Mr. Greer was a friend of yours, correct?" Kensi said.

He stared at her, his eyes blinking away in their enormous sockets.

"Isaak, are you feeling okay?"

"Yeah," he said, not looking okay at all. "Fine."

"Because if you need a glass of water…"

"I don't need nothin'," he said. "And I ain't never heard of him."

"Oh?" Kensi furrowed her brow. "That's kind of odd. Because LAPD investigators looking into the abduction of Theodore Holloway observed the two of you together on several occasions."

He swallowed hard.

"Listen, I'm saying I don't *think* I ever met *that* Erasmo in particular," he said. "I probably know ten, fifteen different guys with the same name."

"Fifteen Erasmos."

"Around that many, yeah," he said. "Maybe more."

Scardella winced. "Mr. Dorani—"

"I'm just sayin' this Greer could've been *any* of 'em—"

The attorney snapped a hand in the air to cut him off.

"Special Agent Blye," she said, "we're heading off into dangerous irrelevancy again. I'm sorry about these terrible crimes. But there's no sound reason my client has to answer questions about them."

Kensi sat quietly a moment.

"You're right about one thing, counselor," she said. "The killings *were* heinous. In fact, I'd call them coldblooded executions." She reached for her tablet and thumbed on the power. "I'd like to show you both some crime-scene photos of Mr. Greer's body."

Scardella frowned. "That's very thoughtful," she said caustically. "But it won't be necessary…"

Kensi ignored her, holding up the tablet so they could see the damaged, bloody face.

Dorani's went a shade paler.

"Oh crap," he muttered in a choked voice. "I can't believe it."

Kensi looked at him. "It appears he was beaten with a club or similar object," she explained. "Then shot point blank through the forehead."

Dorani dropped his eyes to the table, suddenly sobbing aloud.

Scardella gave Kensi an angry look.

"We really *could* have done without that stunt, Agent," she said. "I don't see what you've achieved besides upsetting my client with a gruesome photograph."

Kensi continued to ignore her. She looked straight at Dorani.

"Isaak, I'm guessing from your reaction that you do, in fact, recognize *this* particular Erasmo. Or would you like to see more pictures to be sure?"

"Okay. Enough," Scardella interrupted. "Unless you have something else to tell us about the incidents Mr. Dorani was supposedly involved in, I think we can cut this meeting short—"

"That's exactly what we're doing."

A new and unexpected voice from the doorway now. Scardella glanced in its direction, Kensi swiveling her head around to look as well. Only Dorani seemed oblivious as he kept bawling away with his eyes downturned.

The short, sixtyish woman in the entry stood

looking at the attorney. Her square-cut hair falling neatly over her collar, she looked bright-eyed and businesslike now at an hour when most people were blearily climbing into bed for the night.

"I don't believe we've met, counselor," she said with a polite nod. "I'm Hetty Lange, Operations Manager."

Scardella nodded. "A pleasure to meet you," she said, introducing herself. "But did I just hear you say—?"

"We're letting your client go home until we can better review and prepare our evidence," Hetty said.

Scardella glowered at her. "Wait," she said. "You keep Mr. Dorani waiting here for *hours*, make me suffer through the mother of all traffic jams, and then tell us you still need to review evidence?"

"And prepare," Hetty said. "Yes."

"Did you consider reviewing and preparing it *before* you placed him under arrest—?"

Hetty shrugged her shoulders. "Things happen," she said. "It's an imperfect world."

Scardella's frown deepened. "Ms. Lange, if I may speak my mind, your tactics are reprehensible."

Hetty looked over at Dorani.

"You're free to go until we're ready," she said. "Hopefully nothing unfortunate will happen to you in the meantime."

He glanced up at her.

"Hold it," he said. "What do you mean by 'happen'?"

She turned toward Kensi. "Did you show him any of the crime scene photographs?"

"Yes," Kensi said, raising the tablet in her hands. "Right here."

"Well, then," Hetty said. "What I meant should be abundantly clear."

Isaak looked at her with his huge, teary eyes.

"Lady," he said, "did you see what they did to Erasmo's *face*?"

"Yes," she said. "It's quite an awful sight."

A moment passed. Isaak sat there staring at her. Stared at her some more. At last he slouched forward, folded his arms on the table, buried his face in them, and began weeping uncontrollably.

"I'll talk," he said, his words muffled by his shirtsleeves. "I'll talk."

Status:
SEALED/CLASSIFIED/TOP SECRET

**Videorecorded Statement Of Isaak Ismael
Dorani Taken 10:45Pm (Pacific) by Naval
Criminal Investigative Service, Office of
Special Projects, Los Angeles Station.**
Location Withheld

Interrogated By:
Kensi Blye, Special Agent, Ncis Los Angeles
Martin Deeks, Detective, Lapd (Liaison Ncis)
Henrietta Lange, Operations Manager

Attorney For Mr. Dorani:
Lauren Scardella, Esq., Los Angeles County Public Defender's Office

Q&A
(KENSI BLYE principal interrogator)

KB: Mr. Dorani… that's spelled D-o-r-a-n-i, is that right?
ID: Right. But Isaak's fine. No need to get formal all of a sudden.

KB: Isaak… I'd like to direct your attention to yesterday afternoon, the twenty-second of April, at around three o'clock, and ask your whereabouts at that time.

ID: Three o'clock, um, I was at old man Sutton's place.

KB: The home of Elias P. Sutton? In Santa Barbara?

ID: That's right.

KB: And how did you enter the property?

ID: I went through the side door.

KB: Were you invited into the house?

ID: Well… no.

KB: So you forced your way into Mr. Sutton's home.

ID: It sounds violent when you put it that way. I didn't do nothing violent.

KB: Is it accurate you picked the lock to gain entry?

ID: Yeah.

KB: And was this after disabling the burglar alarm system?

ID: Yeah. But I didn't hurt nobody.

KB: You've made that point, Isaak. Now can you tell me how you took out the alarm?

ID: I used a jackrabbit.

KB: What's that?

ID: One of Erasmo's gizmos.

KB: An electronic device of some sort, in other words.

ID: Yeah.

KB: And who gave it the name "jackrabbit"?

ID: Not me. Erasmo called it that.

KB: For the record, you're referring to Erasmo Greer. A suspected hacker.

ID: Right. May the poor jerk rest in peace.

KB: Isaak… can you tell me if this device was a software-defined radio transmitter?

ID: Huh? A software whatsis?

KB: I'll repeat that for you. A software-defined—

LS: Agent Blye, my client isn't a technical wizard. He already

225

told you the late Mr. Greer provided him with this jackrabbit.
And admitted using it to gain entry to Sutton's home. What
more do you want?

KB: Well, how about he describes it for starters?

LS: Is that really germane—?

HL: If I may interject, counselor… hackers use SDR
transceivers to intercept burglar alarm signals running
from the sensors to their control panels. We believe the
same sort of device put the alarms at Theodore Holloway's
condominium out of commission when he was kidnapped.
And your client now admits he was involved in both crimes.

LS: I understand. But Mr. Dorani admits he used the
jackrabbit. Why do you need him to paint pretty word
pictures of it?

HL: Because we've had four apparently connected murders
in two days. Because we suspect whoever's behind them
plans to kill a great many more people. Because we need
all the information we can get to stop that from happening.
And finally, because your client, who claims he's never
harmed a fly, but can be tied to each of the homicide
victims, has agreed to share whatever he knows with us.

ID: Look. I got no problem describing the contraption if it's
so important to you.

LS: As long as everyone's clear it was Erasmo Greer who
programmed the device. And instructed my client in its
operation.

HL: I don't think anyone in this room is under the impression
he's capable of doing it on his own, counselor.

KB: Isaak…?

ID: It's black and round. Like a weight. With an antenna
sticking up outta the middle.

KB: And exactly how was it used to disable the alarms?

ID: I just brought it with me and turned it on. Erasmo did the
rest with his laptop.

KB: You mean he programmed it to monitor signals from the alarm system?

ID: That's right.

KB: And was Erasmo present at the Sutton and Holloway burglaries?

ID: No, he was in a car a few blocks away with some of the crazies.

KB: Both times?

ID: Yeah. Well, at the old codgers' home they were parked outside the gate. I was carrying a few jackrabbits that day.

KB: What do you mean by a few?

ID: I must've had four, five of 'em when we got outta the car.

KB: "We" meaning…?

ID: Me and the two crazies who kidnapped him.

KB: Isaak, I'll be asking some questions about the people you call crazies in a minute.

ID: Sure.

KB: But about the jackrabbit… why carry so many with you?

ID: That first time?

KB: Yes. At the Bel Air Palms Senior Living facility.

ID: There's a gate where you drive in. And a uniformed hump.

KB: You mean the guard by the visitor entrance.

ID: Ain't that what I just told you?

KB: Not quite, Isaak. It helps us when you're specific.

ID: Okay, gotcha. The hump was a security guard.

KB: Now if you'll explain why you used… did you say four or five jackrabbits?

ID: Right. The easiest way to get Holloway out was through the bushes behind his condo—

KB: Because of the guard out front…?

ID: Right. We figured we couldn't sneak Holloway past him. But they have motion sensors all around the grounds so the fogies don't wander off between diaper changes. Erasmo said he could take 'em offline by laying some jackrabbits in those hedges...

KB: The hedges bordering the village's grounds.

ID: Yup.

KB: And that's how you managed to bypass the sensors.

ID: Right.

KB: Okay, Isaak. I want to get back to yesterday at Mr. Sutton's home. Please tell me what happened there.

ID: My job was to let in the crazies and grab some stuff from his bedroom.

KB: Again, it helps if you're specific.

ID: About the stuff I was supposed to glom? Or we talking about the stupid-ass guard again?

KB: The data storage material, Isaak.

ID: They wanted the computer's hard drive. Plus CDs, memory sticks, anything like that.

KB: And by "crazies"... how about telling me who you mean.

ID: I mean the Armenian whackadoos. Specifically.

KB: Are these people affiliated with a group called the Justice Commandos of the Armenian Genocide? Or the Suicide Commandos?

ID: I got no idea what they call themselves.

KB: How about the Armenian Secret Army?

ID: I told you. I ain't never heard'a no Armenian Nutjob Brigade or whatever.

KB: Never heard them mention any organization...

LS: Agent Blye, I object to this line of questioning. My client's no more an expert on political action groups than he is on the latest hacking technology.

KB: They're global terrorist groups according to the State Department.

LS: I'll take your word for it, Agent. But Mr. Dorani just stated he didn't know whether the people who hired him are connected to any of those organizations.

KB: Actually that isn't quite what he said. But I'll rephrase my question. Isaak, were you aware the people that hired you belonged to a gang or ring engaged in illegal activities?

ID: Lemme put it this way… I knew they weren't the Boys and Girls Club of America.

KB: And did you know why they wanted Mr. Sutton's data storage materials? And Mr. Holloway's for that matter?

ID: Um… ahh… I'm kinda confused.

KB: I was asking about the information on those disks and memory sticks.

ID: (inaudible)

KB: I'm sorry, I missed that. What did you say?

ID: (Mr. Dorani begins to cry)

KB: Would you like a drink of water, Isaak?

ID: No… why…?

KB: Because you seem upset by my question.

LS: My client hasn't said why he's upset, Agent.

KB: How about you let him tell us, counselor?

LS: I believe this might be a good time for a break.

KB: First, I'd like him to answer my question.

LS: Which one? You've asked several…

KB: About whether he knows why his employers wanted data storage add-ons from the Sutton home.

LS: Well, he'll be more able to do that when he isn't choking on his tears. Furthermore, I'm not sure he's capable of reading minds.

KB: I don't remember saying that.

LS: You asked him to characterize his employers' motives.

KB: I asked if he knows why they wanted the computer hardware. If he doesn't know, he can tell me. But a man was killed so they could get hold of it. A former United States senator…

LS: My client isn't a murderer.

KB: You're putting words in my mouth again.

LS: Say what you will, we can't continue if you're going to talk about a crime he didn't commit.

HL: All right, everyone. Perhaps it might be beneficial if we did take a few minutes to regroup.

Questioning resumed 11:05 P.M. (PACIFIC) aforesaid date. Det. Martin Deeks now in the room.

KB: Isaak, I want to get back to why you were in Mr. Sutton's house.

ID: I'll talk about what I was doing for the crazies. But I won't talk about why the crazies wanted me to do it.

KB: Is that how your lawyer told you to respond?

LS: I strongly advise you don't go there. Our attorney-client conversations are out of bounds.

KB: Thanks for the reminder, Ms. Scardella.

LS: You're so welcome, Agent Blye.

KB: (Indicating) I have on this screen a diagram of the home's interior. Can you show me where you entered?

ID: Sure… right here.

KB: That's the east side of the house. Where the driveway's located.

ID: Yeah.

KB: (Indicating) And the pergola here…

ID: The what?

KB: The carport… it's at the head of the driveway. And the east door leads between it and the house, is that right?

ID: Right.

KB: Is there a reason you chose this particular entrance?

ID: Well, it's a long driveway, so it's hard for people on the street to see all the way up to the house. And the carport gave me cover.

KB: From potential eyewitnesses.

ID: Right.

KB: And were you alone when you went into the house?

ID: No.

KB: Who accompanied you?

ID: Two of the crazies.

KB: Can you give me their names?

ID: One of 'em was Matous.

KB: Do you know his second name?

ID: Nope. No clue.

KB: You're sure?

ID: Positive.

KB: And what about the other man?

ID: His name, you mean?

KB: Yes.

ID: I think it's something like David.

KB: Something…

ID: Right. It's got some kind of foreign pronunciation.

KB: And would you recognize these men if you saw them again?

ID: Well, what do you think?

KB: I don't know. You tell me.

ID: I would recognize them. It ain't like I got no brain in my head.

KB: Okay, Isaak. Looking at the layout of the house. When you get through the door, you're in the living room.

ID: Yeah. That's a nice diagram, incidentally.

KB: Thank you, Isaak. Now to the right, there are glass doors leading out to the patio. The dining room and kitchen are on the left, correct?

ID: Exactly.

KB: And beyond them there's a hallway running all the way to the back of the house. With three bedrooms aligned.

ID: Right.

KB: Do you recall which one was Mr. Sutton's?

ID: It's the last room down the hall.

KB: Thank you. Now… can you tell me if anyone was home when you entered?

ID: No.

KB: "No" you can't tell me, or "no" nobody was home?

ID: Nobody was home.

KB: Tell me what you did after entering the property.

ID: I went straight to the bedroom.

KB: Were Matous and the other man with you?

ID: Matous's pal hung back to stand lookout.

KB: Can you show me where on the diagram?

ID: (Indicating) He stayed right about here.

KB: That's in the entry between the dining room and hallway.

ID: Yeah, he could see the doors from there.

KB: The front and side doors to the house.

ID: That's right.

KB: And Matous?

ID: He waited outside the bedroom.

KB: To stand watch for you.

ID: Right.

KB: And what happened next?

ID: I did what I was supposed to do.

KB: Went about stealing the computer hardware…

ID: You could say that, yeah.

KB: Isaak… were any members of your team in contact with Mr. Greer? While you were burglarizing the house, that is?

LS: I think the word "team" is somewhat misleading, Agent.

KB: Really? Does "boy band" work better? Or is "partners-in-crime" more your speed?

LS: Isaak, I prefer you don't speak unless asked a direct question. As for your terminology, Agent, I'll let it stand. But let's state for the record that my client was doing work for hire, and had no philosophical or political affiliation with this group.

KB: To the best of our knowledge. Happy, counselor?

LS: I think we can live with that. In the interest of getting out of here before dawn.

KB: That's very considerate of you. Now once again, Isaak, were any of you in contact with Mr. Greer?

ID: We all were.

KB: All? Can you explain that to me?

ID: We had headsets so we could talk to each other over the Internet. I think Erasmo called it a rope connection…

KB: Rope or RoIP? That's Radio over an Internet Protocol.

ID: If you say so.

KB: But you're saying it was a wireless two-way radio of some kind.

ID: Yeah.

KB: And while in the bedroom, did you receive any instructions from Mr. Greer?

ID: Yeah. He reminded me what to look for. And, like, if I wasn't sure where to find something, or what it was, I could ask him over the radio.

KB: Okay, Isaak. Tell me what you did in the bedroom.

ID: I took everything Erasmo wanted off the desk, outta the drawers… wherever he told me to look. Then I was supposed to open up Sutton's PC and pull out the hard drive. So I opened up its case… used these tools he gave me…

KB: Is something wrong?

ID: No, nothing. It's just, ah… I…

KB: Yes?

ID: Well… what else you wanna know?

KB: The rest of what happened in the house, Isaak.

ID: Can I have a drink of water first? I'm kind of thirsty.

KB: Yes, go ahead.

ID: (Drinks) That's better. Thanks.

KB: You're welcome. So, back to yesterday afternoon. You're in the bedroom opening the CPU…

ID: Right. I lift it off, start unscrewing the drive… and that's when Matous's friend David warns us somebody's coming in the front door.

KB: Did he say who it was?

ID: He didn't know right off. Just heard somebody opening the door. Then Matous told him to hide, and I guess he kind of backed into the hall.

KB: And then what?

ID: Everything stopped. I... I can hardly even describe it. It's like the air around me froze solid... I swear to God, I couldn't move a muscle. I dunno how long I stood there, by the desk. It felt like an hour, but it couldn't've been more than a minute or so. And then... I remember hearing a lady. A lady's voice...

KB: Angelica DeFalco. The housekeeper.

ID: Yeah. She... she wasn't supposed to be there.

KB: How did you know?

ID: That was the information I got. That's all. I just knew.

KB: And was she alone when she came in?

ID: Yeah. Well, she had the old man's dog with her. At first I thought she was talking to a little kid. Colin this, Colin that, c'mere Colin. Her voice all lively and cheerful...

KB: What happened then?

ID: She started to do things around the house. I heard her open the sliding doors...

KB: The doors to the veranda?

ID: Yeah. I guess she was letting the dog out in the yard. Then she went into the dining room, I figured maybe she was setting the table, putting out dishes or glasses. And then...

KB: Go on, Isaak.

ID: She must've heard Matous's pal. Or seen him. They never told me. But she hollered really loud... I'm pretty sure she asked who was there. And the next thing I know, she's saying... begging him... it was something like, "Please don't do it." I'll never forget, she told him... told him she had kids.

Two young kids. And then... ah God... I couldn't believe it...

KB: Isaak...?

ID: Then the gun went off. I remember... there was one shot. And I didn't hear her anymore...

LS: Agent Blye, I think we could all use a little break.

KB: Counselor, for once I'm in total agreement with you.

Questioning resumed 12:05 A.M. (Pacific) April 24

KB: Isaak, now that everyone's back, would you please tell me what happened in the moments after Angelica DeFalco was shot.

ID: I heard the dog out in the yard. Not really barking... it was more like a howl, went right to my bones. And then there was another gunshot. I could tell it was outside.

KB: And then?

ID: The dog stopped making a noise.

KB: Okay, Isaak. What did you do next?

ID: I wanted to leave the place. Just get the hell out. I was scared, but it wasn't really about being scared. The wanting to get out, I mean. I swear to you, I couldn't feel my hands. That poor lady begging... I never in a million years thought anything like that would go down...

KB: Why did you stay, then?

ID: Matous. He told me to finish what I was doing... get the hard drive from the computer. And the look on his face... If you saw it, you'd know.

KB: Know what?

ID: He would've killed me too. Blown me away.

KB: So you continued removing the drive.

ID: Yeah.

KB: Even though you couldn't feel your fingers.

ID: It wasn't brain surgery. I probably had it out in two, three minutes.

KB: And you put the drive in your bag with the rest of the memory storage devices?

ID: Right.

KB: What then, Isaak?

ID: Erasmo told me to take a last look around.

KB: Told you over the RoIP headset.

ID: Exactly. He said to give a once over to the drawers, the desk... check I didn't miss anything important.

KB: And what did you think about that?

ID: Think? I don't understand...

KB: Upset as you were by the gunshots. Wanting to hurry out of there.

ID: Oh. I get you.

KB: So what did you think?

ID: I figured I hadda do it. Because Matous could hear everything I did over the radio.

KB: And you still felt threatened by him.

ID: I figured he'd kill me if I tried to leave without doing it.

KB: And were you able to carry out those instructions?

ID: I... yeah. Yeah. I was done with it just before... you know.

KB: I'm not sure I do, Isaak. How about you tell me?

ID: I had everything in the bag when the car pulled up into the driveway.

KB: Elias Sutton's car?

ID: I didn't know it was him till afterward.

KB: But it was Mr. Sutton.

ID: It was, yeah.

KB: Did you actually hear his car pull in?

ID: I heard it pull in. It's a quiet neighborhood.

KB: Okay, go on.

ID: The rest's kind of a blur in my head. It was so crazy...

KB: Let's hear it as best you can remember.

ID: I remember Matous's friend—David or whoever—saying

on the two-way radio that the old man was home. He wasn't in a panic, these guys're cool customers. But his voice... they knew this was gonna be an epic shitshow. I think Matous told him to hide, and then I saw him in the hall...

KB: Outside the bedroom?

ID: With Matous, yeah. The two of them stood there whispering... I couldn't really hear any of it. Then after a minute Matous came back in. He told me to finish checking the drawers for stuff, climb out the window, and bring everything back to Erasmo in the car.

KB: Everything being the storage media.

ID: Yeah.

KB: Was that all he said to you?

ID: That was it. He was outta the room like lightning afterward.

KB: And did you follow his orders?

ID: No. I already knew I didn't miss anything.

KB: What did you do instead?

ID: I took the cylinders outta the glass case and loaded 'em into my bag. As insurance if I needed getaway money. I thought they'd pull in a sweet sum—and they would've if that squeaker Daggut, God rest his soul, didn't squeeze me dry...

KB: Do you remember anything else, Isaak?

ID: What do you mean?

KB: Anything that happened before you left the house.

ID: I... can I have another drink of water before I answer?

KB: Go ahead.

ID: Thanks. That's better...

KB: Isaak, did you see or hear anything else before going out the window?

ID: Well, yeah. I did. I...

KB: Yes?

ID: I heard the gun again. Pop-pop-pop.

KB: That's how it sounded?

ID: Yeah.

KB: Exactly three pops?

ID: Right. Close together.

KB: Were these shots inside the house?

ID: No. I could tell they were coming from out in the yard, like when the dog stopped making its racket. And then I went out into the hall… for a look, y'know. Don't ask me why, either. I just did it.

KB: What did you see?

ID: Everything. I could see everything. That house, it's real open… look at the diagram. I saw the woman on the dining room floor, and then the old man and the dog through the patio doors. And the blood. There was so much blood…

LS: Isaak, are you all right?

ID: I don't feel so good. My stomach, it's… I think I gotta hit the bathroom. This always happens when I get nervous…

LS: Okay, Isaak. Agent Blye, we're taking another break…

KB: Not so fast.

LS: What do you mean "not so fast"?

KB: Does that statement really need translating?

LS: Please, Agent. Spare me the sarcasm. My client's squirming in his chair…

KB: We're almost done here, counselor.

LS: Be that as it may, I don't think he can wait…

KB: Then let's not waste more time arguing. Detective Deeks will ask a few questions. Hopefully Isaak will answer. And then he can go to his heart's content.

ID: FYI, it ain't my heart I'm worried about.

Deeks thought it did, in fact, look as though Dorani would embarrass himself if he was forced to be seated much longer. But he'd watched the first part of the Q&A in the observation room, and stood quietly alongside the table for the rest, and a quick glance from Kensi had told him this would be a good time to make him a little more uncomfortable.

To hear Dorani tell it, he was a complete victim of circumstance, who just happened to be in the wrong place at the wrong time with some tremendously wrong people. Putting aside that he'd gone in with the clear and deliberate intent of *robbing* the place, and was in the middle of *doing exactly that* when they got their bloodbath underway...

And that wasn't all.

Dorani's defense attorney would surely propose a sweetheart deal for him when the prosecutors got involved, and Deeks had no problem with the OSP endorsing it in exchange for his testimony. But it did not mean he would let him sit there flashing the victim card.

"I'll try and make this quick, Mr. Dorani," he said.

"Please, Detective," Scardella said. "It's late and he's having difficulties."

"Putting it mildly," Dorani said, shifting in his chair. "And Isaak's fine, by the way."

"Mr. Dorani, you mentioned setting up the jackrabbit outside Sutton's door."

"Yeah. And like I said, it's Isaak."

Deeks nodded.

"Then, once it disabled the alarm, you picked the lock."

"You're a good listener..."

"And *then* you led Matous through the house into the bedroom."

"That's how it happened, yeah."

Deeks looked at him, scratching his head.

"The itsy bitsy question tickling my brain is why

you thought no one was home."

"I got no clue what you mean…"

Deeks shrugged.

"Let's press replay," he said. "You told us you didn't expect the housekeeper to be there, right?"

"Right."

"And I'm guessing you figured the same thing was true of Sutton, right?"

"Right. I didn't want nobody getting hurt…"

"So what made you and those homicidal doorcrashers think you'd have the place to yourselves?" Deeks said. "I'm also wondering how you knew its interior layout."

Dorani frowned, turning to Scardella.

"The bathroom," he said. "I'm gonna mess my pants."

Scardella sighed. "Detective, if there's a point to all this, how about sharing it?"

"Sure," Deeks said. "I'm a big sharer."

"Arguably an oversharer," Kensi said.

"And the point I want to share is that Mr. Dorani didn't just offer out his services as a random porch climber," Deeks said. "He was obviously familiar with Sutton's usual routine, knew the killers wanted his data storage devices, and offered to help steal them."

Dorani was shaking his head.

"That's an eensie weensie hallucination," he said.

"Think so?"

"Yeah."

"How about Ron Valli? Is *he* for real?"

Dorani abruptly stopped shaking his head. "Where'd you get that name?"

"Doesn't matter," Deeks said, thinking about the call he'd got from Callen about an hour earlier. "All you need to know is he tried taking his own life tonight."

Dorani stared at him. "I... I don't believe you."

"He was at his cabin in the mountains," Deeks said. "Filled it with gas, and was about to strike a match to blow it up."

"No way," Dorani said. "The guy's too wild about his wife and kid."

"He felt responsible for Sutton's murder," Deeks said. "And thought he'd be blamed for it."

Scardella was looking across the table with displeasure.

"I think your muskrat butt cologne's gone to your head, Detective," she said. "Isaak's been nothing but cooperative. How dare you spring this on us without warning?"

Deeks shrugged.

"Sorry," he said. "It was just sprung on *me* a little while ago."

She frowned and began folding up her laptop.

"We're ending this session right now," she said. "If you intend to formally arrest my client, I want him brought to the county jail, and not kept here like a hostage. Call me when you can promise not to hold back any more information."

Deeks placed his hands on the edge of the table and leaned forward.

"It's your client who's holding back," he said. "We need the truth from him. The *whole* truth."

"And nothing but?"

Deeks met her gaze.

"My dry wit aside, this isn't a joke," he said. "We don't know how many lives might be at risk. But it could be a lot."

Scardella looked at him a moment, glanced over at

Kensi and Hetty, then looked back at Deeks.

"We're done here," she said angrily, and finished packing away her tablet.

Beside her, Isaak stared at Deeks, his eyes wide and fearful.

13

Tomas opened his eyes to find Alysha gone. He'd awakened suddenly in the thin predawn light, and sensed her absence at once.

She was an early riser, so it did not surprise him.

He tossed off his sheets, rose out of bed, and took some fresh clothes out of his knapsack. The public water to the house was disconnected, but there was a working spigot in back. Matous had run a garden hose from the spigot to an outdoor shower stall, equipping it with a small electric water heater.

Tomas paused to pick up his boots and stepped naked and barefooted into the hallway. The house had three bedrooms—the one he'd shared with Alysha, Matous's room, and a third being used for the preparation and storage of explosives. The rest of his comrades were in the living room, dead to the world on the couch and chairs, a couple of them in sleeping bags on the bare floorboards.

Tomas strode quietly to the backdoor and out to the rear of the house. Leaving his clothes on the patio's sandstone tiles, he pulled the shower curtain open and entered the stall.

The platform was wet, the interior of the stall beaded with moisture. When he reached up to touch the showerhead, fat droplets of water dribbled over his fingers.

Alysha must have used it only a short while ago.

Tomas opened the faucet, raised his face into the stream, and let the fresh water run over him. He dressed out on the dusty patio tiles, looking around, his hair and beard drying in the cool desert air.

There were abandoned houses to his right and left—row upon row of uninhabited residences standing, silent and ghostly, across the deserted housing complex. Some of the homes were completed, others just partially built. Driving up in the darkness two nights before, Tomas had seen tracts of vacant, trash-strewn lots and sidewalks overgrown with high brown weeds, children's toys, discarded furniture, and trash cans poking out of them. As he approached the safehouse, a coyote had loped in front of the car and stared boldly at the windshield. He'd needed to tap his horn to frighten it off.

Now Tomas heard a loud, sharp cry pierce the twilit stillness and flinched a little, his neck tightening. The birds had been there since his arrival, but their screams did nothing to ease his discomfiture.

He glanced over his left shoulder. A short distance away, a huge, shaggy vulture was perched atop a shattered traffic light. Further off across a wide open field, dawn was a blood-red stripe along the low horizon.

Tomas strode toward the field. The vulture shrieked at him as he passed, extending its long bare neck from its collar of ragged feathers.

He took a quick look, then averted his eyes from it.

As he came to the edge of the field, he saw it was

patched with flat concrete slabs—the foundations of unbuilt homes, many concealed by weeds. Pipes and electrical cables snaked through the weeds, connecting to nothing.

Alysha stood in the middle of the field watching the daybreak. She had always enjoyed doing that in solitude.

But today she was not alone. A man stood there with her, looking off to the east. Matous.

Something coiled inside Tomas. He cursed under his breath as he pushed toward them through the desiccated, knee-high weeds.

They looked around at him as he approached.

"Tomas," she said. "I thought you were asleep."

"I woke up," he said. "Forgive me."

Her brief, sharp glance made him feel small. He instantly regretted buckling to his jealousy.

"I heard from Azarian," Matous said. "We won't have the information in time for tomorrow's mission."

Tomas stared at him. "Is this certain? After all we've done to prepare?"

Matous nodded.

"It may be in the hands of federal agents," he said. "Naval investigators."

"They *know* of us?"

"It's doubtful," Matous said. "Most likely they're just looking into the death of their old admiral." He paused. "We're lucky to have a fallback."

Tomas shifted his eyes to Alysha. "So our plans hinge on your wind-up trainman?"

"Yes, destiny brought him to us for a reason," she said. "You know it."

"And if we're wrong?"

"We proceed with things anyway," Matous said.

"Hundreds will still die."

Tomas was silent, questions crowding his mind like sudden shadows. Why had Matous chosen to inform Alysha and not him? Had they walked to the field together? Or had he sought her out here?

How would he know her habits? Where to find her?

Tomas noticed she had continued to watch the eastern sky, where the dawnlight was a smoldering orange band beneath the ashen remnants of night.

A vulture shrieked harshly in the distance.

"The birds stir around us," Matous said.

Tomas felt a pulse beating in the hollow of his throat. He could not dispel the questions.

"They are everywhere," he said.

Drew Sarver hopped out of bed at 6:00 A.M. feeling refreshed and full of energy after only a few hours' sleep.

Tomorrow was finally today. Where to take Milena for lunch? He'd been so focused on Poppo's map and the yard tunnels that he hadn't given it the slightest thought.

As he put his coffee on to brew, he was thinking there were a few excellent spots right near Union Station—and within easy walking distance of the yard. A little café that served great soup and sandwiches, a farm-to-table vegan place with a backyard dining area, and a chic pan-Asian food bar where you could watch the chefs prepare sushi and banchan that melted in your mouth. Between those three restaurants, he didn't see how they could miss.

Drew wondered if he should wait till nine o'clock or so and phone Milena to ask her preference, but quickly found himself leaning against it. He didn't want to smother her, and doubted they needed reservations for any of those places.

Besides, they already had enough plans for their date. A little spontaneity in the mix wouldn't hurt.

Now he went to the fridge, poured a tall glass of orange juice, and carried it to the breakfast nook by his kitchen window, parting the curtains to let in the bright, warm morning sunshine. Across the room, his coffee maker made its coffee maker noises.

Yes, he thought, he would leave the great where-to-eat-lunch decision to teamwork. When you were getting to know a person, it was sometimes a good idea to relax and go with the flow.

Anywhere he and Milena went together would be absolutely fine with him.

"I'm thinking we should make an oyster pizza next time," said Nell Jones. "I saw a chef make it on television and it looked… what's a word for something that kills awesome?"

Eric Beale glanced up from the fifty-four cylinder recordings arranged on the lab counter in front of him.

"*Extra* awesome?"

"How about 'X-awesome'?" she said. "Or 'awesome-X'?"

"Well, technically, neither are words," Eric said.

"But strictly speaking 'extra awesome' is two words."

"But the 'X' sounds porny," he said.

"But we're talking about pizza," she said.

"So?"

"Pizza isn't porny."

"But oysters *are* porny." Nell smiled. "Ooo," she said. "They are, aren't they?"

Eric cleared his throat. "Nell, why are we discussing

food porn at four-thirty in the morning?"

"Because we're having one of those moments between sleep-deprived coworkers when inhibitions go flying out the window and anything can happen?"

He considered that. "I don't know," he said. "I'm not feeling that tired."

She locked eyes with him.

"It's an explanation," she said. "Run with it."

Eric frowned. His collar felt suddenly tight around his neck, which puzzled him considering he was wearing a collarless, oversized polo shirt. But he reminded himself there was a weightier mystery to solve. Hetty had asked him to process the Edison records, wondering aloud if they might have some importance in the Sutton case. Importance, that was, beyond being valuable objects stolen from Sutton's home. She'd been a bit cryptic, which was nothing new. Still, Eric was certain there was a lot more than the theft of collectibles behind the murder. Which had led him to suspect there was a lot more to the *collectibles* than being valuable.

About thirty minutes ago, an idea had come to him, appropriately enough, like a light bulb blinking on over his head.

"Nell, listen," he said, motioning at the cylinders. "I arranged these on the counter according to type. Edison's factory used three different kinds of cylinders. The oldest are his Gold Molded cylinders. They were sorta brownish and made of aluminum stearate, beeswax, and ceresine wax… a petroleum byproduct." He paused. "They're in the brown packing tubes to your left."

She pointed her chin at the blue tubes on the right side of the counter.

"And these are…?"

"Blue Amberols," he said. "Edison switched from wax compounds to celluloid in the nineteen-twenties. The newer cylinders weren't as fragile as the originals."

Nell stood looking down at them.

"I only see brown and blue tubes here," she said. "You mentioned three kinds of cylinders."

"The Black Amberols also came in brown storage tubes," Eric said. "They fall in the middle chronologically. They're stronger than the browns and weaker than the blues."

She looked thoughtful.

"Help me get this straight," she said. "First Edison made brown wax cylinders…"

"And packaged them in brown cardboard tubes…"

"Then he made black wax cylinders…"

"And also kept them in brown tubes…"

"And then he manufactured blue *celluloid* cylinders…"

"And changed the packaging. They came in blue cardboard tubes."

Nell lifted one of the Blue Amberols off the counter in a nitrile-gloved hand.

"'Missouri Waltz' by the Jaudus Society Orchestra," she said, reading the label on its lid. "Catchy."

"How about the Orpheus Male Chorus?" Eric showed her another blue. "Featuring their smash hit 'Dixieland Memories.'"

"A must for everyone's stranded-on-a-desert island top ten list," she said. Her expression asking how any of this had the slightest bearing on their efforts to find a killer.

He set down the Blue Amberol, nodding at the brown tubes again.

"Take a closer look at them," he said. "Notice anything different?"

Nell examined them a minute, picked one up off the counter, and shrugged.

"Hmm," she said. "There's no recording artist's name written on the lid. Just a serial number."

"That's because the Edison Company didn't package them with labels," he said. "Unless you were standing at the store display, the only way to identify the artist was to open up the cardboard tube and read a little slip of paper inside."

She looked at the tube in her hand.

"This might be a dumb question... but if I open this up right now, will I hear a horrible disintegrating noise and then feel very sick and guilty?"

Eric shrugged.

"The only way to know for sure is to try," he said. And grinned. "I tried."

She gave him a questioning glance.

"You can open it," he said, holding out a pair of tweezers. "Just don't sneeze, cough, hiccup, or yawn."

Nell carefully removed the lid, saw the paper slip between the tube and cylinder, and pulled it out with the tweezers.

After a second her doubt turned to surprise.

The information about the recording was written, rather than printed, on the insert in faded blue ink.

It read:

E. Sutton
8/30/1945
T-31-445-01

"I don't get it," Nell said. "Sutton must've written this himself. A long time ago judging from the date."

Eric nodded. "Way, way, way, way, *way* back in the

day, phonographs were hyped as being for personal recordings," he said. "Those brown wax cylinders weren't worth the fifty cents they cost if you wanted to score the Jaudus Society's greatest hits. Their wax was so soft, the phonograph's metal stylus would chew up their grooves like a power drill. They were shot after nine or ten plays."

"Are you telling me the admiral was a closet crooner?" Nell asked, although her *expression* was telling him she knew full well where he was going with this.

"It *was* a kind of novelty item, and some people did torture their wives and kids with their ballads and fiddle playing," Eric said. "But they also used the recordable cylinders for drafts of letters, diary entries, favorite sayings…"

"Beep-beep."

"Beep-*beep*? What's that?"

"My contradiction alert," she explained. "You just said people knew the cylinders wouldn't last long. Why bother with the recordings?"

Eric frowned. Nell always blamed her penchant for cutting him off on her Attention Deficit Disorder… but since when did the interruptions come with beeps?

"They weren't usually making them for posterity," he said. "Think of the cylinders as rewritable media— the equivalent of CD-RWs. People would refer to their verbal documents when preparing the written ones, then wipe the cylinders clean."

"You could *erase* these things?"

"Yeah. Well, literally, you'd buy tools that would raze, or shave away, the grooves on their outer layers," Eric said. "Edison boasted that the blanks could be reused a hundred times before they had to be tossed, but it was probably less."

Nell thought about that.

"You said the phonograph needle would ruin the grooves," she said. "What if they were never played? Locked away for safekeeping?"

"They still wouldn't hold up," Eric said. "The brown and black wax became so brittle with age they could shatter in a person's hand with the slightest pressure… I mean, explode. They were also vulnerable to being attacked by fungus and mold—"

"Gives new meaning to Gold Molded," Nell said, and grinned.

He looked at her. "You just stole my line."

"Sorry, couldn't resist." She held the cardboard tube in her hand. "What do you think is recorded on here?"

Eric shrugged.

"Who knows?" he said. He adjusted a table lamp so its brightness shone directly over the tube. "I wouldn't touch the cylinder, it's too fragile. But take a closer look at it in the container."

She immediately noticed the whitish-gray splotches across its surface.

"Speaking of mold," she said.

"Yup," Eric said. "All of Sutton's brown cylinders have it, some worse than others, which ain't good. The stuff eats away at their grooves like Pac-Man monsters eating, uh, Pac-Men." He paused. "Back to the paper slip, if you want my not-so-wild guess—and for what it's worth, that's an index number below the date."

"But it's of no use to us without a key."

"Right." Eric motioned to the other browns. "There are three or four more tubes with handwritten labels, so we *might* find a pattern to the numbers—"

"What if we could listen to the recording?" she said,

cutting him short a third time. "Then we wouldn't need the numbers *or* an index key."

He shook his head. "Okay... *beep-beep*. We've already established that playing the cylinder's sure to mess it up, maybe even destroy it."

"Right," she said. "But I said listen. Not play. There's a difference."

Eric's brow creased, his eyes leaping to hers. A moment later they filled with understanding.

"There is, isn't there?" he said.

Nell smiled sweetly, nodding.

"X-awesome," he said.

"Awesome-X," she replied.

14

Deeks entered the interrogation room at 8:30 A.M. to find Dorani leaned forward over the table, snoring lightly, his arms crossed under his head.

His estimable lawyer had arrived a few minutes earlier looking drawn, caffeine-buzzed, and indignant over having to return to the Boatshed on very short notice... this after spending half the night here with her client, and the rest of it working at home to complete a petition that he be properly charged before a judge or magistrate, and then remanded to the custody of the Los Angeles County Sheriff's Department.

Though Deeks commiserated, he wasn't about to feel too sorry for her. The fact was that he and the rest of the OSP's personnel also had been at it nonstop for an unholy span of hours, trying to solve a case with so many moving parts it was hard to keep track of them...

Ms. Scardella's client being a *key* part. And one of the few they had managed to get their hands on.

"Rise and shine, Isaak," he said now, slamming his palm against the edge of the table. "It's almost go-to-jail time."

Dorani snapped his head up, yawning.

"Nice'a you to give me a shake," he said blearily. And sniffed. "Did I mention this joint smells like clams? Which, nothing personal, ain't any worse on the nose than you."

Deeks grinned as he sat down.

"That's funny," he said. "Positively chucklicious."

"Hey, I got loads more where it came from."

"Cool," Deeks said. "You can write 'em all down on a yellow legal pad while you're doing fifteen to life."

Scardella frowned.

"You said you had some new questions," she said. "Shall we get this latest session underway? Because the longer my client stays here in this room, the greater my inclination to trash my request for a transfer and demand his immediate, unconditional release."

"Based on?"

"More violations of his constitutional rights than there are clams in the sea."

Deeks's smile broadened.

"The merriment never ends," he said, then returned his eyes to Isaak. "One thing…"

"Here we go," Isaak said. "You show me another picture of a stiff, I'm gonna puke my guts out."

Deeks shook his head.

"Actually," he said, "you have a visitor."

Isaak regarded him with the same frightened, goggle-eyed expression he'd shown before the interview broke for the night.

"What kind?" he said.

"What do you mean, 'what kind'?"

"I mean, it ain't somebody who wants to *kill* me, is it?"

"There a lot of people in that club?"

"Funny guy," Isaak said. "Now how about you tell me who this visitor is?"

"How about we just have him come in?"

"I have a better idea," Scardella said. "How about you people stop springing surprises on us?"

Deeks spread his hands.

"Believe it or not," he said, "I didn't plan this."

"Oh, really?"

"Cross my smelly heart."

Scardella looked at him a moment and sighed.

"Say I accept you're telling the truth," she said. "Isaak promised he'd cooperate, not play 'This Is Your Life.'"

Deeks's expression suddenly turned grave.

"Nobody here's slept in forty-eight hours," he said. "This isn't a game. We need your client to talk."

"And if he does?"

"We won't forget."

Scardella hesitated a full ten seconds. Then she turned to Isaak.

"I suggest we proceed, and see who they've brought in," she said. "What do you think?"

He looked at her nervously. Licked his lips. And nodded.

"Okay," he said. "But it better not be my moron Auntie Evelyn."

Ron Valli entered the room first, Kensi behind him. Callen and Sam stayed out in observation with Hetty, thinking five would be a crowd.

Dorani sat there stiffly, staring at them in silence. Tension and surprise mingled in his eyes as Valli came through the door.

"Zak," Valli said. "How you doing, man?"

Dorani gave a mute shrug. He watched Valli

approach the table, taking the chair Deeks had occupied moments before.

A moment passed. Scardella quiet behind her tablet, Deeks and Kensi standing against the wall.

All of them waiting.

Dorani kept staring at Valli across the table.

"You don't look too good," he said.

"You neither," Valli said.

"I been up all night," Dorani said.

"Me too," Valli said.

Dorani smiled nervously.

"Terrific," he said.

Valli smiled back but didn't answer.

Finally he shifted in his seat.

"I had a helluva night," he said, breaking the unearthly silence. "A helluva night."

Dorani nodded.

"I heard," he said. "Didn't know if I should believe it—"

"I was gonna check out," Valli said. "If that's what they told you, it's true."

"I don't get it," Dorani said, shaking his head. "You didn't do anything."

Valli shrugged.

"Sometimes it don't matter with guys like us," he said. "Sometimes it's what they *think* you did."

"But everything's okay?"

Valli shrugged again.

"I'm still here," he said. "I saw Karyn and Lila."

"And they're good?"

"They're good."

Dorani nodded, smiled, turned his eyes down at the table, and abruptly burst into tears.

"Shit," he said, reaching out sideways. "Will

somebody here let me have a tissue?"

Scardella got some out of her bag and gave them to him.

"Zak... listen," Valli said. "I don't know what happened in the admiral's house. All I know for sure's you wouldn't kill anybody."

"I didn't." Dorani wadded the tissues in his hand. "I swear on my life, I thought the place would be empty..."

"I know," Valli said. "I'm telling you man, I do. But they say you were in there with some bad dudes."

Dorani wiped his eyes. "That don't describe 'em," he said. "We're talking the biggest nuts in the nutcake."

Valli was nodding.

"You need to tell these people who they are, Zak," he said. "They—"

"Hold it," Scardella said, turning to Dorani. "You *don't* have to tell anyone anything."

"Maybe," Kensi said, "you should let your client decide for himself."

Scardella shot a look at her. "Let me remind you that he's been very forthcoming to this point," she said. "Meanwhile, you've pulled one stunt after another, and given us no chance to prepare..."

"I wouldn't call Mr. Valli a *stunt*," Deeks said. "He's your client's closest friend. And Isaak used information he innocently gave him to lead Mr. Sutton's killers into his home."

"Again, this is news to me," Scardella said. "Assuming it's true..."

Dorani was trembling.

"Ronnie," he said. "Is that what you think?"

Valli looked at him. "It don't matter right now," he said.

"It does," Dorani said, plaintively. "It matters to me."

There was a momentary silence. Valli took a long, deep breath and slowly released it.

"I told you I was taking the admiral to the cemetery," he said, and inhaled again. "I told you Angie was supposed to have the day off. I told you a whole bunch of stuff about the house…"

"But I didn't do it on purpose. I mean, I didn't think the crazies would *shoot*—"

"Isaak," Scardella said. "We've been all through this story already. It isn't in your interest to repeat it…"

Valli kept his eyes on his friend.

"I'm asking you to tell the agents about those people," he said. "Whatever you know."

"But it won't make up for things. It won't make things right…"

"It'll help, Zak," Valli said. He reached across the table and grabbed his arm above the elbow. "Please. I'm asking you."

Dorani was crying again, covering his eyes with his palms, his cheeks shiny with tears.

"I'm in a spot," he said. "Suppose I talk. The crazies'll kill me. I know they will."

Kensi moved up behind Valli.

"No," she said. "I promise we won't let that happen."

There was another silence. Dorani looked at her across the table. Looked at Valli. Looked back at her for a long time.

"Okay," he said finally, gulping down the lump in his throat. "You were right."

"About what?"

Scardella shook her head. "Isaak, don't. This is a mistake—"

"The crazies call themselves commandos," he said, paying no attention to her. "Goddamn *suicide* commandos."

Kensi kept her eyes on his.

"What else?" she said.

"They want to build a dirty bomb," he said.

"A dirty *nuke*?"

"Right, exactly," he said. "They been planning to set it off here in Los Angeles…"

"Do you know when?"

Dorani swallowed again.

"Not for sure," he said. "But if you guys got some nice Samsonite luggage at home, I'm thinkin' you should hurry up and pack."

15

The OSP's second all-hands-on-deck meeting in as many days got underway at 9:30 A.M., with agents Callen, Hanna, Blye, and Detective Deeks urgently reporting to the Operations Center to find both Henrietta Lange and Assistant Director Owen Granger awaiting them. Also in the room were Beale and Jones.

Granger watched the team file in. A lean, rugged-looking man of about sixty with intense brown eyes, a long taciturn face, and a receding hairline that gave his forehead a high, prominent appearance, he stood near the big plasma screen wearing a navy-blue sport jacket, dark-gray trousers, and an open-collared white Oxford shirt.

His presence reinforced what the agents already knew. The case they were working was now about far more than the bloody double homicide at Elias Sutton's home, and the associated kidnapping of Theodore Holloway two months before. Add the apparent repercussions of those crimes—the killings of the hacker, Erasmo Greer, and the pawnbroker-slash-fence Zory Daggut—and you still fell incalculably short of its full, chilling immensity.

In starkest terms they were now racing against time to head off a terrorist strike meant to bring mass murder and destruction to Los Angeles.

"Okay," Granger said. "Operations Manager Lange has been keeping me updated about your investigation. But we need to see what we've got collectively."

Callen glanced at the enlarged image onscreen. He'd seen right off that it was part of a document written in an old Courier typewriter font—the same typeface used in the OSS/Deep Dive report Hetty had put up the other day.

The document's header, stamped boldly at the upper margin of the page in red ink, read:

SECRET ULTRA
TO BE KEPT UNDER LOCK AND KEY AND NEVER TO
BE REMOVED FROM THIS OFFICE. THIS FORM IS FOR
G2 INTELLIGENCE MESSAGES ONLY

Typed beneath was this:

#224756/18 December 1944
From: Rear Admiral Hideo Kojima {BERLIN}
To: Chief Shigero Matsuoka, Military Affairs
Bureau, War Office {TOKYO}

Due the critical war situation, Commander-in-
Chief Doenitz has conveyed that the number of
nonregular passengers who return to the homeland
via MINAZUKI-1 be restricted to two or three
persons at a time. (U-437)

Based on their necessity to the strengthening
of the war effort, and in view of the cargo to be
transported aboard the ship, my recommendations

```
for the initial passenger list are below:
Technical Commander Haruo Mori
Technical Expert Masahiro Tanaka (assistant to
Commander Mori)
Colonel Daichi Suzuki (aeronautics specialist)
Major Jiro Tarutani (rocket fuel specialist)
```

"That's the decrypt Warren Alders at the Seabee Museum got from the National Archives," Callen said, reading over the document. "A cable from the Japanese attaché in Berlin to his superiors in Tokyo."

"And check out the first name on that list," Sam said. "Haruo Mori's the scientist whose journal Alders gave us."

Hetty nodded.

"Your curator emailed this scan to us last night," she said. "His predecessor at the museum requested—and was granted—its declassification through the Freedom of Information Act." She paused. "The CIA had no knowledge of this intercept, or another one that was boxed away with it. Otherwise, the Agency's watchdogs would have ensured they were still classified."

"Why?" Sam asked. "And how'd the docs slip past them?"

"I believe that's two questions," Hetty said. "The second is easiest to answer. Intelligence was far less centralized during World War Two than it is today. There were no networked computer databases for people like Eric to hack into."

Beale gave a mock shiver from his console.

"Sounds ghastly," he said.

Sam turned to Hetty. "You're saying the information didn't flow through OSS channels."

"Correct," she said. "OSS being the CIA's forerunner,

its records likely would have been handed right over. But the cables were netted by U.S. Army crypto specialists stationed in England, then forwarded overseas to G2 Military Intelligence."

"And after the war they went straight from G2 into the archives with a gajillion other documents," Callen said. "Completely bypassing the OSS."

Hetty nodded again. Meanwhile, Sam continued to study the screen.

"Looks like somebody wrote the word 'U-437' on there in ink," he said.

"Probably an anonymous G2 analyst during the war," Hetty said. "Minazuki is the traditional Japanese word for June."

"The month Alders told us U-437 was scheduled to arrive in Kobe," Callen said.

"Making Minazuki-1 a codename for the sub," Sam said.

Granger nodded.

"The suffix '1' indicates it would be the first of the *Speermädchen* boats to leave for the Far East," he said, turning to Eric. "Okay… I want everyone to see the relevant section on the boat's freight manifest."

The tech tapped his console, bringing up the document on the plasma screen. It read:

#224894/2 January 1945
From: Rear Admiral Hideo Kojima {BERLIN}
To: Chief Shigero Nakamura, Military Affairs Bureau, War Office {TOKYO}

1. I am pleased to inform you that Commander-in-Chief Doenitz has approved our requested passenger list of 18 December. All

four specialists are presently arranging for
travel to MINAZUKI-1's port of embarkation.
2. The freight hold of MINAZUKI-1 will hold
about 35 tons, and German naval authorities
are confident that a watertight compartment
on deck will take an additional 5 tons of
storage. As negotiated with CIC Doenitz, our
total loading cargo will therefore consist of:

- Parts for long-range V-weapons: 12 tons
- Plans and Drawings for the above: 650
  kilograms
- Special steel for rocket and aircraft
  construction: 15 tons
- Insulating material: 1 ton
- Optical glass: 10 tons
- Lithium Chloride: 500 kilograms
- ███████ (sealed barrels): 2 tons

"The manifest was another wire between the Japanese attaché and his boss back home," Granger said.

"What's with the two tons of redacted fun at the bottom?" Sam asked.

"We'll come around to that in a minute, Agent Hanna," Granger said. "But let's look at the numbers. If you add up the weight of the cargo items, it totals just over forty-one tons. One above the German estimate, got it?"

They all nodded.

"The next document you'll see is *not* declassified," Granger said. "It's part of the extensive Deep Dive file prepared by Theodore Holloway in 'forty-five.'"

"We had a peek at it yesterday morning," Kensi offered. "Well, a *short* peek at its *title page*…"

"The folder itself is several inches thick," Hetty said.

"It contains his reports and substantiating enclosures. Among them are ships' logs and charts, prisoner interrogation transcripts, photos taken on inspection of the submarines, action reports, and ULTRA radio intercepts that *were* routed to the OSS... and eventually the CIA. They've kept them under lock and key since the war."

"How'd we get hold of them?" Sam asked.

"They found their way into my hands after Tip Holloway's abduction," Granger said. "I had questions and did some digging."

Sam was silent, the AD's look telling him he was not intending to discuss the type of shovel he'd used for the job.

"Mr. Beale, pull up the U.S. Navy manifest of cargo seized from aboard U-437 at Hueneme, please." Granger said.

Eric nodded. A moment later this appeared on the screen:

```
ENCLOSURE A
12 May 1945
CARGO TAKEN FROM ABOARD U-BOAT 437

Joint Statement of Commander Elias P.
Sutton, USN
and
Theodore Holloway, Project Director, Deep
Dive.

Sheeting (aircraft grade) — 15 tons
Lithium Chloride — 500kg
Insulation material (cork) — 1 ton
Optical-grade glass — 10 tons
```

```
V-2 rocket components — 12 tons
Technical blueprints for V-2 rockets — 650kg

Total weight: 39.15 tons
```

Sam looked at Granger. "Everything jibes aside from those sealed drums," he said. "They're missing. And something tells me they didn't jump off the boat on their own."

Granger nodded. "Since Hetty tells me everyone was briefed about Deep Dive yesterday, I have a hunch you all suspect what they contained."

"Uranium," Callen said.

"Make that uranium isotope two-thirty-five… the only type that's fissile in nature, making it nuclear-weapons grade," Granger said. "It would have been processed into a fine brown powder. With a radioactive half life of seven hundred million years."

"How do we know it was in the barrels?"

"Try because the Germans painted the number two-three-five on them."

"Now there's a clue," Deeks said.

Granger expelled a silent breath. "Several German sailors mention seeing the barrels—between fifteen and twenty of them—at Kiel harbor in the Deep Dive interrogation reports," he said. "The loading would have been done by naval dockworkers, so there aren't any eyewitnesses from the crew who saw them aboard in the hold."

"The sub couldn't have accidentally left them behind," Sam said. "There are shipping officers to keep tabs on everything. And they have a full staff."

"Besides… barrels aren't exactly easy to miss," Callen said. "It isn't like forgetting your wallet in the bedroom when you leave home."

"But Sutton and Holloway both signed off on the offload manifest," Kensi said. "They *must* have known about the intercepted German manifest. And been aware of a discrepancy in the cargo's tonnage and contents."

Granger held his eyes on her a moment, then glanced around the room.

"I have one final document to show you," he said. "A letter from Holloway to General Leslie Groves."

"Wait," Sam said. "Is this the same Groves who headed the Manhattan Project?"

"I think you know the answer," Granger said, nodding to Eric.

He put the letter up onscreen:

From: Theodore P. Holloway, Project Director
To: Leslie R. Groves, Brigadier General
Attachment: 2

20 May, 1945

Dear General Groves,

Our cataloguing of Minazuki-1's (U-437) freight load has been completed and all items removed from the captured vessel. Mindful of the expectation of its special cargo, I am writing to inform you that the barrels described in ULTRA intercept #224894 of 2 January 1945 were not found aboard the hold or deck compartment. Nor were the four Japanese technical experts named in a previous signal aboard the submarine.

Although POW testimony indicates the barrels were seen on shore during preparations for Minazuki-1's embarkation, it is my conjecture that

Germany canceled or delayed the shipment shortly before the boat set sail. The absence of the above mentioned scientific personnel suggests a change in overall plans.

I am aware of the Los Alamos National Laboratory's interest in obtaining the material, and was prepared to expedite its delivery to the facility under armed guard. It is therefore with great disappointment that I report this news.

Attached are German and U.S. Navy shipping/receiving manifests. It seems clear that the former was a working copy and not the Kriegsmarine's final version.

Again, I regret having to share this information with you. We are hopeful that further and ongoing interrogation of prisoners will shed greater light on the shipment's disposition.

Yours Truly,
THEODORE P. HOLLOWAY
T.P. Holloway, Lt.
Port Hueneme, California

"Man oh man," Callen said. "Holloway's lying outright about the Japanese passengers."

"Or Haruo Mori, at least," Sam said. "His journal proves he was on the sub."

"And Holloway tried to burn it," Callen said. "You have to ask why… and what happened to those scientists."

"I think the 'why' is crystal clear," Hetty said. "Holloway's lie about the scientists was part of a bigger deception."

"The uranium *was* aboard the sub when it came into Hueneme," Callen said. "It's the only explanation. He and Sutton deliberately falsified the receipt manifest. Made the barrels disappear."

Sam shook his head. "*Path to Glory*," he said. "I'm thinking they'll have to change the title of the admiral's book if it's ever reissued."

"One thing," Deeks said. "There were around seventy German crewmen. How can none of them have mentioned the Japanese when they were interrogated? I mean, unless…"

"The interrogation reports were altered," Kensi said. "If you're going to hide two tons of uranium and cover up the presence of four scientists, editing the interrogation transcripts is small potatoes."

"You'd think some of the sailors would let something slip after the interrogations," Deeks said. "They had nothing but time on their hands in the POW camps."

Hetty shook her head in emphatic disagreement.

"The submariners took oaths of secrecy to the Reich," she said. "They wouldn't have wanted to talk—it was an act of treason. They also may have been coerced or threatened into silence as prisoners."

"Speaking of treason," Sam said. "Holloway and Sutton ripping off the uranium fits smack into my definition."

"Indeed," Hetty said. "It would have been worth a tidy ransom on the black market back then. The Cold War was beginning, there were a great many nations that would have paid them handsomely for fissile material."

Granger gestured impatiently.

"We can only speculate about their motives," he said. "For whatever reason, it doesn't seem the uranium was sold after its theft. Our concern right now is *where* they stored it."

"The train tracks behind Building Thirty-One at

Hueneme linked up to the national railroad grid," Sam said. "They could have moved it anywhere. Especially with Holloway's family connections."

"Except Isaak Dorani told us not an hour ago that they stockpiled it right here in SoCal," Deeks said. "Not that he's a walking, talking shrine to honesty."

"But his story makes sense," Callen said. "According to him, the hacker… what was his name…?"

"Erasmo Greer," Kensi said.

"Greer stumbled onto the truth about the uranium a few weeks before Holloway was kidnapped," he said. "Dorani claims he gained backdoor entry to Holloway's computer via an online dating site the old hound frequented…"

"A *cheater*'s site," Nell said. "The Lexi Parks website has thirty thousand paid subscribers. Men wanting to discreetly date married women and vice versa."

"And then it got infamously hacked," Kensi said. "Nobody knew who did it or exactly why…"

"But *now* we know it was Greer," Callen said. "Again according to Dorani, he sent malware packets out to subscribers' computers over the Internet, turning their hard drives and cloud vaults into data grab bags."

"And then went poking around for valuable goodies," Deeks said. "Information he could sell or use to blackmail people."

"While he's doing it, Greer lucks into horny, ninety-something Tip Holloway's system," Kensi said. "That's where he finds his notes about the uranium."

"And then he decodes those notes and learns where the drums were stashed away all those years ago," Sam said.

"*Approximately* where they're stashed," Callen said. "The exact location wasn't on Holloway's computer."

Sam nodded. "He and Sutton were slick enough to divvy the information between them so it wasn't all in one place," he said.

"Anyway, when Greer gets hold of the info, he contacts his friend Isaak to see if he can rustle up paying customers," Kensi said. "Isaak's his man on the street…"

"A career wheeler-dealer," Deeks said. "Probably knows every shady character from here to Tijuana…"

"One of them being a guy named Gaspar affiliated with the Secret Army Commandos," Kensi said.

"The *Armenian* Secret Army Commandos," Granger said. "We can't afford to forget that."

Kensi nodded. He was right, naturally. But the one thing all terrorist flakes did, whatever their beef, was foist their real or perceived woes on innocents, bringing on wreckage for wreckage. Her job so often involved dealing with the bloody effects of their violent hatred—and doing it on the run—that she couldn't stop to look at its origins.

"When the Secret Army bit, things got serious," she said. "They were ready to pay for the location of the uranium. But they wanted the *full* location…"

"And Greer didn't have it," Deeks said. "He'd sifted through every byte of info in Holloway's system without any luck…"

"Which left them hoping the old man stored it on external media like a backup drive or memory stick."

"That's why they did the break-in and kidnapping at Holloway's condo," Deeks said. "They were after whatever storage devices they could find…"

"Including Holloway himself," Kensi said. "For all they knew, he'd kept the information locked away in his head…"

"The hardest type of external media to crack, when

you consider it," Deeks said. "Greer basically ran the show. He told the Secret Army he could disable the senior watch systems at Bel Air Palms with his jackrabbits, and had Isaak set them up for him."

"Then he sent Isaak into the apartment to grab the storage devices…"

"While the SA grabbed the old man and drove him out to their hideaway somewhere in the desert," Kensi said. "Unfortunately for them, the information wasn't on the backup media, and Holloway was a lot tougher than they imagined. They couldn't coerce him to talk. Threats, physical force, nothing worked."

"Till they drugged him," Deeks said. "Even then, he didn't totally open up. But he spilled something about Elias Sutton having what they were after."

"So they dumped him in the Mojave and started to plan the Sutton burglary," Kensi said. "Isaak thought it was a nice little fluke that he knew Sutton's driver."

"More than just *knew* him," Callen said. "They were bosom buddies from prison."

"Holy jailhouse serendipity," Deeks said.

Sam smiled a little. "My mom used to say kings and crooks have all the luck."

"Valli didn't have a clue he was being milked," Kensi said. "But he gave Isaak—and the Secret Army— the precise gen they needed for the job."

"Namely the layout of Sutton's property," Callen said. "And a direct line into his daily routines."

Granger was listening closely.

"A second burglary would have been risky even if Sutton wasn't a well-known person," Granger said. "Do we know whether Greer tried hacking Sutton's machine or cloud storage?"

"He did, but there was no backdoor in," Kensi

answered. "Sutton was the polar opposite of a web junkie. He barely used email... didn't shop online..."

"To him the only clouds were the ones drifting around in the sky," Callen said.

Granger grunted. "Any idea why the SA didn't try abducting him?"

Kensi shrugged.

"My hunch," she replied, "is that whatever Holloway said convinced them the info was on his computer."

"They didn't expect Sutton *or* the housekeeper to be home," Sam said. "It was her off day, but she decided to surprise him."

Callen nodded. "Valli says his visits to his wife's grave were always tough on him," he said. "She came to cheer him up."

"And got blown away for her kindness," Sam said.

Hetty sighed into the suddenly quiet room.

"Our problem right now is that we don't know whether or not Greer ever found the information about the uranium on Sutton's computer," she said at length. "I also doubt Holloway will voluntarily share it with us. Certainly not without lawyering up and trying to broker a deal."

"We can't wait for that," Granger said abruptly. "There's no time."

"Isaak says Greer was under pressure from the Armenians to get the info fast," Callen said. "Heavy pressure."

Granger exchanged glances with Hetty, then looked around the room.

"Have any of you noticed the date?" he said.

Sam checked his watch. "April twenty-fourth," he said. "That mean something?"

Hetty's face was sober.

"A little over a century ago today, three hundred innocent members of Constantinople's Armenian community were slaughtered by the military government," she said. "Blame the usual sludge of primitive, senseless reasons—nationalism, ethnic strife, territorial conflict." She paused. "It was the first of several massacres that took a million and a half Armenian lives in Turkish-controlled lands over the next decade."

"At the time Armenia was part of the Ottoman Empire," Granger said. "It went on to be annexed to the Soviet Union after World War One."

"Anybody ask the Armenians what *they* wanted?" Sam said.

"I assume that's a rhetorical question," Granger replied. "The Armenian Justice Commandos formed in the nineteen-seventies. Their M.O. primarily involved attacks against Turkish diplomats and calling for recognition of the genocide by the government in Istanbul. A more violent offshoot called the Armenian Secret Army broadened the terrorist activities throughout Europe. And added Armenian self-rule to their demands."

"After Armenia declared its independence in nineteen-ninety, the Justice Commandos fell out of sight," Hetty said. "But the SA still had angry factions. They insisted the Turks admit to their crimes against humanity and pay reparations to survivors. And that America lead the world in imposing sanctions for noncompliance."

"And we didn't," Sam said.

Granger shook his head. "Too many other battles to fight," he said. "Geopolitics makes for awkward bedfellows. We needed Turkey as a strategic coalition partner during the first and second Gulf Wars, and still do in the war against ISIS."

"The SA's rhetoric hasn't helped their cause, either," Hetty said. "Every now and then they surface to advocate reprisals against the Turks and their allies."

"And what else?" Sam said. "What've they been up to lately?"

"It's widely thought that their funding dried up years ago," Hetty said. "Our intelligence agencies believe they're dormant."

"But we all know better," he said.

"Yes."

"*We* know they've been after the Nazi uranium so they could build a dirty bomb."

"Yes."

"That they kidnapped one person, and killed at least *four* other people trying to get hold of it."

She gave a slow nod.

"Yes, Mr. Hanna," she said. "Four since yesterday."

Sam thought a moment, looking from her to Granger.

"And *today's* April twenty-fourth," he said. "The anniversary of the genocide."

A hush settled over the room.

"What we *don't* know is where the uranium was stashed," Callen finally said. "If they *do* and get their hands on it—or already have it—we're cooked."

There was another deep, heavy silence. Then Nell cleared her throat to interrupt it.

"I think I might be able to help on that score," she said.

It was a little past ten in the morning when Matous entered the ordnance and explosives lab, briefly looking in on his commandos before he left for the railway station.

The small, bare room was lit with bright metal floor lamps. There were two worktables, a long rectangular one in the middle, and a wheeled, stainless steel laboratory table to his left near a wall-mounted gun cabinet. Blackout shades covered the windows.

One of the men, Pavel, sat at the wheeled table loading bullets from plastic ammunition boxes into forty and fifty round magazines. Gaspar, Narem, and Davit were at the other table on adjustable stools, inspecting the half-dozen satchel charges in front of them.

Each of the black nylon haversacks contained eight two-pound bricks of cocrystallized HMX-CL20 plastic explosive, a state-of-the-art formulation that combined high yield with enhanced stability—and produced less vapor signature than other comparable materials. Although the packets would be undetectable to most electronic scanners—and even escape the sensitive noses of bomb-sniffing dogs—Matous had instructed his men to seal them in large Ziploc freezer bags, further tamping down their chemical scents.

Using a screen of proxy buyers, Jag Azarian had acquired the HMX-CL20 from a black market Pakistani arms dealer for an even six thousand U.S. dollars.

Matous himself had purchased the detonating system from KABOOM.COM, a Cincinnati-based e-commerce site specializing in pyrotechnic supplies.

Its six wallet-sized firing modules received their radio signals with small, nubby radio antennas and ran on plain AA batteries. The LED remote control with which Matous would activate them took a single twelve-volt battery.

The system was legal, inexpensive, easily acquired, and patently ordinary.

In a few short hours he would be putting it to extraordinary use.

He watched Gaspar snap open his satchel's outer pouch, pull out its firing module, and closely examine the thin copper wire running from the module to the explosive packet in the bag's main compartment. Satisfied the connection was secure at both ends, he slipped the module back into the pouch and then closed the flap.

The team's methodical preparations gave Matous a sense of calm assurance. When the men left here this afternoon, they would carry many times the destructive power needed for their mission.

In Iraq during the Battle of Fallujah, his Marine unit would clear out blocks of Saddam's Ba'ath Party loyalists with satchel charges of C-4, using a single twenty-pound bomb to level a sprawling, palatial home.

The HMX-CL20 packed significantly more explosive force than C-4, and there would be *four* satchels on the railbed. That made for sixty-four pounds of plastic explosive at the target location, enough to bring down an entire row of houses. The other pair of haversacks—containing thirty-two pounds of explosive between them—would be handed off to Tomas after he brought the hijacked express shuttle in from Union Station.

With the drums of powdered uranium onboard, the shuttle would turn into an enormous radiological dispersal device—a dirty bomb that would annihilate hundreds in the initial blast, and spread a cloud of deadly radioactive contamination across a large, populated area.

"What are you doing here? I assumed you would have left by now."

Matous turned to see Tomas standing behind him in the hall.

"I'm waiting for Alysha," he said. And raised an eyebrow. "She isn't with you?"

Tomas shook his head. "I last saw her a half hour ago. She was doing something to her hair."

"Prettying up for her date?"

"She would slice off your balls and feed them to the vultures for that remark," Tomas said. "And you'd deserve it."

Matous tried not to look too amused.

"You sound a bit defensive," he said.

"She doesn't need me or anyone else to defend her... but let's drop it." Tomas looked him in the eyes. "With Alysha going on ahead of us, I'm a person short. Yuri can't guard the passengers himself while I pilot the train."

Matous gestured toward the man at the steel table.

"You'll have Pavel," he said. "He's already been informed."

"And you can vouch for his reliability?"

"He fought under me in two deployments," Matous said. "There isn't a steadier hand here with a weapon."

Tomas looked through the doorway at him and nodded.

Hearing Alysha's light, quick footsteps, Tomas glanced around to see her approaching in a white peasant blouse, jeans, and sneakers. A purse under her arm, a pair of designer sunglasses up over her forehead. The blouse was made to fall loosely below her shoulder, offering a hint of smooth, toned flesh.

His eyebrows rose. She had darkened her hair so it was almost black and tucked it into a neat French Twist.

"You're ready for your conductor friend," Matous

said. "He'll be spellbound."

Her face was cold.

"I'm being cautious," she said. "I don't want to look the same today as I did yesterday."

Tomas regarded her in silence, his eyes brushing over the curve of her collarbone...

"Is something wrong?" she said suddenly.

"No." He remembered the smoothness of her skin on his lips. "Nothing. You were saying?"

"Just that I'll be in touch." Alysha regarded him for another minute. "Things will develop quickly. You'll need to be fast and adaptable."

Her words, if not her tone, seemed a jab.

"I'm no stranger to action," Tomas said. "You of all people shouldn't have to be reminded."

Silence. She shrugged, turning to Matous.

"Let's go," she said, and strode off toward the front door.

16

"Late in his life, Guglielmo Marconi came to believe in necrophony, or the science of receiving voice transmissions from the dead," said Nell.

"Which isn't *really* a science, but who here wants to argue with someone who kind-of-but-not-quite invented the radio?" Eric said, realizing he'd cut in on *her* for a change.

It was 10:43 A.M. Crammed into a forensics lab with the two intelligence analysts were Granger and Hetty Lange, along with Callen, Hanna, Deeks, and Blye.

Granger studied the contraption in front of Nell, thinking it looked like what you got crossing a garage workshop table with a half-million dollar digital microscope.

Mona, the analyst had called it.

"Tell me that's a necrophone and I'm out of here," he said.

Nell gave a quick laugh. "Marconi's dream was to build a radio receiver that could capture Jesus's Sermon on the Mount out of thin air," she said. "Mona can't do that. But it's the next best thing."

"*Tubwayhun lahvday,*" Hetty said. "It's Aramaic.

Blessed are the peacemakers."

No one said anything for a long moment.

"The clock's ticking," she said. "Let's focus."

Nell nodded, motioning to the wide vertical tubes above the instrument's mounting platform.

"My college friend had it rushed over from UC Berkeley overnight," she said. "She works for Intelligence and Analysis under Homeland Security, and I&A and the Defense Intelligence Agency run a joint project to recover and preserve historic wartime records—ours and other countries'."

"Mona's optics should be able to map the topography of the brown wax cylinders in Sutton's collection," Eric said. "Recreate what's in them—"

"—without physically making contact with their surfaces," Nell interjected, finishing the sentence. "It appears Sutton had a half dozen home recordings, and they're the ones that really interest us."

"The problem's that they're all severely infested with mold," Eric said. "Active mold spores spread easily..."

"And since mold feeds on dead organic material—"

"Like the waxy substance they're made of..."

"It'll have eaten away and disfigured their surfaces..."

"Which could create dead spots in the digital reconstruction," Eric said. "Also, Mona can't see through excessive dirt or mold encrustations. We're betting her predictive intelligence engine can fill in some of the gaps—"

"By looking at the hills and valleys *it* is able to see, and making statistical guesses about what's between them," Nell said.

Eric was nodding. "To give ourselves the best shot

at success, we'll need to clean as much gunk off the cylinders as possible before scanning them…"

"And that's going to be tricky," Nell said.

"*Very* tricky," Eric said.

"How long do you expect it to take?" Hetty asked.

"It's a delicate process," Eric said. "We don't want them to crumble in our hands…"

"How *long*?"

Eric motioned to a stainless steel counter across the room, where he'd carefully removed the cylinders from their cardboard containers and set them out on lab trays.

"There are experts at the Library of Congress who specialize in this kind of physical restoration," he said. "I fired off some red-flagged queries about how to proceed but haven't heard back."

"Have you tried calling them?"

"We just get routed to voice mail," Nell said. "The problem's that the library's underfunded and understaffed."

"This can't wait," Granger said. "Give me your contacts. I'll set a fire under their asses that'll leave them smoking for a month."

Nell nodded, reaching for her tablet.

"One thing I don't understand," Granger said. "What's convinced you two the cylinders will give us the location of the ore?"

"I was about to ask the same question," Kensi said. "Isaak Dorani swears they weren't on the Secret Army's wish list. He only grabbed them as an afterthought, thinking he could roll them over for getaway money."

Eric started to respond but then thought twice about it, interrupting *himself* this time. Admittedly, he was first to notice some of the cylinders were homemade recordings. But it had been Nell who connected the dots.

He lobbed her a glance that said she should be the one to answer, and got a quick, acknowledging look in return.

"We've been working under the hypothesis that the murders of Zory Daggut and Erasmo Greer are both related to the Sutton murder," she said. "Isaak Dorani being the connecting link. Right?"

Kensi nodded.

"So if the killers are the same people–members of the Secret Army—what brought them to Daggut's shop?" Nell asked. "What could they have *wanted* except the cylinders?"

"And why?" Kensi said. "*Why* did they want to get hold of them?"

Nell glanced over at her.

"That's what we think Elias Sutton will tell us," she said.

"If we can make him talk," Eric said.

"Your chaperon's here, Isaak," Kensi said.

It was a quarter past eleven and a pair of U.S. Navy masters-at-arms were waiting outside the Boatshed for Isaak Dorani's transfer to the custody of the L.A. County Sheriff's Department. Blye and Deeks had driven over from HQ only minutes ago.

Dorani looked at her across the table. "They bring my prom tux?" he said. "I'm pretty much a small, though they say I got manly shoulders."

Kensi almost told him he'd have to settle for baggy orange jumps for a while, but bit her tongue.

"You'll be copied via email on the paperwork," she said to Scardella.

The lawyer folded her laptop.

"Thanks," she said. Then hesitated. "Godspeed finding what you need."

Kensi thought a second.

"I have one last question for your client," she said. "It's important."

Scardella sighed.

"The interrogation's over," she said, shaking her head. "I can't allow—"

"I'll keep it off the record."

"On your word?"

"Yes."

The attorney turned to Dorani. "Your choice," she said.

He nodded, still in his chair. "Ask away," he said, looking at Kensi. "Since you promised you'd be nice to my cats."

She sat down opposite him.

"About the SA's safehouse... that's what they call it, right?"

"Yeah. Like it's beneath them to say they got a *hideout*."

She held her eyes on him.

"You told us you were there a few times," she said. "That it's somewhere in the desert."

"Uh huh."

"Can you share anything that might help us find the place?"

He shook his head.

"We been through this already," he said. "I thought you were gonna ask something different..."

"Isaak," she said. "Try to remember."

He sighed.

"My answer's the same as before," he said. "They

drove me out there in a crappy old van... the kind with no windows. Blindfolded me. I couldn't see anything."

"You had your other senses," Kensi said. "Smell. Hearing. Touch. You must have picked up something from your surroundings."

"All I know is it was hot. And the road was full of bumps," he said, expelling another breath. "Listen, believe it or not, I ain't no keener on getting microwaved than the next guy. But I got no more to tell you."

Kensi looked at him a long moment, her hands folded on the table. Then she nodded.

"Okay, Isaak," she said. "If anything comes to you, we'd appreciate you telling us."

He half shrugged, half nodded, and then just sat there in silence.

Kensi stood up, turned to Scardella.

"We're done," she said. "I'll have the guards come in, and you'll be on your way."

"Wait," Dorani said. "I got a question or two of my own before we hug bye-bye."

She waited.

"My cats," he said. "What happens to 'em now?"

"I'm having them brought to foster care," Kensi said. "They'll be fine."

"Yeah, well, my babies don't eat no poison from the supermarket," he said. "I buy their food at one of those pet boutiques."

"I'll pass it along..."

"And they use natural pine litter," he said. "Pour that regular stuff in their box, I'm telling you, they won't poop."

She sighed. "Anything else?"

"Yeah, plenty," Dorani said. "They're used to a

smoke-free environment. No chemicals in the air. Or dust mites, God forbid. And you don't want 'em near freaking little kids…"

"Or little birds," Deeks interjected.

Dorani snapped a glance at him.

"What'd you say?"

"Take it easy, Isaak. I didn't—"

"No." He shook his head. "You said 'birds.'"

"Right, I—"

"*Birds.*"

Deeks looked at him, puzzled. He really was worked up.

"Bad joke," he said. "You know… cats." And motioned with his right hand. "Birds." Motioned with his left. "They don't exactly go, uh, hand-in-hand."

Dorani kept staring at him another minute, then abruptly looked around at Kensi.

"Stop the presses," he said. "I got something for you."

Kensi made two hurried calls on her cell within minutes of Dorani and his attorney departing with the MAs.

The first was a three-way call to Sam and Callen at headquarters. They needed to know what Dorani had told her about the safehouse—and determine whether his recollection could help them locate it.

The second was to Theodore Holloway, who answered his phone on the second ring.

"Sir, this is Agent Kensi Blye," she said, and got straight to the point. "My partner and I would like to drop by and speak with you in about an hour."

"I'm afraid that won't be possible, Agent," he said. "This call comes as a complete surprise, and I have an early lunch appointment..."

"Respectfully, sir, I'd suggest you postpone it," she said.

A pause. Then, slowly, he said, "May I ask what this concerns?"

She wondered if she was imagining the guardedness in his voice.

"It's really best we talk in person—"

"I might have to disagree," he said. "I told you everything I could about my cousin yesterday..."

"Sir, I have questions about Operation Deep Dive."

Another pause at the other end of the line. She heard him pull in a breath.

"*Deep Dive?* What sort of questions? I haven't heard that name in a lifetime."

"Again, sir, I would prefer to wait until we see you."

"Well, I'll tell you right now, it would be a worthless conversation," Holloway said. "I don't know why you're bringing up Deep Dive, but I hardly recall anything about it. That was seven decades ago—"

"Mr. Holloway," Kensi said. "There's no statute of limitations for treason or war crimes."

A third pause.

"This is unbelievable," he said. "You can't be serious."

"I'm dead serious, sir," Kensi said. "I can have you picked up, handcuffed, and brought in for questioning by uniformed officers. Or Detective Deeks and I can come quietly and spare you the embarrassment." Now it was her turn to be silent and she let it stretch. "The decision's all yours."

Holloway said nothing for a while. She heard him shift the receiver to his other hand and wondered if he was about to hang up on her. But instead he blew a long, heavy breath into the phone.

"Come over," he said. "I'll be here."

And then he finally did hang up.

17

"The Mojave has two native bird species with the characteristics Dorani gave us," Nell was explaining to Sam and Callen. "He says he could tell they're very large by the flap of their wings. That they make a shrieking noise louder than any he ever heard from a bird. And they congregate in flocks."

"Large, loud flocks," Sam said.

"Large and loud is how they roll," Nell said. "Specifically the turkey vulture and black vulture."

It was now 11:35 A.M., and the agents had pulled Nell away from the station where she and Eric Beale laid out the Edison cylinders... and where, at that moment, Eric was waiting to hear from Granger about the Library of Congress restoration experts.

"Are we sure only vultures are a match?" Callen asked. "No other kinds of birds? He didn't actually *see* them."

Nell nodded.

"Some might have one or two of those traits, but not all three," she said. "Falcons and hawks are big, and there are several species in the desert. Also the golden eagle. But they're solitary birds of prey.

Vultures are pretty social birds."

"Do turkey and black vultures live in the same areas?" Sam asked.

"Yes, I've seen both species roost in the same Joshua tree while I was hiking and it's sort of creepy," she said. "The black vultures are more aggressive. When they have to compete for food, they'll drive off the turkey vultures."

"So even if we knew which type was hanging out around the safehouse, it wouldn't help us pin down its location," Callen said.

"Probably not, since they're all about the same size and make a big racket," she said. "But there are other things."

"Like?"

"A turkey vulture will pick the highest spot around for its roost. Once it finds one, it'll stick to it for years, or even life. And it can live to be a hundred," she said. "If the birds were perched nearby when Dorani was out there, it means the area's probably developed, and it's eliminated their natural habitat. Otherwise they'd roost out of earshot on trees and ledges. They'll ride the thermals over populated sections when they're looking for food. But they're shy of people and cars. Human activity would scare them away."

Sam rubbed the back of his neck. "So we're looking at developed *and* deserted."

"You know the abandoned subdivisions outside Palmdale and Lancaster?" Callen said. "They turned into ghost towns when the housing bubble burst in Antelope Valley."

"Isn't that around where Theodore Holloway turned up in a rain ditch after his kidnapping?"

They looked at each other a long moment. Then Sam turned to Nell.

"Can we get some hi-res imagery of those developments?"

"The NRO's new Block Four satellites would do the trick," Nell said. "They can bring us in close enough to see the dust churn up when a vulture flaps its wings."

"*That* close?"

She frowned.

"Okay, maybe I got overenthusiastic," she said. "But it *would* show us the bird."

"How fast can you do it?"

"Hetty's the one to ask," Nell said. "She'd need permission from the NRO to re-task a satellite."

"And say she gets it?"

"A single satellite can take lots and lots of photos when it makes its pass," she said. "Once it's positioned, I can have a near-real-time image stream going immediately."

Sam nodded.

"I'll talk to her right now," he said.

Eric received the call from Howie Wallach, an audio restoration expert with the LoC in Washington, D.C., a little before midday. As he listened to his instructions for cleaning the cylinders, he found himself stuck with a somewhat unsettling image of Granger holding a blowtorch to his red, blistered posterior.

"Just don't break the persnickety thing to smithereens like I've done a hundred times," Wallach cautioned before hanging up.

Eric had nervously wondered whether he might have been better off without that added snippet of advice.

Now, twenty minutes later, he perched over the cylinders on a lab stool, slipped his forefinger and middle finger into one wax blank's hollow core, spread them wide, and delicately lifted it up off the tray. Slightly to his right were a spray can of compressed air, and a large aluminum bowl containing a mixture of Labtone detergent compound, technical grade isopropyl alcohol, and de-ionized water. Also on the counter were several small micropile cleaning cloths, a roll of nonabrasive cotton wipes, and a few outspread paper towels.

The cylinder was badly crusted with mold, the growth speckling its grooves like bits of caked white flour.

Reaching for the spray can with his free hand, Eric held the nozzle six inches from the blank and streamed some air over its convex surface, clearing away whatever dust was on it. Next he dipped the cylinder into his detergent solution. As he held it there, fully immersed, he lifted a velveteen cloth off the counter, wet it with the solution, and slowly began wiping it around the cylinder, trying not to apply more than the slightest pressure.

The mold began to dissolve after five minutes, and within twenty minutes every visible trace was gone.

Finally, mindful of Wallach's warning, Eric lifted the cylinder out of the bowl, stood it on the paper towel, and dabbed off the solution with a cotton wipe, not wanting to leave behind any detergent residue.

At last he stretched his arms and exhaled, the tension draining out of him.

He'd not only cleaned the cylinder, but managed to leave it intact.

One down, five to go.

"Howie W., bless your overcooked ass," he said.

And reached for the next blank.

* * *

Alysha's train rumbled into Union Station at one-fifteen, precisely on schedule. Matous had driven her to Via Princessa, one stop down the line from Vincent Grade/Acton, so she could take advantage of the station's more frequent service.

Gathering her purse, she quickly rose from her seat in the first car and looked out her window for the attendant. Sarver was waiting for her there on the platform, where they had arranged to meet up with an exchange of text messages.

"Hey!" he said as the doors slid open. His smile was a little shy. "Recognize me without my uniform?"

Alysha returned the smile and took his hand. He wore an unbuttoned Los Angeles Dodgers road jersey over a longsleeved blue polo shirt. She noticed a tan canvas messenger bag over his shoulder, and a worn, sunbleached ball cap stuffed in his back pocket.

"You look very handsome, Drew," she said, kissing him on each cheek. "I couldn't wait to get here."

He motioned to the sunny blue sky.

"Looks like we've got a perfect day for our adventure."

Alysha met his gaze, nodding, her hand still in his.

"Yes," she said. "Perfect."

"Well," said the Bel Air Palms security guard. "You're back."

"Like *Ahnold*," Kensi said out the window of her SUV.

"Or the ghosts in *Poltergeist*," Deeks said from the passenger seat.

Kensi held her ID out the window, but the guard waved it off.

"My eyes tell me you're the same person you were yesterday. I think Mr. Holloway's at his condo. His assistant got here ten, fifteen minutes ago."

"Murphy?" she said.

The guard nodded. "You can drive right up," he said. "I'll call ahead so they know you're on your way."

She nodded and thanked him.

"Hope Mr. Holloway's hard partying hasn't gotten him in trouble," he said with a sly wink. "I figure he was quite the guy with the moves in his day."

"That sounds about right," Kensi said, and drove on past the booth.

According to public speculation, the U.S. intelligence community's late-generation Block Four satellites boasted optics that could read the license plates of cars. This was hardly a stretch, since declassified photos from earlier spy sats had confirmed they could resolve on objects as *small* as cars.

Sam Hanna knew the satellites could not only see the vehicle's plates, but obtain crystal clear images of its passengers through the windshield, and then identify them with 3D facial recognition technology, or even human skin texture analysis face-rec that turned lines, wrinkles, acne scars, and other distinguishing marks into definitive algorithms.

He studied the pictures on the interactive table in Ops alongside Nell, Callen, and Hetty, thinking they looked as if they were coming from a kite twenty feet in the air, not a low earth-orbit satellite zipping through the upper limits of the atmosphere. He was also thinking the view wasn't pretty—the high-resolution closeups showed block after block of boarded up homes, barbed-wire fences, gang graffiti, trash, weeds, dead tumbleweed… and vultures.

The birds were everywhere, droves of them. Many in the air circling the subdivision's geometrically laid out streets and roads, others perched on rooftops, fences, lampposts, and streetlights. This area very well could be where the safehouse was located, but based solely on the presence of the vultures, the safehouse could be one among dozens, possibly hundreds, they were using as roosts.

"Which of the housing developments are we looking at here?" Sam asked.

"This one's called Flor Linda," Nell said. "It's about fifty miles northwest of us. The closest of two or three."

Sam grunted. "Talk about a burst housing bubble," he said. "The gang tags mean some badass crews are marking turf."

"It's totally *Night of the Living Dead*," Nell said. She shivered. "No one's around but the squatters. And probably the zombies that eat them after dark."

Callen looked at her. "You've been *out* there?"

She nodded.

"I once got lost driving out to Vazquez Rocks and passed it right by."

"On the state route?"

"No, that's where I went wrong. You have to turn off the main road. There's a highway linkup to Flor Linda that was never finished."

Hetty removed her eyeglasses thoughtfully. "Can you bring us in tight on that road?"

Nell nodded, swiping and tapping the tabletop. When the imagery appeared after a few seconds she tossed it up on a wall screen, highlighting either side of the road with red lines.

It wound south off State Route 14 midway between Palmdale and Edwards Air Force Base, the paved segment coming to an abrupt end after the first half mile, where it turned into a pitted gravel and dirt strip.

Hetty studied the flatscreen display, absently rubbing her glasses with a silk handkerchief.

"Dorani mentioned the road to the safehouse was bumpy," she said. "It was the only detail he gave about the drive out. Besides riding in a windowless van."

"Your classic creepmobile," Nell said. "The ideal family vehicle for pervs and killers."

They were all quiet a second. Then Callen turned to her.

"Bring us back to Flor Linda," he said. "We have to keep looking."

18

The drive up to Tip Holloway's condo led to a semicircular parking area with a jacaranda tree in full April bloom. Kensi turned inside to see Murphy standing on the wide front doorstep.

"Didn't the guard say he's been here awhile?" Deeks said, scratching his head. "You'd think he would have a key."

She halted in the shade of the tree, then thought twice and eased the SUV toward the other side of the semicircle.

"No jacaranda love for you?" Deeks said.

She shook her head.

"The pollen is a menace to my paint job," she said. "A *smelly* menace."

Deeks frowned.

"I can relate," he said, reaching for the door handle.

Murphy turned around to face them as they approached, his worried expression noticeable from several feet away.

"Mr. Murphy," Kensi said. "Is everything all right?"

He didn't reply. Deeks saw the sun glint off an object in his hand and furrowed his brow.

"There's his key," he said to Kensi. "So why isn't he using it to get in?"

They quickened their pace. Something was definitely wrong here.

"Mr. Murphy, what's going on?" she said.

He stood there apprehensively as they came up to the doorstep, stopping below him on the paved walkway.

"I can't get in the door," he said at last, wobbling the key. "Something's blocking it inside."

"Have you knocked?"

"Knocked, rang the bell, called on my cell..." He shook his head. "No answer."

"And you're sure he's home?"

Murphy nodded.

"Mr. Holloway knew I was on my way over," he said. "He phoned to tell me you were coming, and that he wanted me here when you showed up."

"That the same key you always use?" Deeks asked, pointing his chin at it.

Murphy gave another nod. "There's nothing wrong with it," he said. "The lock opened okay. But the door's jammed shut."

Kensi stepped past Murphy, tested the knob, pushed the door with her shoulder. It didn't budge.

"Mr. Holloway!" she exclaimed, rapping on it. "This is Agent Blye! If you're home, please open up."

No answer. She pressed an ear against the door, waited, heard no sounds from inside the condo, and knocked again.

"*Mr. Holloway, if you don't answer us, we'll have to force our way in!*"

Nothing.

Kensi moved away from the door, eyeing the sash

windows on either side of it. Then she reached into her blazer for her car keys and tossed them to Deeks.

"The tire iron's in back," she said.

He sprinted around to the SUV's tail section, returning seconds later with the metal rod.

"You two better move back," he said, looking at both Kensi and Murphy.

They did without a word.

Deeks went up to the window, raised the iron from his side, and swung it once against the pane. It shattered with a loud crash, shards of glass pouring onto the lawn and walkway. Jabbing the tire iron into the broken window, he moved it around the frame to clear away the jagged fragments of glass still attached to it. Then he shot a quick glance over at Kensi and hoisted himself through the opening.

He looked around quickly. The living room was empty, everything neatly in place. His eyes swept over the gramophone, the Warhol print. *Tyger, tyger.*

Deeks turned and ran into the hall, peripherally aware of Kensi climbing in the window to his left.

There was a partly open door in front of him. All at a glance he saw the twisted bedsheet looped around its knob, then run over the door's upper edge.

His heart skipping a beat, he rushed up to the door. And then halted for the slightest instant, looking into the room beyond.

Theodore Holloway was suspended there from the sheet, his feet still on the floor. The makeshift noose he'd fashioned was high up around his throat, its knot positioned to cut off his oxygen supply.

Deeks pressed his fingers to Holloway's neck, feeling for a pulse. But he knew the old man was gone. His face was purple, his tongue protruding from his mouth. He'd bitten halfway through it in his violent final throes, bloodying his lips, chin and shirt.

Deeks swooped in a breath and went back into the hallway to untie the sheet from the doorknob. He saw Kensi rushing toward him, and shook his head.

She met his gaze.

"Oh, man," she said. Then opened her mouth to add something more, and couldn't think of any words.

"We better call an ambulance," Deeks said after a second.

Kensi exhaled, nodding.

And reached for her cellphone.

She had chosen a light lunch at the Bean n' Crème coffeehouse on North Alameda, only a block and a half from Union Station.

Drew liked the place. It was clean, warm, and atmospheric in a funky sort of way, with reclaimed wood walls, a tin ceiling, a blond bamboo floor, and alternative rock music playing at an ambient level.

Really, though, anyplace Milena wanted to go would have been fine with him. As long as it had a table where they could sit and talk, Drew figured he was golden.

"So," he said, "how's the food?"

"Very good," she said, and took a small forkful of her black bean and corn salad. "It's just enough to keep me fueled up… I don't want to be too stuffed with a busy day and night ahead of us."

Drew chuckled.

"I know what you mean," he said. "I get downright sleepy after eating big."

She smiled a little, swallowed, then reached for

her jasmine tea and sipped.

Drew took a bite of his chicken wrap, thinking this was as good a moment as any to spring his surprises on her.

"I'd like to show you something," he said. "Well, a couple of things."

She sat quietly, waiting, her eyes on his face.

Drew reached inside the messenger bag he'd slung over the back of his seat, and took out a brand-new Dodgers cap.

"First things first," he said, handing it to Milena. "I picked this up for you on my way to the train station. Hope it's the right size…"

"I'm sure it is." She took the cap from him and put it on her head, adjusting it with a downward tug of the brim. "What do you think?"

He smiled.

"Looks great," he said. "You like it?"

"Love it," she said. "Thank you, Drew. That's a very sweet gift."

His smile broadened.

"While I'm at it," he said, "I want to show you something else."

He reached into the bag again, extracting the map he'd brought in a transparent vinyl sleeve.

"This is a copy," he said, and passed it across to her. "My grandfather made the original a long time ago."

She held the map in both hands, studying it through the sleeve.

The writing on top said:

PIGGYBACK YARD GERMAN POW HOLDING AREA

"I told you about Poppo… my gramps," Drew said. "As you can tell from all the crooked lines and squiggles, he sketched it out freehand." He laughed a bit. "Guess he had a thing against rulers."

She raised her eyes to look at him.

"This map shows the entrance to the underground passageways," she said.

Drew nodded. "And their layout," he said. "X marks the spot, like in an old pirate map. The big difference being there's no buried treasure. Just some dank, dark, crumbly tunnels to nowhere... as you'll see for yourself in a little while."

Her eyes stayed on his face.

"One man's trash is another man's treasure," she said.

Drew shrugged, but he was smiling again. "And one man's Nowheresville another's Dreamland?"

She laughed.

"I can go with that," she said, and forked some more salad into her mouth.

"Nell, wait," Callen said. He quickly read off a set of coordinates on the wall screen. "Give me a closeup right there."

She nodded, already zooming in on a segment of Flor Linda's twenty-three-acre tract of desert real-estate.

It was now 1:20 P.M., and she'd begun her fifth image sequence five minutes ago, methodically organizing the torrent of Block Four satellite photos into a gridded, intricately detailed layout of the subdivision. For Hetty, Callen, and Sam, it was almost like they'd been shrunk down to fit inside a low-flying surveillance drone.

The current sequence had initially presented a

numbing reprise of the abandonment and neglect laid out in the previous four—street after street of decaying homes orbited by scavenger birds, and surrounded by barbed wire, weeds, and refuse.

But now everyone in the room could see what Callen thought he'd seen.

Nell moved in tighter, tighter, all of them watching in silence.

"This is too good to be true," Callen said. He glanced around at the others. "It *has* to be the safehouse."

No one else spoke. Beside him, Sam was staring at the image onscreen...

The tan stucco house.

The battered, windowless white van in the driveway.

And the vulture, dark and hunched, on its roof...

Hetty turned to the agents.

"You'd better get out there right away," she said.

19

The Challenger's big-horsepower engine throbbing, Sam saw two choppers overhead as he turned sharply off the highway link onto Flor Linda's entry road. Wasplike UH-72A Lakotas, they were bristling with thermal I/R surveillance equipment.

The OSP was used to operating in the shadows, Hetty Lange's natural element. But this time Hetty had called in the cavalry.

He glanced at his dashboard's center console, then at Callen.

"Where's the downlink?" he said.

Callen tapped the touchscreen. "I'm entering the access code again," he said. "Think I screwed up when you hit a bump."

"You're blaming *me*?"

Callen shrugged.

"You or the bump," he said. "Same difference."

Sam sped past the derelict properties they had seen in the Block Four photorecon imagery. It was almost 2:30 P.M., a full hour since they'd set out from headquarters, and by now the L.A. County Sheriff's Department's Special Enforcement Bureau tac teams would have established a perimeter around their target.

Callen input the downlink code again. This time the chopper's I/R video stream appeared, replacing the console's GPS view.

The combined daylight and warm temperature made nearly everything in the image radiate in the red and orange wavelengths... the safehouse's roof and walls, the windows, the walks and driveway. The body of the parked van was bright yellow, almost white, from sitting in the sun. Even the dry, overgrown shrubs, grass, and weeds around the house mostly showed red-orange from absorbing the sun's heat, with a few scattered blue and purple spots indicating shadier areas.

"Leader, this is Alpha Bird," Callen heard the helicopter pilot say over the air-to-ground radio. Both he and Sam were wearing lightweight bone conduction headsets that left their ears uncovered. *"I notice your log-in... you with us yet?"*

Callen copied him. "We just cleared the entry road," he said. "What's happening at the target?"

"It looks clear outside on the ground," the pilot said. *"We aren't sure about the premises. Window blinds are down, can't see what's inside."*

Which essentially told Callen what he already knew. He hadn't expected miracles. Thermal sensors could not see through walls—and therefore couldn't reveal whether there was anyone in the house. But they *would* show human heat emissions on the surrounding property, meaning anyone trying to make off, or hide outside, would be detectable.

Callen peered out the windshield as Sam shot along, his tires spinning up dirt and pebbles. A BearCat armored truck was stopped in the intersection up ahead, SEB personnel in olive drab uniforms pouring from its doors. He could hear the commander shouting orders beneath the throb of the Lakotas' rotors.

"We're here," Callen said over the radio. "Hold your positions. Out."

"Got it."

Sam slid the Challenger to a halt yards from the BearCat, exiting his door at once, Callen rushing from the other side. The agents wore light armor over their shirts and had large badges on their belts, the letters NCIS emblazoned on their chests in white to leave no mistake about their identities. Both had assault rifles slung over their arms, Sam a full-size M-4 carbine, Callen an H&K 416 subcompact, his SIG-P226 service pistol tucked into a crossdraw holster on his left hip.

He raced up to the SEB commander. "I'm Agent Callen, this is Agent Hanna."

"Captain Porat," the commander said. He pointed down the side road blocked off by his truck. "Target's fifteen yards up."

"Still no sign of occupants?" Sam said.

Porat shook his head. "We have entry teams onsite. Sergeant Leo's your point there. LASD regulars are in close perimeter."

Callen snapped Sam a glance. "What do you think?"

"We go right in," he said. "Can't waste time."

Callen turned to Porat.

"Hold steady," he said. "Tell your men at the house we're on our way."

Porat nodded. "This is your dance," he said. "Good luck."

The agents sprinted up the road as it curved between several crumbling properties, then saw patrol cars across the blacktop, flashers on, sheriff's deputies milling around them. An SEB entry team was gathered on the front lawn beyond the vehicle cordon. Sam spotted a short, chunky man with sergeant's stripes on his sleeve in the middle of the group.

He trotted up to him. "Leo?"

"Agent Hanna." The sergeant tapped his headset. "The commander told me you were on your way."

Sam gestured toward the house. "What's the situation, Sarge?"

"I've got four men at each entrance, front and back," Leo said. "Can't tell if anyone's inside."

"You ready to move?"

"Yes, sir. At your say-so."

Sam turned to Callen, caught his nod, then turned back to Leo.

"Okay. Let's roll."

The three of them ran across the yard to the front door, heads low, rifles in their hands. One of four armored tacs posted on the right of the door held the ram, the man behind him a ballistic shield. The two at the end of the stack had their semiautomatic weapons ready to fire.

Leo, Sam, and Callen moved to the left of the doorframe, the sergeant talking to the rear breaching team over his throat mike.

"Beta, on one," he said. "Do you read?"

"*Yes, sir.*" Callen and Sam heard, their radios switched to the ground freq now. "*Loud and clear.*"

Sam thumbed his M-4's bolt catch as he waited.

Leo began his countdown. "Three... two... *one...*"

The tac with the ram swung it against the door like a pendulum, slamming it hard under the lockplate, reducing its frame to splinters with a single blow. As the door crashed inward, one of the tacs on the right tossed a flashbang into the room beyond, and then the men went rushing through the entryway, storming in behind their bullet resistant shield, Sergeant Leo, Sam, and Callen following close on their heels.

The room was large and empty, no furniture besides a couch and some recliners…

And sleeping bags. Sam and Callen saw several on the bare wood floor.

They moved deeper into the house with the tacs, hearing the sound of hurried footsteps as Beta Team poured in through the backdoor. Leo shouting terse commands, the two teams moved from room to room, storming through hallways in a rapid, coordinated sweep.

The place seemed unoccupied. There was a bed with pillows and tousled sheets in one room. More sleeping bags in another. The bathroom had soap, toothpaste, and toilet paper. Peering down a hall into the kitchen, Callen saw a trash can filled with crumpled towels, paper cups, and plastic food wrappers.

Unoccupied, but not unlived-in.

Hugging the wall, Sam and Callen moved down the hallway to a closed door, a couple of tacs lining up behind them. Sam tried the doorknob, found it locked, and glanced around at the guy with the battering ram.

The guy moved along the wall to the door.

"Police! Get down on the floor with your hands over your heads," he shouted.

Then he swung the ram again and the door crashed open.

Sam led the way into the room, Callen behind him, buttonhooking to the opposite side of the entryway with his subcompact's barrel outthrust.

Like the other rooms, it was vacant. But its furnishings were conspicuous. Laboratory tables, stools, a metal cabinet on the far wall.

A gun cabinet.

Callen strode over to it, noticed the door was slightly ajar, and pulled it open.

It didn't surprise him to discover it was empty.

He turned to Sam. "Nothing," he said. "There's nothing here. They cleared out and took everything with them."

Sam lowered his weapon, filled his cheeks with air, and slowly let it escape through his mouth.

"Question is," he said, "where'd they go?"

Callen just looked at him without anything resembling an answer, thinking they needed one fast.

Matous checked his dashboard clock as he guided the Savana over the dusty, sunwashed highway blacktop. It was 3:15 P.M., hours earlier than he had expected to be making the trip across the desert. But adaptability was an operational necessity—a basic principle of warfare.

In the Marines, Matous had learned that engagement was friction, and friction created turbulent change. You couldn't always control its tempo. But you had to anticipate the changes and be ready to adjust on the run.

You needed to be mobile.

He looked over at Gaspar, who sat bolt straight in the passenger seat, staring out his window at the yellow, barren Mojave hills. Matous thought he looked nervous, but not overly consumed with fear, and that was all right.

"Are you ready to die, Matous?" Gaspar said after a

while. "Can you honestly tell me you're ready?"

The question caught Matous a little by surprise. He had already turned his mind toward timing and practicalities.

A half hour ago, Tomas, Yuri, and Pavel had swung off the highway into Vincent Grade/Acton, boarding the three o'clock train into Los Angeles. It would put them at Sun Valley around four-thirty—and that was where they would strike.

Tactically, the station was perfect. Seize the train further up the line, and you left time for the Dispatch and Operations Center in Pomona to detect a problem—especially as you began skipping stations. But the off-peak train out of Sun Valley normally bypassed both the Burbank and Glendale stops en route to Union Station, where it was scheduled for a 5:00 P.M. arrival.

That gave Tomas a full thirty minutes before anyone at the DOC even sniffed anything irregular or unusual. It was a good window of opportunity.

He drove on, aware Gaspar was staring at him, waiting for his answer.

Matous considered it now, then tightened his jaw.

"I'm prepared to die for the cause," he said. "And take a lot of other people with me."

Silence. Gaspar looked at him another moment before returning his eyes to the monotonous hills outside.

They said nothing more the rest of the way into Los Angeles.

At 3:30 P.M., an eyestrained, stiff-necked, and sore-shouldered Eric Beale rolled across the room on his lab stool, carrying the fifth and last of the brown wax cylinders from their cleaning tray to the Mona audio restoration scanner.

Eric had started his scans an hour earlier with the only recording whose container bore any markings besides a catalog number: a date written on its lid in faded, barely legible ink—2/17/1921—with three letters—W.G.R.—penned beneath it. Twenty minutes later, his first digital surrogate was complete, and with good results despite the mold damage that had eaten deep into the cylinder's grooves. As Mona's software converted his waveform transcript to audio files, he'd heard the high, ghostly voice of a young boy rise above recurrent flurries of hisses, crackles, and pops, singing along to the accompaniment of a choppy, inexpertly strummed acoustic guitar.

The audio reproduction was clear enough for him to make out the lyrics without a problem:

> *Strange things have happened*
> *Like never before*
> *My baby told me*
> *I would have to go*
>
> *I can't be good no more*
> *Once like I did before*
> *I can't be good, baby*
> *Honey, because the world's gone wrong*

The next three recordings consisted of Sutton's recollection of his maiden voyage aboard a naval warship as a young ensign, an off-key duet of "I'm Sitting On Top of the World" he'd sung with his wife Mara, who he introduced as his "heartbeat" at the top of the number... and a spoken draft of an ardent, and spicy, love letter he'd written to a woman named Cleo, who may not have been his heartbeat, but had obviously made his pulse race.

They were remarkable—and in the case of the letter, *shameless*—glimpses of the former senator's past, but Eric hadn't had time to enjoy them. Not with the city of Los Angeles's *present* threatened by a group of maniacs trying to build a dirty bomb, and the OSP desperately seeking to beat them to the stash of fissile uranium—courtesy of Hitler, Tojo, and a couple of crooked American officers.

Hunched over Mona now, his feet on the chrome rung of his stool, he slipped the fifth cylinder onto the scanner's horizontal spindle and then glanced over at Nell, who was sitting at the system's keyboard/ flatscreen console.

"Oh, throw yourself in a hole, and say here goes nothing," he said.

She looked around at him. "First known use of the expression?"

"*Fibre and Fabric, A Record of American Textile Industries in the Cotton and Woolen Trade*," he said. "The Saturday, November third, eighteen eighty-nine edition."

Nell looked wistful. "I want to eat oyster pizza with you until I can't," she said.

Eric swallowed, his throat suddenly thick.

"We should get this done," he said.

She nodded, tapping her keyboard. An instant later, the cylinder began to rotate under Mona's confocal laser lens—a virtual phonograph needle imaging its grooves in microscopic detail, then sending the three-dimensional profiles to the system software for reassembly as sound files.

Eric lowered his feet from the stool and pushed himself to Nell's end of the table, where a composite map of the cylinder's surface was forming on her display. To him it was like looking at tire prints, each tread representing an individual groove.

"Okay," Nell said. "I'm sending the audio stream to the computer speakers."

He inhaled deeply, staring at the screen.

"Your heavy breathing is *so* sexy." she said, and clicked the keys.

A second later, a deep voice over the speakers:

"This is Admiral Elias P. Sutton, United States Navy, Commander Naval Construction Battalion Center, Port Hueneme. The date of this recording is August twelfth, nineteen forty-five…"

Eric glanced at Nell. He still hadn't exhaled.

"…am preparing this document to log the storage site of the uranium two thirty-five that arrived aboard the hold of the German U-boat codenamed Minazuki-One, and was subsequently diverted from Los Alamos National Laboratory…"

Nell's eyes widened.

"Eric," she said in a trembling whisper. "Eric…"

He finally exhaled, realizing he hadn't breathed in a long time.

"This is it," he said, and then listened to the rest in silence.

20

"That's it up ahead, as if you couldn't figure it out for yourself," Drew said, smiling. "The famous—or should I say famously dumpy—Piggyback Yard. Which must top the list of all-time first date turnoffs."

Alysha laughed, walking alongside him on Lamar Street between the cement plant and the San Antonio winery. She was wearing the Dodgers cap he'd brought her as a gift, her quilted purse slung over her bare, tanned shoulder. Inside the purse was a makeup compact, her forged Milena James passport, and a wallet containing a driver's license and some cash. In a concealed carry belt under the waist of her jeans was a hand-tooled Beltrame automatic stiletto, and a slim, lightweight Ruger LC9 handgun.

"Stop it, Drew," she said. "This is going to be pure heaven."

He looked at her, his smile growing surer. "You know," he said, "I'm thinking you just might be the cure for my nerd insecurity."

Alysha slipped her arm through his.

"You should probably think a little less, and enjoy a little more," she said, walking closer to him.

They continued toward the end of Lamar Street. It led directly to the train yard's access road, which ran toward its entrance between cracked, spalled concrete retaining walls. A railway overpass several yards up ahead marked the division with a wide band of shadow. The graffiti-tagged metal sign facing them from the middle of the span read:

LOS ANGELES TRANSPORTATION CENTER
PRIVATE PROPERTY
NOT A THRU STREET

"Heaven's gate," Drew said. He gestured up at it, then pointed straight ahead toward a sentry booth. "You won't find Saint Peter in there, though. Just an ordinary security guard."

"Will we have a problem getting in?"

He noticed she was no longer smiling, and realized he should have explained.

"We're good, no worries," he said. "Come on."

They approached the booth, the guard stepping out onto the concrete island to greet them.

"Drew, *qué pasa*?" he said.

"*Nada mucho*," Drew said as they soul shook. "Jorge, this is my friend, Milena. Milena, Jorge."

The guard turned and offered her his hand in a more courtly manner.

"Pleasure," he said. "You're the history buff, huh?"

She nodded. "I see I've had advance billing."

Jorge chuckled.

"Me and Drew go back to high school," he said. "When he told me you were coming for a tour of the yard, I thought, 'Girl's in serious trouble.'"

"Oh?"

His look said he was kidding.

"Don't get nervous," he replied. "Drew can tell you everything about this place. I just never thought he'd actually meet somebody who'd want to *hear* it."

She was smiling again.

"I assure you," she said, "I'm a willing victim."

Jorge grinned and checked his watch.

"Well, you two still have a few hours to the Dodger game," he said to her. "Tell me on the way out how you like his tour."

Drew laughed.

"You thinking of charging my victim admission?" he joked.

Jorge laughed, shaking his head.

"The tour's free to all survivors," he said, and motioned them around the lowered barricade.

A moment later, they walked past it into the yard.

"Piggyback Yard," Hetty Lange said. "The world is full of obvious things which nobody by any chance ever observes."

"Sherlock Holmes," Granger said. "*Study in Scarlet*."

Hetty shook her head. "Close," she said. "It's *Hound of the Baskervilles*."

Granger looked at her.

"That's what I thought," he said. "I like keeping you on your toes."

She smiled thinly. It was now 4:15 P.M., and they were standing with Nell and Eric in Ops, where the two analysts had just finished their second playback of the Sutton recording's virtual clone. Kensi and Deeks stood nearby—they'd hastened upstairs from the bullpen after returning with the bad news about Holloway.

"When you think about it, the whole thing makes sense," Eric said from his console. He threw a satellite map of the train yard onto the plasma screen, highlighting the yard's borders in red, then dragging an arrow to its western margin. "This is the coastal shipping line. The uranium would have come south from Santa Barbara here, then been trucked to the hiding place somewhere else in the yard."

Hetty was nodding.

"We assumed it was only a stop along the way," she said. "That the drums were being shipped to a prearranged endpoint across the country."

"But Piggyback was as far as they went," Granger said. "Sutton and Holloway were playing the nuclear market. Salting the uranium away until they could gauge postwar supply and demand..."

"And set their price for the highest bidder," Kensi said.

"We need to sort this out fast," Granger said to Eric. "Run the recording again. Pick it up right after Sutton's intro."

Eric nodded, tapping the console again.

"*...diverted from the Los Alamos National Laboratory pending final disposition,*" Sutton's voice said over the speakers. His inflections were clipped, with a slight British overlay—what was once called New York genteel. "*After much consideration, it was decided to cache the materiel at Deep Dive Alpha Zero One, a former locomotive construction shop in the Union Pacific LATC. The structure was requisitioned for the war effort and deemed highly suitable for storage, as tunnel excavation could proceed from an existing basement—*"

"Okay, pause it right there," Granger said. "Do we know where the shop was?"

"Not exactly," Eric said. "In that way Sutton kind of blew it with this spoken map."

"He had a clear crystal ball for playing the futures market with uranium," Nell said. "But he had no idea the steam locomotive would be obsolete three or four years after the war. By nineteen-fifty all the construction and repair shops were torn down, including the one Deep Dive glommed…"

"Wait," Hetty said, holding up a hand. She had been studying the satellite map as they spoke. "Let's focus on the positive. We *do* know some things that can help us."

She stepped behind Eric's console and dragged the arrow onscreen to the southern edge of the yard.

"The yard's oldest track runs along the banks of the Los Angeles River," she said. "The river's natural grade slopes, east to west, toward central L.A.—laying the line there made it easier for trains moving freight into the city."

Granger's eyes filled with comprehension.

"The general shops would've been built along the main track," he said. "To service the trains after their cross-country hauls."

"Most of them," she said. "I believe some shops went up at the north end as the yard expanded. But if we're playing the odds, I suggest we pull an old map of it from the historical archives and start our search there."

Eric scratched behind his ear. "Aren't those south tracks used by Metroline nowadays?"

"Yes," Granger said. "They cross the river to Union Station. It's the shortest and most direct route."

"Very convenient for someone wanting to haul the uranium into the city," Kensi said.

Silence.

Granger moved his gaze around the room again.

"Once LAPD starts scouring the yard, people will want to know why," he said. "If even a whisper about hidden radioactive material leaks out..."

"...it'll be mass freakout time," Deeks said.

Granger nodded. "We need to keep a lid on this. For now."

"Marty and I can head down to the yard and poke around," Kensi said. She turned to Eric. "When do you think you'll have those old maps?"

"It won't take long," he said. "I'll shoot them over to you as soon as they're downloaded."

Granger exhaled a long, deep breath.

"Let's move," he said.

"We're almost at the tunnel entrance," Drew said. "Not that it's visible from here."

Alysha's pulse quickened. They had crossed a small freight transfer station bordering the Los Angeles River, then turned to follow a high concrete embankment channeling its flow west toward the downtown area and out to sea.

"Where is it?" she asked.

He pointed straight ahead. "See that row of storage sheds?"

She looked. The long, windowless industrial structures—four of them—were lined along the wall as it ran under a sagging, disused rail trestle.

"Yes," she said. "I see."

"It's in the fourth shed," he said. "The last one in the group."

Her dark eyes narrowed. The shed was partly blocked from sight behind one of the trestle's steel pylons, and further hidden by the crisscrossing shadows of its rust-scabbed upper framework.

Drew lowered his hand. "Come on," he said. "I'm sure you'd rather check it out than hear me go on and on."

They continued up the littered path. Walking through the station moments ago, Alysha had observed several yellow forklifts parked around a spur of railroad track. But they were all unoccupied, and there were no trailer trucks or yard workers in sight.

"I hope this doesn't sound ignorant of me," she asked now, motioning toward the track. "But is the transfer station active? It's so deserted."

Drew turned his head to smile at her.

"Not ignorant at all," he said. "In fact, you're very observant." He paused. "Once upon a time, American Pacific employed two thousand yard workers... most of them in giant shops along this stretch. You know how many there are now?"

She shook her head.

"A hundred," he said.

"In the entire yard?"

"And that includes security, not that there's a ton," he said. "Rail freight isn't totally obsolete, but Piggyback's close."

They reached the first of the metal sheds. It stood on a cracked concrete base, its door secured with a rusty chain and padlock. Random pieces of trash were heaped in front—newspapers, junk food wrappers, styrofoam takeout boxes, crumpled cigarette packs, and beer cans.

A squirrel chittered loudly from the shed's roof as they went by, catching their attention.

"He's the neighborhood watch," Drew said. "These

sheds haven't been used in decades."

"Really?"

He nodded. "Back in the Caleb Holloway era they held crossties and rails," he said. "Later on they stored crated cargo. But freight's only allowed to stay in the yard overnight these days, so it never leaves the trucks. There aren't enough personnel for long-term storage."

They walked on into the trestles' patchy shade. At a glance the fourth shed didn't look any different from the rest—its exterior blemished with rust, rafts of garbage heaped against its front and sides.

Then Alysha noticed the chain on the door. It was enclosed in a nylon web, with an integrated lock.

"Modern," she said, motioning to it.

Drew looked at her. "You really don't miss a whole lot," he said. "Somebody replaced the old one."

"Do you know who?"

Drew reached into his pocket for a keyring and thumbed to a tubular key.

"Rocky the Squirrel isn't the only guy looking out for things around here," he said with a wink. Then he turned to the shed. "Are you bothered by creepy crawlies?"

"It depends."

"On?"

"Where they creep and crawl," she said.

Drew laughed and went up to the door, stepping over the brown and green fragments of shattered beer bottles. Turning the key in the lock, he flipped up the hasp and pulled at the door handle. The door squealed on its rotting hinges but opened easily.

While his back was turned, Alysha quickly pulled her cellphone from her purse to check that the GPS tracking was on.

"Ready?" Drew asked after a second, glancing back over his shoulder.

She'd dropped the phone back into her purse.

"I couldn't be readier," she said, and followed him into the shed.

Sam and Callen were driving back to L.A. on the Antelope Valley Freeway when they got an encrypted call from Hetty. In the passenger seat, Callen switched his smartphone to its secure voice mode and compared notes with her over the Bluetooth.

"I don't like this," Sam asked after she signed off.

"Neither do I," Callen said. "If the uranium's at the train yard, and the bad guys get hold of it before we can track them down..."

He let the sentence trail. A short while ago at the Flor Linda hideout, they had watched an SEB bomb dog give its handler a passive alert, instantly sitting down beside him in the room with the lab tables and gun cabinet. Minutes later, a chem-bio sweep team entering with handhelds detected the chemical constituents of smokeless gunpowder... and, worse yet, traces of nitroamine, a high explosive taggant.

It all added up to the people who'd bolted from the place carrying along some awesome firepower.

"It's four-thirty," Callen said. "That leaves seven and a half hours till the anniversary of the Armenian genocide is past tense."

"I hear you," Sam said, eyes on the road. "We've spent two days chasing after Sutton's murderer. But the main thing is to find out what those Secret Army diehards are planning."

"The nitroamine worries me," Callen said. "It tells

us they've got military grade plastic explosives. Half what it takes to build a dirty bomb."

"The other half being the uranium," Sam said. "But we're talking two *tons* of the stuff. Four *thousand* pounds. How are they going to do it on the fly? It isn't like they can pack all that into a suitcase."

"Or even a car," Callen said. "I'm betting on a vehicle, though."

"Say they load it onto a truck… something like an eighteen wheeler," Sam said. "That could do it."

Callen didn't appear convinced. After a minute he sat up straight in his seat.

"Sam," he said. "Think."

Sam gave him a look of dawning comprehension.

"A *train*?" he said.

Callen just regarded him in silence.

Gripping the wheel, Sam jammed his foot down on the gas and sped on toward the city.

21

It was 4:37 P.M. when the Metroline train pulled into Sun Valley roughly on schedule, air hissing through its brake pipes. Barring the unexpected, the train would arrive at Union Station a few minutes after 5:00 P.M.

In the cab car near the operator's cabin, Tomas looked out his window at the almost empty platform. He counted five people spread out along its length, and a group of three young men in tee shirts and jeans at the front end. One was wearing a red Anaheim Angels baseball cap.

As the train drew to a halt, Tomas stood to take his haversack from the overhead compartment. His companions had done so minutes before, looking as if they were preparing to disembark—Pavel moving down the aisle into the third car, and Yuri into the fifth and last.

Now the doors slid open and he watched the three men in jeans board the train. The one in the baseball cap gave Tomas the slightest of nods as he and the other two took seats down the aisle.

Tomas slipped the pack over one shoulder, knowing he had to move fast.

Only a small fraction of the train's seats were occupied. In his walk-through after it left the last stop—Newhall Station—he'd counted thirty-two heads: ten men, thirteen women, four children, and the five conductors. Add four of the seven who'd just gotten on and it made for a total of thirty-six people.

It was an easily manageable number.

But one thing at a time.

He looked down the long central aisle at his car's other passengers. Besides the three men who'd just come aboard, he saw a middle-aged businessman working on his laptop, and a young man and woman in Dodgers jerseys who had been necking since they boarded at Via Princessa. The conductor was also on his level, occupying a single seat at the far end of the car. Finally, he'd seen a woman with an infant in a baby carrier board at Newhall and climb to the upper deck. Otherwise it was unoccupied.

Tomas was certain that none of the riders on his level had taken notice of him.

Reaching into his pack's outer compartment, he slipped out his ghost gun and a balaclava and turned his back to the car's long middle aisle. Then he pulled the mask down over his head, shrugged the pack over one shoulder, and hurried toward the stairwell to the operator's cabin. With the gun close against his side, he swung directly past the CCTV dome, rushed up the short flight of stairs, and rapped on the cabin door twice.

He waited. Once the train left the station, the driver would be automatically locked inside his cabin to prevent an intruder from accessing the controls with the train in motion.

But the driver needed to be able to enter and exit

during stops, so the cabin would be unlocked now.

"One minute, please," he said through the door. It opened slightly and he looked out at Tomas. "Hello, sir... is something wrong?"

Tomas moved closer, placing his free hand on the outside of the door.

"The woman upstairs," he said, motioning back with his head. "It's her baby—something's wrong."

The operator's face grew instantly concerned. He opened the door wider.

Tomas pushed it inward with a hard shove, stepping through into the cabin. He saw the concern on the man's face turn to fear as he brought up his rifle and squeezed the trigger.

The conductor crumpled to the cabin floor, dead, a crimson flower of blood spreading open in the middle of his chest.

Tomas dragged the body around so its foot was wedged in the opening. He didn't intend to be trapped inside.

"The cabin's taken," he said into the mike of his tiny earset. "Get ready to clear out the cars."

"Yes," Yuri replied. "Right away."

Tomas scanned the main controls. The console was identical to the simulator on which he'd practiced in Mexico.

He sat down behind it, checked that the directional selector was on "Forward," and released the airbrake, watching the indicator panel, keeping the locomotive's independent brakes applied. It would take several seconds for the airbrake signal to travel down the full length of the train.

When the rear PSI began rising, he took a deep breath, grabbed the throttle with his left hand, and notched the lever up from Idle to Run 1, feathering the brake with his right hand to counterbalance the surge of the engine.

"This is it, we're rolling," he said into his mike now, his voice tightly controlled.

An instant later, the train heaved forward.

Yuri sat at the end of the fifth car with his back to the aisle, his haversack on the floor between his legs. As Tomas powered the train into motion, he slipped his ghost gun from the pack, shielding it from view with his body as he looked quickly around.

There were six passengers in the car with him—two men in office clothes on the right side of the aisle, a third, disheveled-looking man further up on that side, fast asleep, and a pretty dark-haired Latin woman with two young boys on the left. She was speaking Spanish to the children as she passed them snacks from a large green tote bag. Meanwhile the conductor stood leaning against the door mid-car.

Yuri had not seen anyone upstairs.

He launched to his feet and turned toward the front of the car, holding the weapon ready in automatic mode. As he stepped into the aisle, the conductor instantly noticed the gun and pushed himself off the door, his eyes wide and stunned under the brim of his cap.

"Hey! What are you—?"

"Shut up." Yuri aimed at him, remembering his English. "No more talk."

The conductor froze, staring at the gun in horror.

Yuri's eyes swept the car. The passengers gaped at him from their seats, the mother with her arms around her boys.

"Everyone move to first car!" he shouted, gesticulating with the gun barrel. He leveled it at the office workers. "You two... *now*."

They rose from their seats, one man letting a briefcase slide off his lap to the floor.

Yuri saw the woman hesitate, her arms enfolding the boys. The smaller one had started crying.

He walked down the aisle toward her.

"*Move*," he barked. "Do as I tell you!"

She got to her feet, still holding the boys close to her side.

Yuri herded the passengers up the aisle. As he neared the door to the fourth car, he stopped by the sleeping man in rumpled clothes.

"You!" he shouted. "Open your eyes."

The man blinked awake, giving Yuri a fuzzy, confused look.

"What's goin' on?" he said. Then saw the weapon in his hands. "Hey... c'mon... take it easy..."

Yuri jabbed the gun into his scruffily bearded cheek, pushing his head sideways with its barrel. "Shut your mouth," he said.

The man's lips contorted with fear, a low, tremulous moan escaping them. Yuri noticed the crotch of his pants was suddenly wet, the stain spreading to his leg.

"*Dog*," he said. "Stand up and walk."

The man complied without another word of protest, falling in behind the others.

Yuri followed them through the door and into the next car, his gun to the man's back, resisting the urge to put the filth out of his misery then and there.

* * *

"I swear the shed's even gnarlier than I remember from last time," Drew said over his shoulder. He'd pulled a wide-angle LED flashlight from his messenger bag, switched it to its highest intensity, and aimed it in front of him. "But that must've been two years ago, and I barely leaned my head in for a look."

Alysha ducked away from a ragged, dust-clotted spider web, brushing her hand across her face.

"Don't worry," she said. "I'd think it strange if it were any different."

Drew paused a few steps through the door, his flashlight's beam pouring into the shed.

"You have a point," he said. "I still should've warned you."

She stood there looking around. The shed was dark and dusty, its air thick with a sour ammonia smell she recognized as the odor of rodent droppings. Drew's flash revealed stacks of wooden railroad ties against the wall, scattered rail segments, and jumbles of what she guessed was track laying and grading equipment.

He glanced over his shoulder at her, set his bag on the floor between his legs, and held the flashlight out to her handle first.

"Would you mind holding this a sec?" he said.

She took it from him. "Of course not," she said. "But why?"

He shrugged out of his baseball jersey and offered it to her.

"I know it's big," he said. "But I have sleeves and you don't."

Alysha smiled and took it from him.

"You're a squire," she said, slipping her bare arm into it.

The flash in his hand again, Drew turned deeper into

the shed, Alysha close behind him. He brushed aside more dirty, low-hanging webs, clearing a path through the disorganized heaps of tools, spikes, and fasteners.

They had gone about ten feet when he stopped and angled his flash toward a high mountain of crates to their left. It appeared at a glance to be flush against the back of the shed, but after a moment Alysha noticed the large, dark shadow it cast on the wall. Clearly there was some room behind it.

"C'mon," Drew said, turning toward the crates. "Here's where it gets to be fun."

Alysha forced herself to breathe normally. She could feel her pulse beating under the skin behind her ear.

Drew led her over to the pile and then moved around it. She glanced over his shoulder and saw that it stood four or five feet from the wall… further away than she'd thought.

But as she pressed into the space behind him, her eyes were on the dirty concrete floor. He had lowered the head of the flash, revealing what looked like a rectangular cast iron vent or heating grate.

Drew squatted over it, shining the light on the grate. As she leaned down for a closer look, Alysha could see the caked dirt and grime on its mesh fluttering almost imperceptibly in the slight air current from below.

"Okay if I ask you to hang onto this again?" he said, and wobbled the flash. "If you keep it on the vent cover, it'll be a huge help."

She took it from him, aiming it at the vent.

Dropping to his knees, Drew reached down with both hands, gripped the vent cover by the mesh, worked it until it moved a little, and then pulled on it with a low grunt of exertion.

It came up off the floor without resistance.

The flash poured light into a vertical concrete shaft with a fixed ladder descending into heavy gloom.

Drew propped the grate against the wall and looked up at her.

"I'll go first, you can give back the flash once I'm on my way down," he said. "The tunnel's only about ten feet down, and the ladder's always been stable, but watch your step."

"This is fantastic," she said truthfully. "Just fantastic." Her anticipation was nearly unbearable.

Drew smiled. Then he shuffled around to where he could easily grip the ladder and swung his legs over the edge of the shaft.

As he lowered himself into it, Alysha reached into her bag for her cellphone, sent a preset text message to Tomas, then carefully placed it on the floor outside the opening and followed him down.

Kensi screeched up to the train yard's entry checkpoint at ten minutes to five, the SUV jolting hard as she slammed her foot on the brake.

The guard eyed them from inside his booth.

"Hi," he said. "What can I do for—?"

"Agent Blye, NCIS," Kensi said, cutting him off. She held her ID out her window. "Can you tell us if you've seen anyone or anything unusual here today?"

He glanced at the badge card, then lifted his eyes to her face. "There a reason I should've?"

"We need to take a look around," she said. "Do you know anything about the yard's old general shops?"

He gave her an odd look. "You sound just like my buddy," he said. "If you'd come a half hour ago, he could've told you where they used to be."

Her brow creased. "Your friend was here *today*?"

"Still is. Drew's giving his new girl the grand tour…"

"We have to find him," she told the guard. "Now."

"Stick close to me," Drew said, helping Alysha off the ladder's bottom rung. He thumbed his flashlight to its wide-beam setting. "We should be able to see just fine."

He turned and led the way through the darkness.

She walked almost alongside him, the spread of the powerful flash fully illuminating the tunnel ahead. After walking a few feet, he paused to shine it on the low, curved ceiling.

Alysha glanced up at a row of overhead cage lamps—the same sort of fixtures she'd seen in the smugglers' tunnel that brought her and the others in from Mexico.

"Those lamps still worked when I was a kid," Drew said, his voice loud in the silence. "They fed off catenary lines—the overhead electrical wires you used to see on poles and towers." He slid his beam down over the rough concrete wall on their right, where a vertical cable ran from the ceiling to an old, circular metal switchbox. "Here's where I'd turn them on. But once the city upgraded to underground lines, the flow was cut."

She nodded, then looked down the length of the tunnel. Wide enough to allow for two or three people walking abreast, it ran straight for a number of yards, then crossed another passage, and another beyond, before dead-ending about a hundred yards up.

"Where do the other passageways lead?" she asked.

"Not too far, but they're interesting for lots of

reasons," Drew said. He motioned her forward. "C'mon, I'll show you."

They strode toward the first cross-passage, swatting away cobwebs, their shoes gritting on the broken cement floor. As they went deeper into the tunnel, Alysha felt the stale air rustle around her and glanced up to see grated vents like the one they'd used to access it.

Reaching the junction, Drew shone his flash around the corner to their left.

Her eyes narrowed as she stared down the passage. There were openings on both sides, one every few feet, some with empty metal doorframes. A few still had doors hanging ajar from rusty, partly detached hinges.

Steel doors.

"Here's where it gets good," Drew said, turning the corner. "This way."

He strode toward the first doorless entry. A corroded sheet metal sign was mounted on the wall alongside it, the word stenciled across it readable through a layer of soot:

INTERROGATIONS

Alysha studied the sign a moment, then peered through the doorway into a small, square room with a lamp cage on its ceiling, identical to the ones in the main passage.

"Here's where the German prisoners were questioned," Drew said. He shone the light into the space, then turned to point it at the opposite side of the passage. "*There*'s where they were held."

She crossed over to it with him, saw another sign riveted to the wall:

P.W.T.D.
ROOM A
AUTHORIZED PERSONNEL ONLY

"The acronym stands for 'Prisoner of War Temporary Detention.'" Drew cast light through the door. "Take a peek at this room—it's *much* bigger than the first one."

She nodded, estimating it was three or four times the other's size.

"There are two large detention rooms—A and B—and no wonder," Drew said. "Poppo saw dozens of POWs marched in from the rail spur."

Alysha said nothing. She needed to hurry him along. Tomas soon would be diverting the hijacked train toward the yard.

"You mentioned storage areas," she said. "If you don't mind my asking, Drew… where are they?"

He cocked a thumb over his shoulder.

"Back that way," he said. "They're bricked up, don't forget. But I can show them to you now, if you want."

"Yes, please," she said. "I guess I'm a sap for mysteries."

Drew smiled. "Then let's go," he said, and turned back toward the T-juncture.

They crossed the main tunnel into the branching passage, where his flash revealed a tall, wide archway on its right-hand side. Alysha saw at a glance that it was blocked by a masonry wall.

She moved closer, reading the sign next to the entry:

STORAGE

"This is it," Drew said. "The storeroom. Or one of

them. There are three more bricked up entryways in the passage."

"And you've never gone into any of them? Seen what's inside?"

Drew shook his head. "I would've if they weren't all closed off," he said. "Poppo heard talk the Seabees kept fuel drums down here, but he never saw them himself."

Alysha felt the fine hairs on the back of her neck prickle.

"Say there *are* drums... they would be heavy," she said. "I don't see how anyone could have carried them down the shaft we took."

Drew smiled a little. "Guys were big and strong in those days, but not that strong." He motioned down the passage. "I'll show you the loading ramp at the far end. It has a roll-up door that just looks like a service entrance in the river wall."

"Can it still be opened?"

"I gave up trying when I was a kid," Drew said, shaking his head again. "Somebody put a high security lock on it decades ago, and there's all kinds of junk piled outside."

Alysha stepped closer to the wall, noticing it had been discolored by splotches of dark-green mold and some whitish, chalky substance. As Drew came up alongside her, shining his flash directly on its surface, she watched a large black beetle flatten itself into a gap where the decaying mortar had completely fallen out. Clusters of small, pale insect larvae boiled in other open spaces between the bricks.

"You really *aren't* squeamish, are you?" he said.

"My family was very poor," she said, her tone suddenly detached. "I couldn't allow myself to be delicate."

He seemed uncomfortable. "I'm sorry," he said. "I hope I didn't say anything wrong…"

She restored her game face. "My life has changed," she said. "It's fine, Drew."

He looked relieved. Then he returned his eyes to the wall, touching a hand to the powdery white deposit.

"This is salt from the decomposing mortar," he said. "It wasn't here before."

"You sound concerned."

He shrugged a little.

"It tells me moisture's seeping in here from someplace—probably the river." He pushed several bricks under his fingertips and they wobbled loosely. "See how it's weakened the wall? Sooner or later it could undermine the rest of the tunnel the same way."

Alysha was thinking it would first prove a benefit to Karik's team. She estimated they would arrive in four or five minutes, and wanted to neutralize the conductor before he became a problem.

"That ramp," she said. "I'd love to see it now, Drew."

He smiled.

"Let the grand tour continue," he said, turning up the passage.

She smiled back and followed a step behind him, reaching under her blouse to open her waistpack.

"Kensi, we've got maps of Piggyback," Eric said over her SUV's Bluetooth. "In fact, we have so many our maps have maps. I pulled them from the archives of the L.A. County Bureau of Land Development, the Bureau of Engineering, Department of Public Works—"

"Did you work up a historical overlay?"

"Yes. One merging every source into a single

cool *interactive* map," he said. "With intelligent geo-referencing."

"It's ready now?"

"You and Deeks should have it in your email queues."

She drove past a string of flatcars loaded with brown, blue, and red forty-foot containers. It was less than five minutes since she'd left the checkpoint, where the security guard had been unable to reach Drew Sarver on his cellphone.

"Okay," she said as Deeks pulled the map up on her dash console. "Meanwhile, did you notice where the general shops were located?"

"American Pacific built them all around the yard," Eric said. "But my guess is Deep Dive commandeered one of the big old shops on the west or southwest sides."

Deeks was already checking out the map. "Why there?"

"It's where the coastal line's run since the eighteen-sixties," Eric said. "The drums could have come straight up from Hueneme on that track for a quick offload."

Kensi had been driving west for that very reason, but was still on the north edge of the yard leading off the entrance from Lamar.

"Stay with us, we're on our way there," she said.

And drove on for fifty yards to where the access road forked south, picking up speed as she swung sharply into the turn.

Tomas received Alysha's text message on his cell at 5:00 P.M.—a green apple emoji giving him the go-ahead to proceed with the operation. If she was unable to access the tunnel, or had to call a halt to things for any reason, she would have sent him a red apple emoji. A yellow pear would have notified him to stand by for one of the other signals.

Her position was easy to fix. The tracker application on her phone used two different localization systems— GPS and radio tower-based GSM networking—to transmit its whereabouts within a twenty-five foot radius. Because it wouldn't pull a signal once she was in the tunnel, Alysha had dropped the cell outside its entrance before she descended.

Their plan had so far worked to perfection.

He quickly checked her coordinates and saw she was at the southwestern edge of Piggyback Yard, just below the spot where the coastal line curved up toward Santa Barbara and points north. He was now heading toward her from the east, moving along the yard's southern perimeter at a moderate Run 5. Normally the Metroline's approach to Union Station would go directly past her position before swinging west over the Los Angeles River.

Tomas would ensure the train did not get that far— not yet.

Glancing out the cabin window toward his right, he observed row upon row of parked freight and tanker cars stretched along a commercial siding. The adjacent loading area was filled with huge truck-mounted cranes and winches, yellow and orange forklifts, and a smattering of cargo trucks and other vehicles.

He turned to look straight ahead. The switchpoint lights at the crossover were yellow, indicating the track was aligned for diverging movement. That was likely its default position, allowing operators to pull off the main track onto the siding in the event of an emergency. But an operator needed the command center to authorize such action, and Tomas knew the Pomona DOC would take swift notice of his deviation from the route.

He hoped to keep its suspicions from escalating as long as possible.

"Karik," he said into his mike. "I'm about to initiate."

"How long?"

"Two minutes," he said. "Be ready."

Taking hold of the throttle, Tomas notched it down to Run 4, then Run 3. He eased the train into the crossover, bringing it off the main rail toward the siding.

As expected, the cabin radio squawked almost at once.

"Antelope Zero-Two-One, I repeat Antelope Zero-Two-One. This is Pomona Dispatch, do you read?"

Tomas lifted the handset to his ear and pressed the "Talk" button.

"Loud and clear," he said. His neutral American accent was flawless. "We have a medical situation, Pomona. We're pulling into the yard."

"The hell you are, you can't switch tracks without permission!"

"Pomona, it looks like an emergency childbirth—"

"I don't care, Zero-Two-One. Procedure is to call in. There are medical personnel at Union Station."

Tomas throttled down to Run 1. He needed to end the call right away.

"The passenger needs immediate assistance," he said. "Will update ASAP, Pomona. Over and out."

"Zero-Two-One, hold on a minute—"

Ignoring the dispatcher, Tomas cradled the handset and carefully eased off the main track onto the siding.

Then he gripped the reverser and brake lever and backed up to straighten the train.

Bringing it to a relatively smooth full stop, he turned toward the Selective Door Operation touchscreen on the cabin's right wall. Its interface was nearly identical to those on the simulations—a basic schematic of the train, with the doors of each car simply marked Front, Middle and Rear.

"Karik," he said. "Are you in position?"

"*Yes.*"

Tomas tapped the SDO display, then watched an animated visual of the cab car's front door opening up. An instant later he looked out his window and saw Karik and his men scrambling out into the yard.

He took two deep breaths to fill his lungs.

This is it, he thought. *At long last*.

The Day of Fire had truly begun.

His baseball cap pulled down over his forehead, Karik sprang off the train, his two companions behind him. Their weapons concealed beneath their team jerseys, they walked quickly and silently across the dirt-and-rock berm onto the blacktop of the transfer station, turning toward its southwestern corner.

The siding was to their left now, rows of freight cars to their right, the station's parking area straight ahead of them with its small fleet of forklifts, stackers, and cranes.

Karik saw only a skeleton crew of yard workers—two men using steam pressure washers on the vehicles, a mechanic crouched under a forklift with his tools, and a fourth man standing near an open trailer at the far end of the parking area.

"Petros—stay with me," he said to the tall man beside him. He had to raise his voice over the loud roar of the pressure washers. "Simon, take the workers."

He strode toward the trailer, Petros keeping pace, Simon breaking off toward the cluster of industrial vehicles.

The yard worker outside the trailer was wearing a florescent lime safety vest over blue coveralls, SUPERVISOR written across the front of the vest.

He turned toward Karik and Petros as they came closer.

"Can I help you guys with something?" he asked.

"Yes," Karik said. He nodded toward the trailer's entrance. "We need the forklift keys."

The supervisor stared at him with incomprehension.

"Who are you?" he said. "This is a restricted—"

Karik reached under his jersey for the Glock longbarrel and fired two bullets into the supervisor's heart, the reports muffled by the racket of the nearby pressure washers. As the man dropped to the pavement, blood pulsing from his chest, Petros stepped past him into the trailer.

Karik stood with his back to the trailer, gazing across the parking area toward the industrial vehicles. A yard worker had noticed Simon and cut the flow to his steam hose. Lowering it to his side, he stepped toward Simon as if to ask what he was doing there.

Simon's ghost gun whipped up from under his jersey in a blur. Karik heard a ripple of semiautomatic fire issue from the weapon, saw the worker crumple to the ground in a heap, then watched Simon pivot on his heel and take out the remaining two men with a sustained burst.

He'd needed less than ten seconds to neutralize all three workers.

After a moment, Karik turned back toward the trailer.

Petros was already leaning outside, the forklift keys dangling from numbered tags in his fist.

"Easy," he said, glancing down at the supervisor's body. "They were racked above his desk."

Karik nodded toward the parked vehicles.

"Come," he said. "We need to hurry."

Drew had only gone a few feet toward the loading ramp when he reached a second walled-off archway and stopped dead, shining his flash over the bricks.

"Milena, *look*," he breathed.

Alysha halted a step behind him, slipping her hand from under her peasant blouse, leaving the tiny Ruger pistol in its open pouch. Ready for the kill, she felt the shock of interruption like a sudden dash of ice water on her skin.

She turned toward the wall and lifted her eyebrows. It only took her a second to understand the reason for his excitement.

The middle of the wall was bowed where its salt-and-mold filmed brickwork had loosened, pushed outward from the weight of the bricks above them. She saw chips of crumbled mortar at the foot of the wall.

Drew trained his flash on the section that bulged outward, testing the bricks with his free hand, applying only the slightest pressure.

They wobbled discernibly under his fingertips.

"It was never like this before, not even close," he said. "I'll bet I can get some of those bricks out easy.

But you'll need to hold the flashlight."

She heard her molars click. By now Tomas had surely pulled the train into the yard, and she wanted her conductor friend out of the way before Karik's team broke through to the ramp. But the urge to see the drums—*see* them with her own eyes—was irresistible.

"Of course," she said. "I want to help."

Drew smiled and passed her the flash. "Here goes… hold this sucker steady."

Kneeling to examine the weakened area, he wedged his fingertips around a protruding brick and worked it back and forth, prying it from its slot in the wall. It began to disintegrate almost at once, the fragments spilling to the floor amid clouds of dusty, crumbled mortar.

Alysha saw the surrounding bricks shift out of position as he removed what was left of it, leaving a dark, rectangular gap in the wall.

"We're almost ready," he said, a chunk of the moldering brick in his hand. "I'll take out a couple more of these. Then it's all yours."

She nodded, her fingers tight around the handle of the flash.

Reaching into the gap, Drew pulled out two of the displaced bricks and then set them down intact beside his feet.

Alysha aimed the flashlight into the widened hole.

22

Kensi was approaching the yard's southwestern transfer station when she noticed a Metroline commuter train stopped up ahead. It seemed oddly out of place on the industrial siding.

Deeks was also staring at it.

"Kens," he said. "Do you see what I see, or has this godawful cologne finally gone to my brain?"

"*Godawful?*"

"Hey, we're partners. If I can't tell *you* I'm tired of smelling like a spoiled salami sandwich, what's the point?"

She frowned. "Something definitely stinks here," she said. "Besides you for a change."

"I'm no expert. But if this transfer station's meant for freight trains…"

"Then why's a *passenger* train sitting there?" she said, finishing his thought.

Deeks turned to her. "Do we check it out?"

Kensi thought a moment, her hands on the wheel. She'd noticed a prefab metal shed forty or fifty yards to her left, almost directly under a half fallen railroad trestle. To her right, a blacktop parking lot extended west past the shed toward the river.

"Take a look at Eric's overlay map," she said. "We need to pin down the location of the old general shop."

He studied the display a second, then gestured out his window.

"See that shed under the trestle?" he said. "It would've run all the way from there to the river." He paused, his attention drawn toward the river wall. "Ah, Kens... since when do yard forklift operators wear baseball jerseys to work?"

She immediately knew what he meant. The three forklifts moving toward the wall—or rather their drivers—were as conspicuous as the Metroline train.

"I think the wrongness factor around here just shot off the charts," she said.

"All right," Deeks said. "Drivers first, train second?"

"Sounds like a plan," she said, and veered off the access road into the station, tires screaming.

Alysha centered the flashlight in the opening, Drew half-crouched beside her, both of them leaning forward to peer into the storeroom beyond.

The beam revealed the barrels at once. They stood on a metal pallet in the middle of the room, six of them, their surfaces mottled with rust. From their size, Alysha judged their capacities were fifty or fifty-five gallons.

"I can hardly believe my eyes," Drew said, fascinated. "There's something painted on them... words... can you see?"

She nodded, moving the flashlight's beam over one of the drums. The rust had eaten away some of the letters, but like the stenciled signs in the passage, the writing was mostly legible:

CA TION
HAZ RDOUS M TERIALS

"A seventy-something year old hazmat warning," Drew said. "I wonder what's inside them?"

Alysha looked at him. "I don't know," she lied smoothly. "We should—"

She broke off, a mechanical whine suddenly catching her attention. Drew heard it too, turning his head toward its source.

It was coming from their left, the direction of the exit ramp.

He looked around at her. "Sounds like engines," he said in a confused tone. "Outside the loading door."

Karik's team, Alysha thought. *They're here*.

She offered Drew a replica of his baffled expression, once again lowering her hand toward her weapon, thinking it was finally time to end the charade—and his life.

Then she heard the gunfire erupt outside and everything changed.

Kensi had barely gotten within thirty yards of the forklifts when one of the drivers—a slight man in sunglasses wearing a red Angels cap—glanced around at her SUV, shoved a hand under his jersey, and brought out a very large and dangerous-looking firearm.

She registered at once that it was a Glock 41—the same type of pistol used in the Greer and Daggut killings. As the other two drivers followed his lead, reaching for their own weapons, she saw that *they* were carbine versions of Isaak Dorani's ghost gun.

It all added up to a whole lot of bad news.

"*Hang on!*" she shouted to Deeks, swinging the wheel to the left, right, left, and right, zigzagging evasively as the drivers opened fire on them.

Beside her Deeks unholstered his own sidearm, a Beretta 92 he preferred to the OSP's standard issue SIG, mainly because it had saved his life more than once—which seemed an excellent reason, being how guns were *supposed* to do just that.

He lowered his window. The river wall was about ten yards up ahead now, the forklifts moving between its facing side and the SUV. As he raised the 92 in both hands, Deeks noticed a graffiti-covered rollup door in the wall, drifts of garbage and mechanical junk flush against it.

Then the nearest forklift driver swung his ghost gun around at the SUV, rattling off a burst of semiautomatic fire that pecked loudly into its front end, gouging out large chunks of its carbon-fiber bumper.

"Kensi, *duck!*" Deeks shouted.

"*Way ahead of you there!*" she shouted from the driver's seat. Swerving right, left, right, left…

Besides turning his stomach, the zigging and zagging made it hard for Deeks to get a decent bead on his target. As he swayed back and forth, the driver released another volley, his bullets smashing into the windshield, their impact pounding star-shaped fractures into the glass.

Deeks focused on the driver, forgot about Kensi's swerves making him carsick. Leaning out the window, tucking his head as low as possible, he leveled his gunbarrel, took quick aim, and returned fire with three fluid pulls of the trigger.

The driver flew sideways off his seat in a spray

of red, sailing through the little vehicle's safety bars to land on the blacktop, his arms and legs sprawled limply around his body.

Deeks did not let himself feel even an instant's relief. The other two men had turned their fork trucks around full circle and were bearing straight toward the SUV. Steering one-handed, the rider with the ghost gun poured long streams of fire at the car, the guy in the red baseball cap shooting round after round from his Glock.

Bullets punched into the SUV's windshield, leaving the glass pocked with stellated holes.

"These psychos aren't playing," Deeks said.

"You think?" Kensi said, cutting the wheel hard to the left… and then to the right.

Deeks swayed this way and that again. Then another slice of the wheel hurled him back toward the passenger door. He leaned out his open window, hands wrapped around the Beretta's grip, zeroing in on the man with the ghost gun.

He fired twice, the guy simultaneously discharging a volley from his weapon. Pain seared through his left arm as his attacker tumbled out of the forklift, a gaping wound in the middle of his chest, his vehicle flipping over on its side.

Wincing, Deeks looked down at his bloodied sleeve. "Ouch," he said.

Kensi glanced over at him. "Bad?"

He gulped a mouthful of air, examining the wound. His arm was pulsing with agony.

"How rhetorical is that question?"

Kensi didn't reply. She had turned back toward the windshield, her eyes widening.

"Deeks," she said, one hand dropping from the wheel to unfasten her seatbelt.

"Yeah?"

"We have to bail."

"What?"

"*Bail!*"

Deeks looked up to see the man in the red baseball cap coming straight at them in the forklift with a fixed, stony expression on his face.

Kensi reached across and opened the clasp on his belt, unstrapping him as the forklift came close, closer, *closer*, the vehicle growing large in the bullet-pocked windshield as he reached for his door handle and Kensi shoved him through the door with both hands, then pushed herself backward out her side of the SUV, falling free of it even as he went rolling across the blacktop.

An instant later the forklift slammed head-on into the SUV, the propane fuel cylinder clamped across its front end exploding with a loud roar, an orange gout of flame rising up and up around the rider to envelop him in his seat.

Flat on his stomach, superheated air blowing over him in a wave, Deeks propped himself off the ground with both hands, looked up, saw a fiery cocoon swirling around both totaled vehicles.

Then Kensi was kneeling over him, bracing him in her arms, helping him to a sitting position.

"You okay, Deeks?" she said over the loud crackle of the blazing vehicles.

He was silent, seemingly oblivious to her, gazing past her into the distance.

"Deeks?" she said in a concerned tone. And waved a hand in front of his eyes to see if he could track it. "Are you with me?"

He opened his mouth, closed it. Brought his eyes to her face. Then finally nodded.

"The Metroline train," he rasped. "It isn't there."

"What?"

As he angled his chin in the direction he'd been staring, she turned to look across the blacktop at the siding... and froze.

He was right.

The train was gone.

The shooting outside lasted only a minute or two before the explosion shook the tunnel, sending rivulets of dirt and concrete down from the ceiling.

Drew looked at Alysha, confusion spreading across his face. They were still crouched in front of the brick wall.

"I don't know what's going on," he said. "But we should get out of here."

"Yes," she said, and returned his flash. "I'll stay right behind you."

He nodded. "We'll be fine," he said, turning the light back the way they'd come.

She glanced down at the floor as they stood, snatching up one of the bricks he'd pulled from the wall moments before.

"Better hang onto me." He reached behind himself for her hand. "I don't want to chance us getting sep—"

Alysha smashed the brick against his temple with such force the rotted clay cracked in her grip, sending pieces flying off around her. The blow crumpled him to the tunnel floor.

As he fell onto his face, she bent to take the flash from his loosened fingers, then brought what was left of the brick down on his head again.

"*Never trust*," she whispered into his bloodied ear.

The jagged fragment of the brick resembled a broken tooth in her hand.

After a moment she stood up, let its fragments drop to the floor, and ran toward the main passage.

"Sam, G... give me your position," Kensi shouted over the Bluetooth.

Callen checked the Challenger's GPS display as Sam stitched through traffic with his foot heavy on the gas. He could hear sirens in the background over their phone connection, hear others screaming closer by, see black smoke spindling into the cloudless sky up ahead.

"We're on one-five, maybe a quarter mile from the Main Street turnoff," he said. "Should be with you any minute... what's going on?"

"I'll explain later," she said. *"Listen... there's an L.A.-inbound Metroline train. I think it's been hijacked."*

Sam exchanged glances with Callen. Then the telltale chopping of helicopters drew his gaze toward the upper portion of the windshield. Two LAPD birds were zipping south overhead toward Piggyback.

"You know where it is right now?" Callen asked.

"No. It pulled out of the yard sometime in the past few minutes," Kensi said. *"I don't think the uranium's onboard... again, later on that. We—"*

"Guys, this is Eric," Beale cut in from HQ. *"Can everyone hear me?"*

"Loud and clear," Sam said. "What is it?"

"The Metrolink's operations center has realtime tracking of all their trains," Eric said. *"I'm patched into its system and can toss you their feed—"*

"Eric, forget the feed," Callen said. "Where the hell's that train?"

"It just shot past Union Station and Santa Fe Springs. I mean, it's really plowing along."

"What's next on the line?"

"The last three stops are Buena Park, Fullerton, and—"

Silence.

"Eric? You still with us?"

"Yeah, yeah, sorry. I just realized the last stop's Anaheim… Angels Stadium."

Callen shot Sam a look.

"The Rail Series game," he said.

"Zero-Two-One, this is Chief Dispatcher Popowich. I am instructing you to halt the train. I repeat, you are ordered to halt the train at once. Do you copy?"

Tomas ignored the new voice on the radio and looked out the cabin window, his hands steady on the controls. He had pushed the lever to Run 8, speeding up to almost eighty miles-per-hour—the fastest the Metroline train could travel over the short, old stretch of rail south of Buena Park without certain derailment. Fullerton was the next stop, and Angels Stadium no more than eight miles beyond it.

The target was minutes off. He'd alerted Matous to his progress and let him know they were proceeding without the uranium. With law enforcement personnel descending on the area, he would see for himself that stealth was no longer an option.

"Zero-Two-One, come in. You are in breach of approved movements along the route. Can you goddamned HEAR me, Zero-Two-One?"

Tomas peered up the track, already able to see Fullerton's platforms ahead of him… but that wasn't all he saw. Glancing skyward, he discerned two LAPD helicopters flanking the train, the sun sparking off their windshields as they kept heated pace.

It occurred to him that the police would even now be clearing the station at Anaheim. They might not know everything about the original plan, but their arrival at Piggyback Yard meant they knew *enough* to order an evacuation—and probably cut off service to the line. That meant the death toll would be smaller than hoped for.

Still, the bombs Matous and his men carried were tremendously powerful, their explosive yield beyond anything the authorities might expect—sufficient to wipe a full city block out of existence. The hostages on the train, and anyone near the platforms in the stadium's parking lot would be incinerated. Whether casualties numbered in the hundreds, a thousand, or more, the day wouldn't be forgotten.

Tomas snatched up the handset and raised it to his lips.

"I hear you, Dispatch," he said calmly now. "The train will pull into Anaheim without interference."

"That isn't possible, Zero-Two-One. Permission to enter the station is denied. An automatic block has been established and you are to comply with all signals—"

"No," Tomas said. "The operator is dead and the train no longer in your control."

"What? Are you out of your mind?"

"Dispatch, listen to me. We have over fifty hostages. Men, women, children. Try to stop us and they will die."

"You can't do this—"

"We can do whatever we please," Tomas said. He felt light and floaty, his muscles somehow relieved of tension. "Know this action is taken in the name of the unavenged victims of Medz Yeghern, the Great Crime against the Armenian people."

Tomas heard the dispatcher say something in response, but his words no longer registered. The sounds coming out of the radio speakers seemed faint and distant, like the imaginary wash of waves a child might hear holding a conch shell to his ear.

Lowering the handset into its cradle, he turned down the radio's volume, thinking he'd done almost everything he needed to do.

He would soon reach the station. The rest was up to Matous.

The stadium's parking lot was jammed with vehicles and game goers as Sam turned in from East Katella Avenue at 5:50 P.M., discreetly flashing his badge at the uniformed cops deployed to guard the entrance.

It was now about an hour before first pitch, and with tens of thousands already in the ballpark, and droves more still arriving from every part of Metro Los Angeles, NCIS and its partner security agencies had held off on putting the area into lockdown. The authorities did not want the crowds surging everywhere at once. Therein lay chaos and mass hysteria.

Instead they had decided to keep a lid on the situation—for the present. The platform outside the stadium had been cleared, and service on the entire line suspended due to what was being called a "police action." But everyone in the grandstands would stay in the grandstands. The ticketholder gates remained open, the lot was open to arriving cars, and copious amounts of chile dogs, nachos, and short rib sandwiches were being served up in the concourses and food courts. The game would go on as scheduled unless developing circumstances pointed toward a clear and present threat to the fans in attendance. Let anything slip, alert even a single smartphone-tapping person to the situation, and you could count on the news spreading like wildfire over social media.

It was, of course, impossible to hide the influx of LAPD officers in patrol cars, the SWAT vans and trucks, the bomb dogs and wheeling surveillance choppers. But in an age when the possibility of terrorist attack was a constant, the public had come to expect an escalated police presence at major events.

Driving slowly in from the parking lot's entrance, Sam and Callen could see the stadium across the lot to their right, the railroad tracks to their left, and the foot ramp leading up to the commuter platform just ahead on that same side. People all around them were swarming from the parked vehicles to the outfield gate.

"The bunch that took the train might have an advance team waiting here," Sam said, looking around. "I think we split up. One of us stays in the lot. The other waits on the platform."

"Agreed," Callen said. "Who goes where?"

Sam shrugged absently, still peering out the windshield. He took one hand off the steering wheel and fished a quarter out of his pants pocket.

"Heads or tails?" he asked.

"Heads."

Sam flipped the coin, caught it, and slapped it onto his wrist.

"Tails," he said, glancing down at it.

Callen looked at him. "So how's that matter, since neither of us said where he wanted to go?"

Sam shoved the quarter back into his pocket, turning into an available space.

"Let's start over," he said. "You take the ramp. I take the platform."

Callen grunted and scanned the parking lot.

"You're gonna need some fan gear to blend in," he said. "I don't see any venders around."

Sam quietly eyed the people around them. After a moment he nodded toward a tall, overweight guy in a team jersey and baseball cap. He was getting out of his car with a teenaged boy and carrying a clear bag of snacks.

"Who said anything about venders?" he said, and opened his door.

Callen watched him move briskly up to the guy, exchange a few words with him, then reach for his wallet and slip him some cash.

Seconds later, Sam hurried back to the car with his cap, jersey and bag of snacks.

"Brought you some garbage calories," he told Callen, dangling the bag outside his open window.

Callen snatched it from his hand.

"Thanks, big boy," he said. "What'd you tell him?"

"Undercover security, pay a hundred for your gear."

Callen nodded. "Slick," he said.

Sam pushed the baseball cap over his head, removed his windbreaker, and tossed it into the car. Then he shrugged into the jersey and adjusted it over his holstered SIG.

"I look okay?"

"Like a hundred bucks."

Sam smiled a little.

"A quarter gets you nowhere these days," he said, and started toward the railroad platform.

Callen watched as Sam jostled through the crowd toward the railroad station, presented his ID to a small group of cops at the bottom of the ramp, and went jogging past them onto the platform.

Then his face grew sober. Quickly reaching for his doorhandle, he exited into the lot.

As Callen left the Challenger, a white Savana passenger van drove past him through the lot, then backed into a spot several cars down.

Parking the van directly opposite the ramp to the station platform, Matous stared out the windshield from behind its wheel, taking quick count of the police at the bottom of the ramp.

There were four of them, all carrying standard issue sidearms.

Anticipate changes. Adjust.

He would neutralize them with a single move. There just couldn't be any missteps. While that was true before the original plan was scrapped, his window of opportunity had shrunk drastically. It was too small now for even the smallest mistake.

He looked over at Gaspar, then half-turned in his seat so he could see Davit and Narem behind him.

"On your toes," he said. "We'll have seconds once the train pulls into the station." He paused. "Those police can't and won't know what hit them."

All three nodded their heads, but Gaspar's seemed too quick, too stiff, as though his fear of looking indecisive had far outpaced his confidence.

That wasn't good, Matous thought. But he'd known going in that his cousin wasn't the most solid of the men.

He studied him a moment, then straightened in his seat to look at the police by the ramp, dropping his hand to feel the weapon concealed under his warmup jacket.

The train would be approaching the station by now. He had no time to worry about Gaspar's strength or weakness, or second guess himself about his enlistment. No time to let his attention be diverted for any reason. He needed to fix the mission in his mind and not stray from its execution for an instant.

The only thing left was to wait for Tomas's signal and act…

Act without chance of mercy, he thought, making sure there were no survivors.

In the operator's cabin, Tomas saw the platform rushing up on him and gripped the throttle.

"Yuri," he said into his headset. "Are all the passengers accounted for?"

"*Yes,*" Yuri confirmed. "*They're under my eye.*"

Tomas nodded, working the levers to slow the streaking train.

"Hold on—this won't be gentle," he said, and went roaring into Anaheim station.

The train came in fast.

In the cab car's lower level, Yuri barely managed to keep his legs under him as it juddered wildly over the tracks. Standing with his ghost gun on the hostages, fighting to hold it steady, he saw Petros almost fall onto his face before bracing himself against the side of the car.

Then the train finally screeched to a halt, pulling even with the front of the platform. Screams tore through the passenger compartment—men and women, all of them *screaming* as it took a hard, final lurch. Yuri saw the mother with the two little boys clutch both of them to her chest as she whiplashed violently back and forth in her seat.

"Damn you, you're out of your heads!" This from the scruffy, bearded man who'd been herded in from the fifth car. Seated in the aisle near Petros, he started pushing to his feet. "Let us go!"

Yuri steadied his weapon on him, pointing it down the length of the car. He'd been thinking the man might be drunk or hung over.

"Stay put," he said. "I'm warning you."

The man glowered at him, half off the seat now. *"Screw you. I—"*

Petros triggered his weapon, a short, tight burst at the man's chest that dropped him in a lifeless heap.

More screams, then. The two boys crying out at the top of their lungs, their mother whispering to them in Spanish, pulling them closer as she tried to calm them.

Yuri stared at Petros across the aisle, a silently questioning expression on his face.

Petros caught the look and shrugged.

"I had enough of his mouth," he said. "He was a dead man anyway."

Yuri's eyes bored into his. "All right," he said tightly. "Never mind. We—"

Tomas's voice in his earpiece interrupted him.

"Yuri," he said. *"What's going on down there?"*

He kept looking at Petros. There was no point escalating the problem. "A minor flare-up from a hostage," he said. "It's finished."

The briefest of pauses. Then he heard Tomas exhale into his microphone.

"All right, get ready," he said. *"I'm about to open the doors."*

"Matous," Tomas said over their radio link. *"Zhamanakn e."*

For perhaps five seconds after receiving that signal in their ancestral tongue, Matous sat with his eyes on the police guarding the ramp. There was a crush of people in the parking lot aisle between his van and their post, within a few feet of the platform where the train had come howling in. He would plow right through them.

Zhamanakn e.

It is time.

Matous started to recite the Lord's Prayer, as he had dozens of times before in action with the 1st MSOB. Then he checked himself.

He would not bring God into this fight. Instead, he glanced into the rearview at Davit and Narem and gave them a slight nod.

Zhamanakn e.

Shifting the van into drive, he took hold of the steering wheel and pushed his foot down on the gas.

The van growled forward before anyone in the crowd knew what was happening. Bodies flew everywhere as it tore into them, people knocked into the air, blood splashing the windshield. Arms and legs flailed bonelessly amid the terrified screams. Two of the four police officers at the ramp were directly in the van's path, and Matous rammed its front end into them, crushing them instantly before he stamped on the brake. The other two stunned cops pulled out their guns in defense, shouting for people to run, trying to rapidly gather their wits and provide cover.

Matous would not give them a chance.

He threw open his door, stepping out of the van with his bomb pack on, simultaneously slipping his ghost gun from under his jacket. The others exited at the same instant, Davit on his side, Gaspar and Narem to his right, all four of them striding rapidly toward the ramp in near lockstep, pouring automatic fire at the cops and whoever else was in their path.

The plastic carbine chattering in his upraised hands, Matous took out one of the remaining two cops before he could fire a shot.

That left just a single officer crouched beside the ramp with his handgun, hollering for the civilians on the pavement around him to *move, move, move,* trying to get a bead on their attackers without hitting anyone else.

Having no such compunctions, Matous turned his weapon on the cop as he came within three or four feet of the ramp. Hastening forward, the ghost gun's stock against his shoulder, he took fast aim and prepared to cut loose at him through the crowd.

If not for the gunshot from his left, he would have killed the cop and everyone around nim on the spot. Instead, he saw Davit's head jerk sideways as he fell to the pavement beside him, then turned abruptly toward the sound of the gun, and saw the man in a blue windbreaker with the words NCIS on its front, a semiautomatic pistol wrapped in his hands.

"*Let's go!*" he shouted to Gaspar and Narem.

And plunged ahead onto the foot ramp, swinging the ghost gun around toward their attacker.

* * *

Callen moved toward the ramp from the left in a shooter's stance, leaning slightly forward on the balls of his feet, ready to get his momentum going if he needed to break into a full running pursuit.

The carnage had erupted just as he exited the Challenger, the van slamming into the crowd, the men with the 3D printed carbines hammering the cops and civilians with automatic fire.

After that his actions were almost reflexive. He saw the threat and reacted, drawing his SIG from under his jacket, getting into the stance, his eyes picking the bad guys out of the crowd.

He'd known he would need to find momentary shooting lanes between the bystanders. Aim high or low—for their heads or legs. Their satchels were in the middle, and based on the evidence at the safehouse, they were very possibly loaded with explosive charges. The last thing he wanted was his fire detonating a bomb around hundreds of innocent people.

His first shot was thankfully clear, with people to the right and left but no one except his target in the line of fire. He aimed the gun barrel high and pulled the trigger and the bad guy spilled sideways to the pavement.

That left him with three of them, the one with the hipster beard closest to him, two more a yard or so over on the right.

People running around him in wild, frantic crosscurrents, Callen saw the bearded guy shout something to his companions and then go dashing onto the ramp. As his men hurried to join him another firing lane opened up, someone lifting a child into his arms, creating a gap in the human wall.

He squeezed the trigger again, *low*, the target's legs presenting the best angle this time.

The man's knees spurting blood, he sank down into the crowd.

Two left. But the van's driver was out of sight now. He'd gone up the ramp to the platform, leaving Callen to deal with the guy who'd exited the van's front passenger seat.

"Sam." In his headset.

"Yeah."

"The beard coming your way," Callen said. "He's armed and wired."

"Got you."

Callen broke off and scanned the crowd, his gaze jumping from person to person. He knew the passenger hadn't yet reached the ramp. He would have seen him making his way up.

Then he heard a staccato burst of fire in front of him, the gun barrel jabbing out from behind some moving bodies. He sliced evasively to one side as the crowd parted, people pushing and shoving, running off in every direction...

And suddenly he was standing almost directly opposite the passenger. The guy was no more than ten or fifteen feet away, nothing and nobody between them. He held his ghost gun in one hand, and from the surprised look on his face must have briefly lost sight of Callen before finding himself exposed.

Callen knew he had a momentary jump on him. He aimed his pistol, *high*, ready to take him out—and then stopped cold.

In the split second before he would have pulled the trigger, the passenger had dropped his carbine, letting it fall to the pavement at his feet while raising both arms straight up in the air, the satchel hanging from his shoulder...

But there was something in his hand, his *left* hand, the one that hadn't been gripping the carbine. An object shaped like a fat pen or pencil.

Callen breathed with his SIG still aimed at the guy, poised to fire.

He'd been around the block in his years as a federal agent, worked with the CIA, FBI, and DEA before Naval Investigations...

He knew a detonator when he saw one, and the passenger was holding just such a device over his head, his finger on the button.

Sam was waiting at the front of the platform, crouched behind a large public trash bin, when the bearded man came off the ramp to his left.

He'd spotted the bin moments ago and quickly decided to use it for cover, guessing the hijackers would have moved their prisoners into the cab car. They needed control of that same car to drive the train, and gathering all the hostages there would make it easier to keep an eye on them. Call them crazies, but it was obvious they knew their game. Sam thought they would do what was tactically sound.

It seemed a good bet, anyway... one he made knowing he represented the hostages' best chance. LAPD and FBI rapid-response teams had set up a perimeter around the parking areas, and there were SWAT snipers atop the ARTIC station's glass roof. But ARTIC was hundreds of yards east of the platform. While it might be possible for a crack shot to put a bullet through a window from that distance, Sam doubted only a single gunman was covering the prisoners. Take out one of them, and the others would react, practically guaranteeing a bloodbath aboard the car.

That couldn't happen. He wouldn't *let* it happen.

Granger had wrangled command of the operation, meaning no one would move unless NCIS made the call. And right now he and Callen *were* NCIS at the scene. Like it or not, everything was in their hands.

SOP, he thought.

As the train squealed to a halt, Sam leaned out slightly from behind the trash bin, trying to see through its windows. He glimpsed the seated hostages in the lead car, and their masked captors standing in the aisle with carbines. There were two of them, or two he could see. With the train moving so fast, he figured he could easily miss a few, and that there might be more hijackers elsewhere aboard.

Its doors opened about ten seconds later—but only the middle doors to the first, third, and last of the five cars.

Why *those* three was a question Sam couldn't answer, not with absolute certainty. But he'd been an underwater demo man with the SEALS once upon a time and knew a little about distribution of energy. They would be the right cars to hit if somebody wanted to spread the force of explosive charges evenly throughout the train.

It was a disquieting thought, as if he needed another added to the nasty mix.

He took a deep breath. A few feet to his left, the bearded man was running toward the cab car's open door, ready to get aboard with a gun in his hand and an even deadlier-looking satchel on his shoulder.

He needed to make his move.

Springing to his feet, Sam made a beeline for the car from the opposite direction, shooting up right behind the beard as he reached the door. The guy was about his height and build, but wasn't nearly as wide at the shoulders. Sam was banking on that and the element of surprise as his advantages.

He hit him hard, slamming an elbow and forearm into his back, knocking the wind out of him. Stumbling forward, the beard managed to stay on his feet and spun around to face Sam, standing in the door to block his way.

"Get out of here," he said, raising his carbine in one hand. "Or I'll kill you."

Sam saw the guy coldly size him up, noticing his baseball jersey and cap.

"Lemme *on*, man!" Sam yelled. "I forgot my ticket, gotta get home for it!"

The bearded man stared at him. Then Sam remembered a name. One of the few Isaak Dorani was able to give Kensi during his interrogation.

"Yo, Matous," he said. "How you doin', killer?"

The guy hesitated for a split second, surprise and confusion on his face.

Move. Sam stepped in on him, locking a hand around his right wrist, his gun arm, twisting it sharply as he brought his knee up into his solar plexus.

Matous staggered back into the train, but again stayed upright, hanging onto his weapon.

Sam pushed forward. He heard hostages screaming inside, and knew the other hijackers would be on him any second, but his focus stayed on the man right in front of him, facing him from the door of the car. Their chests almost touching, Matous was raising his weapon again, about to fire it here on the crowded train.

Sam could not give him that chance. Yanking down on the hand with the gun, hoping to loosen its grasp, he snapped a close, crisp uppercut at his chin. But Matous had reflexes and was no slouch at hand to hand, dodging Sam's fist so it only struck a glancing blow, he then thrust the heel of his own hand at his throat.

Sam deflected the jab with his forearm just before it would have connected with the vulnerable area below his Adam's apple. But its force staggered him long enough to give Matous room to maneuver—and then suddenly the hijacker was bringing up his carbine again, the weapon a dark blur in his fist.

Sam needed some separation. Planting a hand on his chest, he shoved Matous backward with all his strength even as he reached under his jersey for his SIG, pulling it out *fast*, firing point blank into his midsection.

Matous stood there with a look of mute surprise on his face, his eyes fixed on Sam's for a long moment. Then his features went slack, his mouth gaping open, his tongue awash in blood.

"*Stay in your seats, EVERYBODY, heads down!*" Sam hollered as a burst of ammunition rattled at him from down the aisle.

Dropping to his knees, he sighted down the barrel of his SIG and fired three rounds at the shooter. The man spun around like a top, his weapon clattering to the floor, but Sam again wasn't about to make himself a stationary target.

He registered the second hijacker just in time, picking up his movement out the corner of his right eye. He was down at the end of the car, his weapon in front of him in firing position.

Still squatted down in the aisle, Sam pivoted on his heels and trigged another three from his pistol.

The shooter went down instantly in a spray of blood.

Sam gulped air, still facing the rear, gazing down the length of the compartment. He didn't see any more hijackers in the car, and that was fine, that was cool, but *somebody* had been driving the train...

He would never be sure whether he moved on instinct, or heard the shooter step out of the cabin. The only thing he did know was that *something* made him launch forward off his knees an instant before the gunfire erupted from overhead, landing on his stomach as the rounds drilled into the floor of the train where he'd been crouched a split second before. Rolling onto his back and lifting the SIG in both hands with a single fluid movement, he aimed up the stairs leading to the operator's cabin, and fired at the man with the carbine standing outside it.

The man lurched and grabbed his chest with one hand, his weapon falling loosely to his side in the other. Then he came toppling down into the aisle, his arms and legs striking dull metallic clanks on the stairs.

Sam jumped to his feet, passengers screaming behind him in the aisle.

"*Stay put!*" he urged, shooting his arm out at them like a traffic cop. "*You'll be okay!*" and then scrambled over to where the man had fallen onto his back, pulled the ghost gun from his slackened fingers, and touched the side of his neck to check his pulse.

There was a faint throb, too faint. Sam knew he wasn't going to last long.

The man stared up at him, his eyes glassy and unfocused, their pupils dilated. Sam saw his lips move a little, a dry groan escaping them. He was struggling to speak.

He put a hand under his head and tilted it up off the floor. The guy's mouth worked, opening and closing, opening and closing.

Sam still couldn't understand him.

"Go on," he said, leaning closer. "Try again."

He reached up, weakly clutching Sam's elbow. Sam could see the effort on his face.

"*Thank... you*," the guy rasped.

Then he took a series of rapid, shallow breaths and shuddered violently, his hand dropping from Sam's arm to the floor.

A second passed. Sam checked his pulse again, felt nothing, let his head sink back down, and rose to his feet.

"You got it," he said, turning quickly toward the hostages.

"The train's secured, hostages are safe," Sam said over the radio. *"What's your situation, G?"*

Callen held his gun steady on the guy with the upraised detonator. He wasn't exactly sure of the answer to what seemed a very simple question.

"Let me get back to you," he said.

The guy stared at him in silence. The crowd of civilians had evaporated in a hurry, the police having tightened their perimeter around the station after the carnage broke out, guiding everyone in the area to safety across the parking lot.

Leaving Callen alone here with this crazed human bomb, and the bodies of the people who'd been killed.

He watched the guy over the SIG's barrel. The hand that held the detonator was trembling above his head, which Callen supposed could mean he was having second thoughts about pushing the button, or might conversely indicate he was getting ready to do it.

It occurred to him, however, that he easily *could have* done it by now—and hadn't.

Whether that was cause for optimism, or merely a desperate hope, he was taking it.

"I have a brilliant idea," he said, watching him closely. "You drop the detonator, neither of us gets blown to pieces."

The guy didn't respond.

"Think about it," Callen said. "Your people on the train already gave up…"

"No." The guy looked at him. "You're lying."

Callen said nothing. *Let him wonder*, he thought.

He held the gun on him. Steady, steady, aiming for his heart. The guy facing him with his arms up in the air, his hand suddenly shaking hard around the detonator. How long had it been since he pulled it out? Three minutes? Four?

Maybe he really *didn't* want to push the button.

Maybe.

Callen took a deep breath. He was thinking this was the second time in as many days someone was threatening to blow himself up in his presence. It wasn't exactly the sort of thing he wanted to make a habit.

Not that anyone was confusing this homicidal maniac with Ron Valli.

"Listen, it's just you and me here," he said. "Why waste a perfectly good bomb?" He shrugged. "Two jamokes like us won't even make the evening news."

"Shut up," the guy said. "Just shut up."

Callen wanted to be careful not to push him over the brink, but the guy still hadn't pressed the button, hinting at the possibility that he could be doing something right.

"Sure," he said. "After I ask you one question."

The guy stood there.

"You really want to die?" Callen said.

Silence.

"Seems your friends decided it wasn't for them…"

"Stop," the guy said. "I told you. Stop lying."

Callen watched him, noticing the beads of perspiration on his face.

"The train's still over there in one piece," he went on, nodding toward the platform. "You know I'm telling the truth."

The guy kept looking at him.

Callen stared into his eyes, trying to get a read on his thoughts. What was it trial lawyers always said? Never ask a question if you don't already know the answer.

He hoped he was right about knowing the answer to his.

"So," he asked. "*Do* you? Want to die, that is?"

The guy stood there dripping sweat, his face seeming to pull apart as he grew increasingly upset. Then he lowered the detonator in his trembling fist, bringing it down where he could look at it.

His grip so tight his knuckles had paled.

Callen held the gun on him. Steady, steady. For whatever good that would do if he pushed the button.

A long moment passed. Callen heard pounding in his ears. The guy was just staring at the thing in his hand, not moving at all. Then, finally, he unclenched his fist so the detonator clattered to the ground, spreading his fingers apart to show Callen his empty hand.

"I don't want to die," he said. "I don't, I don't…"

Callen took two giant steps toward him, rushing forward, keeping his gun trained on his chest. Kicking the device across the pavement, he gestured for the cops waiting around them to move in.

They swarmed over the guy in an instant, pulling his arms around his back to slap on the cuffs.

"Yo, G, you all right…?"

It was Sam again over the headset, his voice anxious.

Callen expelled a deep sigh of relief, holstering his gun.

"Yeah," he said. "Everything's under control."

Kensi dropped down off the ladder rung to the bottom of the tunnel, her SIG semi in one hand, the flash/laser attachment mounted beneath its barrel splashing light into the darkness around her.

Deeks followed a moment later, descending arduously as he hung onto the ladder with his uninjured arm, four members of a joint NCIS/FBI tac team lowering themselves into the venthole entrance behind him.

"I'm not sure your coming down here's the brightest thing," she said, looking at his arm. The ambulance techs who'd arrived at the transfer station had wrapped an elasticized emergency bandage over his wound, but she could see spots of blood seeping through the fabric. "That bullet left more than a nick."

Deeks's feet touched down on the concrete.

"Nick, schmick. Besides, we both know *you're* the brightest thing down here."

She shook her head.

"You're nuts," she said.

"But lovable." Deeks peered down the tunnel. "Welcome to the Underworld."

Kensi reached into her jacket pocket for the burner phone she'd found above them on the floor of the storage shed. Then she waited for the tacs to come off the ladder.

"Okay," she said in a low voice. "Let's do this. Stay alert."

Kensi and Deeks in the lead, the group moved down the tunnel, two abreast, their automatic weapons bristling outward, rail lights beaming ahead of them.

They had to stay on their toes. It was safe to assume that the phone belonged to the Metroline conductor's honeytrap date. It was likely that she had used the phone's tracker as a homing beacon for the men on the forklifts. Kensi was also convinced the most recent text sent from the phone, with its apple and pear emojis, was a coded signal to those men, the train hijackers, or all of them.

Add everything together and it was impossible to know who and what they would find here in this tunnel.

Reaching a T-junction now, she swung the gun-mounted flash to her left and right.

She stopped, her flash still aimed toward the right. There was a dark shape near the middle of the passage. Something—

She angled the beam onto it.

No.

Some*one*.

Sprawled there on the floor.

Her flashlight beam glanced off a shiny black pool around the motionless figure.

Blood.

She exchanged a glance with Deeks.

Cutting to the right, they hurried down the passage, two of the tacs sticking with them, the other pair staying back to guard the junction.

They crouched over the figure. It was a man on his side, curled into a near-fetal position.

"Crap." Deeks dropped to his haunches, picked up an object near his head, showed it to Kensi. "I guess we know what hit him."

She expelled a breath. It was a chunk of brick. The blood on it left no question about how it was used.

Nodding for the tacs to keep their lights on the man, she thumbed off her pistol flash, slipped the weapon into its harness, and reached down to feel for a pulse—

"*Hlppp.*"

Kensi's eyes widened. Her fingers hadn't yet reached his neck.

"*Plsss h-hllp... meee.*"

"Drew?" she said. "Are you Drew Sarver?"

"*Y-y-yesss...*"

She moved her hand away from his neck and instead placed it gently on his shoulder.

"It's okay, Drew. Be still," she said. "We're the good guys."

EPILOGUE

Midnight. The San Gabriel Mountains.

A strong breeze played over the surface of Jag Azarian's infinity pool, causing its reflected constellations of stars to expand and contract.

Azarian and Alysha sat at a poolside table, staring at the speckled water, his back to his living room. It was open tonight, the transparent arc of its glass wall retracted.

"We missed one moment today," he said turning to her after a long silence. "But only one. There will be others."

Her eyes met his. "Is that what you sincerely believe?" she asked, sounding unconvinced.

He spread his hands. "It's what I choose to believe," he said. "I see no other way to move forward... do you disagree?"

She shrugged.

"The past is dead, and the future is nothing. I won't harbor the conceit that there are moments beyond this one."

Azarian was silent again. He let a hand settle on the leather portfolio envelope in the center of the table.

or identity papers and travel
d. "Two hundred-fifty thousand
ple bank accounts." A pause. "I've also
reservations for us. A lodge in the Salzburg
that doesn't exist in the public listings." His gaze
had not left her face. "The mountains are beautiful
in springtime, but we needn't ever leave our suite to
delight in our stay."

She smiled a little and sat very still.

After a moment he leaned closer to her. "I know your
history with Tomas," he said. "Did you love him?"

"Let it go," she said.

"I ask only because of what your love means to
me…"

"And I told you how I feel about the past," she said.
"Besides, I sense your eagerness to leave the country
isn't altogether romantic."

"There will be a massive investigation into today's
events. I doubt it can lead to me, but some distance
from California can't hurt right now. It's good to be
light on one's feet."

Alysha's eyes went to his. She kept them there a
long time. "The Alps sound delightful."

He nodded, lightly touching her hand. "We can get
a head start on those delights tonight," he said. "Let's
go inside."

She smiled and gave a slight nod back. "Let's."

Rising to his feet, Azarian turned to Alysha, reached
out to slip an arm around her waist…

And then his eyes widened.

She was pointing her Beretta at his chest, standing
at point blank range.

"What are you doing?" he said. "Are you out of
your mind?"

She shook her head.

"I'm merely heeding your advice," she said. "We need to be light on our feet, and there are too many men hunting you. That makes you a dangerous weight."

He shook his head a little. "I love you," he said. "You have my heart."

Alysha just looked at him, her eyes flat.

"The heart is a useless thing," she said. "Be grateful I'm ridding you of its pains."

The gun jerked twice in her fist.

She took the portfolio envelope off the table, and slipped off into the darkness of the night.

"Hey," Kensi said carrying her coffee into the bullpen. "Something's different around here."

Deeks looked at her.

"Whatever do you mean?" he said.

She walked over to him and sniffed.

"The air's back to being plain old stale," she said. "And odorless."

Deeks smiled a little. "So," he said. "You like the animalic-free me?"

Kensi shrugged.

"Every little bit helps," she said.

His smile widened. His injured arm freshly dressed, Deeks was standing with Callen, Sam, and Hetty in the area between the agents' desk cubbies, where the team had gathered for an informal morning huddle.

"If I may interrupt," Hetty said, sipping her tea. "I want to quickly debrief everyone on what's gone on since yesterday."

Silence. Despite their whistling past the graveyard, Kensi, Deeks, and everyone else in the room had an

...heir eyes. They had averted a
..., saved countless lives, but no one
...elebratory mood. Despite their efforts
... people had still died, leaving far too many
...i ones to grieve.

At the OSP, where it was all part of the job, humor was a coping mechanism, the only way to fend off the grimness they encountered on a routine basis.

Some days it worked better than others.

"I take it everyone's seen the televised news feeds coming out of Piggyback Yard," Hetty said now, looking from face to face.

Callen nodded.

"Hard to miss it," he said. "A hidden uranium stockpile, guys from Homeland in HazMat suits emptying it out... it screams ratings."

Sam sighed. "This could get ugly for the CIA," he said. "Somebody there vaulted off the Deep Dive records at Holloway's say-so."

Hetty regarded him over the rim of her teacup. "It will be an embarrassment to them for a news cycle or two... nothing more," she said. "The cowboys rode off into the sunset long ago."

"And with Holloway gone, I'm not sure anyone's left to tell us who was responsible," Kensi said.

"The moral being that justice has a shorter half life than uranium?" Deeks said.

Hetty looked at him.

"We saved many more lives that could have been lost," she said. "Leave justice to the courts."

There was another silence.

"How's that poor guy we found in the tunnel?" Deeks asked after a moment. "Drew Sarver."

"I just got off the phone to the hospital and the

doctors think he'll be okay," Kensi said. "But there's short term memory loss. He doesn't have a clue how he wound up in the tunnel. Or remember the femme fatale who left him for dead."

"The one that got away," Sam said, shaking his head. "She's stone cold. A professional killer."

Hetty sighed quietly.

"Some say there are always loose ends in real life," she said. "Others believe things eventually sort themselves out."

Callen looked at her. "And you?" he said.

"I want your case reports filed in an hour," she said.

The agents watched Hetty start toward her office, then suddenly turn back around to face them, her eyes flashing behind her glasses.

"The best antidote for pondering life's grand design is aged Scotch whiskey, you know," she said. "I'll have a bottle in my office when you finish those reports."

ABOUT THE AUTHOR

Jerome Preisler has written over thirty published books of fiction and narrative nonfiction, including all eight titles in the *New York Times* bestselling Tom Clancy's Power Plays series, and the first two novels in the forthcoming reboot of Net Force, based on Mr. Clancy's original series.

His narrative nonfiction includes *All Hands Down: The True Story of the Soviet Attack on the USS Scorpion, Code Name Caesar: The Secret Hunt for U-Boat 864 During World War 2, Daniel's Music: One Family's Journey from Tragedy to Empowerment through Faith, Medicine, and the Healing Power of Music,* and *First to Jump: How the Band of Brothers was Aided by the Brave Paratroopers of Pathfinders Company.*

www.JeromePreisler.com
Facebook: www.facebook.com/
JeromePreislerBooks

NCIS™: LOS ANGELES

BOLTHOLE

Jeff Mariotte

A brand-new original thriller tying in to the hit TV
show, *NCIS: Los Angeles*. When a Navy counselor
paying a home visit to a former Navy SEAL finds him
inside his house, tortured and murdered, NCIS are
called in to investigate. Meanwhile, a bank hold-up
goes bad downtown and an LAPD officer is shot. The
cop is a friend of Deeks', but a trace on the getaway
vehicle shows no connection between the crimes, that is
until NCIS dig deeper.

Available November 2016